P9-CQU-551

SHOU

Shou

by

Deborah Shlian

Joel Shlian

toExcel
San Jose   New York   Lincoln   Shanghai

Shou

All Rights Reserved. Copyright © 1999 Deborah & Joe Shlian

No part of this book may be reproduced or transmitted in
any form or by any means, graphic, electronic, or mechanical,
including photocopying, recording, taping, or by any
information storage or retrieval system, without the
permission in writing from the publisher.

Published by toExcel,
an imprint of iUniverse.com, Inc.

For information address:
iUniverse.com, Inc.
620 North 48th Street
Suite 201
Lincoln, NE 68504-3467
www.iUniverse.com

ISBN: 1-58348-759-X

Printed in the United States of America

Acknowledgments

We would like to express our very grateful thanks to our dear Shanghainese friends Hao Cheng, and Hua Qi Han and Qing and Qing Nan Zhou whose personal experiences and special understanding of life in China today have greatly contributed to the factual contents of this book; to Chu Yi Wong who served as a model for Lili and tirelessly read and reread the manuscript.

There are others still in China who we will have to thank anonymously for fear that official knowledge of their help might cause reprisals. Although more than ten years have passed since the massacre at Tiananmen, many of those involved in the student movement still have legitimate concerns for their own safety or for that of their families. Nevertheless, we are indebted to each of them and appreciate their candid exchange of ideas and experiences.

Deborah and Joel Shlian

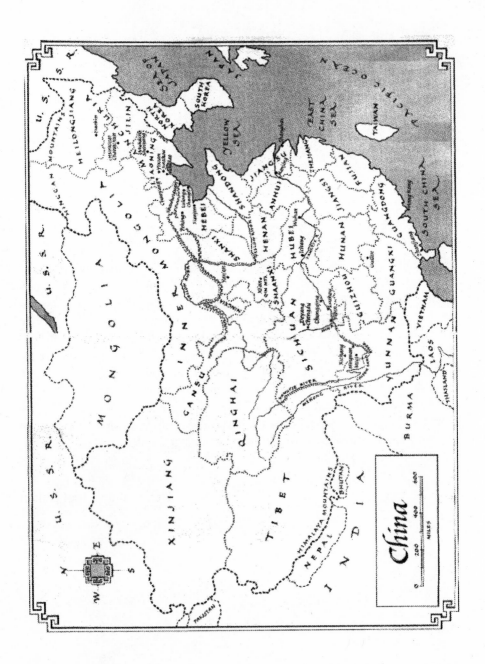

A Guide To Pronouncing Chinese Names

The official system of romanization... used in China today is known as Pinyin. It is now almost universally adopted by the Western media. Although non-Chinese may initially encounter some difficulty in pronouncing romanized Chinese words, many of the sounds actually correspond to the usual pronunciation of the letters in English. The exceptions:

c: is like the *ts* in 'its'

q: is like the *ch* in 'cheese'

x: has no English equivalent, and can be best described as a hissing consonant that lies somewhere between *sh* and *s*. The sound was rendered as hs under an earlier transcription system.

z: is like *ds* in 'fads'

zh: is unaspirated, and sounds like the *j* in 'jug'

a: sounds like 'ah'

e: is prounced as in 'her'

i: is pronounced as in 'ski'

(written as *yi* when not preceded by an initial consonant).

However, in *ci, chi, ri, shi, zi* and *zhi*, the sound represented by the i final is quite different and is similar to the *ir* in 'sir', but without much stressing of the *r* syllable.

o: sounds like the *aw* in 'law'

u: sounds like the *oo* in 'ooze'

e: is pronounced as in 'get'

u: is pronounced as the German *u* (written as *yu* when preceded by an initial consonant)

When two or more finals are combined, such as hao, jiao and liu, each letter retains its sound value as indicated in the list above, but note the following:

ai: is like the *ie* in 'tie'

ei: is like the *ay* in 'bay'

ian: is like the *ien* in 'Vienna'

ie: similar to 'ear'

ou: is like the *o* in 'code'

uai: sounds like 'why'

uan: is like the *uan* in 'iguana'

(except when preceded by *j, q, x* and *y;* in these cases a *u* following any of these four consonants is in fact *u* and *uan* is similar to *uen*)

ue: is like the *ue* in 'duet'

ui: sounds like 'way'

Examples:

A few Chinese names are shown below with English phonetic beside them:

Beijing	Bay-jing
Guilin	Gway-lin
Xi'an	Shi-ahn
Qing Nan	Ching Nan

Foreword

Eternity and Longevity Symbols

The Chinese have numerous symbols for longevity, including peach charms which are worn by children to bind them to life. The gentle, smiling star-god of longevity is pictured surrounded by mushrooms that give immortality and holding the fruit of *P'an t'ao*, the peach tree that blossoms every three thousand years. The *shou* is a familiar symbol of longevity. This character is seen in all arts and crafts of China as a decorative motif. There are over one hundred ways of writing it and occasionally a garment will be embroidered with the different forms. It was considered a rare token when the Emperor granted his ministers copies of this character written in his own hand.

THE OLD DUST

The living is a passing traveler;
The dead, a man come home.
One brief journey between heaven and earth,
Then, alas! we are the same old dust of ten thousand
     ages.
The rabbit in the moon pounds the medicine in vain;
Fu-sang, the tree of immortality, has crumbled to kindling
     wood.
Man dies, his white bones are dumb without a word
When the green pines feel the coming of spring.
Looking back, I sigh; looking before, I sigh again.
What is there to prize in the life's vaporous glory?

Li Po (A.D.701–762)

According to Chinese folklore, there is a rabbit in the moon, which is pounding the elixir of life.

PROLOGUE

May 3, 1949
Shanghai, China

Shanghai was a city on edge. Nervous gossip and anxious speculation electrified the air. Dr. Ni-Fu Cheng sensed tension even in the lunch time banter of his tenured colleagues at the Institute. No one knew which way the political winds would blow this time.

For three days the wireless screamed of valiant Nationalist soldiers fighting in the southern cities. North China's Daily News countered with unqualified praise for the great army of shoeless peasants crossing the Yangtse River to capture Nanking. Would Chiang Kai-chek be forced to retreat? Would the foreign devils finally be driven from Shanghai forever? Would the People's Liberation Army fulfill the promise of a new China? Maybe, Ni-Fu thought. But he couldn't take a chance—not with his daughter, Su-Wei. She was all that was left of his family. She *had* to live.

"You should get out yourself, old chap. It isn't safe," his friend, Denton Browning had warned.

But Ni-Fu couldn't leave Shanghai. Not yet. Thank goodness Browning managed to get Su-Wei an evacuation card.

Hoping to melt into the anonymity of the pre-dawn shadows, Ni-Fu urged the ten-year old along the wide boulevard of the Bund toward the freighters docked at the edge of the Huangpu River. He'd let the child linger too long saying good-bye to her *amah*. They'd have to hurry not to miss the ship's sailing.

A hot sea breeze, thick from humidity even the night's rain could not abate, exacerbated their already ragged breathing. He scanned the river, searching past the barges, lighters, sampans, godowns and junks until he spotted the rust-streaked New Star at the far end of the dock. Opposite, Pudong was shrouded in early morning mist, its smoking factory chimneys resembling silent sea wraiths with gently undulating hair.

A plaintive cry arose from the little girl whose cheeks were wet with perspiration. "I'm tired, father."

"Just a little more, my child. We're almost there." Ni-Fu refused to stop until his daughter was safely aboard the freighter.

The air was rich and heavy with the familiar sounds and smells of the quayside: rickshaw-pulling hawkers beckoning to would-be customers, gangs of grunting, sweating coolies shouldering giant loads balanced at each end of springy bamboo poles, sweet incense smoking and food cooking on charcoal braziers. Ni-Fu watched spirited peasants from the countryside hustle potatoes and chickens. Only their cardboard signs with scribbled prices inflating a dozen times each day spoiled the ordinariness of the scene.

As always, clusters of beggars outlined in the faint early morning light, their matted hair and bare feet blackened with grime, slept silently by the side of the road like stray cats. They'd been there under the British, the Japanese and the Guomindang. Passing the sleeping figures, Ni-Fu wondered if they'd still be there now that Mao was so close to Shanghai.

The image reflected in the shop window surprised him. Only thirty-five, but already his jet black hair had more than a touch of gray. He sighed. Too much had happened too quickly. In less than a week he'd lost his wife, his newborn son and his younger brother. Too soon to feel the depth of his pain.

A hand touched Ni-Fu's shoulder. Turning quickly, he was relieved to see his friend.

"You're late, old chap." Browning smiled at Su-Wei. "Thought you changed your mind."

Ni-Fu shook his head. "I have no choice." He spoke with an acquired Oxford accent.

Browning nodded. "Nor I. The white man's Chinese domain is no more." He mopped the moisture from his brow with a silk handkerchief. "Bloody hot—even for May. Hardly a breath of wind."

Ni-Fu offered his friend an envelope filled with yuan. "For your kindness."

"Nonsense," Browning responded, refusing compensation. "What I've learned can never be repaid. You are a great doctor and teacher."

"What will you do now, Denton?"

"Me? I was meant to be a good English country doctor. I'll set up practice in Surrey, find a wife, have kids and spend my weekends tending a vegetable garden. I'll become famous for the biggest tomatoes in the county." He laughed at the thought, then turned serious again: "I only wish we could have tested your theories in the laboratory."

Ni-Fu shrugged.

Two long blasts from the freighter stacks.

Browning picked up his leather valise and reached for Su-Wei's hand. "We'd better board or we'll miss the boat."

Su-Wei began to weep. Although she knew a little English, she spoke in Chinese. "I don't want to leave you, father. Please don't make me go."

Knowing he might never see her again, Ni-Fu stared at his child as if to burn her image into his memory. Lovely Su-Wei. As beautiful as her name which meant poem and flower. The Chinese in him wondered if the geomancer hadn't been right after all: "You must call your beautiful child 'ugly' or the Gods will punish you for the sin of pride". But the scientist in Ni-Fu refused to believe in *feng shui* or *joss* or any of that superstitious hogwash. He smiled at his daughter: "You'll be safe in America".

"Don't worry, old man. Once we get to Hong Kong, I'll put her on the first boat to San Francisco and wire your sister to meet her." Browning patted Ni-Fu's arm. "She'll be fine."

"Who will care for you if I leave?" Su-Wei asked solemnly, her eyes glistening.

He looked at this grave, almond-eyed child forced to grow up so quickly and he yearned to tell her he was on the verge of a great discovery, the key to a secret that would free mankind forever. But he knew she was too young to understand and he didn't dare let Browning know that he'd already begun testing his theory.

Instead he pulled a jade locket on a gold chain from his pocket and fastened it around her neck. Inside he'd placed a picture of his wife so the child would not forget. "Do you know what this means?" he asked, pointing to the gold Chinese letters?

"Shou? It means long life," said the child, wiping a tear that had trickled down her cheek.

Ni-Fu put his arms around his little daughter and held her close. "Wear this always and never forget that you are Chinese," he whispered in his native tongue. "Someday you will return to your country and we will be together again". He kissed the child good-bye.

Browning took Su-Wei's hand. "I'm afraid we must go." Turning to Ni-Fu: "Take care, my friend. God knows what these Communist buggers are going to do when they take over."

Ni-Fu stood at the dock, shading his eyes against the early morning glare as he watched his small daughter slowly disappear up the gangplank.

Moments later she stood at the railing next to Browning. Ni-Fu waved. "Don't worry about me," he said, knowing they couldn't hear him over the din of the quayside.

Another whistle and slowly the boat edged from the dock, its screws churning the brown water into a scummy froth. Willing back tears though his heart ached, he smiled at his only daughter. Don't worry, he thought. No one will hurt me. Not as long as I can find the secret of *shou.*

BOOK ONE

THE PRESENT

The now, the here, through which all future plunges to the past.

James Joyce: Ulysses II

ONE

January, 1989
Beijing, China

"Idiots! A simple task. I send two young soldiers to extract a little informa- tion from a helpless old man. What could be easier? Yet they return saying he refuses to cooperate? I tell you, Comrades, I don't know what's become of this younger generation. They're not made of the same stuff as the three of us. They're weaker. Softer."

As if to punctuate his point, the Foreign Ministry chief took a deep drag on his cigarette, savored the unfiltered tobacco, then gathered a bolus of saliva in his mouth and launched it, aiming it into the spittoon on the floor by his desk.

The two men in the overstuffed chairs facing the deputy minister's desk nodded.

"You are right, Comrade Lin," agreed General Pei-Jun Tong. "Deng's open door policies cause our children to forget our sufferings. His reforms bring spiritual pollution and immoral behavior. Instead of *shuo ku* , my son wants only to talk of his new business ventures with the West. He has no interest in hearing about the evil social conditions before the revolution.

"Ziyou shichang. Free markets." The general shook his head. "Imagine owning his own factory. Thank goodness old Mao is not here to see the death of his dream for China."

"Deng says it does not matter whether the good cat is black or white, as long as it catches mice," Peng Han reminded his fellow Long Marchers.

The deputy minister jumped up from behind his desk with the furious energy of a man thirty years his junior. His fist slammed the desk, scattering papers and upsetting the tea cup perched on the edge. "Of course it matters! We sacrificed everything for the Party and our country. If we lose our ideals now, we are no better than those foreign devils!"

A girl in pigtails and a white jacket appeared with a thermos of boiling water. Soundlessly she refilled the deputy minister's tea cup and offered some to his guests.

The men waited for her to leave before continuing.

"I couldn't agree more, Comrade Lin," Peng Han said. "Our numbers have dwindled. Deng has stripped the Party of most of our old allies. In my section of the Intelligence branch there are few of us left." He sipped his tea. "Ironically, it was the wave of student protests as much as our work behind the scenes that helped to discredit Hu Yaobang last year."

The Foreign Minister shook his head. "You are too hard on yourself, old friend." All three knew it was political suicide to openly disagree with Deng's economic reforms. Instead, they'd had to clandestinely destroy the reformers. "Without your work, Hu Yaobang would never have been ousted."

"Peng Han is right about one thing. It's more difficult than ever to keep things as they were," the old soldier lamented. "Deng forgets the bedrock of Mao's philosophy: political power grows out of the barrel of a gun." Tong rubbed his balding temple. "He has slashed the army's ranks by a million and with so many of the old Marxists retired, we have fewer seats on the Politburo."

"Precisely why we are meeting today." Deputy Minister Lin fingered the collar of his crisp gray cotton Zhongshan tunic. Although foreigners knew it as the "Mao jacket", it had actually been designed by some junior political officer from the cities. When Mao adopted it as his preferred uniform, almost a billion people dutifully followed his lead. Only in the last few years had many resumed wearing more Western styles, especially the young. To Lin, who clung to the old way of dress with the same tenacity that he clung to the old way of thought, it was a sensible, functional garment—cheap fabric, comfortable cut.

He pulled the jacket over his matching slacks. "Thank goodness the new head of the Xi'an Institute is still loyal. With Professor Cheng's discovery we will regain control of the Party." He cleared his throat with a noisy flourish, then spewed another frothy mouthful into the spittoon. "We *must* get him to talk."

"I agree," Han replied, tugging his own jacket. Although all three men ate far more than the fifteen hundred or so calories the average Chinese managed to exist on, only Peng Han's belly rippled under his Mao suit. "But torture is not the way. If, as he claims, there is no written record of his research, we need him alive and we need his cooperation."

"Any word from the young doctor you sent in as lab assistant?"

"Chi-Wen Zhou is slowly gaining the professor's trust."

"It's been months," the general reminded.

"Such things take time. After all, the young man is not family."

The deputy minister suddenly interrupted: "What about relatives?"

Han took a deep breath and opened the file he'd brought with him. "Dr. Cheng's wife and son died in childbirth. His brother was killed fighting with Chiang Kai-chek. One daughter, Su-Wei escaped to the United States before Liberation."

"And now?"

"According to our intelligence she lives in San Francisco," he said, reading the prepared notes. "Widowed, one daughter Li Li Quan. Su-Wei was recently diagnosed with cancer."

"Could she survive a trip to China?" asked the general.

Han thought a moment wondering what plan his old friend was conjuring. "I suppose."

The general nodded. "She might provide just the incentive our friend needs to talk."

"Perhaps we could persuade her to return home," Han said.

The deputy minister spent a long time staring at nothing while the aromatic steam from the bitter, dark red tea called Iron Dragon permeated his sinuses. Finally, he looked at his friends and smiled. "Daughter, maybe even granddaughter. Yes, comrades. Perhaps we could."

*   *   *

Washington, D.C.

When a few weeks later a visa request came across the American Consul's desk, he gave it no more attention than any other in the stack. After all, since Nixon's visit in 1972, Chinese students and professors were crossing the Pacific in growing numbers. Recently, the concern of the PRC had become how many of their best and brightest were electing to stay in the States.

But that was not the Consul's worry. If Dr. Seng's government agreed to let him go, the American Consulate would not interfere. Provided, of course, that the man wasn't a spy. That was why, as a matter of course, the Consul now asked his secretary to make a copy and send it to the CIA in Washington.

*   *   *

Seoul, Korea

At the north entrance to Beihai Park, David Kim impatiently watched hundreds of ice skaters enjoying their Sunday afternoon on the frozen lake. Checking his gold Rolex for the second time in five minutes, he wondered if this meeting was a mistake. Would his father approve? He wasn't sure. Up to now the senior Kim had dealt with the Chinese himself, always strictly through bureaucratic channels. It was the kind of tedious red tape that made many Westerners leery of doing business here.

But then Kim was Korean, with an Easterner's understanding of the finer points of negotiation. Over many years, David's father had carefully cultivated relationships within strategic Party-connected organizations, so that now Kim Company was one of Korea's largest family owned *chaebols* or business conglomerates with a firm toehold in a country of one billion untapped consumers.

"Forty years ago, these same people invaded our country and tried to impose their will. Today they buy our TV sets, our textiles, even our MSG," Kim reminded his number one son before sending him off to Beijing. "No longer will the world be conquered by guns. This time, the admirals and generals will wear finely tailored suits; their weapon, economics, their battlefield, world markets."

Although David understood his father's obsessive drive to beat an old opponent at this new game, the younger Kim was impatient for money and power. He was impulsive. A gambler. That's why he was waiting in the insufferable January cold. Tong's mysterious note suggesting a clandestine rendezvous had been too intriguing to pass up.

"*Annyong haseyo!*"

David whirled to face a thirtyish looking Chinese man with a tousled thatch of black hair and sharp cheek bones, dismounting from his black one-speed Flying Pigeon bicycle.

"Speak Chinese," he snapped, annoyed not only by the man's lateness, but by the way his padded cotton jacket and baggy blue trousers contrasted with his own impeccable cashmere coat and Pierre Cardin suit. Lee Tong hadn't even bothered to shave. Hard to believe such a man owned his own factory.

"Anyone hearing Korean will assume we're spies and I don't think even your *hou-tai*," he said, referring to Tong's party connections via his father, "will protect you."

"Sorry." Tong nervously checked the crowd before lighting an unfiltered Kent. He too had second thoughts about this meeting.

David winced as Tong grasped his cigarette between thumb and forefinger. Vulgar, he thought. Like some low-class coolie. "Why all the secrecy? Aren't you satisfied with the agreement made between Kim Company and your plant?"

"You have been most generous. This has nothing to do with MSG." He took a long drag, then lowered his voice. "Recently I overheard my father, General Pei-Jun Tong, talking with two former Long Marchers. What I learned could make us both very rich men."

At that moment two motorcycles and sidecars filled with Public Security Bureau police officers passed the park entrance. Tong stopped talking, following their progress.

"It's okay," he said, lowering his voice. "They're just cruising." Still, he took David's arm, guiding him towards the bridge. "If you're not walking, they think you're up to no good."

*   *   *

Xi'an, China

From his window in the Shaanxi Provincial People's Hospital, Ni-Fu Cheng could barely make out Xingqing Park on the eastern outskirts of the city. When he was first sent to Xi'an some thirty-four years ago, he spent many hours walking among the trees and flowers that grew on the ancient site. Once the official residence of the Tang Dynasty Emperor Xuan Zong, Xingqing Palace's one hundred twenty-three acres had long ago been replaced by an art gallery, reading room, tea house, small lake and children's playground.

Ni-Fu loved to come there. At first it was simply to drink in the beauty, to read and think among the singing cicada. There were great possibilities then and his heart was filled with hope. In recent years he sought the shelter of the park for different reasons. The peace he found there helped to drive away his growing sadness.

But, at age seventy-five, he was locked inside the Xi'an Institute, deprived of even that small pleasure. He turned to catch the cool winter breeze and was just able to discern the edges of the buildings that made up Jiaotong University. Off and on over the past thirty years he had taught science and medicine there, reveling in the exchange of ideas with eager young men and women, hungry for knowledge. And for over thirty years he'd managed to keep his longevity research a secret.

Damn Dr. Seng. Too bad that he had taken over the Institute. Too bad he understood the implications of Ni-Fu's work. And too bad that like a good puppet of the Party, Seng had been only too eager to ingratiate himself with the elders.

Damn. Well at least, Ni-Fu had had the foresight to hide his papers where no one would find them. Not even the torture he'd endured had loosened his tongue.

Ni-Fu thought he caught the voices of some of his young students outside. How he missed them. To Ni-Fu, they were China's most precious resource, the hope for his country's future. To old men like General Tong and his fellow Long Marchers, this young generation was the single greatest threat to their existence. Their fear had made Ni-Fu a prisoner. He was to produce their salvation: a potion to literally cheat death; one that would enable them to live long enough to suppress this young generation as they themselves had been suppressed over forty years before.

Tears came to Ni-Fu's eyes as he considered the futility of his life.

TWO

One month later and some twelve thousand miles away, two men sat nursing brandies after lunching at the White Owl, a fashionable Georgetown restaurant. Although they'd known each other for a long time, had gone through Wharton's MBA program together, each had followed different paths.

Charlie Halliday joined "the Company" as he liked to think of the CIA, while Martin Carpenter became vice-president of Aligen, a top US pharmaceutical company. Each had the kind of perfectly chiseled features that made you think BMWs, cable-knit sweaters and weekends at the Hamptons. They could have been twins—except that Halliday's thick hair had turned to gray years ago, while Carpenter's was still as black as when they were school mates two decades earlier.

Halliday wondered whether the years had really been so kind to his old friend or if the color was an artifice required for his corporate image.

His friend smiled. "I know you didn't haul me half way across town just to buy me a hot lunch, Charlie. What's up?"

"I hear your company's looking for a new Tagamet."

"We're always looking for a box office bonanza. Coming up with a new billion dollar pill every few years is exactly what makes us one of the big boys in the drug business."

"I also hear you're in trouble, Martin," the CIA man said, pointedly lowering his voice. "Aligen has spent over three hundred million on R&D for a herpes cure that the FDA still hasn't approved."

"We're almost there."

"Almost only counts in horseshoes, my friend. If Aligen doesn't come up with a winner soon, your company's going to be in deep financial shit."

Carpenter's eyes narrowed. "Since when does *your* Company care what happens to *my* company?"

"Since we learned the Chinese may be on to a pharmaceutical miracle."

The waitress offered refills. Carpenter waited until she left before responding. "I suppose you have that on the highest authority?"

"That's what they pay me for," Halliday said. "Look, Marty, I know you just spent the morning trying to convince the FDA to expedite your phase three trials. Unsuccessfully, I might add."

"Lousy bureaucrats. Christ, don't they know that in this business timing is everything? I've got deadlines and all they care about is paperwork. Paperwork!" The veins in Carpenter's neck distended as if to emphasize his frustration. "This AIDS epidemic has taken most of the steam out of the Herpes scare." A bitter laugh. "Today you *thank* the doctor when he says you have Herpes or the clap!"

Halliday's smile was sympathetic. "I know that patents on two of your highest margin drugs are due to expire this month and every generic manufacturer is ready to enter your markets."

"We plan to sue."

"Marty, we both know Aligen is undercapitalized and over leveraged. You can't afford long, drawn out litigation. You've gotta come up with a new drug that'll knock the socks off the competition. Something that can't be copied and something that's really new." The CIA man leveled cool blue eyes at his friend. "I can help."

Carpenter snapped to full attention. "I'm all ears."

Making certain no one was near enough to eavesdrop, Halliday removed a manila folder from his briefcase. He placed a picture on the table of two men in white lab coats, arms around each other. Carpenter guessed the Chinese in the picture to be in his thirties and the Caucasian to be somewhat younger.

"Dr. Ni-Fu Cheng. Brilliant physician, teacher and medical researcher trained in England during the '30's. Returned to Shanghai about ten years before Mao and his boys took over." Halliday pointed to the picture. "Dr. Cheng was also something of a history buff. Qin Shi Huangdi, known in the West as Ch'in, first emperor of China, was obsessed with immortality. He sent repeated expeditions into the Eastern Sea seeking the elixir of life. When he died, he was buried in a tomb surrounded by seventy-five hundred life-sized terra-cotta soldiers."

"Yeah, " Carpenter said, interrupting, "I've seen pictures in National Geographic. Pretty amazing." He smiled wryly. "Of course since the old boy died, I assume the mission was a failure."

"Well, that's just it. No one thought this quest for immortality was more than a man's mad obsession. Until Dr. Cheng. As a student at Oxford he spent hours holed up in historical archives—liked to read original documents. By chance he came across a two thousand year old account of Qin's search written by the emperor's personal physician. Certain clues suggested one expedition had discovered a substance that prolonged life. Cheng was impressed enough to ask his Oxford professors to support a research project."

"With little more to go on than a few so-called clues in a two thousand year old document? Pretty far-fetched," Carpenter said, shaking his head.

"Exactly the reaction of the academics. Advised Cheng to concentrate on learning medicine."

"I take it he didn't listen."

"He did at first, but after returning to China as an M.D. in the late '30's, Qin's obsession had become his own."

"How do you know all this?"

"Denton Browning is the other fellow in this picture. An English doctor who worked with Cheng in China until Mao took over in '49. He was Cheng's student. Just before the Communists swept into Shanghai, Browning returned to England. MI-5, the British Secret Service, debriefed all new arrivals. Browning testified Cheng spent all his spare time reading and rereading the document, trying to reproduce this secret formula." Another dramatic pause as Halliday emptied his glass.

"Well?" Carpenter prompted, betraying his growing interest. "Did he?"

"MI-5 didn't think so. From Browning's account forty some years ago, it seemed clear that Cheng was far from developing anything concrete. He had theories, but that was all. A low priority file was opened that collected dust for years. With the isolation of China until the '70's, it was virtually impossible to keep track of people like Cheng. Then about ten years ago, Cheng's daughter living in LA received word that her father was dead."

Exasperated: "For God's sake, Charlie. Don't tell me that's the punch line."

Laughing. "You always were a bottom line man." Halliday leaned forward conspiratorially. "Three weeks ago MI-5 intercepted an internal memo from the Chinese Foreign Ministry. Cheng is very much alive, but under house arrest in Xi'an. The memo alludes to a major breakthrough Cheng is apparently unwilling to reveal. "

"You think he's hit the jackpot?"

"We do." Halliday removed two more pictures from the manila folder. The first was a snapshot of a sixtyish looking round-faced Chinese man in bermuda shorts, high socks and sandals. "This is Dr. Seng, Director of the Xi'an Institute. Our British counterparts believe Cheng is being held there. Three weeks ago, Dr. Seng, a known Chinese Intelligence operative, applied for a visa to the U.S."

"How is his visit tied to that memo?"

Halliday placed the last photo on the table. "It happens that Dr. Seng plans to visit LA Medical Center where Dr. Lili Quan is a resident."

Carpenter whistled softly.

"Quite a looker," Halliday agreed. "She's Dr. Cheng's granddaughter," he said. "The Company thinks Seng is here to somehow lure Lili Quan to China. Probably in the hope that her presence will make her grandfather talk."

"A mighty convoluted scheme, if you ask me."

"That's because you think like an American. In fact, it's totally consistent with the Chinese way of doing business."

Uncomfortable, Carpenter shifted his gaze from Lili's picture to his friend. "This is all very interesting, but how the hell do I fit in? Cloak and dagger is way out of my league."

"Just keep an eye on Dr. Quan for us. With China-US relations normalized, we can't afford another Iran-Contra scandal. Covert operations must be hands off these days." He smiled at his friend. "And since your company funds medical research at LA Medical, we thought Aligen could have a certain presence there."

"I see, " Carpenter said. "I assume I get something in return for my troubles?"

"Ever the businessman," Halliday chuckled. "If Cheng has discovered the secret to long life, we want it for the U.S. As far as the Company is concerned, if you help us get it, it's yours. Aligen will have the drug of the century. You win, we win." Halliday snapped his fingers to summon the waiter with the check. To Carpenter: "Not a bad deal, don't you think?"

"If you're right, " Carpenter responded, "I'd say not bad indeed."

THREE

March, 1989
1:00 P.M.
LA Medical Center

The chaotic, undulating blips on the overhead EKG monitor suddenly went flat.

"Doctor, we're losing him!"

The senior resident appraised the straight line on the oscilloscope. "V. fib to asystole." The systolic and diastolic readouts were falling rapidly. The patient's respirations grew shallow.

"Damn!" She stopped closed chest cardiac massage and grabbed the paddles on the portable defibrillator. "Stand back."

Doctors, nurses, technicians, all stood clear of the bed while the resident delivered a 400 watt-second jolt to Mr. Sanderson's heart.

"Don't give up, damn it," she exhorted the unconscious patient.

The line across the bluish screen of his monitor remained flat, his own color still the dusky hue of near death.

"Shit." The resident reset the defibrillator.

The nursing supervisor checked her watch. "It's been over thirty minutes, doctor. No one will blame you for calling it off."

"Stand back," the resident snapped, simultaneously sending another burst of electricity to the patient. "Come on, come on!"

This time the EKG monitor responded—first one beat, then two, then three—each perfectly formed and evenly spaced.

The nurse shook her head in awe. "My God, you did it. He's back in sinus rhythm."

Almost as dramatically, Mr. Sanderson's coloring improved, his breathing grew strong and steady. Within another minute, his eyes fluttered open. "Who the hell are you?" he demanded from the resident injecting a bolus of lidocaine into his intravenous line.

"That's the doctor who just saved your life." The nurse smiled.

"I told them no female doctors." He pushed the resident's hand away. "And I certainly don't want any damn Chinks working on me." The man glared at her. "Now get out!"

"Well, I can see our patient is feeling better," the resident calmly announced, heading for the door. "I'm late for morning rounds."

Just outside the room Lili Quan leaned against the wall and closed her eyes, willing back tears. No matter how much Sanderson's comment hurt, she refused to lose control. For her, that would mean losing face. Funny, she thought . Losing face. How Chinese.

A tree must have bark to live, a man must have face.

In all her twenty-seven years she rarely thought of herself as anything but a perfect American. She was born in San Francisco, loved hot-dogs, baseball and Bruce Springsteen, insisted on public school as a kid, double majored in American literature and genetics at Wellesley and focused on the problems of the aging in America in her medical residency.

Opening her eyes, she caught sight of her reflection in the opposite window, then just as quickly turned away from it. All her life she had avoided mirrors. That was when she saw the long eyebrows brushed like feathers over crescent shaped eyes; the thick, lustrous, straight shoulder length raven black hair, the tiny nose and the golden skin. The fact that she was beautiful never seemed to register. It was being different that bothered her.

Banana.

Taunts from the old neighborhood: "yellow on the outside, white on the inside". They didn't care that she hadn't taped her eyelids like some of the Asian girls she knew. But, damn it. She *was* American. Through and through. She didn't even speak Chinese for God's sake.

"Dr. Varney, call admitting…. Respiratory therapy to the ER…. Dr. Clark to the OR…."

She savored the familiarity of the page operator's voice. Here, within the hospital, she wasn't different. No matter what the Sandersons of the world thought. Here she belonged. She'd worked hard to secure her place. Through college and med school she'd driven herself to the limit. Now seven months into her final year of residency, she had just one more hurdle: the geriatrics fellowship. With that experience she was virtually assured of a position on the faculty—one of the few women afforded such an opportunity. Then maybe someday she might even make chief of medicine. Not impossible. Only Ed Baxter, the other senior resident and of course, Dr. Trenton, department chief, stood in the way of her dreams.

"I think you forgot this."

"What the…" She turned to the tall, lanky figure beside her.

"I don't know which is more dangerous," he said, handing Lili her Bioeffe helmet, "resurrecting bigots or riding motorcycles."

"The former, I assure you," Lili declared accepting the helmet. "So you heard?"

"Dumb bastard doesn't know how lucky he was you managed his cardiac arrest."

Lili studied Dylan O'Hara's handsome all-American, blue-eyed, blonde haired features for a moment, wondering how she could explain what she was feeling. They'd only met three weeks before. She hardly knew him well enough.

"Thanks for the vote of confidence, but don't give it a second thought…" She shrugged, as much to convince herself. "Tell me what a researcher is doing on a medical floor."

"Looking for you. How about dinner tonight? Since we met at that house staff party I've spent every minute at the lab. We could both use some time off. "

"I don't know…"

"You have to eat."

"I planned to grab something from the cafeteria on my way home. I've been on call the past two nights."

"Don't tell me. You're prejudiced against first generation Irish Americans."

"But you don't…."

"I don't *look* Irish?" he teased. " My mother's side was Norwegian."

"I see. And I suppose one of your long lost relatives was a Viking," she replied. Lili was just 5 foot 4, so at 6 foot 2, Dylan towered over her.

"Scout's honor," he said, smiling. "Now that we've got my genealogy out of the way, will you join me?"

Lili found herself returning his smile. "Okay, but I'll need to get home early."

"Great. Pick you up at six o'clock." Dylan's stare was an intense azure blue. Avoiding his gaze, Lili checked her Timex. *Damn*, she thought, feeling her cheeks redden. He'd succeeded in manipulating feelings she'd just as soon keep in check. "I'd better get going," she recovered. "I'm presenting and I dare not keep the chief waiting."

"Sure. See you tonight."

"Six." Lili nodded, then pushed past the double doors and entered the brightly-lit corridor where nine other white-coated interns and residents had gathered for bed rounds.

*   *   *

Seoul, Korea
one day earlier
6:00 am

David Kim entered the modern glass tower that housed Kim headquarters, nodded to the sleepy looking guard behind the reception desk and proceeded to the bank of elevators at the rear of the lobby. Outwardly calm, he pushed the button with some trepidation. He had no idea why his father wanted to see him, but he suspected news of his gambling debts had reached the senior Kim's ears. He only hoped he wasn't in danger of losing his inheritance.

The elevator doors opened. At 6:00 AM it was empty except for the white gloved operator. "*Annyong haseyo*, honorable Mr. Kim." She performed the customary respectful half bow.

Although beautiful, she was like all the other hundreds of white gloved young women that worked at the menial jobs within the company—simply a pretty fixture.

"Good morning," David replied automatically. "Top floor."

"*Kamsa hamnida.*"

The ride in the Kim elevator was swift and smooth. In less than twenty seconds it had climbed to the 42nd floor. He barely had time to straighten his hand-tailored three piece Saville Row pinstripe suit, custom silk shirt and Cardin tie in the mirrored panels before the elevator doors opened.

Another bow and the doors closed again. Alone, he stood at the oak-paneled entrance to the executive suite. No matter how often he visited these offices, they always filled him with awe, as though the rooms themselves reflected the enormous power of one man. Perhaps to punctuate that power, his father had placed a CRT screen just outside the suite. Already it was flashing the latest quotes on the South Korean composite. Kim Company was made up of private and publicly held entities, shares of which traded in Korea, though as with all Korean firms, foreigners were barred from direct ownership. Over all of this, Shin-yung Kim exercised absolute control.

David entered the outer waiting area -a large open space magnificently decorated with antique oriental rugs, original French impressionist paintings and chamois leather chairs. Each of two secretaries had a solid rosewood desk fitted with intricate intercom and Fax capabilities and computers to download information from any one of the twenty-five Kim factories around the world in milliseconds.

A private door led to a dressing room with cedar closets, and beyond a tiled bathroom including a marble hot tub, stall shower, redwood sauna and a fully equipped exercise area. Another door opened to a small private dining room, tastefully decorated with muraled walls, where David's father entertained business associates. A third door led to Shin-yung Kim's inner sanctum. Too early for either secretary, David passed through the outer area and entered his father's private office unannounced, his heart pounding as he turned the brass handle.

"Late as usual," his father remarked from behind a hard carved mahogany desk and without looking up from his stack of newspapers. Like his son he was impeccably dressed, but his was a silk suit handmade by a local Korean tailor. One manicured hand covered the Wall Street Journal and the Hong Kong Reporter which had already been devoured.

He was in the middle of the Korea Times when a petite young woman who could have been the elevator operator's twin wheeled in a breakfast cart. The covered dishes contained bean-paste soup, steamed and seasoned vegetables, roasted beef, pickled cabbage called kimchi, grilled fish and rice. Despite his otherwise sophisticated tastes, when it came to dining, the senior Kim preferred exclusively Korean fare.

"One cannot speak coherently of important matters on an empty stomach," he said, staring directly at his son. Though a small man, his round face had a sculptured look, long forged into an intimidating hardness.

David nodded, trying to relax. "Sit," his father gestured.

The white gloved waitress prepared two place settings of Limoge china and polished filigreed European silver, then poured one cup of ginseng tea from an acid-etched silver server.

"Tea for my son," he ordered. "Then leave us. I don't want to be disturbed."

David took a seat in one of two easy chairs facing his father's desk and waited like a dutiful son. When they had each finished a cup of the energizing brew, the old man pointed to the walls of glass through which they had a 360 degree view of Seoul. "Look," he said.

To the north, rose the lofty peaks of Bukhan Mountain, to the south, the green hills of Namsan Mountain, while below the mighty Han River flowed west to the Yellow Sea. Down at street level over nine million people bustled like ants among the giant skyscrapers, grand hotels and crowded highways.

"What you see was ruin thirty years ago. In the time span of this world, that is but a single breath." He paused to be sure David grasped the point.

"You are like so many young people these days—impatient for riches, but without understanding of short and long-term goals. To succeed you must take time to gain the trust of those with whom you do business. Like a cat, quietly stalking a mouse, awaiting the right opportunity to pounce."

He pulled a folder from the middle drawer of his desk. "These are checks drawn by you in the last month on South Korean Bank. 10,000,000 Won, 20,200,000, 5,000,000 and 4,800,000." The balance came to 80 million 500 thousand Won or $170,000. "And this," he said, removing another document from the folder, "is the balance sheet and income statement from our MSG operations."

David's discomfort grew.

"Last year we controlled almost two thirds of the foreign market. This year—even with expanded manufacturing capability in China—we have barely made any gains."

"We are meeting our projected quota." David realized his protest was weak.

"Meeting, but not exceeding. I moved those factories to China because of rising labor costs at home."

"Yes, but now that Deng has allowed some private enterprise, many Chinese are setting up their own factories—hiring away workers from our shop. They're...."

The senior Kim waved away his son's explanation. "When you fall into the water, blame yourself, not the stream." Shin-yung Kim stood up and walked to the window. "Like Phoenix, Korea has risen from the ashes." His voice resonated with feeling. "Not because others helped us. It happened because people like me made it happen."

"I understand, father."

"Do you?" The old man shook his head and sighed. "You young people have never known suffering. You never saw what they did to our cities." He clenched his fist. "We took back our country from enemies and made it our own."

The senior Kim now turned to face David. "When I started this company, I knew nothing about business. I was a farmer from the village. But I did understand that once the war was over, our people would be hungry. Soon we expanded the small sugar refining plant into processed food and MSG. Within no time we became the number one food company in Korea. Five years ago I saw the Japanese steal the electronics market from the Americans. I knew nothing about electronics." He laughed. "But I was convinced we could do even better than our former enemies." His eyes burned with the brightness of a winner. "I appointed my sister's son to head the division. Now Kim Electronics is the number one producer of microwave ovens."

"You have done well, father."

"We have done well, but we are not finished. We must pass other nations! We need young men of vision to take our economy beyond our borders. Otherwise, we are doomed to become dependent on others once again."

Shin-yung Kim looked at his son. After six daughters from two wives, he finally had a male heir—a gem in his father's palm. All of Shin-yung's dreams and hopes rested on the boy who, according to the Confucian tradition of familial hierarchical order, would have the highest priority for inheritance. He knew he'd spoiled this child of his middle years, given him everything he asked for. But he'd also sent him to the best schools, even to the United States to learn Western views of business. Now he expected a return on his investment . His tone was stern: "*Hwankap* comes in just three months. I will have completed my zodiacal cycle of sixty years."

"Yes, father, I know."

"I want to celebrate this auspicious birthday knowing it has indeed been a fruitful life."

"You are still a young man. You will have many more years yet."

"Perhaps, but it is tradition that at sixty a man is considered to have completed the cycle of active life. I would like on this landmark day to turn over Kim Company to my only son and heir." The senior Kim's charcoal eyes were deep and lustrous as they bore into his son's very soul. "Tell me how this is possible when you waste your time and money at the gambling tables in Macao?"

"I know I have disappointed you, father." David lowered his head. "I promise to follow the correct path from now on."

Shin-yung Kim's eyebrows lifted. He was no stranger to his son's promises. But this promise must be kept. "The government is pressuring the-*choebels* by raising our cost of capital. Unless we show greater profits, we'll be forced to divest our unsuccessful businesses." He placed a firm hand on his son's shoulder. "If in three month's time you have improved our China operations, I will hand you the chairmanship of this company. If not, I'll have no choice but to disinherit you and give the business to my sister's firstborn."

David stood and bowed politely. "I understand, father."

One last comment as David reached the door: "Of course I don't have to tell you this is the last time I will cover your gambling debts."

*   *   *

LA Medical
1:45 P.M.

Although bedside rounds were part of the daily routine in virtually every teaching institution in the United States, at LA Medical they had become a dreaded ritual. That was because Dr. Richard (Tex to his friends) Trenton, newly appointed chief of the division of geriatrics, was also ex-army and fond of putting his 'raw recruits' through their paces. He said this would make them better docs. Lili thought it was an unnecessary form of hazing that should have been banned along with razor straps and Dunce caps.

Today the chief seemed in a particularly vindictive mood. As the young doctors moved from bed to bed reporting their cases, Trenton grilled each resident unmercifully, asking particularly difficult questions, never satisfied with their answers. The group gathered outside the room of a patient Bill Webster admitted the night before. Lili was glad it was he and not herself on the hot seat at that moment.

"Dr. Webster," Trenton barked. "And I use the term *doctor* advisedly. "Did you by any chance look in a mirror this morning?"

Several of the residents laughed on cue. Lili watched sympathetically as beads of perspiration dripped from the poor intern's brow.

"Sir?"

"Your clothes, Webster. They look slept in."

"Well, as a matter of fact, sir, I was on call last night and I had six admissions and I didn't have time to...."

"To what?" Trenton interrupted. "Groom yourself?" Trenton moved his Ben Franklin half-frames further down his thin, aristocratic nose, as if viewing the wretched intern through a microscope. "Young man, a doctor must first *look* like a professional. How can you instill confidence in your patients when you look like a handyman?"

Lili thought the question all the more pointed noting the contrast between poor Bill Webster and Tex Trenton. As always, Trenton was impeccably dressed. Today he wore a finely tailored blue suit that hugged his lean body. His graying hair was thick and brushed back from his high forehead, accenting a classically handsome face. His demeanor was crisply rigid, obviously learned in the military.

On the other hand, Lili guessed that Bill Webster's normally unruly red curls hadn't seen a comb for days and the stains on his short white jacket that only partially hid a growing paunch, probably contained a mixture of residue from patient body fluids and cafeteria fare. Not a pretty sight.

"If you look sloppy, you think sloppy." Trenton handed the first year resident the patient's chart. "We'll skip this case until evening rounds. Webster, I want you to take a STAT shower. Then put on some fresh clothes and get down to the clinic."

The disgraced intern seemed rooted to the spot.

"On the double, Webster."

"Yes, sir."

Watching poor Bill shuffle back towards the residents' quarters while Trenton lectured the group on proper decorum and dress, Lili wondered how subjecting him to ridicule would ever produce a better doctor.

"Psst, Dr. Quan?"

It was Sam Gould in the next bed. Eighty years old and until this admission, he'd never set foot in a hospital. "That's how I made it to eighty," he told Lili when she examined him four days ago. Then he had been full of false bravado. Now he was all smiles. "I know you skipped me since I'm getting out today, but I wanted to thank you for everything."

You should thank Dr. Philips. He repaired your hernia."

"Sure, he's a great surgeon, but *you 're* my doctor. You explained the procedure to me, so I wouldn't be afraid. And it was you who sat on my bed after the surgery and held my hand."

"And I thought you were asleep," Lili teased.

Winking. "Can't blame an old man for wanting to hold onto a beautiful young woman, can you?"

"Come on, your wife can give me a run for my money."

The old man nodded. "Sixty years with my Sadie and she still makes my heart go pitter-pat. Three great kids, five grandchildren and one great-grand-child." He looked at Lili. "Family, Dr. Quan, is worth everything in this world."

Lili gave Mr. Gould's hand a gentle squeeze. "You take care of yourself. I don't expect to see you back here."

"You can count on it."

In the hallway, Lili smiled to herself, thinking of his words: *You're my doctor.* Wasn't this what medicine was really all about?

Trenton's voice snapped her back to reality. "Dr. Quan?"

"Yes?"

"Ready to present?"

"Yes, sir."

Lili led the group to the next room and waited until the small, white-coated army had reassembled around the bed. Positioning herself so that Trenton could not easily see the patient, she began a recitation of the vital information, simultaneously monitoring the chief's expression.

"This sixty-three year old white female was admitted yesterday with a diagnosis of progressive change in mental status. Her symptoms included increasing lethargy, weakness, slowed speech and depression. Physical exam was significant for a mini-mental status score of fifteen out of thirty, dry skin, dry hair, large tongue and delayed deep tendon reflexes."

Satisfied that Trenton's expression had not yet registered disapproval, Lili proceeded. "EEG on admission showed a generalized slowing of wave forms. Lab studies confirmed markedly reduced thyroid function. Within several hours of starting appropriate therapy, the patient became fully alert."

"Way to go, Quan," one of the first year residents whispered approvingly. "Sharp diagnosis."

Lili smiled her thanks. Then, as if on cue, the frail looking woman who had appeared to be sleeping, opened her eyes. "Has Kennedy been buried yet?" she asked.

Lili stiffened. Don't blow it now, Margaret, she prayed.

"Did I miss the funeral?" the patient persisted.

"By about twenty-six years," Ed Baxter quipped. "Don't you remember? Dallas, 1963, the grassy knoll?"

Lili avoided Trenton's gaze. She threw Baxter a look of reproach.

"Poor Martha Mitchell. She should never have married that bastard."

"Your patient's a real loon," Baxter said soto voce.

And you're a real pain in the butt, Lili would have liked to tell the resident. Instead, she removed the hammer from the pocket of her white coat and pulled up the bed covers to reveal the patient's feet. "As you can see," she said tapping along each Achilles tendon. "The reflexes are now brisk."

"I have to make poo-poo."

"It's okay, Margaret. We'll call the nurse."

"Poo-poo now!"

"Dr. Quan, what is your patient's name?" Trenton demanded, suddenly edging closer.

"Uh, Margaret Manley, sir."

Trenton snatched the chart from her hand and flipped through the pages. "This patient is from the Cook Nursing Home—the *same* patient we discussed last week. Isn't that right, Dr. Quan?" he asked, his growing displeasure unmistakable.

"Why yes."

"And unless *I'm* becoming demented, doctor, I distinctly remember telling you that the patient had an untreatable disease."

Even if Baxter hadn't rolled his eyes, Lili knew a confrontation was now inevitable. She also knew from the uncomfortable fidgeting of her colleagues, that she was on her own. She stared directly at the chief, converting her fear to defiance. "Are you saying that just because Mrs. Manley has Alzheimer's disease, she is not entitled to the same level of medical care as any other patient?" Lili's voice quavered.

Trenton's hazel eyes narrowed. "Dr. Quan," he said, his tone cold, "your emotionalism is entirely out of place and unprofessional. In these cases one must recognize when a specific diagnostic workup or therapeutic modality has exceeded its usefulness."

"You're talking about rationing care."

"I'm talking about reasonable and prudent care, doctor. If we did a brain biopsy on Mrs. Manley today, what do you think we would see under the microscope?"

Knowing where the discussion was leading, Lili reluctantly responded. "The cerebral cortex would show atrophy with wide sulci and dilated ventricles."

"And?" Trenton prompted.

"And the senile plaques and neurofibrillary tangles typical of Alzheimer's disease."

"Exactly," Trenton said, nodding. "This unfortunate lady has structural changes in her brain that doom her to progressive deterioration of personality and intelligent behavior."

"But what about her hypothyroidism? If I hadn't treated her, she would have died."

"Perhaps that would be for the best."

"Isn't that playing God?" she persisted.

"Young lady, physicians make medical decisions affecting patients' lives all the time."

"Dr. Brotwell would never have…"

"Dr. Brotwell is no longer chief of this division," Trenton responded. "And it was precisely because of his inattention to the economics of medicine that he was replaced. Now I suggest you discharge Mrs. Manley back to the nursing home. The rest of you," he said to the other young doctors, "get down to the clinic. Dr. Baxter will precept. We've got a full schedule today."

Grateful for an excuse to flee the uncomfortable scene, everyone scattered within moments. Only Lili, Trenton and Margaret Manley were left in the hospital room. Trenton had reached the door when he turned. "Dr. Quan, you know I could have you dismissed from the program for your behavior this morning."

Before Lili could respond, Trenton had vanished through the door.

For a few moments after he'd gone, Lili simply stood in silence.

"I made in my pants," Margaret whined.

"Great," Lili sighed, reaching for the nursing call button. "That's just great."

*   *   *

Seoul, Korea

David Kim hurried from his father's penthouse office suite to his own smaller office several floors below. His secretary was not in yet, so he dialed the airport himself. "Book me on the evening flight to Beijing."

"How long will you be staying, sir?"

"I don't know," David replied, hoping that Lee Tong would have the news he'd promised and they could consummate their deal quickly. After all, he only had three months to show his father that he was the man to take over Kim Company.

FOUR

Newport Beach, California
5:45 PM

Charlie Halliday sat on a chaise nursing a Dewars over ice as he watched Walter DeForest complete his fifteenth lap across the length of the Broadmoor Hotel pool. Each stroke sliced neatly through the water. Five more laps and he'd quit. No more, no less. It was a routine from which the old man had not deterred for most of his adult life. In fact, when DeForest had recently moved his business from Houston to the west coast, he'd bought this hotel just to have a place to workout close to his office building across the street.

Halliday looked down at his glass, turning it over in his hands. Funny how things had turned out. Twenty years before he'd thought Martin Carpenter the fool for joining a two-bit company called Aligen. Halliday was off to save the world. Now Carpenter was one box away from the top of the organizational chart at one of the largest pharmaceutical companies in the country. And Halliday? Here he was, a forty-fifth birthday looming and behind him, two decades of pushing papers across a metal desk in a company no less bureaucratic than the post office. Not exactly what he had in mind when he joined the CIA.

Halliday drained his drink, picked up a towel and waited for DeForest to pull himself from the water.

"Thanks, son."

At seventy-three, Walter DeForest was an imposing figure—tall, straight-backed with cool, clear eyes and a robustness that came from a lifetime of discipline mixed with more than an occasional medium rare steak and the best Honduran cigars money could buy.

"The reunion is four months away and I've only got to drop ten more pounds," he said, patting his still sizable paunch. "195. That's what I weighed when I graduated Wharton fifty years ago. I've got fifty grand riding on this. "He motioned to the poolside waitress. "Gin and tonic, dear."

"Certainly, Mr. DeForest." Her obsequious tone evidence that his reputation had preceded him.

"Did I tell you how I retired five different times in my life?"

Yes. And how you made and lost vast fortunes. And how you were on the board of seven of the largest companies in the country. And how you are probably the richest man in America today, bar none.

Halliday had heard it all, many times, but he shook his head. For others, this kind of talk might seem like mere puffery, but Halliday had verified his claims. Everything DeForest said was gospel. Including the fact that he'd started with just five dollars in his pocket fifty years ago and turned it into fifty million as a wildcatter in Midland, Texas. From there he'd formed and sold several corporations, moved on to mergers and acquisitions and finally real estate development.

"Lost more than one fortune, that's for sure. But I always managed to land on my feet. That's why they call me the cock-eyed optimist. I'm not afraid to take risks." He winked at the waitress who'd returned with his drink. Affecting a Texas drawl: "Hell, I ain't afraid of nuthin'."

If *that* were true, Halliday thought, he wouldn't be here. The fact was, therewas one thing DeForest did fear and that was dying. And for all his wealth, Walter DeForest couldn't buy longevity. Until now....

*   *   *

Los Angeles, California

Lili shed her hospital whites in the nurses' locker room (more than a decade beyond the feminist's movement and still no special arrangements for women physicians), pulled on a pair of levis and a T- shirt, and hurried out to the hospital lot. She stopped to tuck her thick black hair under her helmet before straddling her Enduro 250.

An unexpected March inversion formed a thin veil of smog and humidity over the LA basin. Accumulated heat radiated from sidewalks and buildings so that at six o'clock, it was almost as hot as midday. Still, she revved up slowly, snaking her way carefully around the packed cars and out onto the main street. The hospital administration frowned on anything bigger than mopeds and Lili knew her 250 XLE could intimidate even the most understanding bureaucrat.

So she followed the rules—at least until she left the University campus. Then, if she hadn't been late, she'd have headed north, away from her apartment. It was something she did most every evening after work—riding on Mulholland Drive just before sunset. Here she could fly along the edge of the world, deftly maneuvering her bike at sixty miles an hour, the wind screaming against the sides of her helmet like a wild animal. She was always awed by the spectacular beauty as the final rim of gold settled on the horizon and then disappeared. Only on these nightly rides did she experience the exhilaration she imagined a bird must feel soaring just above the clouds. Tonight, she hurried to get home.

It happened in a split second. The Yellow Cab careened down Gayley as her bike entered the intersection of LeConte. She had the green light, but the cab raced toward her. She gunned the throttle, shifted her weight to the back of her seat and pulled up on the handlebars, perfectly balanced on the back wheel. With expertise born of years of practice, she sprinted across the intersection.

Never stopping, the cab disappeared down Gayley. Just ahead of Lili a bus left the curb. Jesus, she thought, she was going to slam into it! Instinctively, she extended her left leg and angled her bike outward, producing a controlled slide-out that stopped her dead, narrowly avoiding a collision.

Her heart pounded as she pulled herself off the street. Except for a few scratches, nothing seemed to be broken. She noticed the bus had stopped and a small crowd was gathering.

A policeman appeared. "You okay?"

"You shouldda watched where you were going, bud!" the bus driver shouted.

"As it happens, I saw everything, bud," the officer snapped at the driver. "The fault was yours." He opened his pad and started writing. When he finished, he handed a ticket to the man. "This is a warning. Next time, look before you pull away from the curb." The officer turned to Lili who had just removed her helmet and was shaking her long hair free, "Luckily she handled that bike of hers like a pro."

Most of the gawkers concurred.

"Sue him," an older woman carrying groceries in a string bag advised. Her heavy accent suggested Russian origins.

"I'm fine," Lili insisted.

The woman nudged her as if a confidante. "Come on, it's American way." She lowered her voice. "Perhaps your neck or back hurts tomorrow. You will have lost opportunity."

Lili shook her head. "Thanks, but I'll be okay."

"All right, folks, let's clear out. Show's over." The officer approached Lili. "I hate to say it, but the old lady's right. These days everybody is suing everybody else."

Lili tucked her hair back into the helmet. "Not me."

He stared at her for a long moment. "You know you really are a hell of a biker."

"Thanks."

"You should consider entering some of the cycle races out here."

Lili smiled. "I'll think about it."

He waved as she headed home.

By the time she turned off Wilshire onto Tenth Street and pulled into her narrow underground parking space, she was exhausted. She wondered if there was time for a cool shower before her date with Dylan. Checking her watch, she realized she was more than a little late. She probably should have called, but she'd been on the phone for hours with nursing homes.

Not surprising, it was easier getting Mrs. Manley out of the home than back in. The son and daughter both refused to take her. They had their own families, their own lives. "She's got MediCal. Isn't the state responsible?" They never even came to see her in the hospital. *Yes, Mr. Gould. Family was everything in this world. If you were lucky.* Well, Lili thought, she'd deal with it tomorrow. Tonight she'd try to relax.

Digging into her pocket for her key, she cursed the fact that she couldn't afford a high-rise with valet parking and better security. As it was, the best thing she could say about her living situation was its location in rent-controlled Santa Monica, just five-minutes from LA Medical. Otherwise, what the real estate agent had called 'cozy living near the ocean' was actually a six hundred square foot box on the third floor with a view of an all-night Taco stand and a parking lot. In fairness, except for her books, some momentos and a few photos on the walls, Lili had made no attempt in the two years she'd lived there to convert the tiny space into home. She never had time. For her it was merely a convenient place to store her things and sleep between clean sheets on those few nights she was not on call.

Hurrying inside, she pushed the elevator button. Two minutes. Three. Damn, wherewas that elevator? After a few more minutes of foot tapping, she decided to take the stairs. When she came up on the third floor landing, she had a clear view of her apartment at the opposite end of the hallway. A crack of light seeping out onto the hall carpet from beneath the front door caught her eye. Something was wrong. She'd pulled the shades down yesterday morning to keep the heat out. Her heart raced as she inched forward.

Slowly she turned her key in the lock, quickly snapped the door open and pressed her back against the wall as it swung noisily on its hinges. She held her breath. Nothing. Bright sunshine spilled out, filling the hallway. No shadow played across it. She listened to the silence.

Cautiously, Lili tiptoed through the doorway. Inside everything appeared exactly as she had left it—except for a half-filled glass on the coffee table. White wine.

Dylan was staring at her. "Are you all right?"

"All right? Jesus Christ, Dylan," she breathed, "you nearly scared me to death." She slammed the door, her heart still beating wildly. "Don't tell me. You moonlight as a cat burglar."

"On the contrary. When I got here it was after six. I knocked. No answer. Then I noticed your door unlocked." His eyes were so direct. "I thought someone had broken in."

"But I'm sure I locked it," Lili stammered, feeling foolish. Nothing looked out of place. "At least I think I did."

Dylan shook his head. "A single girl—alone in the city. You've got to be more careful. Here," he said pouring her a glass of wine, "you look as if you could use this. Then I suggest a relaxing shower. " His smile dazzled as he added: "Don't worry about me. I'll occupy myself."

Lili was nonplussed. She knew she ought to be angry at this strange young man who simply walked in and made himself at home. Yet something about the way he made it all seem so natural charmed her. After all, he did say the door was unlocked and he was concerned about her safety. It wasn't as though he was a thief.

Struggling to control her emotions, she accepted the wine, emptied the glass, then excused herself to shower and change.

                    *   *   *

Newport Beach, California

"So," DeForest said, staring down at his veined hand, crisscrossed with the delicate lines of age. "Did he go for it?"

"Hook, line and sinker," Halliday reported. "Just like you said."

"Good." He pulled an alligator cigar case from his pocket, unwrapped a Hoyode Monterrey and held it under his nose, inhaling the rich aroma. "Then Carpenter suspects nothing."

"Nothing. As far as he's concerned this is a covert CIA operation."

"Well, that's almost true," DeForest chuckled, his whole belly shaking. "And you," the old man's eyes bore into Halliday's as if reading his mind, "any second thoughts?"

Halliday returned the gaze. He'd had plenty of time for second thoughts. When he'd met Walter DeForest at a business school reunion two years ago, the man had sized him up with that same look: *Never work for a company you can't own.* A lifetime of slaving away in the gray corridors for men with small minds and smaller pocketbooks. More than enough time.

It didn't matter anymore. In a few months he'd own the world. A proper reward for being the right man in the right place at the right time. "No," he said. "None at all."

*   *   *

Los Angeles, California

As Lili entered her building, a man, ostensibly snoozing in a rented white Ford parked just outside, sat up. He stared at the doorway for a moment, making certain she wasn't coming out. Then he stretched and got out of his car, crossing to the Taco stand on the opposite corner.

He found a pay phone and dialed a special number the GTE system couldn't trace. He listened for the ring on the other end, humming Imagine to himself.

"Yes?"

He recognized the voice. "I found her."

"Good. Don't lose her."

The connection was abruptly cut and the man sauntered back to the Taco stand. He was dying for a burrito.

*   *   *

When she emerged from her bedroom fifteen minutes later, Lili found Dylan examining the trophies on the hall mantel.

"American Motorcycle Association #1 Junior and Senior Champion, first place, Motocross, Southern California Championship, June, 1987 and another in 1988. Pretty impressive."

Lili thought of the policeman suggesting she take up racing and smiled. "I guess I've done all right."

"Are you going for a win in '89?"

Her smile flattened. "With every-other night and weekend call schedules Tex Trenton just introduced, I'll be lucky to get in an hour or two of riding this year." She shrugged. "Maybe it's just as well. Racing can be a pretty expensive hobby."

"Not to mention a dangerous one."

Her dark eyes flashed. "Only if you're not good."

"Self-confidence doesn't hurt either," he countered. "Tell me, since it's not for the thrill of danger, why *did* you take up racing?"

"I suppose it was my way of rebelling."

"Against what?"

Lili cocked her head reflectively. Maybe it was just the wine, but suddenly she wanted to talk, to tell someone how she really felt. Sighing: "Oh, mostly against what I thought my parents represented—all the old ways they'd brought from China. They wanted me to be a good Chinese daughter, to study hard during the day, take Chinese classes in the evenings, marry a nice Chinese boy. I didn't want anything to do with their traditions. When a couple of All-American types from school took up cycling, it seemed a perfect opportunity to belong."

"And did you?"

A bitter laugh. "Hardly. The kids still called me Chink." Lili brushed a stray wisp of raven colored hair from her forehead. "But that just made me more determined to be the best damned biker around."

Dylan glanced at a grouping of photographs on the wall. "Your parents?" he asked, pointing to a Chinese couple in a formal pose. The gray-haired man in the chair appeared at least thirty years older than the woman standing behind him.

Lili nodded. "My father died when I was ten. My mother was his second wife."

"She's very beautiful." Dylan looked at Lili who had changed from her hospital whites to an emerald green pants suit that complemented her coloring and figure. "Like her daughter."

A bittersweet smile. "Except for looks, we're as different as rabbits and tigers."

"Rabbits and tigers?"

"Legend has it that Buddha summoned all the animals of the world to appear before him promising those who paid him homage would have a year named after them. Only twelve animals came, so there is a cycle of twelve that is repeated over and over. The animal ruling the year in which you were born is said to exercise a profound influence on your life. As the Chinese say, 'this is the animal that hides in your heart'.'"

"I see, "Dylan said, fascinated. "And your mother was born in the year of the rabbit."

Lili nodded. "The rabbit is considerate, modest and thoughtful." She looked at her mother's picture for a long moment. "Certainly all the qualities my mother possesses. She's not a boat rocker."

"And the tiger?"

Lili felt her cheeks redden. "The tiger is full of vigor and the love of life, passionate, daring, and unpredictable." She turned away, embarrassed at having revealed too much. "Anyway, it's my mother who believes in all this nonsense. Not me."

"I don't know, "Dylan said. "A little superstition never hurt anyone."

This time when Lili looked up at Dylan there were tears in her eyes. "My mother has pancreatic cancer."

"I'm sorry." His voice was gentle.

"Because of her foolish superstitions she's refused medical treatment. It's her *joss*, she says, to die now. Just like it was her fate to lose her parents, to come to this country all alone, to live with an elderly aunt who forced her into a loveless marriage with a man old enough to be her father, to..." Lili bit her lower lip in an effort to stop the flow of tears. "She accepts everything too easily."

Dylan moved to put his arm around her. "Somehow I have the feeling she wouldn't accept me with the same equanimity."

Lili saw the cornflower blue eyes twinkle and laughed in spite of herself. To her mother, all Caucasians were foreigners, waigorens. "You're right."

"Something also tells me that wouldn't stop *you*..."

Now the eyes were searching, waiting for her answer. Dylan's face was very close. Too close for her to prevent the kiss. Even if she'd wanted to. The touch of his lips on hers was like fire and she found herself responding. In their closeness she felt his heart beating as wildly as hers, as if his pulse were her pulse, linking them, melting into one another.

She closed her eyes, at once overwhelmed and frightened by his effect on her. No rational explanation. She hardly knew him. Yet there was no mistaking the attraction. Was it the familiarity of his kindness, the danger in his unpredictability, the foreignness of his blonde all-American handsomeness? Or was it something more? Right now she knew only one thing for sure: she was glad he had come into her life. It had been a long time since she'd felt that way.

Opening her eyes, she sensed the warmth of his breath on her cheek, saw him watching her. "Not bad, Dr. Quan."

Lili returned his banter. "I'm strictly an amateur."

"Then I guess we'll have to try it again some time." His lips brushed lightly across her forehead. "They say practice makes perfect." An impish grin.

Lili smiled as she removed her hand from his. "I won't deny it was good, but I generally make a habit of getting to know someone before the first kiss."

"Easily remedied. What would you like to know?"

"Everything."

Dylan laughed. "It's a pretty short story. But I'll tell you what. Grab your purse and I'll give you all the sordid details on the way to dinner."

*   *   *

A few moments after Lili and Dylan had pulled from the curb in Dylan's red Mazda Rx7, the man in the white Ford did the same, staying just close enough to follow without being seen.

*   *   *

Although they had been riding in silence for some time, it was a comfortable silence two friends might share. Amazing, Lili thought. Although they'd just met, she didn't feel the need to fill empty space with idle chatter. Instead, she scrutinized Dylan's handsome profile as the city lights illuminated it in flashes: strong chin, aquiline nose, and a shock of thick blonde hair brushed casually over a broad brow. The fingers that held the steering wheel were long and delicate. A study in contrasts, she thought.

"I'm ready for that short story," she said when they had stopped at a red light. "But first one question."

"Sure."

"You said you were first generation Irish."

"That's right."

"Yet Dylan is a Welsh name."

"Sharp lady."

"I *was* an English major at Wellesley. Dylan Thomas has always been one of my favorite poets."

"My mother's as well," Dylan replied. "An extraordinary individualist she used to tell me. Wanted me to grow up to be like my namesake. The problem is *she* didn't know he wasn't Irish. Worse, *she* didn't know the Welsh have always sided with the British and…"

"And the British hate the Irish," Lili interrupted.

"Let's just say, they usually don't drink in the same pubs."

"So how did your mother get away with giving you such a controversial name?"

Dylan's laugh was measured. "Norwegians have a stubborn streak almost as fierce as the Irish. Besides I was born during one of my father's drinking binges. When he came to, Dylan was officially on my birth certificate."

"Your mother sounds like a woman after my own heart."

"If you mean, a fighter, that she is."

"And your father?"

"He left Belfast at seventeen. Not much work for an uneducated Catholic kid in a Protestant town. Came to Chicago where his uncle pulled a few favors with the democratic organization to get him work with the city."

"What did he do?"

Dylan stared meditatively at the street signal. "Dad called it civil engineer, but garbage man was what he was."

"Honest work," Lili said matter-of-factly.

"Sure. Labor omnia vincit improbus."

Remembering Vergil from college, Lili translated the Latin: "Labor conquers everything."

"Not everything."

"How do you mean?" she probed.

Dylan was silent for another moment, as if hesitating and then, seeming to yield to impulse, began to describe his background. "I was born on the wrong side of the tracks. North Chicago. St. Gregory's parish. Not everyone was Irish. It was a melting pot for new immigrants. That's where my parents met—mom's folks were fresh from Norway. They got married, had eight kids, played Dennis Day records on Friday nights and served soda bread and butter for breakfast. I went to Quigley North with the Catholic sons of other blue collar workers and worked summers as a busboy at the fancy country clubs. That's where I met the sons of the LaSalle Street lawyers and stockbrokers."

Dylan's knuckles whitened as he gripped the steering wheel. "Of course they never invited me to their homes on the north shore." His tone became bitter. "So superior. Like I came from another world."

The switch astonished Lili.

"I guess I did. None of their fathers came home smelling of garbage with their hands so callused by manual labor that they felt like sandpaper." Another uncomfortable pause. "I hated them for looking down at me and yet, I wanted to be just like them." Dylan glanced at Lili. "You probably can't understand that."

A wry smile. "More than you think."

"I spent everyday at the library and every extra dollar on books, determined to be better than any of them. Dad never understood that working for the city wasn't good enough for me. Luckily I managed to get a college scholarship to Georgetown, then a military scholarship to Bethesda Medical."

"That's pretty impressive," Lili said. "But how did you end up in research?"

"To be honest, I never really liked medicine. Not the people part. I was good in the classroom, but dealing with patients just didn't turn me on the way it does you." They turned east onto Wilshire Boulevard. "For me, med school was just a ticket out of poverty." He stared at her for a moment, then looked away. "During my last year of med school I needed a summer job. There was a professor working in immunogenetics at Bethesda who needed a tech. I got hooked on the main histocompatibility complex."

"The what?" Lili asked. She'd majored in genetics in college, but her background was more basic.

"MCH- that's the master genetic control of the immune system. I'm working on a theory that the MHC may be one of the gene systems controlling aging."

"Tell me more," Lili urged, fascinated.

"You're sure? I can bore the hell out of people when I get started."

"I'm sure," she said, pleased at the change in his mood.

"Well, we know that certain substances—superoxide dismutase or SOD and the mixed-function oxidases—protect against damage by free radicals that cause age changes while cyclic nucleotides are involved in cell differentiation and proliferation. We also know that all three are on the same chromosome and are genetically linked to the MHC. In humans, they're found on chromosome 6; in mice, it's number 17."

Lili considered his explanation. "Let me see if I understand. You think because the substances are all genetically linked, these chromosomes may be the focus for age changes."

Dylan shook his head. "Brains as well as beauty. You really are a quick study. I haven't broken the code yet. But somehow the MHC regulates DNA repair. When the process breaks down, the result is a decreased immune response."

"That would certainly explain the increase in certain infections in old people."

Dylan nodded. "Two hundred years ago the average American lived to be thirty-five. Today we can expect to reach seventy."

"Like the Bible said: three score and ten."

"I think we can improve on the good book, Lili. By finding the key to what turns these genes on and off, we might be able to control the rate of aging, prolong human life span to one hundred twenty, one hundred fifty, who knows how long."

"You're serious."

"Deadly serious. The eagle and swan live to be one hundred, the carp and pike are believed to reach one hundred fifty and the whale leads the mammalian group at five hundred years. I tell you, Lili, with a four-fold increase in the over sixty-five population since the turn of the century, there'll be literally millions clamoring for access to it. Nobel prize. Fame and fortune." He smiled, caught up in his own fantasy.

Lili didn't know what to say. Extending the longevity of mankind through genetic engineering. She couldn't even begin to comprehend the enormity of such a discovery. Certainly, if Dylan was right , the stakes were high indeed. What wouldn't most people give to live longer, to see one more sunrise, one more glimpse of a child, one more moment stolen from the inexorable passage of time? "Are many others doing this kind of research?"

"Until about ten years ago, the field was pretty much dominated by pseudo-scientists and charlatans. Now every country is seriously pursuing aging research. But we've got the jump on all of them. As long as our grant money keeps coming."

I'd think this kind of work would be easy to fund."

"Yeah, but medical research just isn't a priority right now. This year's total budget for cancer research is twenty-four times smaller than the thirty-nine billion dollar R & D funding for the Department of Defense."

"Guns over butter," Lili observed wryly.

Dylan maneuvered the car onto Gayley Avenue. "These days wrangling money is a full time job. Thank God for Tex and his Washington connections. When we lost the NIH grant, he pulled strings with some drug company to fund the work. That's how we ended up in Los Angeles."

"You mean Dr. Trenton?" Lili asked at the same time that she realized they were headed back to the LA University campus.

"Yeah. He's the professor I was talking about. When I met him he was one of the few people doing serious research on aging. His wife had Alzheimer's. He was desperate to find a cure."

"I didn't know," Lili said.

"He doesn't ever talk about her now. She died in a private institution in Arlington, Virginia."

"That's too bad."

He stopped in front of the Faculty Club entrance.

"Is this where we're having dinner?" Lili asked, knowing that only university faculty belonged to the swank campus eating club.

Dylan nodded. "I guess I forgot to tell you. The chief's invited some of his research staff to meet the drug company rep."

Lili panicked. "Do you think this is a good idea? If I remember our orientation correctly, Trenton's number one rule: no fraternizing among the troops."

"I'll admit he can be a stickler for rules," Dylan agreed. "But you've got nothing to worry about. This was his idea."

"You're kidding."

"I'm serious," Dylan said, turning off the motor. "He's also invited some visiting physician. Apparently, this guy's interested in meeting a few of the clinical staff."

Lili looked at Dylan, weighing whether she ought to tell him about her run-in with Trenton that morning. "One question."

"Shoot."

"When did Dr. Trenton actually suggest I come to this dinner?"

"Yesterday," Dylan replied, getting out of the car.

Great. That's just great, Lili thought as she watched him circle to her side of the car.

He offered his hand. "Why? Is there a problem?"

She forced a smile as she stepped onto the curb. "None at all." Except for the fact that she was already on her way to ruining her own career with Trenton and she now might take Dylan down too.

*   *   *

David Kim was already in the air when Charlie Halliday tried to reach his contact in LA.

*   *   *

Some thirty years before, the Faculty Club had been the recipient of a significant part of some wealthy alum's endowment to the University. Apparently the only stipulation was that between each course at dinner, a peach sorbet be served. That tradition still persisted along with the impeccable service, soft classical music and the often quotable conversation. Within the impressive glass and stone structure, heads of state sat with CEO's and chiefs of academic departments as equals.

Lili and Dylan were ushered to a private dining room where they found most of the forty or so other guests already at a buffet table overflowing with succulent international delicacies: Moroccan couscous, Indonesian satay, Greek moussaka, Russian caviar; served at the bar, a half dozen wines and a serious champagne. Looking over the crowd, Lili realized most of the group were from the medical research staff. Except for Ed Baxter who had just cut in line ahead of them, she was the only clinician.

"Quite a spread," Baxter observed, loading up his plate. "Guess our invitation means we're both still in the running for the geriatrics fellowship."

"Guess so," Lili responded, hoping Dylan hadn't heard.

Luckily, he was engrossed in conversation with a young Indian PhD. "Lili, this is Dr. Saleh. Bodie perfected his southern accent working on his doctorate at Duke."

"Charmed, I'm sure," Bodie said, affecting Tennessee Williams. "Y'all come by my lab anytime."

"He's into glucose transport," Dylan whispered, as they continued down the line past the salads to the entrees. At the bread table, Dylan introduced Lili to Elaine Morgan, a buxom biochemist from Harvard whose cool smile turned to stone when she realized Lili had come with Dylan.

"I hope our boy genius hasn't bored you with the wonders of the MHC," Miss...."

"Dr. Quan," Lili prompted.

"Oh yes, Dylan did say you were a medical doctor. But of course, clinicians are *really* ignorant when it comes to understanding what it is we scientists do." Her saccharin smile did not belie the barracuda.

"Don't you know what Plato says about ignorance?" Lili questioned.

"Excuse me?"

"There are two kinds of ignorance: simple ignorance which is the source of lighter offenses and double ignorance which is accompanied by a conceit of wisdom." Lili leaned forward and lowered her voice so Elaine had to move closer to hear. "I hope yours, *Dr.* Morgan," she said, returning the fake smile,"is the former."

Dylan was still laughing a few moments later as they headed for one of the round tables in the adjoining room. " You really are something."

"Yes," she replied, distracted. Tex Trenton was approaching them.

"Dr. Quan," he said, extending his hand. "I'm delighted you could make it this evening."

Lili returned his greeting, surprised he had chosen not to mention the morning's incident.

Trenton guided them to a table where he introduced them to Martin Carpenter, Vice President of Aligen International and to Dr. Ma-Yan Seng, a visiting professor from China. " Dr. Seng is medical director of the Xi'an Institute at Shaanxi Provincial People's Hospital. Dr. O'Hara is a research associate and Dr. Quan is one of our medical residents."

He turned to Dylan. "Dr. O'Hara. If I could have a word with you. Excuse us for a moment," he said, leading Dylan to a corner. Lili watched, wondering if they were talking about her. I *am* getting paranoid, she told herself.

At the same time, the moon-faced Chinese professor stood and bowed to her. *"Ni hao ma."*

"I'm afraid I really don't speak Chinese," she said, matter-of-factly. "I understand," the professor replied in perfect English, the slight Russian intonations virtually indiscernible except to the best linguistically trained ear. "It is a hard language to master, harder still to maintain in a foreign land."

Something about his look made her feel uncomfortable. Even defensive. Lili realized his words had been spoken so softly, they were meant for her ears only. The others were engaged in polite small talk that included the obligatory comparisons of west versus east coast living, the latest basketball scores and the sorry state of live theater.

"Laid back…"

"…great weather."

"Too many sprouts!"

"Can you believe those Lakers?"

"If Shakespeare were alive today…"

"….he'd probably be Neil Simon…"

"…or Sidney Sheldon!"

Polite laughter.

"I understand your company funds some of the research here, doctor." Lili addressed Carpenter.

"I'm strictly 'mister'—Wharton MBA. I leave medicine to people like yourself." He smiled. "And yes, this is just one of twenty some university and private foundations Aligen sponsors. Our company spends close to three hundred million dollars a year on R&D."

"I never realized how much research in this country is privately funded," Lili replied, thinking of her earlier conversation.

"It's the American way," he said, observing Dr. Seng's implacable expression. "If a major new product is developed at just one site, we've more than justified our investment."

"From what Dr. O'Hara tells me, his work on aging seems very promising," she said, putting in a good word for Dylan who had just returned to the table with Trenton.

A self-effacing gesture from Dylan. "Well, I haven't found the fountain of youth yet. "

Carpenter turned to the visiting professor. "I guess you haven't either, Dr. Seng or we'd have heard about it."

"Pardon me?" The strange expression that flashed across Seng's face was so fleeting that everyone but Carpenter missed it.

"The Xi'an Institute. I assumed it was a research facility."

Recovering quickly: "We do some research, but not in areas requiring sophisticated technology. In that sense we are still far behind your country." He turned to Lili. "I suppose in your terminology, you'd call our approach more holistic."

"That sounds very modern," Lili remarked.

"Actually holistic medicine is not a Western creation. Plato's original notion of holistic treatment was much like the Chinese concept of medical treatment."

"How so?" Carpenter asked.

"Chinese medicine seeks the harmony of yin and yang—the union of body and mind."

"Interesting."

"It has been proven through historical documents that ancient Chinese physicians took socio-cultural causes of disease seriously. Early on, they noticed the effect of emotions on the body."

"Very enlightened," Lili said.

Seng smiled at her. "I understand you're interested in geriatrics."

"I plan to specialize in diseases of aging."

"In China we do not view aging as a disease," Dr. Seng responded.

"But what happens when people can no longer care for themselves?"

An enigmatic smile from Seng. "I suppose we Chinese are an odd lot. We believe when our children grow up, they not only must respect their elders, but care for them if necessary."

Lili experienced the discomfort she felt earlier as Seng watched her.

"Have you ever been to China?" he asked.

"No." And she didn't plan to.

"Perhaps you might like to spend a few months at the Xi'an Institute as a visiting fellow. You could learn much from our approach to aging."

Trying to be polite: "I'm sure I could."

"A thought occurs to me," he said. "A young resident from Harvard was scheduled to come in April and canceled at the last minute. You could take his place."

It was preposterous. "I couldn't leave LA Medical now."

"I'd grab an opportunity like that," Carpenter interjected. "Wouldn't you, Dr. Trenton?"

"Dr. Quan is merely a junior resident. It would be more appropriate when she's further along in her training," the chief replied, speaking as though Lili wasn't there.

The nerve of the man, she thought, feeling like a child who'd been chastised. For Dylan's sake she held her tongue, though Trenton's supercilious air infuriated her. But for the fact that she had no interest whatsoever in seeing China, she had half a mind to take Dr. Seng's offer. If only to spite old Tex.

Dr. Seng was saying something.

"I beg your pardon?"

"I said I'll be in Los Angeles for the next week." He handed her a card. "Here's my number. If you change your mind, call me. Any time."

"Thank you."

Someone tapped her on the shoulder.

Lili turned to Ed Baxter. "What?"

"I just got beeped for your patient."

"Who?"

In a voice loud enough for everyone to hear: "Margaret Manley."

"What's the problem?"

"You didn't write for restraints. Apparently she got confused and fell out of bed. Nursing is fit to be tied."

Although Trenton said nothing, his expression reflected disapproval.

Lili jumped up, eager to avoid further damage to her career. "I'll take care of it."

"Let me give you a lift to the hospital," Dylan offered.

"No, please. Stay. It's just a few blocks. I'll take the campus shuttle." She made her excuses to the guests at the table and hurried out.

Jesus, Lili thought, as she waited for her ride. What else could go wrong today?

                    *   *   *

The answer came an hour later after she'd finished examining Mrs. Manley. Fortunately, the accident hadn't produced any fractures or even a serious head injury, just a few bruises. But the patient had hit her head. Standard procedure required a neurology consult and skull X-rays. This meant Mrs. Manley wouldn't be leaving LA Medical for a few days. It also meant Trenton would definitely not be pleased.

                    *   *   *

Even Dylan's message on her answer phone wishing her a good night's sleep and suggesting dinner "just the two of us" the following evening failed to overcome her sense of impending doom.

FIVE

March, 1989
Beijing, China

Breathless, Peng Han burst into the Foreign Ministry office. "I have news."

Deputy Minister Lin nodded toward the chair in front of his desk. General Tong was already seated. "Sit down, old friend." He offered Han a cup of tea.

"Fortunately in my section of the Intelligence branch, reports still must go through me." Han smiled as he handed Lin a handwritten memo.

"So, Dr. Seng met the daughter."

"Yes, but how can you be sure he'll convince her to come to China?" the General asked.

"Comrade General, I know you would prefer we kidnap her and be done with it." Han savored a sip of the steaming tea in his cup before speaking again. "Just trust me. Our plan will take time. The daughter must be skillfully recruited and managed. If she comes on her own, we'll accomplish our mission more easily and," he added pointedly, "without alerting others outside our group."

"But once she's here...."

"Once she's here," Han completed Lin's thought, "her life will be of little consequence."

"Yes, I suppose your approach is correct," the General acknowledged.

Even Lin nodded in agreement.

Han took another sip. "I know it is."

*   *   *

Seoul, Korea

This time Lee Tong was waiting impatiently when David Kim arrived at Beihai Park.

"Sorry, I wanted to be certain I wasn't followed."

Tong looked around the park. He was sure the people watching their children playing near the water were not spies. "It's safe. These days most anti-government activity is centered at the universities."

"Oh, I hadn't heard."

Despite assurances, Tong lowered his voice. "Just a bunch of intellectuals," he sneered. "They think because they go to college they understand what this country needs."

"And what do they think this country needs?"

"Right now, they ask for nothing. They're just meeting and talking. But who knows what trouble these hooligans might stir up."

Like demanding that *guan dao* be banned, David thought. Well, it was none of his business. "I've thought about your offer and I'm prepared to make a deal."

Lee Tong looked around before responding. "Equal partners."

"Once you get me the elixir."

"I need something in writing."

David smiled. "You said the students are getting roused up. Suppose someone were to get hold of a contract between a Korean company and the son of a well-known party member? Or worse, suppose the agreement was to steal a drug that could prolong the lives of the common people, but the parties planned to exploit the drug for their own gain?"

"Well, when you put it like that..."

"There can never be written documentation of this transaction. Not until the drug is safely out of the country."

Tong appeared to relax. "Very well."

"When do you think you'll have the formula?"

"Within the next three months," Tong whispered.

Three months! Exactly his own deadline. "Your sources are reliable?"

"Impeccable."

David nodded and the two men shook hands to seal their bargain.

"*Zhu ni yun*," Tong said, wishing them both good luck.

"*Zhai jian.*"

As he left the park, David couldn't help but smile. His luck was indeed good. If all went as planned, before his father's sixtieth birthday, he would claim his rightful place as head of Kim Company. And that, he thought, as he headed for the airport, was certainly something to celebrate.

SIX

Lili's prediction had been right on target. First thing the next morning she was told to report to Dr. Trenton's office. Although he was still in the lab, his secretary insisted that she wait. Sitting in his inner sanctum, her eyes scanned the spacious room. The furnishings were surprisingly austere: two plain chairs facing a massive steel desk. Well, Trenton *was* ex-Army, Lili thought.

Behind the desk a medium sized window framed a smog-filtered view of the LA University campus in the foreground surrounded by the Santa Monica mountains. On the far wall was a row of perma- plaqued diplomas, documenting Dr. Trenton's ascent through the medical academic hierarchy: Bethesda Medical School, Kimbraugh Army Hospital internship, residency and geriatrics fellowship, then back to Bethesda as chief of service. Next to these was a simply framed document stating that Colonel Richard Trenton had been honorably discharged from the United States Army in 1987 and just below, a row of bookshelves filled with the latest medical tomes.

Lili rose to examine the titles: Harrison's Medicine, Schwartz's Surgery, Nelson's Pediatrics. She removed a copy of Principles of Geriatrics Medicine and began flipping through it when she noticed a small black and white photo caught between the pages. Although, faded, the picture was clearly Trenton as a younger man—perhaps about thirty, Lili guessed—with the same aristocratic features, but without the coldness around the eyes. He seemed happy, almost smiling. He had his arm around a beautiful woman with delicate features and a smile that even on the two dimensional surface projected an almost palpable warmth. Could she be his wife, Lili wondered, thinking of her conversation with Dylan. So young to have a disease like Alzheimer's.

"Be sure to put that back where you found it."

Lili spun around to face Trenton who had entered without a sound. He removed his white coat, hung it behind the door, and sat down behind his desk. Closing the textbook, Lili replaced it on the shelf. Then she returned to the uncomfortable straight-backed chair.

For several minutes there was absolute silence as Trenton flipped through his desk calendar, making occasional notations. When he finished, he buzzed for his secretary to take it. Only then did he look up to acknowledge Lili's presence.

"Dr. Quan, I had been told that you were one of LA Medical's best, but I've been very disappointed in your performance these last few days."

The sun from the window behind his desk cast Trenton's face in a play of light and shadow so Lili could not see his expression. There was no question, however, about the coldness in his tone.

"Look, if you're talking about sending Mrs. Manley back to the nursing home, I tried," Lili began. "In fact I spent several hours yesterday making calls. Even the Cook facility was reluctant to take her."

"And why was that?" That supercilious tone again.

Lili fidgeted. "She's on welfare."

"Exactly! LA Medical has to eat the major portion of her care now -including a CAT scan and MRI."

"Dr. Trenton, the fact that she fell out of bed was an unfortunate accident. But I couldn't allow nursing to put her in restraints. It's a barbaric practice."

"It's common practice in hospitals across this country," he said evenly. "And it's my rule in this hospital that patients with dementia are kept in restraints."

"That doesn't make it right," Lili insisted. "Mrs. Manley was terrified of being tied down."

"Dr. Quan, you don't know your place here," Trenton snapped. "You're a resident. Your job is not to second guess me. You have a long way to go before you are even in a position to make any administrative decisions."

Lili felt her cheeks redden. "What is it you're really angry at me for, Dr. Trenton? For asking questions? For thinking for myself? Or for simply disagreeing with you?"

"I have tolerated your impertinence long enough, young lady," Trenton hissed. "Since I became head of geriatrics you have repeatedly questioned my rules." He pointed his finger at her. "If you continue, I promise you you'll not only lose the geriatrics fellowship next year, but you'll be out of this hospital before July. Now get out!"

Shocked, Lili backed away. She opened the door and hurried down the corridor as tears welled up in a mixture of fear and rage.

Behind her, Tex Trenton slammed the door shut, grabbed the phone and dialed Washington.

*   *   *

Macao
one day later
midnight

David Kim had exchanged about $100,000 worth of Won for pataca before taking the 11:00 PM jet foil from Yaumati dock in Hong Kong. Less than forty-five minutes later, the glass and aluminum beast had skimmed due west across the Pearl River estuary to Macao Wharf. Because it was a weekday, the tourist crowds were modest. David could easily find a place to stay later. Now he headed directly for the Macao Floating Palace, a sea-soaked dragon that was one of four no-limit casinos open round the clock for craps, roulette, baccarat, keno, chemin de fer, dai siu (big, small), the slots; anything a gambler might desire.

Fifty percent of Macao's government revenues come from taxes paid by these establishments, patronized almost exclusively by Hong Kong Chinese.

Most Macao hotels take the precaution of asking that bills be paid in advance, since there is always the risk that patrons will lose their last cent at the gambling tables. The streets surrounding the casinos are strategically lined with pawnbrokers so that unlucky gamblers can trade their rings and watches for a one way ticket home.

David made his way inside, where the sound was a metallic roar of one-armed bandits devouring change. Plastic dice tumbled on the green felt of crap tables as stick men changed numbers and gaming chips were stacked, shuffled and collected. He accepted a cocktail from a narrow-eyed waitress in a tight-fitting sarong and moved toward a row of slots where a small fragile-looking Chinese woman was feeding two "hungry tigers" simultaneously, mumbling profanities with each pull as if they were incantations. After watching for several minutes it appeared her curses were of no avail.

"Bad *joss*."

David whirled to find an exotic-looking Eurasian smiling at him. Her short Mary Quant haircut accentuated the elegant planes of her face. David admired her green silk brocade cheongsam, the diamond bracelet and matching earrings at the same time that she seemed to be sizing him up.

"I haven't seen you here before." She looked no more than nineteen or twenty, but her low throaty voice suggested years of experience.

"That's because I usually frequent the Hotel Lisboa."

"And tonight?"

"Tonight I plan to break the bank," he said, downing his first drink and accepting another from the waitress in almost one fluid motion. "I'm looking for a Fan Tan game."

The beauty raised one plucked brow. "Ah, you are celebrating a big business deal."

"How did you know?"

She touched the collar of his Brioni suit. "Successful looking man like you. I merely guessed."

David leaned over, speaking in a conspiratorial whisper. "I'm on the verge of a multimillion dollar deal." He waved his hand in an expansive gesture. "Maybe multibillion."

Her laugh was like tinkling bells. "You are a lucky man."

"David Kim was born lucky."

"Any relation to Kim Company?"

"My father started the firm thirty years ago. I'm his only son and heir."

"In that case, Mr. Kim, perhaps you'd like to join the fun over there." She nodded toward the middle of the room.

He followed her to the Fan-tan game where a sign in Chinese suspended over the table read: "No limit." Except for the house dealer acting as banker, all four men at the table had their jackets off and their shirt sleeves rolled up. Three perspired visibly as they placed their cards around the joker, face up, in the center of the table.

"Mind if I join?"

A heavy set mustachioed man with a pale, Z-shaped scar etched along his right cheek, looked up. A bottle of Dom Perignon was buried in a bucket of ice at his side; a long cigarillo hung from his lips. "We play heavy stakes at this table, my friend." He was a mixed-race Macanese whose English had a Portuguese accent. "Minimum ten grand a bet."

The Eurasian girl took a seat behind him and whispered in his ear. She opened her satin Chanel handbag and tossed ten more chips into a pool. David guessed they totaled $200,000.

David felt his adrenaline pumping. They say the Chinese are insatiable gamblers. But to David, this is where he felt most alive. He summoned the waitress who exchanged his pataca for $1000 chips, then, took off his hand-tailored silk suit jacket, sat down and anted up thirty chips. "No problem. Deal me in."

*   *   *

LA Medical

Lili found herself walking aimlessly down the hospital corridors, avoiding the stares of any who might detect the tears. There was as much anger in them as humiliation, but she refused to indulge either. Instead, she forced herself to take several shallow breaths. *Calm. Calm. It wasn't my fault. It was Trenton who lost control .*

She turned a corner and kept walking. She had to talk to someone. Before she realized where she was headed, she'd reached the door to the immuno-genetics lab. After several knocks, she entered. The large room was filled with rows of granite countertops where a couple of white coated techs were busily pipetting. They didn't seem to notice Lili.

Off to one side were several glassed -in cubicles that served as offices for research staff. Dylan's was in the far corner. From where she stood she could see him sitting, his back to her, hunched over his microscope. She made a move towards his closed door when she realized someone else was in the tiny room, peering into a set of lenses on the other side of the table. Elaine Morgan!

Lili stepped out of direct view. Damn! she thought. Why get so upset? Elaine and Dylan were colleagues. Doing research together. Besides, Lili reminded herself, she certainly had no claim on Dylan. They'd only been out once and that hadn't exactly been a huge success. So why was she feeling betrayed?

She watched as Elaine got up, walked to Dylan's side and bent over to look in his microscope. Lili froze. Something Elaine said made Dylan smile. They were so close. Suddenly, Elaine's lips touched Dylan's. They were kissing. Lili could only stare. How stupid she had been. Thinking there could be something between them.

All she could think of was escape. As she ran from the room, she tipped a glass beaker. The breaking glass made everyone turn, including Dylan. But by then, Lili was almost out the door. She missed Dylan's anguished look and Elaine's triumphant smile.

*　　　　　*　　　　　*

Macao

The stack of chips that three hours earlier had once towered all around David Kim had dwindled to very few. Without counting, David figured he'd won

$110,000 and lost $200,000, so he was down $90,000. Still, he wasn't panicked. Not yet.

"Do you feel lucky, my friend?" asked the mustachioed man, pouring David another glass of champagne.

The others at the table had dropped out, having already anted up everything they had into the pool. David downed the bubbly liquid in one thirsty gulp. It was his fourth glass and his head felt pleasantly light. He was still in control. Just. Words slightly slurred: "What did you have in mind?"

"A private wager. Just between us. Only corner bets. One hundred grand. Loser pays three to one." He motioned to the Eurasian beauty who emptied the silk sack into her lap.

Slowly, almost sensually, David thought, she counted out one thousand chips while, equally slowly, the fat man scooped them from her, then placed them on the left-hand corner of the joker nearest the banker. That meant the winning number would be 1.

"Well?" The man took a long drag on his cigarillo and blew smoke across the table.

David felt the rush, the sense of excitement he always experienced at moments like this: the incomparable gambler poised on the very edge. He knew his luck was about to change. It had to. "I'll have to write a check." His most engaging smile. "I've got a sweet deal going guaranteed to make millions. No billions." He laughed, holding his finger to his lips. "Shh, it's a secret."

"No checks, only cash," the banker declared.

David pulled a leather pouch from his pocket and removed a small case containing a pad of red ink and a stamp that constituted his legal signature. "My tojang," he explained, pushing it towards the fat man. "My father is the president of Kim Company. In three months I take over." He smiled. "Believe me, I'm good for the money."

The man blew a blue smoke ring past him. "I'm sure you are," he said, inspecting the *tojang*, then nodded to the banker who handed David $100,000 in chips.

With as much calm as he could muster, David placed his bet on the right hand corner nearest the banker. It didn't matter that his father would never back up his bet. His number would come up. David felt it in his bones.

All eyes were on the Eurasian beauty as she thoroughly shuffled the deck, then handed the cards to the banker who cut a large packet off the top and began counting off the cards in groups of four. When he could no longer count a complete set of four cards, the cards remaining would determine the winning number.

David watched with growing excitement. *Come on 4,* he prayed.

*   *   *

Los Angeles, California

Running out into the sunshine, Lili sought to escape the oppression of the hospital. She couldn't. bear facing another patient or meeting another colleague. She needed to be alone.

Still wearing her hospital whites, she wandered aimlessly down Westwood Boulevard, staring into shop windows, lost in her own thoughts. At Weyburn she turned left , crossing several streets until she was in little Holmby Hills, amid modest two and three million dollar mansions that stood behind hand-wrought iron gates. The few housekeepers, poolmen and gardeners she passed viewed her with suspicion, but she didn't notice, preoccupied with her own thoughts.

She'd only wanted to do what was best for Mrs. Manley. Lili knew she'd been right to admit her to the hospital. With or without insurance. The doctor's responsibility was to her patients—not to their pocketbooks. Of course she regretted the accident. Thank God, Margaret would be okay. Although that didn't impress Trenton. He couldn't really throw her out of the program. Not after all her years of hard work. Could he? She wanted the geriatrics fellowship so much. She deserved it. Ed Baxter was no competition. It wasn't fair.

She turned into an alley thinking she'd never felt quite so rejected or isolated. No one to talk to. She was such a fool. For so long she'd kept her emotions in check—not permitting herself the luxury of a relationship. She'd learned before how easy it was to get hurt. So why had she let Dylan get close? Why?

"*Ten cuidado* !"

Lost in her musing, Lili didn't hear the warning or see the white Ford come barreling down the alley. It was only the quick reflexes of the Hispanic gardener, pulling her onto the bed of impatiens, that saved her life.

"*Tienses que tener mas cuidado.* You must be more careful, senorita," the old man said, helping Lili up.

"*Gracias.*" She was still trembling long after she'd thanked him and hurried back to the hospital.

*   *   *

In his rearview mirror, the man in the white Ford watched his target. Although shaken, she was in one piece. He knew his contact would not be pleased. That was why he decided to wait before calling in his report.

*   *   *

Dylan caught up with her on the ward after rounds. "Lili, I need to talk to you!"

"There's nothing to say."

"I've been looking for you everywhere."

"Well you found me." She was walking so fast, Dylan almost couldn't keep up.

"I wanted you to know that what you may have seen wasn't really what it appeared."

"You don't have to explain."

"I want to. Look, I know you're upset."

"I'm not upset." Lili fabricated a smile. "Forget it." She turned the corner.

"Do you still want Mr. Sanderson's IV to run KVO?" one of the floor nurse's asked as she passed the nurses' station.

"No, he's stable. You can DC it, " Lili replied. "Oh and why don't you move him in with Mr. Martinez? I've got an admission through the ER that's going to need isolation."

"The Sanderson family ordered a private room," the nurse stated.

"Tell them Dr. Quan ordered this one." Lili grabbed the patient's chart to write her note, then hurried down the hall toward the elevator. Dylan was at her heels.

When she reached it, Dylan spun her around to face him, his arms firm on her shoulders as if afraid that she would dart again. "Lili, listen to me. Elaine Morgan knew you were there. Ever since I came to LA Medical she's come on to me. Not that I've led her on, mind you, but Elaine is not a lady who likes to lose. Then last night she saw us together, not to mention your one-upping her at the party." His eyes met hers. "She set us both up."

Lili laughed at his earnestness. After what she'd experienced, it all suddenly seemed unimportant. "I guess I was being a little foolish. I don't usually play the jealous hussy."

"So I'm forgiven?"

"There's nothing to forgive. Right?"

"Right." His smile reflected genuine relief. "Then we're on for dinner? "

"As long as you're cooking."

"Six o'clock."

"Your place."

                    *   *   *

Neither Dylan nor Lili noticed Tex Trenton standing just beyond the nurses' station, frowning as he watched them together.

                    *   *   *

Macao

"Number 3 wins."

There must be a mistake.

David's expression reflected his disbelief. Sure he would win, he'd bet everything. The lovely lightheaded feeling suddenly became a dreadful pounding in his skull. *Jesus,* he thought. *I'm ruined. Father will disinherit me.*

"I can't pay," he whispered, as much to himself as his opponent who suddenly threw back his head and laughed.

"Can't pay?" It was the maniacal laugh of a man on the edge.

The others around the table laughed with him, as much to ensure that they wouldn't be singled out as because they saw any humor in the moment.

"You would tell Paulo Ng you cannot pay a debt?"

David recognized the owner of the casino. Everyone had heard stories of the bastard son of a Portuguese sailor and the Chinese peasant girl whose family had sold her into prostitution in order to retrieve them from the indignity of bankruptcy. As a child, Ng's mixed blood had made him an easy victim. Before he was out of short pants, Ng had stored up enough bitterness and indignation to make him dangerous and volatile.

After watching his mother starve in the back alleys of Macao, he'd vowed never to be hungry again. From pickpocket to self-made tycoon, Ng was reputed to have made millions smuggling anything the market would bear: gold, weapons, even opium. He was also said to be ruthless—the scar on his cheek, the only evidence of his ever coming up less than a total winner in a fight.

"I'm a little short of cash at the moment," he stammered.

"That's not an excuse I can accept." The voice was controlled, but cold as ice. He turned to the Eurasian beauty. "Camille, our young friend looks like he could use a good night's sleep. Find him a nice room upstairs. A little rest and I'm sure he'll think of a way to settle his account."

The woman reached into her bag and handed David a card that read: Macao Association of Exporters and an address.

"My villa," Ng said. "Meet me there tomorrow morning at ten."

"And if I don't?" David asked softly.

Ng's eyes were suddenly fierce. Anger tweaked the corner of his mouth. "Thinking of not coming?" He slowly poured himself some champagne. "Do you hear that?" he asked as the liquid bubbled from the bottle and drained into his glass. This will be like the sound of your life running out." Standing, the other men at the table followed. "I think I will retire for the evening." Although he smiled, his words were anything but friendly: "Ten sharp or you die."

Long after Ng and his entourage had left the casino, David could still hear the sound of his maniacal laughter.

           *   *   *

Los Angeles, California
7:00 PM

"You really do cook, " Lili declared as they relaxed on the couch in Dylan's sparsely furnished living room after dinner. He'd given his recent move and work as the reason for the lack of decor. Everything except a few books and his kitchen utensils were still in boxes. Cooking, he told her, was his way of relaxing and, he'd added, with an impish wink, charming women. Well, she had to admit, tonight she was charmed. "Caesar salad. Coq au vin. Even fresh flowers on the table. I'm really impressed."

"Next time a little more thyme in the chicken, a little less garlic." Dylan affected a French accent. "Le sauce—she is supposed to marry, never dominate."

"Well, I'm no gourmet," Lili admitted, "but I thought it was perfect. Even the wine is delicious," she said, taking another sip. "Is it French?"

"French? My dear I'll have you know you're drinking one of California's finest late harvest Rieslings—a very rare dessert wine. The grapes were grown just north of San Francisco in the Napa Valley. To get the sweet flavor, the wine maker must leave the Riesling grapes on the vine hoping for a warm, light rain that will sometimes cause a beneficial mold, botrytis cinerea, to form on the grape skins."

"And what happens if the mold doesn't form?"

"In that case, the rainwater would be absorbed into the grape roots of the wines, swelling the berries and decreasing their concentration. That would yield a thin wine that would sell for far less than grapes harvested earlier or grapes that do have the mold. Of course, a really heavy rain could wipe out the crop altogether."

"Sounds pretty risky."

"Yes, " he said raising his glass to inspect the golden colored liquid, "but if the wine maker is willing to take that risk and he's lucky, the result is a luscious complex sweet wine that is highly prized by connoisseurs."

"To a prize worth the risk," Lili said, emptying her wineglass for the second time.

"A little more?"

Lili nodded as Dylan poured the late harvest Riesling into her glass. She felt more relaxed than she had all day. Relaxed enough to finally tell him about her run-ins with Trenton. She was so sure of an endorsement that his reaction surprised her.

Dylan listened, then leaned back on the sofa, closed his eyes and massaged the growing pain in his temples. "Talk about risk taking. Taking Trenton on. Especially in front of the house staff. What were you trying to do? Commit medical suicide? "

"Let's not be melodramatic. Besides," she said taking a sip of wine, "Trenton's the one that lost his cool, not me."

Dylan leveled clear blue eyes at her. "Lili, If there's one thing I've learned about medicine, it's that you go with the flow or drown. Trenton is a powerful guy. Why go out of your way to upset him?"

"Trenton may be powerful, but he's not omnipotent."

"He is well connected in Washington. That means he can get millions of dollars in grant money and that, my dear, makes him omnipotent at LA Medical."

"Don't you think he was wrong about Mrs. Manley?"

"It's not that simple."

"To me it is. Corny as it may sound, Dylan, I became a doctor to save lives. It scares me to see bureaucrats like Trenton making decisions about patients based on their finances not their health. "

"Welcome to the age of cost containment."

Shaking her head. "Never."

Dylan sighed. "How did such a beautiful, brainy kid like you get so naive?"

"I didn't go to the school of hard knocks like you," she retorted.

"You want to view the world as black and white, good guys and bad guys, right and wrong. It's not that simple."

"It is if you're right."

Her head turned slightly so that the flat of her cheek was outlined in the soft room light. Dylan studied Lili's delicate Asian features for a moment, struck by the fiery flash of indignation in her dark eyes. He shook his head. "Beautiful, naive and hard-headed. Just my luck. I had to go and fall for a real woman of the 80's." He smiled. "Dr. Quan. I think I'm in love."

Lili was caught off guard. Dylan's spontaneous declaration suddenly took the edge off her anger. She searched his face, half expecting mockery, but the blue eyes were guileless, the smile on his handsome face sincere. For a long moment she stared directly at him. Her heart was hammering. His arm was around her lightly. It tightened. He kissed her, gently at first, then with more urgency. She wanted to respond—did, then pulled away. "I'm sorry," she whispered. "I can't."

"Want to talk about him?"

As if reading her mind. "What….?"

"The guy that hurt you?"

Flustered: "How did you…"

"How did I know? You have it written all over that beautiful vulnerable face of yours."

Lili looked directly at him. "It was a long time ago."

"Seems you haven't gotten over it."

Lili cocked her head reflectively. "Does one ever get over rejection?" An unconscious sigh, remembering past pain. "I met Darryl Hamstead in Boston. He was at Harvard studying economics, I was at Wellesley delving into American lit. We were inseparable. Even talked about marriage. Then I met his mother."

"And she felt you didn't fit into the pedigree?"

"The Hampsteads are a Mayflower family. Darryl's mother was a Daughter of the Revolution. You know, to my face she couldn't have been more charming. Said how happy she was to meet me. Offered me tea and cucumber sandwiches on her best china. Then she sent me into the kitchen on some invented errand while she had a heart to heart with Darryl."

"I take it you eavesdropped."

Lili nodded. "Told him she had nothing against minorities. After all, she said, many of the people who worked in the Hampstead Mills were lovely Blacks, Spanish, even Orientals. When I returned from the kitchen, Darryl and I were no longer a couple."

"Darryl's loss."

She shrugged. "It never would have worked anyway."

"How so?"

"Darryl hated Hemingway."

A questioning look from Dylan.

"He was a business major. Except for the Wall Street Journal, he didn't read anything more challenging than the TV Guide. He thought my studying American Literature was a waste of time."

"I have a confession to make," Dylan said seriously.

"Oh?"

"I'm a nut for the *Old Man and the Sea*."

She looked at him. "Why?"

"Is this some kind of test you make all your prospective suitors pass?"

"No, I'm always curious about why people like his work."

Dylan shrugged. "Why? I guess because the old man wins. He gets the fish."

"But the sharks eat it."

"Still a win."

"You know they say that Hemingway felt man always loses in the end, but what really counts is how he conducts himself while he's being destroyed."

"I see. Does that mean that I am destined to lose if I try to kiss you tonight?"

Lili laughed.

"You have a nice laugh. You should make a habit of it. "

He leaned over and kissed her cheek. She didn't move away and he pulled her into his arms. "Don't be afraid, Lili…please…" He kissed her face and her lips and her hands and she felt herself wanting to give in to her feelings. To let go. She was definitely attracted to Dylan and after her close call with death today, the idea of being near someone was appealing. Still, something made her push away.

"I'm not afraid," she whispered. "Not of you. It's me. I'm not ready."

"I understand."

For a moment Lili felt a little disappointed he wasn't persistent.

As if reading her thoughts: "I understand for now. But you owe me another dinner."

She smiled. "That's a promise."

*   *   *

Macao

One of the casino bouncers escorted Camille and David to an upstairs suite. After showing them in, the three hundred pound former Sumi wrestler left the two alone. David had no doubt that he was still close by, probably just outside the door. Damn. It hadn't been a good night.

Camille, who had headed for the oak-paneled bar at the far end of the opulent living room, turned and smiled. "What are you drinking?"

David's head was spinning from too much champagne. "I think I've had enough."

"The evening is still young," Camille protested, filling two glasses with brandy. She hovered over the drinks so David never saw the white powder she poured into his glass. By the time she offered it to him, the particles had dissolved completely. "I'd like to get to know you better." Her look was full of sexual promise.

A frequent visitor to Macao's brothels, David had no illusions about Camille's trade. Still, none of those girls came close to her beauty. She was strictly high-class, he thought, appraising her long legs and round curves. "*Tangshinun yeppum nida.*" Very pretty.

"*Kamsa hamnida.* Thank you, sir." She raised her glass. "Now what shall we drink to?"

"*Ihaehaseyo?*

"Sure I understand you. I spoke Korean and French as a baby."

"Oh?"

"My mother was from Pusan, my father was from Marseilles. I also speak some Portuguese, Chinese, English, even a little Russian. It's a big world out there," she said huskily. "You never know when a word will come in handy." She touched his glass with hers. "To money."

"I'll drink to that," he laughed, taking a long pull on the drink.

"It sounds like you're going to have a lot soon."

"*Tashi malssum hae chuseyo?*"

"Money. That deal you mentioned in the casino. You said you were going to make millions."

"I have a big mouth when I drink."

Watching him under long, thick eyelashes: "How about another?"

He focused on her lips for several moments, fascinated by how slowly the words were forming in her mouth.

"Another?" she asked again.

"I...no..." He was starting to feel strange—as though every sense had been heightened: the bitter sweet taste of the liquid on his tongue, the melodious sound of her voice, even the beating of his own heart lub dubbing like a drum in his chest. He loosened his tie. "It's hot in here."

"Why don't you get comfortable?" she purred, turning down the lights and flipping on soft radio music. "I'll meet you in the bedroom."

The room was all bed—king-size with pale blue satin sheets and a real mink coverlet. David hadn't removed his jacket and sat down on the bed before Camille appeared at the doorway with a second dose of her potion.

"You know, it *is* hot in here," she said, handing him the drink. Smiling, she unzipped her tight dress, slipped it off her shoulders and let it slide down to her ankles. "That's better."

She wore a strapless bra, black lace garter belt and silk stockings which she removed with the slow allure of a stripteaser while David watched, totally hypnotized. First she unhooked the bra and dropped it to the floor revealing high, round breasts with nipples the color of milk chocolate and a waist so tiny he felt he could encircle it with only one hand. Never taking her eyes off him, she put one of her fingers in her mouth, sucked on it, then rubbed the wet tip over each nipple, until both were hard and pointing.

David swallowed.

She lifted a leg onto the bed to balance herself as she inched the silk stocking down, exposing bare skin. Since she wore no panties, David could see the tight little V of her black pubic hair and the soft, giving flesh it covered. He was aware of his breath coming in measured gasps. She did the same with the other leg, taking her time, her lips twisted into a mocking smile, knowing the effect her act was having.

She turned and unhooked the garter belt, bending so that the soft light played down the curve of her back and buttocks. Finally she faced him again, wearing only the diamond bracelet and earrings.

Perfection, he thought, reaching out to touch her.

"Not until you finish that drink," she scolded.

He emptied his glass, still watching her.

"Good boy." Camille moved close. He could smell her exquisite fragrance. With a casual, yet precise gesture she might have used to shake hands, she reached out and laid an elegant hand directly over his crotch. "Now, tell me about that sweet deal of yours."

"Sweet...? What?" His thoughts seemed hazy and distant. The room itself refused to stay still, its walls dissolving as Camille's voice receded down a long, narrow cavern. "I need to lie down."

"I think you'd enjoy yourself more if you just sat still," he heard the cavern announce. He was vaguely aware of her dexterous fingers unbuttoning his clothes, their tips stroking his flesh as she removed each garment. When he was naked, she knelt before him and took his limp penis in her mouth. Her lips and tongue worked together. Within moments, it began to twitch and grow in her wet warmth. Like an obedient child, he sat silently, eyes closed, abandoning himself to the novelty of the passive role, feeling only the pulsation between his legs. "Wonderful," he murmured.

"It's the drug," she whispered.

"Drug?"

"Ecstasy. You must abandon yourself to it. Tomorrow you will not remember."

What was she saying? He didn't understand. Didn't want to. Not now. Only feel.

"Ah." She smiled, abruptly removing him from her mouth. *"Now* I see you want me."

He opened his eyes and stared down as his erection, fascinated as Camille enclosed it with the palms of her hands and drew him down with her onto the bed. The repeated caresses of her silken fingers on his engorged shaft felt so exquisite that he gasped with pleasure. And when she stroked his hardening nipples with her warm, moist tongue, he thought he would explode in her hand.

"Not yet," she insisted as she rose up on her knees just above him, her hips arched, her thighs open, an unmistakable invitation. "You must learn to take your time. Concentrate." She opened a jar of oil on the bed stand, dipped her hands in and began massaging him.

Yes, *slow down.* It felt so good, her oiled fingers rhythmically kneading the muscles of his neck, his shoulders, his chest, then his hips. So *good...* "Umm."

"Tell me your secret."

"Secret?" He reached for her breasts, the flesh so soft he thought his hands would melt into them, but she twisted away.

"First tell me about the money you're going to make." She was caressing the underside of his scrotum.

Money? He didn't want to think about anything but the delicious sensations growing between his legs as her fingers continued their work.

"Tell me and I'll make it feel even better."

"Secret," he giggled, staring up at the dazzling splurge of light and shadow playing off the ceiling. "Very pretty."

"Look at *me* ! "

"What?" He watched her raise her body and with the skill of a trained gymnast, lower herself onto him.

"Will you tell me?" Moving slowly up and down, thrusting her pelvis, her soft buttocks pressing on his thighs. Up and down.

"Yes, yes!" What was she saying?

"Tell me."

He was so close.

"Focus on my voice. I need to know your secret."

"Yes, yes!" Her voice. But he could only concentrate on feeling. "Yes!" And then without warning, his climax came, exploding within her. So suddenly, it racked his entire body with spasms of tortured pleasure. He closed his eyes, completely spent.

"No!" Camille hissed as she watched David fall asleep with her still astride. She looked down at him with disgust. Pampered son of a wealthy man. Didn't have to fend for himself the way she did. But then she was a survivor.

She climbed off his flaccid penis. Merde! She couldn't believe it. So much work for nothing. No self-control. She probably shouldn't have given him that second dose.

After a quick shower, she searched David's suit pockets for some clue, some evidence of his secret deal. Except for the tojang, there was nothing. Merde! She'd have to try her other sources. Ng had warned her not to come away empty-handed.

Ng always got what he wanted.

*   *   *

It was nearly dawn when Camille slipped quietly into Ng's darkened master bedroom and sat on the bed beside him. When she began to gently massage his shoulders, the fat man rolled his massive body to his side and took two of her fingers in his mouth, his teeth gently caressing the tips.

"You took your sweet time," he murmured, his eyes still closed. He had her fingers in his mouth, his teeth gently teasing the tips.

"The drug didn't work. I tried everything, yet he told me nothing."

The pressure from Ng's teeth increased until Camille gasped. "You're hurting me!"

He released her fingers from his mouth, but held her hand in a firm grip. "You're not going to tell me you came with no information, are you, pretty one?" His grip was like a vise.

Camille shook her head. "You worry too much, cheri."

"Worry is a wasted emotion. I simply like to cover all the bases."

"So you've taught me." She pulled his hand to her lips and kissed his fingers. "I placed a long distance call to your old American friend. He was most willing to help a fellow pirate. The file on Kim will be faxed to you within the next two hours."

Ng turned on his back and opened his eyes. "That shows real initiative, my dear. I am impressed."

"I told you, I have a good teacher."

"You did well."

Camille's sultry voice whispered: "Why not let me do what I *really* do well."

There were no complaints from Ng as he watched her unzip her dress, letting it slip it off her magnificent body and slide quietly to the floor.

SEVEN

Macao
10:00 AM

Squeezed into a mere six square kilometers, Macao has the sleepy quality of a Mediterranean outpost, recalling the Iberian peninsula more than Asia. But there is also a sense of the sinister: of dark mystery and decadence that lies hidden along the lovely tree-lined cobblestone avenues and behind the quaint terraced red and ocher villas.

That was the feeling David had as he stepped out of the taxi and approached the entrance to Ng's home. No memory of the real events of the past evening, he'd awakened bathed in sweat, having dreamed of his own torture. Forced to reveal his secret, he could still hear his screams of protest. Sweet Jesus. He was a gambler, yes. But a hero? He rang the doorbell and waited, his knees trembling with fear.

*   *   *

Los Angeles, California
10:00 PM

The beep of her hospital pager pierced the silence. Lili sat bolt upright in bed from a dead sleep, unsure where she was. She'd been dreaming of Dylan, making sensuous love with him, falling asleep entwined in his arms. As if they'd always slept that way. She switched on the lamp and checked her watch: 10:00 PM. She was quite alone in her own bed.

Reaching for the phone, she dialed the hospital and waited for what seemed like an eternity before the operator answered. "This is Dr. Quan. Someone paged me?"

"Yes, doctor. It's San Francisco General. Your mother's been admitted."

"Jesus!" Lili said, hanging up and dialing Northern California information. Once she got the number, she tried to track down the admitting doctor. When she'd finished the call, she dialed Dylan's number.

"Did you change your mind?" he joked, obviously pleased to hear her voice.

"It's my mother. She collapsed at home and was taken to the Emergency Room. I've got to catch a plane to San Francisco." Although there were no tears, her voice was shaking.

"Let me drive you to the airport."

"No, that's silly. You've got to work tomorrow. I'll call a cab."

"You're sure?"

"Sure. There is one favor you could do for me."

"Anything."

"Tell Dr. Trenton what happened. It's too late to call him tonight and I don't want him to think I went AWOL."

"Don't worry, Lili. I'll take care of everything on this end. You just hurry back."

*   *   *

Macao
noon

"Let me tell you the problem I'm up against," Ng said, reaching for his coffee.

David sat awkwardly across the table from his host. Instead of being tortured or killed, he'd been greeted at the door by Ng dressed in a double-breasted white linen suit and Panama hat cocked to one side. Looking and playing the part of the perfect, if somewhat rakish host, the fat man hugged him to his barreled chest like a long lost brother, then insisted on a tour of his Moorish-style villa.

For three quarters of an hour he led David from room to room, pointing out the expensive treasures he'd acquired over the years: hand-woven wool rugs and traditional Kashgar carpets, priceless cloisonné vases that took ten artists six years to create, Italian marble bathroom fixtures, hand-carved cherry wood, solid brass doors, even a 24-carat, gold-plated dragon that stretched eight feet across his Louis the Fifteenth vintage bedroom set.

Finally Ng took him over a wooden bridge that crossed a waterfall into the dining room for a sumptuous luncheon of sea urchin, squab in oyster sauce and nine friendly vegetables. Just the two of them. During the meal they exchanged polite if somewhat awkward niceties. Now that coffee had been served, however, it seemed that Ng was ready for serious talk.

"For the past hundred years Macao has been Hong Kong's weak sister. We've had to manipulate trade behind the scenes. Once the British hand the island over to the Chinese there are those who believe Hong Kong will be finished. Many have already left and many more are contemplating leaving."

He wiped a spot of cream from his mustache. "With change comes opportunity. It is time for the weak sister to take her rightful place—to be the new window on the West. Of course," he added, "at the same time providing a lucrative flow of money into the PRC." He leaned forward, locking his eyes with David. "But it's got to be on the up and up."

The fierce look in Ng's eyes, made David squirm.

"As a respected son of a wealthy man, you can not know the infamy of being a bastard. All my life I've had to endure the condescension of men with less than half my wealth and not even a modicum of my talent."

Although Ng spoke in a cool detached manner, David could feel his repressed fury. He hoped it wouldn't suddenly focus on him.

"To command the favor I desire, I must have the proper front. A company ready to move into major international markets; one that commands the respect of all the world's players." He snapped his fingers and Camille appeared—it seemed out of nowhere—with a manila folder labeled KIM COMPANY. "That's where your firm comes in."

David almost dropped his cup. So here it was. Ng wanted Kim Company. What would happen to him now? A thin line of sweat appeared over his upper lip. All color drained from his face. "Kim Company is not mine to give away."

The dangerous scarred face smiled. "I've said nothing about your giving Kim Company away."

"Then, what exactly do you want from me?"

"First, I want to hear all about that sweet deal you mentioned in the casino. Worth millions."

"Idle boasting," David protested. "I was drunk."

"Precisely why the mickey failed to loosen your tongue."

David looked at Camille who avoided his stare.

"Loyalty is something I demand from everyone who works for me," Ng remarked. "Unfortunately, even a beautiful woman could not separate you from your secrets."

"I really don't know what you're talking about."

Ignoring him, Ng nodded towards the folder. "And there was nothing in these documents." He smiled sweetly. "So you see, you must tell me everything now. Then we'll see exactly how we can structure our new partnership."

The man was mad. "There's nothing to tell," David whined. "Honestly."

"Why not let me be the judge?"

Whispered: "I can't."

For the first time the amiable host dropped his polite manner. "You are hardly in a position to refuse, my friend. Remember, you owe me $300,000."

"If you give me time, I'll find the money."

Ng shook his head. "You surprise me. A good bargainer recognizes when he's met his match." The smile as menacing as the words: "You already know what will happen to you if you refuse."

David shuddered, his mouth dry with fear as he contemplated the torture Ng might use to make him talk. He was a coward after all.

"Well?" Ng held his eyes.

"All right. I'll tell you what you want to know."

Ng eased back in his chair, regaining control. "Of course you will."

*   *   *

Los Angeles, California

When Lili left her apartment twenty minutes later, she was unaware of movement in the dark shadows of a closed shop across the street. Hooded eyes watched her step into a waiting taxi. As it pulled away, a tall man stepped from the shadows, and entered his car parked nearby. He followed Lili all the way to the PSA terminal at LAX.

*   *   *

Macao

After hearing David Kim's reluctant account of his meetings with General Tong's son, Ng jumped up from the table and began pacing. "The secret of longevity." He rubbed his hands together. "Judas Priest. " He couldn't help himself as he suddenly began to roar with laughter. "The gods have spread fortune upon us, my friend."

The thought of the control he could have over all the rude Hong Kong Chinese, the mindless communists on the mainland, the miserable Europeans—everyone who'd ever treated him with disdain- sent waves of delight through his body. What would heads of governments or major corpo-rations pay for a secret that would allow them to wield their power that much longer? The possibilities for exploiting such a drug were staggering. He laughed hysterically as David watched in miserable silence. When he'd finally spent his mania, Ng sat down again.

"You're sure Lee Tong can be trusted?"

David nodded. "Without me he has no way to get the elixir out of China."

"What kind of financial split did you arrange?"

David avoided the fat man's penetrating gaze.

Ng exploded with laughter again. "I knew it! You plan to sell him out." David remained silent.

"You conniving son of a bitch! Once he hands you the elixir, you simply have it analyzed and set up your own manufacturing outside China. Lee Tong will have no recourse. Even guandao has its limits," he said, referring to the so-called 'official' racketeering engaged in by the sons and daughters of Chinese party members. "If he reports you, the government will hang him as a traitor."

Ng took David's continued silence for confession. "Perhaps I underestimated you." A cold smile. "You and I share qualities of selfishness and greed that bode well for a profitable collaboration."

Surprised by his sudden temerity, David finally spoke. "You agree that once I have the secret I will no longer need Lee Tong. Tell me why I need you?"

Ng took his gold cigarillo case from his pocket and offered one to David who declined. "The question that comes to mind, my young friend, is once I obtain the secret, why will I need *you* ?" Ng pointed to the folder on the table. "I've spent the last few hours checking out Kim Company. I was not surprised at what I learned. Like so many Korean companies, you are on the brink of disaster. "

"We have had some recent setbacks," David conceded, "but things aren't that bad."

Ng flicked his gold lighter. The dragon etched on the side seemed to be spewing fire. "Perhaps not yet." Though he stopped talking for a moment while he lit a cigarillo, the pirate never took his dark eyes off David. "The soaring won, massive wage hikes, high interest rates and costly strikes are crippling Korea's export machine."

He took a deep puff. "At best, Asia's most ferocious tiger is getting its fangs blunted. At worst, Korea could plunge into its first recession in a decade, setting back its dreams of emerging as a major industrial power." He blew smoke toward David. "Today Daewoo Group, tomorrow Kim Company."

"Daewoo has no choice but to keep shipbuilding in Korea. We have been able to relocate our plants."

"Even after moving your textile plants to China, you've continued to lose market share worldwide," Ng countered. "You didn't expect competition from within China. With strikes at home and falling exports, Kim Company has major cash flow problems."

David looked bewildered. It was not Ng who had underestimated him, but the other way around.

As if reading his mind: "You are surprised that a pirate and a smuggler reads the Wall Street Journal?" Ng's laugh had a bitter edge. "I may not have the education a rich father like yours could provide, but I keep my eyes open and, "he added pointedly, "I only gamble when I can't lose." He crushed his half-smoked cigarillo in the saucer under his bone china coffee cup. "As I said, you may need me more than I need you."

David tried to remain impassive. "I'm listening."

"If this secret is everything you think it is, its market potential is unlimited."

"Don't you think I know that?" David asked, a look of disdain filling his face.

"Recognizing a market is one thing. Knowing that market is quite another. You don't know beans about the drug business. Kim Company's distribution networks for textiles, electronics, even food processing products can't be used for the pharmaceutical industry. You need distribution channels that can reach every major world market. You also need the kind of capital you can't get right now in your country." Ng smiled inwardly, certain the conversation was going his way.

"And you can provide all that?"

Ng nodded. "Capital and connections I have plenty of."

Wary: "Then what is it you want?"

"Just respectability," Ng said matter-of-factly. "I propose we set up a jointly owned subsidiary of Kim Company funded by me and run by you. I would act as an unpaid advisor."

"I see," said David, aware that Ng meant to set up a money laundering operation. "You realize my father would never approve of such a venture. He believes Kim Company must always remain Korean owned. His allegiance is first to his country."

"And yours?" Ng asked, with nothing but a hint of a benign smile on his lips.

David stared at him, understanding the opportunity the smuggler presented. His father's talk of obligation to country was from another era. A businessman had to look beyond his own borders—not only for markets, but when necessary, for partners. He took a cigarillo from Ng's open case. "Money dictates its own allegiance."

"Indeed!" Ng smirked. "Well, no need to worry. We'll keep my involvement secret until you take over the company in three months time."

"Good. By the way, do you have a name for this new venture?"

Ng sat for a moment, savoring his cigarillo and reliving all the injustices and rejections heaped on him over the years. With this company he would finally gain respect as well as wealth. No one could destroy that. No one. "I propose to call it Zee Enterprises, he said, rubbing the Z-shaped scar along his right cheek. "Any objections?"

David nodded agreement, happy the name would preserve his anonymity.

Ng smiled. "Fine. My lawyer will draw up the papers." He extended his hand. "Kim, my boy, it looks like we're in business. My sixth sense tells me we're both going to have good luck!"

David shook hands with the pirate, relaxing for the first time since he lost the Fan- tan game. Perhaps Ng was right. Perhaps his luck *was* finally turning after all.

EIGHT

San Francisco, California
4:50 AM

There is something ominous about the darkness and silence of a hospital asleep.

It was nearly 5:00 A.M. before Lili arrived at San Francisco General. The corridors had slipped into the eerie half-life suffused with the soft lights and muted voices that herald the end of the night shift; the beginning of the morning routine. Lili walked down the long hall towards the nurses' station, past closed doors which muffled an occasional cough or moan—a counterpoint to the rhythmic beeping of cardiac monitors and respirators. In the distance she saw two orderlies talking, although no sound actually reached her. Moving towards them, Lili was momentarily struck by the odd sensation that she was caught in some endless tunnel, with no beginning and no end.

"Visiting hours aren't until ten," came a voice from behind her.

Lili spun around to face a nurse wearing a starched white uniform and an expression to match.

"I'm Dr. Quan. My mother was admitted last night." Lili hoped the authoritative tone overcame her casual appearance. When she'd gotten the call, she'd simply slipped into the clothes she'd worn to dinner: blue jeans and a Wellesley T-shirt.

Hesitant: "Well, I don't know…."

"CA of the pancreas, Nurse," Lili read the woman's name tag, "Thatcher. My mother's dying. Please, I flew up from LA, I've got to return for rounds in a few hours."

The starched expression softened. "Of course. She's in 210. Bed B."

"Thank you."

Lili found the room just around the corner from the nurses' station. The moment she entered, the smell was overpowering, so pungent and nauseating it made the air seem heavy. Lili recognized the odor of rotting tissue mixed with the sweet, syrupy smell of scented talcum powder—a vain effort to counter the stench. It came from Bed A where an obese woman lay snoring, seemingly oblivious to her infected right lower leg exposed to the air. Probably an uncontrolled diabetic, Lili thought, tiptoeing past to Bed B.

Someone had left the side-rail down. Lili found her mother asleep, a tiny figure enveloped in white covers, one arm hanging limply over the edge of the bed. With her mouth half-open, the lines in Su-Wei's face smoothed so that she looked like the young girl on Lili's wall—frail and innocent. Except that her skin was saffron colored—the jaundice indicating that the cancer had caused a serious obstruction. Her breathing was so shallow that Lili leaned closer to be sure she was still alive.

"Ma!" Whispered sharply.

Slowly Su-Wei's eyes opened. She blinked. "Li Li is that you?"

Instinctively, Lili started to react to the Chinese pronunciation of her name which meant flower. From the time she was old enough to insist that she preferred the Anglicized 'Lili', it had been a source of contention between them. Like her not wanting to learn Chinese:

How can you be a good Chinese daughter if you don't know your own language? Asked in Mandarin.

I'm a good American daughter. Answered in English.

Now, seeing her mother's wasted body and obvious suffering, suddenly all the misunderstandings, all the harsh words were forgotten—made insignificant by the fact of her dying. "How are you?" she asked.

"Buddha has not been smiling on these old bones." Su-Wei winced as she experienced a jab of pain. Despite her devotion to the Christian God,

Su-Wei had always retained her amah's respect for Buddhism. Now that she was near death, her affiliation seemed to have shifted entirely to Buddha.

Lili gently pushed an extra pillow under her mother's head and bent to kiss her cheek. "Why didn't you call me?"

"I didn't want to be a burden."

Lili also knew the common Chinese superstition that one entered a Western hospital only when death was imminent. "I would have come sooner."

"You are here now." Su-Wei eased herself up. "Help me, Lili. Take this necklace I wear and put it on your neck. I want you to have this. It was my mother's. Inside there is a picture of her."

"But it's yours. Since I can remember, I don't think you've ever taken it off." Lili looked at the jade locket on the gold chain.

"Your grandfather gave it to me after she passed away. He told me to wear it always and never forget that I was Chinese. I want you to wear it now so you won't forget."

Lili blinked back tears. "You're going to be okay." As if her words could nullify the inevitable.

"You were always a foolish child." The same scolding tone she'd used when Lili was six. "I know somehow you blame yourself for my dying. This guilt, child. In this you are wholly Western. It is my *joss*."

Joss! Damn her ability to accept her untimely death with such equanimity. Lili wanted to scream 'unfair' at the top of her lungs. Do not go gentle into this goodnight, mother!

Su-Wei raised a hand to prevent Lili's response. "Our whole family is gone, Li Li. And now I have no more time." She eased herself back on the pillow. "I am very tired and I must tell you what your grandfather told me. I was only ten when he put me on a big ship to America. He said he'd send for me when it was safe and we'd be together again, but it was not to be. I don't even know where he is buried."

She stopped to catch her breath. "Ch'uing tou-chi—the past, child, is a window to oneself. Remember, if you are Chinese, you can never let go of China in your mind. Someday I hope you will return to China for me. I will live in you now."

Lili took her mother's hand in hers.

"Promise me you will do these things, Li Li."

Lili choked back tears.

"Promise."

"I promise," she said softly.

"You are a good Chinese daughter," Su-Wei whispered, closing her eyes as if in sleep. Then, with an obscene abruptness, she was gone.

*   *   *

Outside the room, the driver of the white Ford also witnessed Su-Wei's dying. While Lili stood crying softly over her mother's body, he took the elevator to the lobby and located a public telephone.

His contact listened quietly for a moment before shouting: "Fool! Did I ever mention trying to kill her?"

"The alley was narrow, I didn't think…."

"I don't pay you to think. You were hired to follow the girl. That's all. Did anyone see you?"

"No one. I'm sure of it. I flew on another airline."

The voice on the other end spoke more softly now. "All right. Keep a tail on her. But that's it. Don't try anything. The mother's death may just change my plans."

The receiver went dead before he had a chance to ask what that change might be. It didn't matter. Like the man said. He wasn't getting paid to think. He replaced the phone in its cradle and took the elevator back up to the fifth floor.

NINE

San Francisco, California

Three days later, Lili was still moving in a kind of sleep-walk, outside a picture of calm, inside a sense of loss and loneliness that she couldn't explain. So long expected, her mother's death should have been easier for her to bear. Su-Wei had left this world with the same quiet acceptance she had shown all her life. The spirit of the rabbit would now reunite with her ancestors in heaven. Su-Wei had told Lili that that knowledge should lessen her grief—that she should be happy for her now that she would be at peace. But Lili found it difficult to let go, so she distracted herself with preparations for the funeral.

The coffin was the most ornately carved teak that the funeral home offered, painted in the most garish colors and it was placed upon a motorized palanquin that resembled a pagoda on wheels. Lili had hired a few dozen professional mourners dressed in the white robes of sorrow to precede the hearse, banging gongs to drive away the evil spirits and to follow along behind. They wailed with such sincerity, one might suppose they knew Su-Wei.

A small bonfire surrounded by a scarlet altar accepted their offerings—paper replicas of the earthly necessities Su-Wei would need on her journey: cooking pots, chickens, money. That gesture affirmed the unbreakable continuity of the eternal generations of the Chinese race.

If you are Chinese, you can never get China from your mind...

At the Church the formal Anglican service was punctuated with cries of such forlorn pain that the stained-glass windows shook in their steel forms. The priest, who served the Chinese community, did not bat an eye.

At the cemetery there were two ceremonies, Anglican and Buddhist and Su-Wei was lowered into the ground, her name and her Chinese chop already engraved on the smooth plaque in the ancient stone next to her husband's. As the casket slowly descended, the mourners stepped back to make sure their shadows did not fall across it.

Lili thought her mother would have been satisfied—besides the thirty hired mourners, there were representatives from her own friends including Mai Li Fong, her old Mah Jongg partner and Mr. Wu, the fish man. A dozen or more uninvited Chinese children scattered through the ceremony to witness the shooting of the firecrackers. Dylan had wanted to come too, but she'd discouraged him. Somehow she felt his presence might be too awkward. Besides, she really wasn't ready to think about their relationship.

At some point she became aware of a male presence close beside her. Looking up, expecting somehow to see Dylan despite what she'd said, she was surprised to see Dr. Seng. He smiled and took her arm. "I heard of your mother's death. It is most unfortunate."

Standing at the graveside, Lili didn't think to ask how he had found out or known where to come in San Francisco. At that moment, if she was aware of anything, it was the Chinese gravediggers waiting respectfully in the trees, ready to fill the gaping hole in the earth. She was also too numb to notice the two men who seemed to melt backward into the crowd.

*   *   *

LA Medical

The hospital operator didn't recognize the caller who placed the STAT page. Nor did she think to ask his name. As she explained to Ed Baxter when she finally tracked him down, he was lucky for that. She wasn't his God-damn private secretary. LA Medical didn't pay her enough. Her job was simply to relay messages.

*   *   *

Xi'an, China

The white crane spreads its wings.

He stepped back as quietly as a cat, whirling his arms in his loose-fitting Mao jacket.

Hand strums the lute.

His body relaxed and extended, swaying slowly like a tree in a gentle breeze.

Grasp the bird's tail

Head erect, torso straight, toes in line with the knees, back leg extended naturally.

Part the wild horse's mane on both sides.

Yin and yang. The gentle shifting of weight to reach the balance.

High pat on horse.

The mind tranquil, yet alert. Combining vigor and gentleness. Like reeling off raw silk from a cocoon.

Needle at sea bottom.

He breathed deeply and evenly as he made a closing form. Then, still in a semi-squatting position, Ni-Fu turned to face the young man who had been waiting quietly in the doorway. "Old Mao said there is more to life than *tai-chi chuan*. It is only there to prepare you for the rest of the day."

"You were fortunate to have known such a great leader."

The old man nodded, standing erect now. "On the other hand, Mao never really understood that the ancient movements, like the Chinese people, have transcended everything in China-famine, dynasties, revolutions, even the Gang of Four."

*   *   *

LA Medical

Breathless, Ed Baxter ran into Dr. Trenton's outer office, almost colliding with his secretary on her way to lunch. "Sorry I'm late," he apologized.

"Late?"

"Yeah for my meeting with the chief. I was paged not more than fifteen minutes ago. The operator said Dr. Trenton wanted to see me." He was still hyperventilating, but managed to smile.

Miss Prim, as rigid as her name, did not return the expression. She prided herself on knowing exactly where Dr. Trenton was supposed to be every minute of the day and this so-called meeting was not on his schedule. She frowned at the second year resident. "I'm afraid there must be some mistake…"

Just then, Tex Trenton appeared at the door of his inner office. "Oh, Miss Prim, I'm glad I caught you. Would you mind mailing this while you're out?"

"Certainly, sir." She took the envelope and started out the door as Trenton turned to reenter his office, both ignoring Baxter.

"Dr. Trenton," the resident called. "I'm here for our meeting."

Trenton looked at Miss Prim who managed to throw Baxter a surreptitious glare a split second before directing an embarrassed look at her boss. "Dr. Baxter claims he is here to see you, but I have nothing on your calendar."

"I was paged," Baxter insisted. "The operator said you wanted to see me. If it's about Mrs. Manley—well, I took care of everything. She's been readmitted to the nursing home. You know, since Lili, I mean, Dr. Quan's been out of town, I've been carrying her load and mine. Not that it was any problem. I'm delighted to help the team," he gushed. "I mean…"

The chief raised a hand in an effort to stop the flow of words. "All right. You're here and I've got a few minutes."

"Don't forget your appointments," Miss Prim reminded, checking her desk calendar. "2:30 with Dr. O'Hara; 3:00 with the vice-president of Aligen."

"Thanks, Jenny," Trenton said, summoning Baxter into his office. "Enjoy your lunch."

The spinster secretary nodded, giving Baxter one more disgusted look. She was sure he had made up the whole thing. Meeting indeed! In her twenty-five years as secretary to many department chairs, she'd met her fill of Ed Baxters—anxious-faced, fast-talking, back-stabbing senior residents all trying to climb to the top of the medical power pyramid.

*   *   *

San Francisco, California

After the service, Dr. Seng walked Lili to a waiting cab. "My invitation for you to study in China is still open," he said as Lili stepped into the taxi.

"Thank you, but I can't think about that just now."

"Of course, I understand." He closed the car door for her. "I'll be returning to Los Angeles this evening. You have my number if you change your mind."

She gave the driver an address, then turned to Dr. Seng. "Thank you for coming to the funeral."

The professor leaned in the window of the cab and looked at Lili. "Please don't think me insensitive. I merely wanted you to know that we would welcome your coming home."

For an instant, Lili wondered whether there was a hidden meaning to Seng's words, but as the cab pulled away, she turned her thoughts to other issues.

*   *   *

LA Medical

"Dylan, how long have we known each other?" Tex Trenton asked.

"Since I was a kid knocking around DC trying to find myself. You gave me my real start."

Trenton nodded. "In many ways, you're the son I never had."

"Thank you, sir."

"That's why this feels so awkward."

Dylan watched the chief, wondering where the conversation was headed.

"I understand your research has hit a snag."

"Where did you hear that?"

"I read your notebooks."

Red-faced: "How dare you? That's *my* work!"

In contrast to Dylan's flash of anger, Trenton's tone was soft and evenly modulated. "Do I need to remind you? When you asked to come to LA Med and work with me again, we agreed on the conditions. Aligen funded the research on aging based on *my* reputation. Until you make yours, I'm the chief and I'll read any notebook I see fit."

"It's just that I wasn't ready to tell you anything. It's true I've had a temporary setback. But nothing that can't be worked out."

"I'm scheduled to meet with Martin Carpenter from Aligen in less than thirty minutes. He's expecting results and at the moment I can't deliver a thing."

"What's the hurry?"

"Carpenter has already intimated that unless we have something on the MHC code soon, the company may discontinue our funding."

"They can't do that!"

"They can do anything they damn well please. It's their money." He looked at his protégé. "Perhaps your mind isn't entirely on your research."

"I don't understand."

"Perhaps you need to spend less time with Dr. Quan."

Dylan's face reddened again. "Is that what this is all about? My spending a few evenings with Lili Quan?"

"What this is about is your need to do better work. And from what I hear, Dr. Quan's work could use a little more attention as well."

"I saw Ed Baxter leave your office. If you're hearing anything negative about Lili from him, you know he's got an ax to grind."

"As a matter of fact, Baxter's observations have confirmed my own growing concern about Dr. Quan." He pointed to an envelope on his desk. "A letter from an unhappy patient."

Dylan shrugged. "Every doctor turns off a patient now and then."

"Bob Sanderson isn't just any patient. His family is one of the largest contributors to this hospital." Trenton paused. "Look Dylan, I'm not about to tell you what to do with your personal life, but, if you're really serious about your research, you'll have to give it 110%. Discipline," the ex-Army man said, "is the only way to achieve your goals."

Trenton got up, signifying the end of the meeting. "I'm glad we had this talk," he said, walking Dylan to the door. "We are close to an answer. We can't afford to waste any more time." A fatherly pat on the back. "Can I count on you?"

Dylan looked at his mentor for a moment before replying. "Of course."

Trenton smiled. "Good." But, the moment he was alone again, his smile was gone. Returning to his desk, Tex Trenton picked up the phone. Damn, he thought, as he dialed. So many administrative headaches. No one seemed to grasp the enormity of his job, the constant pressures, the need to appear omniscient. Jesus. If he didn't manage every last detail, *nothing* got done.

*   *   *

San Francisco, California

The cab ride from the cemetery to Chinatown took Lili more than the five miles. It transported her back in time so that when the driver turned onto Grant Avenue she was ten years old again, playing in the alleys behind restaurants and curio shops. As she stepped from the cab she suddenly remembered how on Chinese New Year when money was plentiful, the older boys would bicycle out to the riding academies in Golden Gate Park, hire horses for three dollars a day and ride back to Chinatown, galloping down this avenue like cowboys. Lili thought it was wonderful and wanted to join them, but her mother would shake her head and say,"*san fun meng*", the Chinese equivalent of "one foot in the grave".

Even after all these years, the neighborhood looked the same: the Hai Wu Fish Market, the Hong Chun Company where the two Chun sisters produced hand-made Chinese dresses—today more for tourists than locals, Tang Mu's jewelry shop. Even Old Saint Mary's Church was still on the corner of Grant and California, although you could see the new TransAmerica pyramid in the background.

It was on the second story of a three story stucco box near the corner of Grant and Pine above Eu's bakery where Lili was born and spent most of her childhood. On balmy days, the windows would all be open and the apartment would smell of *char siu bao* (pork filled buns), *galai gock* (curry puffs) *sui gai dahn go* (sponge cake) and *malai go* (steamed egg cakes). But now, when she pushed open the front door, the windows were shut tight, the air still and odorless.

For a moment she stood in the foyer, taking in the emptiness, unsure of where to go. She half-expected to hear her mother's voice, scolding her for being late, glad that she had come. But there was only silence as she moved from room to room. Stepping into the kitchen, Lili envisioned her mother in her apron as a younger woman, anxious to see that her daughter ate a good hot five course meal before heading off to study.

"I'm not hungry."

"Every grain of rice you leave in your bowl will be a tear that you shed before the day is out."

"You're making that up."

"Chinese never lie."

She entered her mother's bedroom. Funny, long before her father died, this had always been her mother's room. Everything reminded Lili of Su-Wei: the hand-crocheted coverlet, the ivory comb, even the wall-paper with the medallion design in pale yellow. She recalled her mother telling her that the ancient Chinese had invented wallpaper and that it wasn't until the 14th century that wallpaper was introduced into Europe. *You must always be proud that you were born Chinese.*

Lili picked up a bobby pin from the dresser and thought of how each morning she'd stood impatiently as her mother pulled and twisted her thick black hair until she'd formed two tightly plaited pigtails.

Why can't I wear my hair short like the other girls.

You are not like the other girls.

It was a never-ending battle expressed in her growing up years: *Am I of my mother's race or am I an American?* Her mother speaking Shanghainese, learning only pidgin-English, raising her in the standard of Chinese woman-hood, confined within the doctrines of Confucius that her highest reward was to be the matriarch of a large, respectful family. *It is for your own good.* No one in China dreamed of being unmarried.

The American principles of freedom and independence were taught in grade school. Lili learned that qualities such as individuality, self-expression and analytical thought were the rights of all Americans. *I want to choose my own way.*

Lili noticed an old rectangular black lacquer box on the night stand. She sat on the bed and picked it up. Although she'd seen it there since she'd been a child, she'd never touched it. No one had told her not to, but somehow she'd sensed this was her mother's special treasure—something she'd brought with her, hand painted with rose and blue-colored swans, all the way from Shanghai.

Opening its hinged lid, Lili discovered within its imperial yellow velvet and satin lining, several old papers, letters and photographs. She recognized her parents' marriage license and their insurance premium booklet, but the letters were all in Chinese which she couldn't read, so she could only wonder at their contents. Her mother had rarely talked of her life in China. But when Lili was nine, she found her mother crying over a letter she'd just received.

Su-Wei told her it had come from the Chinese government. "They say my father is dead," she'd sobbed. "He promised to send for me, but he never did. Now everyone in China is gone."

It was the only time Lili ever recalled her mother crying. After that, Su-Wei unpacked the camphor chest she'd always kept filled with clothes, shoes and other necessities for her eventual return to China and never spoke of her sadness again.

Lili picked through the few photos. There were several she'd never seen before: one of Lili's father in his Sunday suit. Probably brought to Su-Wei's aunt by the old woman who made the match. Lili wondered what her mother felt when she saw this picture for the first time. Did she even think to protest a forced marriage to a man more than twice her age? She picked up a snap-shot of her parents standing side by side, not touching, looking directly into the camera, but registering no sense of emotion- just acceptance.

At the bottom of the box was a small snapshot of Su-Wei as a child. She couldn't have been more than ten. Funny, how much she looked like Lili.

What was even more striking was her expression—dark eyes radiant, confident, carefree as she held her father's hands. It was also the first time Lili had ever seen a picture of her grandfather. He was handsome, with jet black hair and serious eyes. Su-Wei had told her he was a doctor—*a great professor- you can be proud of your ancestors.*

For several moments, Lili stared at her mother and grandfather holding hands. Su-Wei was so happy once. Then Lili stood up and began wandering from room to room, running her hands over objects barely remembered: a lace tablecloth, a silk pillowcase, a rosewood chopsticks box. Odd. She had grown up here, but curiously felt no attachment.

Now perhaps she was beginning to understand. She had fled this house the minute Wellesley accepted her because she'd been ashamed of her mother— her old-fashionedness, her reluctance to learn English, her insistence on clinging to the old ways. Lili left because she didn't want to be like Su-Wei the rabbit—so accepting of her *joss*. Like the half-emptied bottle of pain pills still on the bathroom counter. Or maybe Lili just never appreciated what losing parents and country had meant to Su-Wei.

Lili returned to her mother's bedroom and closed the lacquered box. Sitting down on the bed, she felt in her pocket for the jade locket her mother had given her and held it by the gold chain. She knew the intricately carved gold letters stood for shou, the Chinese symbol for long life and almost laughed at the irony. Her mother had died so young.

But, of course that was not really why Su-Wei kept it so close to her heart all these years. Lili opened the locket and stared for a moment at the tiny portrait of a beautiful Chinese woman. She'd never seen a picture of her grandmother.

Remember, if you are Chinese, you can never let go of China in your mind.

My God, Lili thought recalling her mother's last words, how little she really knew of her roots.

She placed the locket around her neck.

Someday I hope you will return to China for me. I will live in you now.

Lili opened her purse and found the card Dr. Seng had given her. Remembering his words today: *I merely wanted you to know that we would welcome your coming home .*

Oh God, she thought as she reached up and touched her cheek. She looked in the mirror. Only then did she know that the wetness was her own tears, that she was crying as she could never remember crying.

And sobbing, she suddenly understood that she was now all alone in the world.

TEN

Los Angeles, California

One week later, Dylan paced the tiny space in his lab office. "Lili, you can't be serious."

"I've never been more serious, Dylan," she said, sitting at his desk.

"But to leave your residency in the middle of the year. Trenton, will never let you go."

"As a matter of fact, I met with Dr. Trenton. He seems to feel I could use some time off, " she replied flatly, "Something about not being able to keep my mind on my work."

"Come on. You know where that came from."

Lili held up her hand. "I know about Baxter. I know about Sanderson's letter." She looked directly at him. "I even know about Trenton's little talk with you."

"Why didn't you tell me?"

"What good would it do? As long as you and I are seen together, Trenton's going to be on your case."

"But…"

"Look, let's face it. My leaving now would solve everybody's problems."
"What about us?"

"Not now," Lili snapped, a raw nerve exposed. "My mother's dead. I'm all alone. I need time."

"I'm sorry about your mother, Lili."

"Not as much as I am," she said sadly. "So much of my life was spent fighting her." Lili's voice shook. "… what she represented. I owe her this trip." She bit the corner of her lower lip. "Maybe it's time. Time to go home."

"When are you leaving?"

"Tomorrow. I've arranged to sublet my apartment. I've bought my ticket and before Dr. Seng returned to China, he expedited my visa."

"You've thought of everything," Dylan said, walking over and pulling her up from her seat. "Lili, I don't want what we've started to die."

"Dylan…"

He put a finger to her lips. "I think I understand how you feel. I know what it's like to feel lost. Without roots." He put his arms around her waist. "Look. I've got two weeks vacation coming. Why don't I meet you there in a month or so. You could show me around."

"I don't know."

"It's not as if you're going to the end of the world," he said and Lili laughed. "Well, what I mean is it's not as though you can't write or call or even FAX me- just to let me know how you are and when it would be convenient for me to come. "

Lili gave him a hug and sighed. "Thanks for being my friend."

"For now." Dylan kissed the top of her head. "Just remember. You can always count on me."

*   *   *

Beijing, China

The Foreign Ministry chief was lost in thought when he turned to face General Pei-Jun Tong who had been waiting quietly in the doorway. "You have news?"

"Everything is going as planned, Comrade."

"The granddaughter?"

"She should be here within three weeks."

Lin nodded. Everything *was* going as planned. Still, it never hurt to have a back-up plan. That was why, when the general had gone, he pulled an Intelligence dossier from inside his desk.

* * *

Washington, DC

A few days later, Carpenter and Halliday met in the park just opposite the Washington Monument. Although it was only early April, the warm days had already brought the first blush of cherry blossoms. It was the nicest time of year, thought the CIA man as he listened to Carpenter's report.

"Everything worked just as you said. Even better than you planned."

Halliday watched a small girl struggle with the string of a kite, a bright blue Mylar shark. "How so?"

"Well I was thinking about her mother's dying. You knew she was terminally ill. But her death just now seemed the catalyst for Dr. Quan's decision to go to China. It was perfect timing."

The shark was moving dangerously close to the trees. Distracted: "Yes, it was."

"I guess I've done my part."

Halliday did not respond.

"How shall I keep in touch?"

Halliday turned to face his old friend. "You know the saying: 'Don't call us...'"

Carpenter nodded. "I understand." He deliberately lowered his voice. "This clandestine stuff makes me nervous. I don't know how you've done it all these years."

Halliday shrugged. "It becomes habit, I guess."

The men shook hands and Carpenter departed for his car, slowly disappearing in the distance. As Halliday watched him grow smaller, he thought of his friend. Assuming the events of the last few weeks were serendipitous, a result of 'perfect timing', luck! Fool, thought Halliday, observing the shark dip, then glide on the breeze as the child skillfully moved it away from the cherry trees. He smiled to himself, understanding what Carpenter never could: experts left nothing to luck—not Mrs. Manley, not Baxter, not Carpenter, not even Su-Wei's passing. Everything had been part of his plan.

*   *   *

Xi'an, China

Ni-Fu Cheng did not have the heart to go on.

He felt the heaviness of the world on him with each breath. When he was young he could have pushed the stone up the mountain no matter how many times it fell back to the bottom. Like Sisyphus, he persisted despite failure upon failure. At the same time he was able to reassure those in power that though he was close, he was not yet there.

Now that he had finally perfected his discovery, the prize seemed pointless. Since his "house arrest" three months before, he had slowly learned the truth about China. Just last week he was told of a new plan to rid China of all "spiritual pollution" among China's youth. He shuddered to think of how he would be contributing to their downfall. So many destinies in the palm of his hand.

Ni-Fu reconsidered his lifetime of sacrifice for China. Was this really the country he had spent forty years trying to save? For what purpose? So that evil old men like General Lin could subjugate the masses? Perhaps, he thought now, it is I who am evil.

Ni-Fu stirred as he heard footsteps. With his back to the door, he could not see who it was.

"Dr. Cheng?"

"Yes?"

"I've brought you your dinner."

"Thank you, Chi-Wen, but I'm not hungry."

"You haven't eaten for five days. You need your strength or you will die." The old man sighed. "I don't care."

"But your work…"

"It doesn't matter anymore." He pointed to the wooden chair beside his bed. "Please, come sit." He smiled as the young man came into his view. "There are few left to trust these days. I am grateful for your company."

BOOK TWO

THE PAST

THE POET THINKS OF HIS OLD HOME

I have not turned my steps toward the East Mountain
for so long,
I wonder, how many times the roses have bloomed
there....
The white clouds gather and scatter again like friends.
Who has a house now to view the setting of the
bright moon?

Li-Po

SWIMMING

After swallowing some water at Changsha
I taste a Wuchang fish in the surf
and swim across the Yangtze River that winds
ten thousand li.
I see the entire China sky.
Wind batters me, waves hit me-I don't care.
Better than walking lazily in the patio.
Today I have a lot of time.
Here on the river the Master said:
"Dying -going into the past- is like a river flowing."....

Mao Zedong, June 1956

ELEVEN

Saturday
April 15, 1989
Hong Kong
5 AM

Flecks of mauve, indigo and gold as if from a painter's brush streaked the early morning horizon as the huge, ungainly bird swept low from the south aiming for the single fingertip runway of Kai-Tak airport. Peering from her window, Lili held her breath, wondering how the 747-SP floating so slowly down through the clouds didn't just fall like a dead weight into the gray South China Sea. Below her, sampans, junks and snakeboats slid silently by, while up ahead cargo ships from all over the world were steaming toward the Kowloon peninsula.

"Five more minutes."

Lili smiled at the woman seated on her right. Ms.—she'd emphasized her liberation—Dorothy (call me Dottie) Diehl, a Dr. Ruth look-a-like and a retired geography teacher from Long Beach was finally going to see all the exotic places she'd taught about. She pointed to a lined copybook. "I plan to write it all down. Everything. Who knows, if it's good enough, maybe I'll even sell it. Start a whole new career." She laughed self-consciously. "You don't think I sound foolish?"

"Of course not. Many artists began their careers in their...," Lili searched for just the right word.

"Sunset years?" Dottie suggested, giggling good-naturedly. She even laughed like Dr. Ruth. "Thirty-five years I gave those kids. And for what, I ask you?"

It was a rhetorical question.

"You know," Dottie confided, not missing a beat. "Years ago geography was an important subject. *Very* important. No less respected that any of the three R's—reading, writing, arithmetic. But today..." She shook her head. "My Lord, today, most young people couldn't even tell you where Florida *is* on the map." She tsked. "And they don't care. Not unless Guns 'N Roses are appearing at the Forum and they need a ride."

Lili suppressed a smile.

Ms. Diehl sighed. "I just don't know what this young generation is coming to." She took the plastic cup from her breakfast tray and finished her fourth Bloody Mary. "Calms the nerves," she'd told Lili when the trip had started. "I'm a terrible flyer.

Anyway," she continued after renewing her courage, "I'm free now. Left everything behind—house, car, ex-husband. There's nothing holding me back." She looked at Lili. "Am I talking too much?"

"Oh, no, not at all." Her chatter had made the fourteen hour flight pass more quickly.

"Tell me," she said, clutching her Guidebook to Asia, "is the Far East as exciting as they say?" Another self-conscious titter : "I'm not talking about the ancient ruins now."

"Beg your pardon?"

A conspiratorial whisper: "Asian men. I hear they're real tigers in bed."

"Well..."

A flash of indigence in her bloodshot eyes: "If you think sixty-five is over the hill, young lady, well think again."

"I wasn't thinking anything," Lili soothed, biting her lower lip to hide her amusement. "It's just that I've never been east of New York."

"Well then, you're in for a treat..." Dottie tapped her guidebook. "I'm joining a tour tomorrow. Three weeks through China by train and boat. Cheaper than booking through the States and not just the usual tourist sites. This is off the beaten path."

"Sounds like fun."

"Where are you going?"

"Oh, I'm flying directly from Hong Kong to Xi'an."

"Without seeing any of the country?"

"I'm not making the travel arrangements."

"Didn't you tell me your people are from Shanghai?"

"Yes, but that was forty years ago," Lili replied. "There's no one there now."

"Still, you should see where your family came from ," Dottie pressed. "You've come half way round the world. Be impulsive. Just say you're taking a little detour before starting your work."

Unwilling to argue, Lili produced a noncommittal "We'll see."

The captain's voice over the loud speaker: "Ladies and gentlemen. fasten your seatbelts. We are about to land."

As they were waiting to disembark from the plane: "Don't forget what I told you. China Products. Opposite the Central Market. That's where you'll get the best value. Nathan Road is strictly for tourists."

"I'll remember."

In line for customs: "Oh and if you decide to see some of China, you can buy a ticket and get your travel permits at the CITS office in Kowloon." Dottie stopped to tell the immigration officer this was her first trip to the Orient. His response was a disinterested nod and a perfunctory stamp of her passport. "My tour leaves at 10:25 tomorrow morning," she yelled before she was swallowed up in the crowd.

"Staying in Hong Kong long?"

"Excuse me?"

The customs officer was processing passports without looking up.

"A few days. I'm a doctor. I'll be studying at the Xi'an Institute. For about three months." She wasn't sure he needed so much information, yet she didn't want to appear secretive.

The young officer interrupted his processing rhythm to stare at Lili. For a moment he seemed to look right through her. Then he checked and rechecked her passport picture, reconciling it with the young woman standing before him.

"I know, it's a terrible shot. I just decided to come to China….," Lili stammered, conscious of the impatient movement of people behind her. "I didn't have time to get a good one."

Without another comment, the officer stamped her entry visa and waved her through. "Next."

Once she passed customs, Lili maneuvered her luggage through several groups of tourists, each clustered around guides waving colored flags. Beyond them several individuals held placards with the names of arriving passengers. Not expecting to be met, she almost missed the card with her name on it.

"I'm Lili Quan," she said to the formally dressed chauffeur.

He bowed. "Welcome to Hong Kong." He spoke English with a clipped British accent.

"This must be a mistake."

"You *are* Dr. Quan?"

"Yes, but…."

"Good," he said, picking up her suitcases and began heading out of the terminal. "I am to take you to your hotel."

"I have reservations at the Holiday Inn."

The chauffeur shrugged. "My instructions are to take you to the Peninsula."

"The Peninsula Hotel?" Lili almost had to run to keep up with him. "I can't afford that."

The chauffeur placed her luggage in the trunk of the green Rolls Royce limo, then spoke in a tone that defied argument: "You are a guest of the PRC."

*   *   *

Xi'an, China

"Please, professor, just a little more. The soup will give you strength."

Ni-Fu Cheng looked up at the young man trying so valiantly to keep him alive. Over the past six months he'd become very fond of Chi-Wen. Although deprived of a formal education by Mao's Cultural Revolution, Chi-Wen was naturally bright. Ever the teacher, Dr. Cheng delighted in the opportunity to expand his horizons.

Together they'd read books Chi-Wen smuggled in from the professors' old library: the classics, science, geography. Chi-Wen's English had improved under the professor's tutelage. So much so that they'd even argued philosophy and religion in that strange sounding foreign language: Ni-Fu, the romantic scientist, Chi-Wen, the practical Taoist.

The old man thought of him not only as the surrogate for his own lost children, but for all the lost children of China. "You know," he sighed, "I have always believed China to be the most wonderful country on earth."

Chi-Wen nodded. "My father used to say 'the East is the place where things begin, where the sun rises, where the wind is born'."

"It is also a place that has been betrayed too often." The old man looked directly at his young protégé. "Everywhere there are old men with power—not because they are wise or just, but simply because they are old men."

"I have been taught to respect my elders," Chi-Wen said woodenly. "Not to question."

"Sometimes questions are important."

Chi-Wen looked away to ladle another spoonful of soup.

"I'm not hungry," Cheng said, tears filling his eyes. He'd given up everything to discover the mystery of *shou,* to give mankind the gift of longevity. So much. His home in Shanghai, his family and now his freedom.

His tears suddenly turned to an irrational hysterical laughter. Ironic, wasn't it? As an old man, he realized change was essential to launch China into the twentieth-first century. He looked at Chi-Wen, appreciating his fear, wondering how to make him understand that without the cycle of ages, change would never occur.

*   *   *

Hong Kong

Some say the Peninsula Hotel is Hong Kong, standing like a beacon on the tip of Kowloon, facing the Star Ferry that carries thousands each day to the Central District on Hong Kong Island. This grand old lady of world hotels, "the Pen", was built in 1928, when travelers took many weeks and trunks to reach Hong Kong. A colonial institution, it maintained the British tradition of understated style, good taste, grandeur and elegance.

Twenty minutes after leaving the airport, Lili's limo had maneuvered through thick early morning traffic, then joined the Peninsula's fleet of green Rolls Royce limousines parked in the fountained driveway where several chauffeurs idly buffed headlights. A white-clad page boy held open the etched glass doors as she entered the ornate columned and gilt-corniced lobby, reminiscent of Europe's great railway lounges.

Although it was not quite 7:30 AM, smartly suited men and women sat at marble tables, sipping steaming cups of coffee while perusing the latest economic news in the Hong Kong Journal. By early afternoon, the scene would change to high tea with British scones, cucumber sandwiches and a string quartet.

"Welcome to the Peninsula, Dr. Quan." The desk manager was a sleek-haired Chinese whose name tag said, 'Mr. Wong'.

"Thank you, Mr. Wong, but…"

"Your room is ready. The bellman will take your luggage."

Before Lili had a chance to register another protest, the manager turned to help a Texas businessman and his wife who wanted to switch to a suite on the harbor side. "I'm afraid we're all booked, sir."

"Look pal," the Texan shouted. "For eight hundred US big ones a night, I don't think it's asking too much to be able to see the goddamn water."

"But sir…"

"Don't 'but sir', me. We came all this way to see the sights and hell, we're gonna to do just that," he bullied.

The manager held his ground. "I wish I had more rooms to give."

"Why don't you check your computer."

Wong was polite, but firm. "I know we're booked."

Fascinated, Lili watched the apparent standoff when she saw the Texan slip a large bill across the counter.

Checking that the concierge had his back turned, the manager carefully palmed the bribe, then switched on his computer. "Actually I think there is something on the fifth floor."

"I thought as much."

"A win-win situation."

Lili wheeled around to see a white-suited man in line behind her, preparing to light a cigarillo. "I beg your pardon?"

"The manager saves face and the Texan gets his room. Win-win."

"I see."

"Especially in this part of the world," the man continued. "It's essential that everyone's special needs be satisfied."

"Dr. Quan?" The bellman was standing in the open elevator.

"Oh, yes. Excuse me."

As she reached the elevator, Lili turned to get another look at the strange man with the mustache and the Z -shaped scar on his face. Except for the trail of blue smoke from his cigarillo, there was no trace of him at all.

*   *   *

As soon as the elevator doors closed, a young Chinese man sitting at one of the marble tables, folded his copy of *Renmin Ribao* (The People's Daily) and headed for the lobby pay phone.

*   *   *

The room valet deposited her bags in a large, high-ceilinged bedroom, turned on the TV, set the air-conditioner on cool, opened the curtains and then disappeared, returning with an elegant fruit basket and a sandalwood box filled with wrapped designer soap.

"Gifts from the management. And this," he said, pulling a sealed envelope from his jacket pocket, "was delivered just before your arrival."

"Thank you." Lili reached for a few dollars from her purse, but the valet declined the tip, assuring her "everything had already been taken care of".

He was gone before Lili opened the envelope which contained a plane ticket to Xi'an via Beijing dated for the next day. Although there was no note, its source seemed obvious.

"Damn it," she said out loud. Rather than appreciation, Lili was suddenly angry at Dr. Seng's apparent generosity. She hadn't asked for any of this—not the Rolls Royce limousine, not the room in this world class hotel with its marble bathrooms, not the free ticket to Xi'an. She would have preferred to pay her own way at the Holiday Inn. None of this made sense to her. She didn't understand Seng's motives and what she didn't understand, she didn't like.

Confused, she opened the sliding door and stepped out on the balcony. It was only mid- April and already there was more than a trace of the humidity that would become unbearable by June. Lili removed her sweater and took a deep breath. She could smell the dahlias in bloom. Her eyes drank in the sights. From the sixth floor, she could see Kowloon, hazy through a humid gray mist. Across Victoria Harbor, a Star Ferry pulled away from the pier.

"Damn it," she declared again. "I'm lucky to be in this fabulous town. I might as well enjoy it." She returned to her room and headed for the shower. Today she'd see the sights. Tomorrow she'd think about Dr. Seng.

*   *   *

Paulo Ng was a man who trusted no one. Once he had seen Lili, he was satisfied that so far, David Kim's information was accurate.

*   *   *

After a quick shower, Lili changed into jeans and a T-shirt and headed for the hotel lobby where the concierge advised her to start her exploration of Hong Kong with a half-day city tour. The air-conditioned double-decker leisurely circled the island, making obligatory stops at Victoria Peak, the Typhoon Shelter, Repulse Bay and Aberdeen while passengers listened through plastic earphones to commentary taped in almost any language from English to Swahili.

At the Central District, Lili decided to take off on her own, weaving through the crowds on foot. Her guidebook described Hong Kong in hackneyed epithets—"a cement jungle", "a bustling port", "a capitalist paradise". What struck Lili, as she headed across Connaught Road was the noise. The streets throbbed with competing sounds, all seemingly set at maximum volume: the staccato clickety-clacks of Mah Jongg tiles; the beat of rock, pop, soul—even Cantonese opera; the blaring of Mercedes and Rolls Royce horns; the pounding of jackhammers and pile drivers; a dozen tongues and dialects vying for the ears and eyes of ever changing crowds.

Surprisingly, no natives among the throng seemed upset by the din. It was as if they possessed some inner barrier to the cacophony. Or perhaps they were simply too busy trying to succeed in this laissez-faire economy to notice. After all, in Hong Kong, the acquisition of money was a mania from beggar to business tycoon.

In the four-story Central Market, the noise was intermingled with the smell of everything from eels and crabs to quail and chickens. Lili stopped at one stall to watch a man in a greasy apron slit a black carp lengthwise in one deft movement so that the heart was still beating and pumping blood.

"You like?" he asked. "Very fresh."

"I see," Lili acknowledged, feeling queasy. It was close to one PM and she realized she hadn't eaten since before five o'clock that morning.

Just beyond the market she located a restaurant, packed with like hundreds of diners eating, reaching, shouting and gesturing for *dim sum* as Chinese waitresses wheeled trolleys filled with these ancient fast-food savories past their tables. Several bamboo poles were strung across the width of the dining area for patrons to hang the wicker cages of pet song birds out for their daily airing. As she sipped tea, Lili relaxed, finding their musical chirping a pleasant counterpoint to the clattering of the trolley trays.

"*Fun gwor?*" A serving girl asked as she uncovered one of the steaming bamboo baskets.

Lili nodded, accepting a plate of three steamed rice flour triangles filled with pork, shrimp and bamboo shoots. Delicious.

Another trolley rolled by. "*Pai gwat?*"

Lili realized her seat on the aisle gave her easy access to the besieged serving girls. "Thank you." The spare-ribs with red-pepper sauce were even better.

"I'd leave room for the *saan tat*. if I were you. It's the best hot custard tart you'll find anywhere."

"Excuse me?" Lili looked around, but by the time she realized the voice had come from just behind her, there was no one there. The table had just been vacated because the waiters hadn't yet cleared the stack of empty dishes and baskets. Lili searched the restaurant, but her view was obscured by the press of people still waiting to be seated.

"You want *saan tat?*" A waitress was asking.

"What? Oh, yes, sure, I guess so."

The waitress distracted her so that she missed the man as he left the restaurant. She wouldn't have seen his face since his back was to her, but she might have recognized his white suit and the blue smoke from his cigarillo.

*   *   *

Lili also missed the young Chinese cadre seated across the room watching as she finished her dessert.

*   *   *

After lunch, Lili explored the boutiques and sophisticated westernized stores along D'Aguilar Street and the tiny shops up and down Stanley Street and Hollywood Road that all seemed to sell stereo and VCR equipment, cameras, jewelry or watches.

Eventually she reached Possession Street marking the border between Central and the down-to-earth old Chinese section of Hong Kong called The Western District. According to her guidebook, although Western was the very first district settled by the British, malaria soon decimated their numbers. By 1848, this area was a haven for Chinese immigrants.

Wandering down the narrow streets with their chop and jade carvers, opera costumers, fan-makers, pottery-shapers and egg-roll bakers, Lili felt she was as close to traditional Chinese urban society as she was going to get in this otherwise ultra-modern city.

Turning onto Bonham Street West., she found a Chinese apothecary. Inside, the dusty shop smelled of ginger, seaweed and incense.

"May I help you? My name is Ching-yi."

Lili spun around to face the local herbalist. The old man was missing his left eye, a not very well-made glass bulb filling the socket. "Just looking."

Ching-yi was quite happy for her to investigate his potions. "Of course. Take your time."

Lili looked at dozens of glass jars containing pickled bears' claws, otters' penis and snake's gallbladders.

Ching-yi pointed to an ancient wooden cabinet near the far wall, its tiny drawers filled with many of the two thousand traditional remedies used to promote health and vigor. "Dried snake," he said, pulling out one of the drawers. "For chest pain." Dried lizards mixed with green pellets filled another. "Best remedy for cough."

He opened several more, explaining that powdered armadillo relieved morning sickness; elk horn, his recommended therapy for stomach complaints. He had racks of pungent smelling roots, snake venom antidote, tortoise shell, sea porcupines and bats pinned up with their wings outstretched. Also dried birds' heads, mushrooms, bottles of leaves and slimy-looking things in oil.

Finally, he handed Lili a mixture of freshly ground rose petals mixed with sugar. "This will keep you fit and strong," he assured her.

"How much?"

"For you? A gift."

Even though Lili assumed the mixture was only worth pennies, she felt compelled to pay.

The man thought for a moment. "The rose petals are free. But for two dollars I will read your fortune."

Lili smiled. Saving face. "Sure, why not."

"What do you want to know?"

"You tell me."

The man nodded, took her right hand in his and gently traced the tiny lines in her palm. "I see that you have come from very far away."

Lili almost laughed. With her Levi jeans, Greenpeace T-shirt and LA Gear aerobic shoes, it didn't take a soothsayer to guess she was a tourist.

"But your journey has just begun."

"Yes, I plan to…"

"You are going home," he said in a low voice.

Dr. Seng's words. Annoyed: "If you mean I'm going to visit China, I guess you could say that."

The old man was not listening. Still holding her hand, he closed his one good eye. "When you look outward, you see the past. I wish to see the future."

His breathing slowed as he seemed to fall into a trance. Finally: "It is a very difficult and dangerous journey."

"And why is that?" Lili asked, amused by the man's showmanship.

"Difficult because the path is long and winding. You will lose part of yourself before you find yourself. Just be wary of new friendships. The most cunning adversary first seeks to be your closest ally."

Lili felt the man's body shake. To her it seemed like bad theater, but then what did you expect for two dollars? "And why is it dangerous?" she prompted.

"Dangerous because the journey ends in… in…" He pulled his hand away as if been burned by her touch.

"How does the journey end?"

The man opened his eye and looked at her for a long time. "I'm afraid that is all I can say. But you must not undertake such a trip in the year of the snake. Unlucky for travelers."

"How does the journey end?" Lili demanded.

Almost a whisper: "It ends in death."

"That's ridiculous," Lili declared, suddenly angry at herself. "I'm not going to change my plans just because of some superstitious hogwash." She paid him his two dollars and turned to go. "Thank-you."

The old man frowned as he watched her disappear down the alley. Foolish young woman, he thought. She should listen. Two dollars was a cheap price for saving a life.

*   *   *

Back in her hotel room, Lili placed a person-to-person call to Los Angeles. Dylan wasn't home, so she left a message on his answer phone. "Slight change of plans. I'm taking a train tomorrow to see a little of China on my own. I probably won't arrive in Xi'an for a week or two. I'll write when I get there."

The phone clicked off before she had a chance to say she loved him or even that she missed him. Just as well, she thought. She needed more time to sort out her feelings.

Now back to our regularly scheduled program…

Lili had the volume turned down and her back to the TV, so she missed the news announcing that earlier that day seventy-three year old deposed party leader, Hu Yaobang had died of a heart attack. According to the reporter, Beijing students were pouring into the streets to demand democracy.

*   *   *

As customary, whenever an American requested to travel alone to China, the American Embassy in Hong Kong received a copy of the itinerary. Less than ten minutes after Lili's itinerary arrived, it was faxed to Washington, DC.

*   *   *

Beijing, China

Because the young cadre followed Lili to the CITS office, his Beijing boss was aware of Lili's change in plans. Now the Foreign Minister sat facing the two other men in the room, his round face humorless, his voice tight. "This is a very delicate operation. I don't have to remind you that we can't have this young woman running all over China, unsupervised."

General Pei-Jun Tong scowled. "We should have kidnapped her the minute she landed in Hong Kong. We'd have the secret by now."

Peng Han shook his head. "Patience, general. We must not be like the mantis seizing the cicada—blinded by greed."

The Foreign Ministry chief put the palms of his hands together as if in prayer. "Our comrade is right. The strategy proposed was correct. Remember this had to be a clandestine affair. Except for Dr. Seng, no one outside this room could know. That meant getting the girl to China without alerting the international community. Now it means getting her to Xi'an without alerting enemies in our own country. Force is not the answer. At least, not yet."

"You have a new plan, comrade?" Pei-Jun Tong asked.

Lin studied his hands for several moments. "The young man who you had installed as Dr. Cheng's lab assistant."

"Chi-Wen Zhou?" Peng Han offered.

"Have him flown here tonight. Tomorrow I will personally brief him. Then I'll arrange to have him meet Dr. Quan's train in Shenzhen and escort her to Xi'an."

"He *is* trustworthy," Han conceded.

"He is also young and handsome," the deputy minister added pointedly.

*   *   *

Hong Kong

For several hours after calling LA, Lili sat on her hotel balcony, staring at the city, illuminated by the neon sky. Tonight the stars' light was particularly clear; Hong Kong shimmered before her like an iridescent jewel.

Lili was suddenly struck by the fortune teller's words: *When you look outward, you see the past...* All this light from the stars had traveled millions of years to reach earth. She was indeed looking into the past. This same light illuminated China just beyond the distant hills. *Ch'uing tou-chi*—the past, her mother had said, is a window to oneself.

She stared at China winking in the distance and wondered why she was going. What did she expect to find? She sighed, trying to sort out her feelings. Did she want to spite Tex Trenton? Or had Dylan come on a little too strong too soon? Perhaps it was the fortune teller warning her not to go? Or was she simply fulfilling her mother's dying wish? Maybe there was something in Dr. Seng's telling her to come home?

Did she want to deal with her present or look for her past? Lili wasn't sure. She only knew she had to find out.

TWELVE

Sunday
April 16, 1989
Beijing, China

The Foreign Ministry chief scrutinized the young man standing before him. Lin had reviewed the dossier prepared by Peng Han. He knew Chi-Wen Zhou, thirty-three, son of an intellectual, had been sent to the countryside during the Cultural Revolution for reeducation and now worked for the government. During the past year he'd been posted at the Xi'an Institute. His superiors all described him as 'quiet and respectful.'

Six months ago Lin had agreed to let Peng Han install Chi-Wen as lab aide to Dr. Cheng. He was to get the old man to reveal his secret. Peng Han insisted Chi-Wen was making progress, but time was running out.

That was why Lin decided to meet the young man himself—to confront him, to look deep into his eyes, to study every corner of his features like a *fung shui* man divining the true nature of his soul. After all, Chi-Wen was going to be pivotal to their scheme. Such a handsome Chinese face. Thick black hair, serious dark eyes. And his name: Chi-Wen. Chi meant 'unique'; wen, 'gentle, learned'. A true son of China.

The old man lifted a hand. "Please, sit down." When Chi-Wen made no move, he added. "I won't bite, you know."

Tea was brought and Lin waited while Chi-Wen took a few sips before continuing. "I trust your father's sister is well?" His owl-like eyes fastened on Chi-Wen. Fan Zhou was Chi-Wen's only living relative.

"She is very happy in her new apartment."

The deputy minister nodded. "And you, Chi-Wen. You are happy working for Dr. Cheng?"

"He is an excellent teacher."

"I understand you have passed the qualifying exams for medical school."

"I would like to be a doctor."

"I see." The deputy minister leaned forward, speaking in a low, confidential tone. "You know this can be accomplished." Of course he knew. After all the government controlled every citizen's education, housing, employment and residency.

The old man waited until he saw Chi-Wen suck in a breath of air. "On the other hand, places are hard to get. So many qualified."

The sigh was audible.

Good. Now I have him. Mao always said 'kill the chickens to teach the monkey'. It was easy with Chi-Wen's group- the so-called lost generation. They understood the lesson. Only a word here or there was needed. It was the younger ones he had to worry about. But that was another story.

He handed Chi-Wen a picture of Lili Quan. "This is the granddaughter of Ni-Fu Cheng. She will help us accomplish what you could not."

*   *   *

Outside, on the eastern side of Tiananmen Square, in front of the Museum of the Chinese Revolution, a class of elementary boys and girls listened to their teacher explain the growth of communism in China from its birth to its ultimate triumph. Not far away, several students from Beijing University were marching back and forth carrying homemade big-character posters or *dazibao* .

Some expressed grief over the death of Hu Yaobang: '*Those who ought to live have died; those who ought to die...*'

Others professed guilt at not supporting him in 1987: '*When we were deprived of your post, why didn't we stand up?*'

Still other placards quoted Abraham Lincoln, Thomas Paine and the Chinese Constitution : *"Government of the people, by the people, for the people", " Give me liberty or give me death!", "Freedom of speech, press and association and the right to demonstrate."*

"Ironic," Lee Tong quipped, lighting a fresh cigarette from the butt of his last one.

"What do you mean?" David Kim asked.

"Where do you think these students learned this?"

"How should I know?"

"On TV. They see your student demonstrations in South Korea."

"What do they want?"

Lee Tong shrugged, reading one of the slogans. "Who knows? Right now they're asking for 'a sincere dialogue with the government', whatever that means".

David laughed. "It sounds like the harmless rambling of student intellectuals."

"I suppose you're right," Tong said, unwilling to reveal his worst fears. It was the placards denouncing cadre children who considered themselves above the law that disturbed him most. In China one could never be sure when the wind would change. If for some reason the students' did get Deng's ear, who knew how well Tong's *hou-tai* would serve him.

*   *   *

Hong Kong

At the Hunghom Railway Station, Americans were outnumbered by large groups of Chinese travelers seated on rows of hard benches. All waited patiently for the train to Guangchou- most with cardboard suitcases, some with live chickens, a few with electronic souvenirs from Hong Kong.

"Are you our guide?" The question came from an older woman wearing a bright pink cotton warm-up suit that stretched across a generous rump and ample bosom.

"Excuse me?"

"Lili!" Dorothy Diehl pushed through the crowd. "You decided to take my advice."

"Yes, I could use an introduction to China before I start work."

"Are you joining our tour?" the fat lady asked.

"No, I'm traveling on my own. I only have a week or two."

"Well, at least ride with us to Guangchou," Dorothy insisted, turning to her companion. "Charlotte Miller, this is Dr. Quan. We met on the plane from LA. She's a doctor who's going to work in China. Lili, Charlotte is a retired history teacher from Ohio."

"Asian history, my dear." Charlotte corrected Dorothy before she turned to inspect Lili. "You're a doctor?"

"Yes."

"So young," she clucked. "You must be very bright. I should ask you about my back..."

A smiling bespectacled Chinese woman with a plastic China International Travel Service badge on her blouse, interrupted.

"Tour #5?" The woman spoke English with a lilting Shanghai accent. "China Off the Beaten Path." Charlotte raised her tour brochure.

"Yes, that's it," the guide said. "I am Miss Pu."

They traded introductions.

"So old! So fat!" Miss Pu remarked to Charlotte. "You must be very prosperous and have very good fortune."

"Actually the opposite, but it's nice to know my years and pounds are valued in your country."

Miss Pu looked around. "Is everyone present?"

With the air of a general, Charlotte led them to the far corner of the large waiting area where a coterie of blue-haired seniors sat guarding their luggage. The 'hello my name is' tags worn on their chests made the group look like elderly campers.

Lili counted ten taking the tour.

Alice and Virgil Fosbent were celebrating their fortieth wedding anniversary in two weeks. "First time we've been outside of Bangor," Alice told the group. "Except, for Virgil's two years in the Pacific during World War II. He was in ordinance. For the Flying Tigers. Right, Virgil?"

"Eh yup."

"Virgil just retired from the Post Office. Said he wanted to see China again before it was too late. Right, Virgil?"

"Eh yup."

The Witticks were another story. Shirley and Morris from Brooklyn, in their late sixties, wore matching jogging suits and 'I've climbed the Great Wall' tee shirts. "You'll love China," Shirley cooed. "This is our second trip. It's a whole lot cleaner than Cairo and the people are so friendly."

"Not like the Russians," Morris complained loudly. "You'd have thought the KGB was behind every tree. They were that scared to talk to us."

"They never smile," Shirley said, pulling out a set of snapshots. In the foreground of each stood Shirley and Morris in their jogging outfits. There they were in Borneo, in New Zealand, in New Guinea, in Dehli, always waving, usually slightly overexposed.

"See. Here we are in Moscow. The subway is just gorgeous."

"A work of art," her husband agreed.

"Here we are at the Pyramids. The ones on the camels are the Bessemers from San Pedro. Lovely couple. He was in insurance like Morris. Casualty, wasn't it, Mo?"

"Right, babe."

"Anyway, their son is a chiropractor in Los Angeles." She looked at Lili. "Maybe you know him."

"No, I'm afraid not," Lili said, inwardly groaning at the thought of even a few hours with these people.

Betty Lou Chandler was an attractive widow from Baltimore. "My husband was in aluminum siding," she confided. "A killing business. Never made it to retirement. His heart couldn't take the stress."

"Mine was in scrap metal. Just as bad." Althea Doolittle from Memphis had a drawl that stretched words like rubber. "Quadruple bypass and they couldn't save him."

Both widows carried identical Brownie instamatics.

"At least you had husbands," Abigail Brooks, the librarian from Butte, Montana whined.

"You tell 'em, honey," Charlotte encouraged, looking covetously at the single male in the group. Edmond Hawkings, an anemic looking retired CPA in polyester pants and white patent leather shoes, hailed from Tucson.

Lili noticed that Alice Fosbent grabbed her husband's hand possessively, a warning that this one was off limits.

"I've got more than enough to go around for all you ladies," Morris Wittick bragged.

His wife rolled her eyes. "He thinks if he doesn't use it he'll lose it," she chuckled.

"Are you married, Dr. Quan?" Charlotte asked.

"Not yet."

A unanimous sympathetic sigh from the single women in the group:

"A gorgeous girl like you?"

"Hard to believe no one's grabbed you up."

"Men today…"

"…they don't know a good thing…"

Lili accepted their comments affably. "I guess I've been too busy working."

Charlotte shook her head. "Take advice from an old fool. Don't put it off too long or you may end up alone."

The train whistle blew leaving Charlotte with the last word. All order suddenly collapsed as everyone began pushing and shoving to board. As the group moved from the platform to their assigned car, Miss Pu whispered to Lili.

"I don't speak Chinese," Lili stated matter-of-factly.

Ah, huaqiao, the guide thought, shaking her head. She studied Lili for a moment, not sure what to make of this overseas Chinese who didn't speak her own language. But she was curious enough to want to ask: "Such personal questions. Don't they make you feel uncomfortable?"

"In America people like to know about one another. "

"It isn't considered rude?"

Lili smiled. "Not at all. They're just being friendly."

"Americans make friends easily, don't they?"

"Yes"

The tour guide was silent for a moment. "In China, old friends are safe."

Lili suddenly thought of the fortune teller's warning: *You must be wary of new friendships* and wanted to probe further, but Miss Pu had disappeared down the aisle, checking that all her charges were properly seated before the last whistle blew.

*   *   *

Beijing, China

Chi-Wen closed his eyes as the military aircraft began its takeoff from Beijing Airport and imagined the meeting he had with the deputy minister. He had never met the man before, but knew him as he knew all Chinese government bureaucrats: squat, round-faced with narrow owl-like eyes. He knew the counterfeit smile and the soft words, each sentence a line of dialogue in a play of make believe, meant only to manipulate and deceive.

He had known and accepted it for so long. Then why question? Because suddenly a sense of dispossession engulfed him. Why now? He'd survived the Cultural Revolution. Correction. He had endured. Men like Lin had taken away his childhood with all its hopes and expectations until only *ren* was left—to endure. And he had endured, retreating into himself, hiding all his sorrows where none could see until he was able to endure the pain, the irrationality, the seeming endlessness of the nightmare. Until he felt nothing.

Until six months ago.

That was when they sent him to Dr. Cheng—to infiltrate his lab, to gain his trust, to learn his secret. He had gone willingly. After all, they had given his father's sister, his only living relative, a decent place to live, canceling out the disgrace of his rightist family. It meant a reprieve from a life of utter isolation—almost worse than her time in prison. No longer did she have to tolerate the snubs of friends and neighbors, the talk in whispers meant to be heard. *She is Fan Zhou, sister of one of the Stinking Ninth. A damn intellectual herself. Don't speak to her.*

How could he allow her to suffer again? To cooperate was Chi-Wen's duty. *Duty is what makes this country great.* He had agreed to betray a man he had never met before.

But that was then. In the past six months he had come to know Ni-Fu Cheng -perhaps in some ways better than he had ever known his own father. He had learned from him. Not just about science and literature, but about life itself. And he had begun to feel again. Just enough to wonder whether the professor was correct when he said: 'sometimes questions are important'.

Did he dare?

You have been selected for a very special assignment.

He looked at the picture of Lili Quan.

She is Dr. Cheng's granddaughter . She is now the key to his secret.

She was very beautiful.

We hope you will make her want to stay in China.

He and Dr. Cheng and Lili Quan—all pawns in the old men's game. *Everything will continue—your aunt's apartment, your job, your future as a doctor- As long as you cooperate. The degree of your assistance in this matter will be a test of your sincerity.*

Did he dare to question? Or would he simply continue to endure? He wasn't sure even as the plane headed into the clouds on its way to Guangchou.

*   *   *

The express hugged the Tolo Harbour coast, chugging its way toward the Chinese border.

It was very hot and as the train rumbled on, the ceiling fan only served to push a humid breeze through the compartment. That didn't stop the female attendant who appeared with a tray of large tea mugs, each with its individual lid. One for every passenger, along with a small bag of tea leaves was placed on a small table by the window. Out of politeness Lili did not refuse when a few minutes later, the woman returned, this time with an aluminum teakettle and poured steaming hot water into her cup of tea leaves. After all, when in

Rome. And no one knew better than Lili that *cha* , green tea with no cream or sugar, was as integral to life in China as coffee was in the States.

While some of the group continued to share their life stories, others agonized over whether watches and rings needed to be declared or how many yuan equaled a Hong Kong dollar. Every few minutes, Miss Pu would interrupt, pointing out those sights she felt should not be missed while Dottie made frantic notes in her lined copybook.

From her window seat, Lili observed the names of passing stations—Mangkok, Kowloon Tong, Shatin, Ma Lui Shiu, Taipo Kau, Taipo Market, Fanling, Sheung Shui. Miss Pu explained that these were the "new territories": twenty-seven miles of curving hills bordering on the water's edge, slapped up concrete neighborhoods with red paper- plastered doorways to ward off evil and capitalist enterprises, still owned by Hong Kong, nervously awaiting 1997 when the People's Republic would reclaim it as her own.

"We're in China!" someone yelled excitedly as the train crossed the border. A cheer from the group.

Lili didn't know what she had expected, but there was no barbed wire, no barricades. The space on the China side of the border was sunny and open. What did change was the scenery. As she peered through the window, the narrow dusty road that paralleled the train track was suddenly dense with every kind of traffic except for private cars. Buses, vans, tractors, horse and even donkey-drawn carts heaped with furniture, vegetables and live animals, vied for position with bicycles ridden by solemn faced men, women, boys and girls. Only the bike riders were able to squeeze around passing traffic coming in the opposite direction. Lili perceived all this as a slow moving army purposefully traveling in straight lines, all seemingly directed by hidden agendas.

The landscape itself was open and almost treeless. Neatly ordered green fields sprawled outside occasional villages with houses made of mud; dirt alleys ran between. The train passed flooded rice paddies where Hakka women in black "pajama" suits and wide-brimmed, silk-fringed straw hats stooped over in fixed and silent postures like cranes with their beaks down, fishing in shallow water. Two boys operated a chain-driven water pump that , according to Miss Pu, had been in continuous use in China since the first century AD.

Ever the teacher, Charlotte chimed in: "You know, the Chinese are responsible for many modern inventions—the iron plow, the umbrella, the spinning wheel, sliding calipers, movable type and the printing press, paper money, the seismograph. They even made the first kite two thousand years before it was seen in Europe. Amazing, isn't it?" she said, pointing out the window, "for a people so advanced at one time, how primitive all this seems?"

Lili had to agree. It seemed light years from Hong Kong—as though she'd suddenly gone through a time warp. In less than an hour she had traveled from one of the most international cities in the world to a place withdrawn from the rest of the world. Ancestors of this peasant women had been farming this same earth for thousands of years. And apparently in the same back-breaking way.

She stared at a man riding his water buffalo home and thought: *I am going home.* The words of Dr. Seng and Ching-yi, the fortune teller.

And her mother's: *Someday you will return to China for me.*

She was returning to China—a place she'd never been, a people she'd never known. Yet her eyes were misty. Odd. It was almost as if this scene evoked some long-forgotten memory.

*   *   *

Xi'an, China

Ni-Fu hovered somewhere between sleep and wakefulness- a kind of fugue state brought on by his prolonged fast.

His daughter, Su-Wei, was standing on the deck of the ship, crying. Just as he remembered. She was so beautiful. Like her mother.

Don't leave me, father.
Don't cry, child.
I'll never see you again.
Of course you will.
Who will take care of you?
I'll be all right. As long as I can find the secret.
Father...

"Su Wei!" he called. But no sound came. He strained to call to her, but there was no response.

And then she was gone.

From the darkness, Death called his name—whispering seductively, like a long-lost lover, arms outstretched: *Come to me, come to me.*

Yes. He was ready. He wanted to go. *I am coming.*

At that moment he saw her: Qing-Nan. Only once in the past forty years had he seen her and then, as now, she appeared to him in a dream—a shadow, larger than life. *It is not your time, husband,* she whispered. You *must not give in to death.*

But I have the power to save China.

By dying?

He closed his eyes, ashamed. Yes.

No! You can save China only by living.

I am nothing. Less than a speck in the vastness of time and space, hardly known, quickly forgotten.

You have the power to save China.

I am too old.

Death reached out to him again, but Qing-Nan pushed her aside. *Husband, I helped you once, didn't I?*

Yes, you made me understand the secret.

Qing-Nan nodded. Then *listen to me now.*

I am listening.

You must not let the secret die with you.

Who shall be its keeper? Chi-Wen?

You will know very soon.

The image was less clear now. Please tell me.

Very soon....

Slowly, the vision evaporated. Only the memory remained. Ni-Fu opened his eyes. "Chi-Wen?"

"He is not here, professor."

Ni-Fu recognized Dr. Seng standing over him. "I have brought you some soup," Seng said, putting the tray down beside his bed.

"I am not hungry."

"I think you may feel differently when you hear what I have to tell you."

*   *   *

Guangchou, China

The same chaos that had erupted in Hong Kong was replayed the moment the train stopped at Guangchou station. Arriving travelers laden with bundles, babies and birds, almost trampled one another getting out of the ramshackle train terminal as those who had come to greet family or friends clamored to get in.

"After we pass through customs," Miss Pu explained, "you will be officially in China. You may not take any ordinary Chinese money or Ren Men Bei into the country, but you can convert US traveler's checks or cash." Turning to Lili: "Overseas Chinese are processed there." She pointed to the far side of the station.

"I guess I'm on my own then."

"We'll be in Xi'an in three weeks," Abigail said, checking her itinerary. "At the Golden Flower Hotel."

"Maybe I could stop by the Xi'an Institute for an acupuncture treatment," Charlotte suggested.

Dorothy winked at Lili. "I'll fill you in on my exploits." She giggled. "And maybe you'll find a husband."

" Out of a billion people, there's bound to be one man here for you, " Althea Doolittle drawled.

"If not, I'm available," Morris Wittick quipped.

Lili laughed as she left. Poor Miss Pu had her hands full with these boisterous American seniors.

She wound her way through the tumult and sweaty confusion until she found the customs area for Overseas Chinese. She thought it odd that this group should be separated from the rest of the travelers until the suave computer executive in front of her explained that as *huaqiao*, overseas Chinese had special status. "They put on company behavior for us," he said, adding, "at least for a little while."

"How do you mean?"

"They won't spit near you in the streets and on the overnight train, they won't strip down to their underwear."

Lili laughed.

"That all changes once they relax and see that you look and sound like them."

"I don't speak Chinese. Only a few words."

The executive nodded. "In Singapore I only speak English." He pointed to the old man in front of him, explaining that he was accompanying his aged father who had escaped in 1947. "Dad's still sentimental about China," he said. "He has no family, but he's looking forward to returning to the village where he was born."

He frowned as his father opened his suitcases and boxes for the Chinese soldiers in green uniforms and red-starred caps. "That's typical of these first generation migrants. They want their countrymen to think they are rich and important, so he's brought the villagers TV sets and bicycles. He even plans to give a banquet for the whole place." Exasperated: "In Singapore, he's just a lowly store clerk."

Lili wondered if her mother would have been the same way had she had the chance to return. "How do you feel about coming to China?"

"Me?" He seemed surprised at the question. "I guess I feel a kind of pull," he said after a few moments. "Strange isn't it? My wife was born in Singapore , but she thinks I'm nuts. 'Why visit that lousy country? Why not the US? Or Europe?' And my kids feel the same way."

The executive's turn was next. He opened his suitcase, his carry-on, then his briefcase, all the while tapping his foot impatiently. He whispered to Lili: "Their way is different from ours. They work and think slower." The immigration officer finally waved him through. "You'll see," he said as he turned to leave.

"Next?"

A moment later, Lili did see. The customs official stared at her documents for several minutes, then shook his head.

"What's the problem?"

"You had a direct visa from Hong Kong to Xi'an."

"Yes, but I decided to change my plans." Lili pointed to the new stamp. "See I have permission to visit Guangchou, Shaoshan, Wuhan, Nanjing, Suzhou and Shanghai."

This prompted a conference in Cantonese with his colleague who shook his head. "Highly irregular."

Unsure, they summoned a pigtailed young woman in an Army uniform. "My name is Lieutenant Bao. Please follow me."

Lili was led to a smaller room sparingly furnished with a cushioned chair and one threadbare davenport. "I will need your travel papers and passport."

"But why?"

"My supervisor will check on you."

"Good God. Check what? I'm just a doctor. It's not like I'm some kind of spy."

Miss Bao looked at her for a long time.

"Look, can't I just talk to your supervisor? I'm sure I can clear up any problems in a few minutes."

"Not during *xiu si*."

Lili barely contained her impatience. "And what is *xiu si*.?"

The young woman explained that from noon until 2:00 PM most people had their rest period and couldn't be disturbed. *Xiu xi* , it seemed, was an immutable institution in China.

Lili checked her watch: 12:15. How would she fill her time?

"Please complete these entry forms."

"I just did."

"We would like duplicates, please."

Lili felt a rising desire to scream, then began to laugh.

"Are you unwell?" the young woman asked.

"No, no I'm fine," Lili managed, still laughing. Perhaps it made sense for China to be so entrenched in bureaucracy. After all, this was where paper and printing were invented.

"Would you like the floor fan to be turned on?"

Lili nodded. The temperature was at least ninety degrees in the closed space.

"I'll bring you hot tea in just a moment."
Great. That's just great. But this time she stifled her laughter.

*   *   *

Beijing, China

General Tong stood with his hands behind his back as he looked through the foreign minister's office window facing Tiananmen Square.

"Chi-Wen is enroute to pick up the girl and Dr. Seng has talked with the professor. That is good. But this," he said pointing to the scene outside, "is a troublesome complication."

"We've dealt with these kinds of demonstrations in the past. Why worry now?" the foreign minister asked.

The general turned to face his two comrades. "I'm worried the students may muster support outside the intellectual group. There are many elements in the party who see ideological laxity as an opportunity to make yet more changes. "

Peng Han nodded. "I share your concerns, old friend. That is why I have begun a campaign against such spiritual pollution."

"How?"

"Trust me." An enigmatic smile on his peasant face: "And read the evening paper."

*   *   *

Guangchou, China

"Dr. Quan?"

Lili was startled awake by the hand on her shoulder. Somehow the heat combined with a heavy lunch of steamed rice, chicken, prawns and soup served to her in the waiting room had produced postprandial fatigue. Before long, Lili had nodded off in the overstuffed chair. Now she rubbed her eyes, trying to shake off her drowsiness.

"Dr.Quan?" The male voice had a soft British accent.

Lili opened her eyes and focused fully on the young man who stood over her: a tall, thin Chinese, with thick black hair and intense, dark eyes that were starting to make her feel uncomfortable. "Where is Lieutenant Bao?"

"She's gone off duty."

"Off duty. What time is it?"

"Almost 6:00 PM."

"Shit!" It just escaped.

The young man looked perplexed. Perhaps his schoolroom English hadn't included expletives.

"What about my papers and my passport?"

"I've got them," he said calmly. "We can go now."

Suspicious: "What do you mean *we*?"

"Didn't Miss Bao explain?"

Annoyed: "Explain what?"

"You were detained until my plane arrived from Beijing."

Lili stood up. Face to face, he wasn't quite as tall as she'd first guessed - probably around 5'10", but he was more handsome. Dressed in a short-sleeved cotton shirt, she could appreciate his sleek muscularity and broad shoulders. "Who are *you*?"

"Forgive my manners." He extended his hand. "My name is Chi-Wen Zhou. Dr. Seng sent me to escort you to the Xi'an Institute."

Lili refused the handshake. "Escort? You mean a nursemaid," she said , letting out her pent-up frustration. "Why don't you just go back to Dr. Seng. Tell him I'm perfectly capable of making the trip on my own."

Chi-Wen frowned. "I'm sorry if I have offended you, Dr. Quan. In China, travel is often quite difficult. Especially to the cities you wish to see. Dr. Seng merely wanted you to have a pleasant experience."

"I've already planned my itinerary."

"That's no problem. Just consider me your faithful servant."

If Chi-Wen hadn't delivered that line so earnestly, Lili might have burst out laughing. Servant indeed. It sounded ludicrous coming from a Communist.

Chi-Wen had already picked up her suitcase. "Tonight you will stay at the White Swan Hotel. It is very nice. I will be at the Hongfeng."

"And why is that?"

"You are a special guest. The Hongfeng Hotel is for Chinese".

"I see you've taken care of everything."

"If arrangements had not been made ahead of time, you would never have found a room. The city is full. The annual Trade Fair is taking place."

Lili had never considered this. Still, she resented being controlled. Even more, she resented Chi-Wen's equanimity. She silently followed him as he directed her to a line leading to the exit. "What now?"

"The lady must take your ticket."

"Why?"

"Pardon?"

"Does a used ticket have any value?"

"I suppose not."

Feeling peevish, she said: "Then tell her I don't have one."

Chi-Wen didn't respond, but Lili gestured empty-handed when they'd reached the woman and smiled.

The smile was not returned. Instead, the woman looked at Lili for a moment, unsure what to do and then with a tired motion, waved them on.

Lili felt triumphant. "See, you don't have to blindly follow rules."

"You're in China now," Chi-Wen said quietly. "You should stop thinking like a Westerner".

*   *   *

Beijing, China

Just before retiring for the evening, General Tong perused his copy of the official newspaper, People's Daily. A front page commentary responded to Sunday's protests without describing them. He found what he was looking for at the conclusion of the article—a warning that "social turmoil can only do good to a small number of people with ulterior motives and do harm to China's modernization."

Peng Han's campaign against spiritual pollution had begun. Satisfied, Tong turned out his bedside lamp and fell into a deep, dreamless sleep.

*   *   *

Guangchou, China

Lili lay awake most of the night. After checking in at her hotel, Chi-Wen left, saying he would pick her up first thing in the morning. Alone, she'd showered, called down to room service for a light dinner and tried to sleep. But her mind wouldn't rest. Her excitement at finally being in China was tempered by the fact that she was no longer on her own. She couldn't help wondering how Dr. Seng had tracked her down and why? Did he have some ulterior motive or was it as Chi-Wen had said—simply a thoughtful gesture?

And what about Chi-Wen? Who was he? Except for saying that he worked at the Xi'an Institute, he'd barely spoken to her. He was certainly good looking—really quite handsome. In the train station and at the hotel she had noticed the flirting glances from more than one brazen young woman. But there was something about him she couldn't quite figure.

Lili didn't remember which writer once said the best way to convey a man's character with a minimum of strokes is to draw his eyes. Despite Chi-Wen's impersonal tone and distant manner, his liquid eyes expressed a certain vulnerability Lili found intriguing. He was so different from the overly confident Chinese boys she knew at home. Even Dylan. Chi-Wen Zhou was clearly a complicated guy.

She yawned. *Knock it off, Lili Quan. You didn't come to China to find romance. You came to work and see a little of the country of your ancestors. Besides, remember the warning of the one-eyed fortune teller: 'Be wary of new friendships. The most cunning adversary first seeks to be your closest ally.'*

Ridiculous nonsense. Still, Lili thought as she finally drifted off to sleep, it wouldn't hurt to be wary of this young man.

*   *   *

Sleep eluded Chi-Wen no less than Lili.

An hour after going to bed he was still thinking her photograph didn't begin to do her justice. The black and white photo didn't capture the luxuriance of her thick raven colored hair, the lustrous glow of her skin or her magnificent bright eyes. Standing slim and straight, she exuded a kind of natural sensuality of which she was totally oblivious . He had never seen a woman so lovely. Their proximity in the taxi had taken his breath away when he felt her thigh innocently pressed against his. She was attractive and he was attracted. In spite of himself.

But he also sensed something dangerous about her. This brash young American Chinese who refused to follow rules. A woman who thought you could force things to happen. As though you could control your own fate.

This was China. He meant it when he told her she needed to think differently here. That is, if Deputy Lin's plan was to succeed. *And* if, Lili Quan was going to survive.

THIRTEEN

Monday, April 17, 1990
Guangchou, China

Chi-Wen had described the White Swan Hotel as "very nice". It was much more. It had an opulence that easily rivaled Hong Kong's Peninsula—from the lobby with its twenty-five foot waterfall that dropped beneath an ornamental temple into pools flickering with goldfish, to expensively appointed lounges where Western and Hong Kong businessmen signed contracts with new Chinese partners, to the shopping arcade that sold mink coats to tourists who would return home proclaiming the "charm" of the mainland, to its Japanese restaurant where one could spend the monthly salary of a Chinese clerk and still emerge hungry.

This is not the real China, Lili thought as she waited for Chi-Wen and a day of sightseeing. Chairman Mao's headquarters, Dr. Sun Yat Sen's Memorial Hall, the historical Pavilion museum didn't represent China either. Lili yearned to leap beyond the clichés to see China as it really was; to walk along the streets and take the measure of the country in the faces of its people.

She checked her watch: ten to nine. If Chi-Wen was a good Chinese host, he'd arrive precisely at nine. She had time to leave a message at the desk and disappear for a little sightseeing on her own. Five minutes later she crossed the graceful stone-arched bridge linking the center of Shamian Island with the mainland.

Guangchou slopes southward in the curve of the Pearl River. Amid the din of river traffic, auto horns and bicycle bells, its diasporic citizens tread main streets flanked by rows of dilapidated four and five story buildings with ornate facades. Hanging gardens cascade from upper stories that jut over the sidewalks while every roof sprouts a made-in-Japan TV antenna. Lili realized many of these formerly imposing mansions had been divided into apartments, while others had been converted into tiny factories producing everything from cardboard boxes to playing cards.

Paralleling the main streets, suspended billboards—the new Great Wall of China—enticed consumers with the latest model washing machines, video cameras, even car stereos—most out of reach of the average Chinese. A radio cost the equivalent of three months' salary; a bike—one year's. With a new sensitivity to the nuances of marketing, the #3 Watch Factory was renamed Elegant Watches for Women; Coca Cola once 'Bite the Wax Tadpole' was now 'Tasty to Evoke Happiness'.

"You have US dollars?" a tousle-haired youth in tight jeans and a bright colored T-shirt whispered.

No sooner had she waved away the illicit money-changer when two more enterprising boys offered to sell pocket calculators at "half-price."

Lili shook her head, wondering whether this kind of hustling was the result of Guangchou's proximity to Hong Kong. She'd heard that 80% of the city's population had relatives who regularly supplied them with foreign goods. Or was it simply that, as her mother often said, the Cantonese were not only smaller in stature than their northern cousins, but in integrity as well.

Just off the boulevard, she discovered a network of narrow *hutongs,* the distinctive alleyways evocative of old China. Lili had the sense of being drawn into the past as she entered another, quieter world of small, clean white-washed houses whose occupants sat on stools in the cobbled sidewalk, talking as they cleaned chickens and washed clothes. The women smiled, but did not call out. An old man pushed his grandchild in a squeaky bamboo per-ambulator resembling a birdcage. Along the pavement an infant urinated through trousers ritually slit open between his legs to the smiling indulgence of everyone nearby. Isolated vignettes.

An hour later, she emerged onto Beijing Road, another main thoroughfare where she wandered past movie theaters featuring *Rambo* and *Superman*, into a large bookstore filled with young people browsing among endless rows of paperbacks. In the section for translated foreign literature and Chinese fiction, they stood silently, three and four deep, their selected books held close. Only the political counter with tomes of Marx, Lenin and Mao was uncrowded.

Lili checked the single stand of works in English where *War and Peace* was shelved in unlikely partnership with *Dracula* and *Huckleberry Finn* Surprisingly, she found a translation of *The Old Man and the Sea* . Deciding it would make a nice souvenir, she took it to the counter where the young woman at the abacus was engrossed in an English version of *The Scarlet Letter* translated as *A Red Letter*.

"American?" the girl asked after looking up and noting Lili's 'Born in the USA' T-shirt.

"Yes. Are you enjoying the book you're reading?"

"Very much. It's so sad."

"Hawthorne had a lot to say about the hypocrisy of American Puritan morality."

The girl's wrinkled brow betrayed confusion.

Lili smiled. "The author felt that women were not treated fairly."

"Women always suffer." She told Lili she had studied English at Zhongshan University, hoping to get a management job at one of the better hotels. "But those usually go to men."

"Are men preferred?"

"Everywhere. Even to get into college, girls must have at least five percent better marks than men."

"I thought men and women were equal here."

"Oh, we get equal pay, but men get better jobs. In China there is a long history of men being considered better. Years ago women would tell their daughter-in-laws when they bore a girl child: 'You had flowers, next time bear fruit.' And now with the one child policy, most people want boys."

Lili had heard of female babies being drowned by mothers in peasant villages, but assumed such practices were no longer tolerated.

"Do you have a boyfriend?"

Lili shook her head.

"Me either. Arranged marriages are mostly gone, but it's still hard to make friends with boys."

"Why?"

"Rumor mongering. That makes it difficult for a boy and girl to get close. Nobody trusts anybody."

Lili thought of Miss Pu. *Old friends are safe*, she'd said.

"A few years ago a public reading by your American poet Allen Ginsberg was canceled at the University because the Communist Party of Guangchou said he was spiritually polluted."

"But why?" In the United States in 1989, the message of this '60's veteran of bohemianism seemed quite benign.

"Because he wrote that it was good to have the freedom to speak openly and to love openly. If we had listened to him speak, the Party said we would have become spiritually polluted too."

"But I see boys and girls holding hands on the street," Lili protested.

"Things are improving." The cashier lowered her voice. "But old ways must change."

"Do you think they will?"

The girl looked around, though no one was near enough to hear. "There's a demonstration at the university this afternoon. See for yourself."

"I'll try."

Chi-Wen walked to the counter, breathless. "I've been looking for you everywhere. Why didn't you wait for me?" he demanded.

His anger surprised Lili, but she refused to show contrition. She never asked for an escort. "I left you a note."

"But I told you I would come at nine."

"I wanted to see the city on my own."

"Didn't you think I'd take you wherever you wanted to go?"

A few hours ago, it hadn't seemed such a big deal. She wasn't sure why Chi-Wen was so upset. But then she hardly knew this young man. "I'm sorry."

"Finish paying for your book," Chi-Wen said abruptly. " I'll wait outside."

As he walked away, the girl at the counter leaned over and whispered conspiratorially. "You have to teach your boyfriend or he'll always think he's boss."

"He's not my boyfriend."

The girl winked. "You should teach him anyway."

*   *   *

Xi'an, China

When he awakened, Ni-Fu found food waiting for him on the low table by his bed. Hot tea, a steamed bread roll, a bowl of thin rice gruel. Hardly fancy, but after a week of almost nothing, it provided the nourishment he needed. He ate slowly, savoring the break of his fast almost as much as he had savored the news last night.

Could it be true? He wanted so much to believe Dr. Seng. His heart had filled with sorrow when he learned his darling Su-Wei was dead. But then, for all these years she had been dead to him. It was the new generational link that gave him hope enough to empty his bowl. A granddaughter living in America! Lili Quan. She was coming to China. He closed his eyes and sighed. His dream. It all made sense. Now he knew to whom he must deliver the secret.

He guessed what his jailers had in mind. Greedy men, certain that his potion would guarantee them power. He knew why they were bringing Lili to China, why they had waited to tell him about her.

He held his tea, staring deeply into the green leaves that clung to the bottom of the cup. They were right about one thing, he thought. He was not ready to die now. Not just yet. He had to be very careful. Not for himself. It was Lili Quan whom he needed to protect. And if Seng's words were to be believed, he had at least a week to figure out how.

*   *   *

Guangchou, China

Outside Chi-Wen's anger seemed to have abated, though he remained cold and detached. "I've made arrangements to take the night train to Changsha."

"Thank you."

"We'll see the historical museum, but I don't think we have time for Mao's headquarters."

"That's okay. I'd prefer to see the university." She saw Chi-Wen's frown and added, "that is, if you wouldn't mind."

Chi-Wen stared in silence before responding: "As I said last night, we'll follow your itinerary."

"Good." Though somehow it seemed a dubious victory.

On the way to the university, they stopped for lunch at a small *xiaochi* or fast food house that specialized in noodles and dumplings made fresh. As they watched, the pastry chef placed a huge lump of dough on his head and with a flashing knife in each hand, rapidly shaved off thin slices. To Lili, it was an exciting if somewhat unnerving performance. Chi-Wen's expression, however, was unreadable.

When they sat down to eat, Lili tried unsuccessfully to engage Chi-Wen in small talk: "What do you do at the Institute?"

"I'm a technician."

Wondering if his reticence was simply shyness, she made another attempt. "Do you enjoy the work?"

Again he hesitated, but this time she sensed he was unsure what to say. "I suppose."

Lili thought she saw a look of pain pass over his eyes, but it was gone quickly. They finished their Cantonese flat rice noodles in silence.

The walk to reach Zhongshan University, south of the city, took close to an hour. Lili was surprised how much the campus reminded her of LA University on a warm spring afternoon: students cycling, some with Sony Walkmen in their ears, others sitting under eucalyptus trees studying, a few girls and boys holding hands, one or two even sneaking a kiss. At the middle of the campus was the *sanjiaodi* or triangle area, where a small crowd had gathered.

"What's happening?"

As they drew close, Chi-Wen asked, "Did you know about this?"

"The girl in the bookstore mentioned a demonstration. I thought it might be fun."

"Fun?" Chi-Wen glanced curiously at her for a moment. "Shit!" he whispered.

"What?" Although she was sure she'd heard correctly.

"Nothing. Come on."

At least a hundred students squatted on the lawn while several organizers perched on crates, addressing the group with hand-held megaphones.

"What are they saying?" Lili asked.

"That one is the leader." Chi-Wen indicated the first speaker whose voice shook with passion.

The student pulled out a pen and a blank piece of paper and drew four concentric circles in black ink. "Here," he was saying pointing to their center, "are a very few good leaders."

Lili watched as he placed more X's in the wide track of the second circle. "Here are thousands of senior cadres. In every ministry. Most of them are at least sixty, some well into their eighties. Old men with no education. They will neither change their ways nor hand over power. We'll have to wait forever for them to die."

The student pointed to the third circle. "Here are most of the Old-Hundred-Names; those who suffer without complaining. And here are we." He pointed to the outermost circle. "Six hundred fifty million under age thirty-five—the young of this country who must work for change."

Lili listened as Chi-Wen translated. That number was over twice the entire population of the United States.

"He urges students to think independently about politics," Chi-Wen explained.

"Anything else?" Lili asked, sensing that Chi-Wen left something out.

Reluctantly: "He chastises those who were uncritical during the Cultural Revolution. We must hate as well as love, he says. He urges students to boycott."

"You think they will?"

Chi-Wen shrugged.

"What about you?"

"I am not a student," Chi-Wen replied with surprising bitterness. "Look. This doesn't concern you. It's late. We must check out before the train leaves at 7:00 PM."

*   *   *

Seoul, Korea

Shin-yung Kim read his son's monthly production report with unmitigated pride. David indicated MSG production had risen almost twenty percent since March. He projected capturing seventy-five percent of the foreign market by year's end. That's more like it, the senior Kim thought. Perhaps David would keep his promise after all.

He filed the report and buzzed his secretary. "Miss Chang?"

"Yes, honorable Mr. Kim." Although it was already 6:30 PM, Kim's personal secretary wouldn't think of abandoning her post before the chief departed.

"I'm through. Why don't you go home?"

"Thank you. sir. *Annyong hasimnika…*"

"Good night."

Kim flipped off the intercom and rubbed his brow. His headaches were getting worse, but he refused to take the pills Dr. Ahn prescribed. They dulled his senses. He wanted to stay alert. The old physician said he should retire early, enjoy the time he had left, but Kim had no intention of leaving the helm of Kim Company. He was determined to stay alive until his sixtieth birthday—until his son could take over the choebol.

He winced as a sharp pain lancinated his temples. Ordinarily he might work another few hours, but tonight a little relaxation couldn't hurt. In fact, he hoped a bottle of *soju*, a good meal and a *kisaeng* girl might be just what the doctor ordered.

*   *   *

Guangchou, China

They left Guangchou on the night train.

A Chinese version of "Green Green Grass of Home" bounced over the speakers as Chi-Wen guided Lili past the clamor of several hundred travelers struggling to push through the Hard Sleeper turnstile. He helped her climb aboard the Soft Sleeper car filled with party cadres and People's Liberation Army officers whose leather briefcases and finely tailored "common soldier" uniforms distinguished them from ordinary workers jamming the carriages next door. Lili was surprised that class consciousness was so evident in this classless society.

There were six, four-person berths in the car- two uppers and two lowers. A dirty red carpet ran down the aisle; a thin green one covered the floor of the compartment Chi-Wen indicated was theirs for the night. Thick cotton quilting lay in rolls at the end of each bed; the mattresses were wrapped in a grayish white sheet, held in place by snaps and decorated with a row of fringe.

"You take the upper bunk," Chi-Wen offered. "It's more comfortable."

"Are we sharing this compartment?" she asked, eyeing the close quarters.

"You, me and two others," he replied as a middle-aged man with a rasping cough entered.

The man announced that he was a traveling railway supervisor. He was dressed in a heavy cotton suit despite the heat and the fact that the overhead fan was not working. Within moments he removed his clothes until he was down to his undershorts. Lili almost laughed aloud. Obviously the supervisor didn't realize she was "company". She was sure of it when he hopped onto the bunk opposite hers, hawked loudly, then nonchalantly expectorated a huge bolus of phlegm onto the carpet.

"What is she saying?" Lili asked, indicating the high-pitched voice that followed the music over the public address system.

"Comrades, we welcome you to your journey. Do not spit everywhere..."

Lili's laughter was uncontrollable.

*   *   *

Macao

All eyes were on the small white ball as it bounced from number to number.

"Red thirty-two."

"Too bad, cheri," Camille said sympathetically.

David Kim shrugged and placed another bet. Black twenty. The roulette wheel turned again.

"Red thirteen."

So what if he was down. Ng had given him carte blanche in his casino. So far the Macanese pirate had proved true to his word—having funded their new joint venture to the tune of two hundred forty million Hong Kong dollars, the equivalent of roughly thirty million US dollars. Everything was going as planned. Dr. Quan was in China. With Ng's capital, he'd increased wages in the MSG factory and boosted production. The general's son promised to deliver the secret to him well before his father's 60th birthday. Then he would head Kim Company and all his worries would be over.

"Perhaps you'd have better luck tonight with chemin de fer."

David smiled at Camille. "Sure, why not?"

*   *   *

Guangchou to Changsha

Dinner on the train was a nondescript meal during which Lili tried to draw Chi-Wen out with no more success than she'd had earlier. There was so much she would have liked to ask him, but he had erected an impenetrable barrier between them. So she contented herself by gazing through the dining car window as dusk's light melted over the landscape until a young couple indicated by gesture their desire to sit at their table.

"Of course," Lili smiled.

A waitress placed bowls of noodles in front of them which they ate with the relish of the famished. Both had mastered the efficient eating style of chopsticks: forearms on the table, leaning forward, distance from dish to mouth reduced.

The young man used his chopsticks as an arrhythmic baton, gesturing to Lili as he spoke. "Are you an American?" he asked in English.

"Yes."

He explained that he was a purchaser for a machine tool factory, adding, "Someday I will have my own business."

He wanted to learn enough English to converse with the new wave of foreigners anxious to resume commerce with China. "There are many more opportunities with Deng's new reforms."

"You speak English well."

Lili's compliment produced the Chinese obligatory self-effacing response: "No, I speak only a little." Then the young man turned to the plain looking young woman beside him and smiled. "We are on our honeymoon."

Although neither looked barely out of adolescence, Lili recalled Miss Pu's explaining to the tour that Chinese law forbade marriage before a man had reached twenty-two and a woman twenty. "How nice."

Haltingly, the young man explained how he had met his wife on one of his business trips to Guangchou. "She was leaving her government office when I saw her. I knew immediately I would ask her to register."

"Register?" Lili turned to Chi-Wen for clarification.

"In China, a man and woman desiring to contract marriage must register with the marriage registration office."

"Ah, you knew you were going to propose," Lili said to the young man. After several months of courtship by letter, they married and were now honeymooning at his home for a week.

"Where is home?"

"Wuhan," he replied, expertly snaring his slippery noodles between chopsticks. "I want my family to meet my bride. She must return to Guangchou."

"Why?"

"Because her job is there."

"Can't she change jobs?"

The young bridegroom was flustered by Lili's question. Chopsticks poised over his bowl, he gazed into the distance of the loud, smoky car.

"Dr. Quan, in China it is not permitted to move from job to job or from city to city," Chi-Wen said evenly. "You follow your prescribed path."

"You mean a married couple must live in separate cities?"

Chi-Wen nodded.

"When do you see each other?"

"Once a year husbands and wives are allowed 'marital leave'."

"Once a year?"

"When we retire we can make a home together."

"That's ludicrous," Lili said. "How do you stand it?"

"Chinese adapt," Chi-Wen said simply.

"And you?" the new bridegroom asked, hoping to change the subject.

"I beg your pardon?"

"Where are you going?"

"I'm on my way to Changsha to see Shaoshan where Mao Zedong was born."

"Everyone used to visit that village," he replied. "Today no one does."

Lili would have asked why not, but she knew she'd already been too forward. Besides, the young man indicated that they ought to be getting back and his wife obliged with a giggle. After all, they only had a week together before they would begin a long separation.

As the bride turned to leave, she spoke to Chi-Wen in Chinese. His response was a firm head shake, but Lili noted the violet blush racing from neck to hairline. After they'd gone, Lili asked what was said.

"She asked if…uh…if we were engaged," he stammered.

"Oh. I see." The second person that day who wanted to make them a couple.

Ten minutes later, they returned to their compartment to find a fourth passenger sound asleep, snoring loudly in his bunk. From the uniform hung neatly on the hook by the door, Lili guessed he was a high ranking officer in the People's Liberation Army. The railway supervisor was also sleeping, his cough intermittently punctuating heavy breathing. Apparently he had brought his own food, evidenced by the peanut shells and cake crumbs covering the floor. The car stank from cigarette smoke.

While Chi-Wen began a modest strip tease, Lili hopped up onto her berth, switched on the overhead gooseneck lamp and brushed her hair. Her eyes were closed, but when she opened them she caught Chi-Wen's stare. For an instant, she shuddered at the power of his glance. Then he broke the spell, quickly turning off his light and disappearing into the bed below.

Odd fellow, Lili thought as she picked up the copy of *The Old Man and the Sea* .

A whisper from the darkness: "Dr. Quan?"

"Yes?"

"I suggest you not stay up too late."

"Why is that?"

"The public address goes off at 5:00 AM."

"Thank you." An afterthought: "May I make a suggestion?"

"Of course."

"If we are going to be traveling companions, you might as well call me Lili."

*   *   *

Macao

Paulo Ng was watching the casino floor action on a video monitor when the cashier knocked.

"Mr. Kim now owes the house thirty thousand dollars. Shall I continue to extend him credit?"

Ng opened his drawer and pulled out the red ink and stamp that constituted Kim's legal signature. He had extracted the *tojang* from Kim as a form of collateral. Now he stared at it, mulling over his options.

The cashier was still waiting. "Sir?"

"Know your enemy and know yourself; then in a thousand battles you can never be defeated. "

"I beg your pardon?"

"An ancient Chinese saying," Ng told the cashier. "Give him anything he wants," he said, sucking on a fresh cigarillo. "For now."

Ng waved the cashier out in time to catch David losing another hand of chemin de fer. He shook his head. The young man was bright, but he didn't know how to gamble. And that could be a problem—for David *and* for Ng.

The Macanese pirate blew a fresh smoke ring across the room, never taking his eye off the action below, thinking how he loathed this smooth, pampered young man. Well, he had to control his emotions—at least for now. He still needed David. Once he had the elixir, that situation would change. If David proved to be more of a liability than an asset, he would prove to be expendable. In that case, Ng thought, it would be wise to have a contingency plan.

*   *   *

Guangchou to Changsha

Lili.

Her name, like her laughter, was musical. Long after Lili had turned off her light and fallen asleep, Chi-Wen lay in the blackness of the compartment, tossing and turning, filled with conflicting emotions. Telling himself he had to keep his distance—for her sake as well as his own.

Still, when he finally slept, Chi-Wen dreamed of a woman with hair that flowed like a dark rain over her shoulders.

FOURTEEN

Tuesday, April 18th
near Changsha, China

The exhortation to awaken came at 5:00 AM through the ceiling loudspeaker with a blast of martial music followed by glass-splitting local opera in falsetto, with plenty of gongs and static. Lili groaned and groped for a switch to turn the system down before she realized where she was. China is on Beijing time, so dawn had not yet crept into the eastern sky. When she opened her eyes, she saw the compartment bathed in the incandescent glow of three gooseneck lamps. The supervisor and the army officer were gone. Everyone had stripped their pillowcases and bedding, folded up blankets and sheets to help the railway personnel prepare the train for its next ride.

Chi-Wen, dressed in slacks, was in the midst of *tai-chi chuan*. Smoothly his arms rose, his fingers extended as he began to weave slow circles before his face. His eyes closed, the slow, graceful movements, conscious of the ripple of his muscular shoulders. He hardly seemed to be breathing. So quiet. Turning, twisting, gently dipping.

Suddenly aware of the thumping of her heart, she admired his fluid grace, hoping to catch his eye again, to share another secret glance.

When his ritual was complete, Lili said: "That was beautiful."

Chi-Wen didn't turn , but the quaver in his voice betrayed embarrassment. "You'd better wash up. We're on the second shift for breakfast."

The washroom was separate from the toilets. It contained a row of basins and mirrors where men and women stood side by side as they shaved, brushed their teeth and combed their hair. No wonder there was no word for "privacy" in the Chinese language, Lili thought as she elbowed a position for herself.

From somewhere outside, a piercing scream transcended the cacophonous chorus of garglers.

Suddenly, Chi-Wen appeared. "Come quickly, please."

Lili followed him. "What's going on?"

"There's a sick child in the dining car. Hurry!"

Lili pushed through the crowd, shouting that she was doctor.

"*Yi shen...*" Chi-Wen translated and a path quickly opened.

A little boy, no more than three or four, lay on the floor, his flat Cantonese face growing cyanotic, his black eyes round with fear. Lili knelt beside him, feeling for a pulse. Thready, but present. With her ear close to the child's mouth, she could hear the straining sound of air forced against a barrier. The boy was choking, dangerously close to losing consciousness.

Lili forced his mouth open, swept a finger deep inside, hoping to dislodge a piece of food blocking the upper airway. There was nothing.

"Get me a chair!"

Chi-Wen shouted in Cantonese. A chair immediately appeared.

Lili grabbed the child, sat on the chair and lay the choking boy's face across her knee. She delivered several gentle thumps with the heel of her hand between the child's shoulder blades.

Nothing.

"*Aii-ya, aii-ya* !" The agonized cries of the mother, watching helplessly nearby.

Several more thumps and a tiny peanut popped from deep in the child's throat. It neatly arced across the dining car, landing on the floor several feet away. The little boy squirmed from Lili's grasp and was grabbed by his mother.

A crop of smiles blossomed into fresh tears.

"*Xie, xie,*" the mother sobbed her thanks.

An older man dressed in a Western suit came over and bowed formally. Chi-Wen translated: "You have saved my grandson's life."

"I'm happy I could help."

The man waved away her modesty, shook her hand, then exchanged a few words with Chi-Wen.

"What did he say?" Lili asked.

"You see that poster?" Chi-Wen asked, pointing to a picture on the wall of a woman with an unusually large bosom holding a young boy.

"Yes."

"The inscription reads 'she is a good comrade. She has only one child."

Lili glanced over at the grandfather smiling at his grandson, his look filled with love.

"That boy is the only child in his family."

Lili , remembering what the girl in the bookstore had said, understood the enormous value placed on this one male child's life.

"That was wonderful, Dr. Quan, I mean Lili." Chi-Wen said.

And then, as if Lili's saving the young boy had suddenly freed his unwillingness to talk, he told her how he, too, wanted to be a doctor, how he had passed the entrance exams and hoped to enter school.

It was only when Lili asked why he hadn't gone to medical school earlier that she caught his trace of uneasiness. "I...uh...circumstances prevented it."

"You mean the Cultural Revolution?"

Chi-Wen's jaw visibly tightened. He took a deep breath, started to speak, then changed his mind.

"At least you'll go soon," she said encouragingly.

The train whistle, indicating their arrival at Changsha station, saved him the necessity of a reply.

Five minutes later, they descended from the carriage. "We'll need to change for Shaoshan here," he said.

"What tune is the clock tower playing?" Lili asked.

Chi-Wen studied her speculatively. "You don't know?"

"No."

"It's called 'The East is Red'."

Though curious, the melancholy in Chi-Wen's voice put an abrupt end to Lili's questions.

*   *   *

Newport Beach, California

The wealthy industrialist evinced little surprise at the second overseas call he received. After listening to the proposition, DeForest agreed a meeting was in order. And as soon as possible.

*   *   *

Shaoshan, China

One day in 1966, over one hundred twenty thousand Chinese wearing red armbands and Mao buttons, completed a four day pilgrimage from Changsha to Shaoshan, waving flags and singing ditties set to music from the Little Red Book. More than twenty years later, Lili and Chi-Wen arrived in Shaoshan on an empty train. The young bridegroom on the train was right, Lili thought as they walked from the barren station through the large parking lots devoid of buses, past the huge statue of the "Great Helmsman" in the park providing shade for a lone billiard player to the almost-empty Shaoshan Guest House. No one *does* visit this village any more. So vacant and quiet, it reminded her of a stage with a struck set.

The next day and a half as they explored the various Maoist shrines confirmed her initial impression: the duck pond where he swam, the field which he plowed, the old schoolhouse where he studied, the house in the glade where he was born were all but abandoned. In seventeen of the Mao Museum's eighteen rooms, the leader's early life was displayed in great detail through pictures and captions: his school days, his job, his travels, the death of his brother, the Long March, the war, his first marriage. However, his entire chairmanship from 1949 through his death in 1976 was telescoped in the last room. Not only was there no mention of his other two marriages, but Jiang Qing of the Gang of Four was airbrushed out of the photographs.

In the museum shop Lili asked the clerk for a Mao Badge.

"We have none."

"How about *The Little Red Book*?"

"All sold."

"Will you be getting any more?"

"Those are out of fashion," she explained through Chi-Wen. "They're history."

"Well, ask her what she has?"

The clerk pointed to counters filled with razor blades, cigarettes and men's underwear.

"No souvenirs?"

The woman opened a box and pulled out several key chains with color photos of Hong Kong movie stars.

"Never mind," Lili said on her way out the door. An hour later she and Chi-Wen sat in the almost empty hotel dining room. "Amazing," she declared as she tasted her bean curd and cabbage.

"It's chili peppers that give Hunan food bite."

"Yes, it *is* spicy, but I was thinking about the last few days here—the sense that everyone wants to forget Mao Zedong existed."

"Not forget," Chi-Wen spoke carefully. "Just placed in the proper historical context."

"And what is that?"

"A man who did great things for our country, but who also made...mistakes."

"Like the Great Leap Forward?" she asked, referring to the economic fiasco of 1958 that led to millions of Chinese starving to death.

"Yes."

"And the Cultural Revolution?"

Wary now: "That too."

"Tell me what it was like."

"Is this part of your sightseeing?" he asked accusingly.

"No," Lili replied, meeting his troubled gaze. "I'll admit I *am* curious. But I want to know what is was like for you."

"Please."

Chi-Wen closed his eyes for a moment. This strange, beautiful young woman isn't really here. I'm just dreaming, he thought. But when he opened them again, Lili was still there, her wonderful, dark, honest eyes searching his face, proving that he had not conjured her up out of his desperate need for companionship, understanding, and perhaps, even love.

"Please, Chi-Wen."

He began haltingly, trying to decide where to cut into the story of his life.

"I was nine in 1966, when everything started. Actually eight, by Western standard," he corrected.

Lili nodded. She was aware Chinese added a year to age, the so-called womb-time period.

"Four years later, I was sent off to a work camp in central Mongolia. It didn't have a name. Just a number. '345'. They called us 'Soldier Farmers'. Volunteers for our country."

He spoke without pauses, as if once started, he was unable to control the avalanche of feelings stirred by old memories. "We were told to learn from the peasantry. But we didn't live with the peasants and we rarely worked with them. They resented our eating their meager rations of food, so we were isolated in tiny mud huts, ten to fifteen in one room.

The cold. That was the most difficult part. I can still remember the raw nights. No heat or electricity—only one oil lamp for the group. Every morning at five, our leader would blow a whistle, wake us to exercise before breakfast. First, though, we had to sing a verse of 'The East is Red'."

Caught up now in memories, Chi-Wen began to sing the Maoist revolution song in a soft voice: "The east is red from the rising sun, In China appears Mao Zedong, He is our guide, He leads us onward to build a new China...."

As he translated, Lili suddenly understood Chi-Wen's reaction the day before. The song was clearly evocative of years of suffering.

When he finished, he continued. "Even though the food was tasteless, I ate—mostly what we called black wheat—corn and flour made from sweet potato. We worked hard and had unbelievable appetites. I even gained weight " He laughed at the thought since now his wiry body was almost too lean.

"We spent most days cultivating vegetables or potatoes or wheat. Sometimes there were no crops to tend and they made us repair roads. In the wintertime when the fields were frozen, we were sent to Ulan Cu Hai, a large lake in Inner Mongolia. When the lake froze, we went out onto the ice to cut down the tall reeds which had grown around the shore. The reeds were used to make paper and thatch for roofs as well as mats we slept on in summer to keep cool. The peasants were expert weavers.

Nothing kept us from our daily routine—not the cold, not the wild dust storms that came out of nowhere and lasted for days." He looked at her sympathetic expression and shook his head. "No need for pity. It was no worse for me than for thousands of others."

"But to be separated from families and denied an opportunity to attend college. You'd have a right to complain," Lili said.

"Now, yes," he acknowledged. "But in those days, being stalwart was considered very revolutionary."

"What did you expect when you were told you were going away?" Lili asked.

"People's Liberation Army soldiers came to our middle school and told us conditions in Mongolia were wonderful. They said we could ride horses every day and go walking in the grasslands; that it was a nice place to live and we would be allowed to come back home and visit our families every year. But, of course, it wasn't so. Once we were settled, they told us that unless we married in Mongolia, we could only return home once every three years."

"You must have been homesick."

His smile was sad. "When I first arrived, I was full of imagination and a sense of possibility. I believed we had an obligation to reshape our world view through hard physical labor—like Chairman Mao had done as a boy. I thought such work would help harden our spirit and resolve. I studied Chairman Mao's teachings diligently and I worked hard. But as time passed, I became less sure this was the only way to help China. I missed school. The girls were peasants who held contempt for intellectuals. And I often thought about my mother at home alone."

Lili studied him, wondering whether to ask why she was alone when Chi-Wen continued.

"My father had a hard time during the Cultural Revolution. Mao decreed nine categories of enemy: landlords, rich peasants, counterrevolutionaries, bad elements, rightists, traitors, foreign agents,

capitalist -roaders and the Stinking Ninth—the intellectuals. Father was an intellectual, singled out because he was an English professor at Fudan University."

"What did he do?"

Chi-Wen looked at Lili and shook his head. "No American can ever understand. He didn't *do* anything. My father was a wise and gentle man. Unfortunately, he was also very literate. They said he hurt China. They made him wear a dunce hat and walk through the streets reciting 'I am a cow's demon' all day."

"An evil spirit?"

"From Chinese mythology. Mao first used this expression to describe the intellectuals during the Anti-Rightist Campaign of 1957. He said they were evil spirits in human form when they pretended to support the Communist Party. When they criticized the Party's policy, they reverted to their original shapes. During the Cultural Revolution, it was applied to anyone considered politically deceitful."

For a few moments Chi-Wen sat silently. His eyes seemed haunted by memories still not remote enough in time to have lost their dark shadows. "I even participated in criticizing my own father," he said finally.

"You were young."

Chi-Wen waved away her attempt at consolation. "They subjected him to hours of 'struggle sessions', demanding he admit things he'd never done. When he wouldn't, they beat him."

Lili thought she saw a tear appear at the corner of his eye.

"Mother didn't know what to do. She loved the Party and never believed they would hand down the wrong verdict. It was an agonizing dilemma. Her traditional Confucian sense of family obligation told her to defend her husband, while her political allegiance required that she damn him. In the end, Party loyalty won out and she declared him an enemy of the state and demanded a divorce.

Father couldn't take the shame. One day my mother found him hanging from a cypress tree." Chi-Wen's voice cracked. "She blamed herself and stopped eating. A few months later she was dead too." The tear found its way down his smooth cheek. "I felt so...bitter," he faltered. "...at my parents, at myself, at Chairman Mao..."

Without thinking, Lili reached out and took Chi-Wen's hand in hers. Silently she cried for him, for all that he had lost—his childhood, his education, his family, his happiness.

"....Because I could not succeed in banishing these feelings from my heart, I felt tremendous conflict. How to make harmonious the need to serve one's country with the need to serve oneself. I still don't know the answer." For a long time, they sat facing one another, holding hands. Two people from opposite cultures. And yet, Lili thought there was something in Chi-Wen that made her feel as if she were looking at herself. At what her life might have been if she'd been born here.

*   *   *

Later that evening as they rode the train to Wuhan, Chi-Wen's thoughts were in turmoil. He had made his peace with life in China and now Lili was turning everything upside down. He had never before encountered anyone who had the temerity to be so direct, to confront feelings and ideas head on as if they were never meant to be hidden or unspoken. Yet he found her directness oddly intriguing. How different she was from the shy, tongue-tied girls he knew. He couldn't help feeling something unique had brushed against the orderly fabric of his life and he would never be the same again.

Everything was slipping, events rearranging themselves without his conscious will. Suddenly, after so many betrayals that he had learned to trust no one; after so many years of *ren*, of enduring without feeling, he was telling this stranger about his past, his fears, even his hopes.

As the train pulled into the station, he told himself again, as if the thought alone could make it so, that he was not falling in love with Lili Quan. Then she smiled and he knew he was only fooling himself. It was already beyond his control.

*   *   *

Wuhan, China

When Chi-Wen made his required telephone call to the foreign minister at 10:00 PM that night, he dutifully reported the events of the past three days including the university demonstration in Guangchou, leaving out only the hand-holding at lunch. Whatever guilt he felt at this omission was pointless, however, since Lin had received a more complete account of all his activities an hour earlier.

*   *   *

Thursday, April 20th
Xi'an, China

"Ah, Dr. Cheng, so good to see you up and about."

"Dr. Seng." Ni-Fu's smile was genuine. He was glad to be back at work. Especially happy to be with his patients. Eagerly anticipating the arrival of his granddaughter.

"Do you mind if I observe your rounds? No matter how many times I watch your examinations, I am always impressed by how much you learn from a mere touch of your hands."

Ni-Fu nodded, though he suspected that a man who carried the title of vice-chairman of the Revolutionary Committee as well as Medical Director was more likely interested in chaperoning than in expanding his medical horizons. Trained in England in the 1930's, Cheng had become expert at bedside diagnosis, a skill almost entirely supplanted by Western medicine's emphasis on technology. Dr. Seng, who studied in the Soviet Union, was less inclined to place hands on the patient.

He walked to the next to the last bed in the small ward. As in most hospitals in China, each patient was expected to provide his own sheet, pillow and cotton quilt. It was a practice that, to Cheng, increased the already dangerously high rate of infection. But like so many new ideas felt intuitively by oldtimers to be counter-revolutionary, his argument fell on deaf ears.

The wheezing of the elderly man lying prone on the sheet was unrelieved by the array of hot glass cups arrayed across his back. Cupping—a favorite therapy Seng learned in Russia. Though relatively useless, it did give relief. After a careful listen through his stethoscope, Ni-Fu agreed that symptomatic relief for this patient's severe lung disease was all they had to offer. "Are you a textile worker, Mr. Yi?"

"Yes," he wheezed. "Twenty-five years I worked in Number 5."

And breathed in cotton dust, Cheng surmised. "Byssinosis," he said naming the disease that would likely kill Mr. Yi, within a few years if not months.

"I agree," Dr. Seng declared. "But I'm anxious to hear your diagnosis for this last case. The rest of the staff is stumped."

Rising to the challenge, Cheng followed him to the last bed occupied by a 60 year old woman who had propped herself high up on pillows. "Do you feel better that way?" He took hold of her hand as they spoke.

Mrs. Sun nodded. "It burns when I lie down."

"How long have your fingers been swollen?"

"My mother also had 'wind in the bone'," she replied, referring to the Chinese explanation for rheumatism.

Except that this wasn't the ordinary osteoarthritis typical of aging. Cheng noted the leathery appearance of Mrs. Sun's skin and her generalized muscle wasting. "Do your hands and toes turn blue when it's cold?"

Although the woman laughed, her face registered no expression. "I'm always cold. My husband says it's because I'm from the South."

When he'd finished listening to her heart and lungs, Cheng turned to Dr. Seng. "We ought to talk outside."

"I take it you've made a diagnosis?" Seng asked.

"Yes, although I need to check my texts from England. It's been more than forty years since I've seen a case of diffuse scleroderma."

Seng had never heard of the disease.

"That's because it's so rare in Asia. But I saw many cases in my training. Mrs. Sun's response to cold, the tightness of her skin, the loss of expression in her face, the muscle atrophy, the arthritis, even her gastrointestinal symptoms could be attributed to scleroderma."

"What causes it?"

"Overproduction of collagen, though that's never been proven." So long cut off from his colleagues beyond China, he added, "At least not to my knowledge."

"And the treatment?"

"It's too late for steroids. Besides they would aggravate her esophagitis. I'm afraid we can only offer her symptomatic relief. If she's lucky, she'll have a remission and live another five or ten years. Her heart and lungs don't appear to be involved yet."

"Impressive," Dr. Seng acknowledged. "It's always enlightening to be at the bedside with you."

Not wanting to spend another moment with this fawning bureaucrat, Cheng turned to go. "That's where I should be right now."

"Of course. But I hope you will spend tomorrow in your lab. Everyone is anxious to see your research proceed."

Everyone, Cheng thought bitterly. Seng really meant Lin and his two treacherous comrades. Damn. Time was running out. He only had a few days to set a plan in motion.

*   *   *

Wuhan to Suzhou

At Wuhan, Lili and Chi-Wen left the train and boarded The Golden Line No. 10, a rusting five-decked steamer that would carry them toward Shanghai. Only April and already the heat and humidity justified the area's reputation as a "furnace" of the Yangtze. The boat was crammed with over twelve hundred Chinese citizens, most traveling fourth class. The galleries, lined with twenty-four bunks, lacked even the minimal comforts offered by Lili's second class two-berth accommodations. First class had apparently been eliminated entirely as a concession to equality.

Still, despite the squat toilets and lack of hot water, it was a rare opportunity to mingle with a cross section of the population. As she chatted with passengers driven on deck by the heat, Lili found a fascination with America:

"What does the name Wham! mean?" a teenager asked referring to the rock group that had recently toured China.

"We love Coca-Cola...."

"...and Kentucky Fried Chicken..."

"...and *Hunter*!"

Lili was simultaneously amused and offended by the notion that such mundane fare represented authentic American cultural exports to these Chinese.

Many were simply anxious to practice English learned from weekly television broadcasts, awkwardly testing a language that demanded the use of pronouns, active and passive voice and plurals: "Wife is happy to meet. He is likes you."

Lili's attempt at Mandarin was no less bungled. Since Chinese is a tonal language with four separate pitches, it matters whether one says *ma* with a flat, upward, swooping or diving inflection. In one tone it could mean "mother", in another, "numb", in a third, "horse" and yet another, "scold". The passengers laughed good-naturedly when Lili's misplaced tones and awkward emphases brought sugar and tobacco at dinner in lieu of soup and salt. Suddenly she wished she hadn't dropped Chinese as a child. Thank goodness Chi-Wen was there to smooth over her gaffes.

"Excuse me." A middle-aged man wearing wire-rimmed eye glasses timidly dropped down on the bench beside Lili. "I couldn't help overhearing you. I very much like Americans." He leaned over, keeping his voice low. "When I was growing up during the Korean War, I was taught to hate Americans."

"What changed your mind?"

"Your Mr. Nixon."

"How's that?"

The man explained that he worked as a bookkeeper in a Nanjing hotel. Once Nixon re-opened China to Western tourists, he met many Americans and thought they were very nice. "Some even invited me to visit their homes."

"Will you travel to the United States?" Lili asked.

"It is not so easy to get a visa," he replied. "Tell me, is it true that you can travel from city to city without letters of permission from your government?"

"Yes."

"And do you have *jumin weiyuanhui* ?"

Lili looked to Chi-Wen.

"Neighborhood committees," he translated.

"You know, the man said, "to make sure you only have one child; to watch your comings and goings."

"No," Lili said. "We don't."

"What about work. Can you switch jobs if you are not happy?"

"Absolutely."

The man shook his head in wonder. "Three times makes a tiger."

"I beg your pardon?"

"It's a Chinese expression," Chi-Wen explained. "If things are repeated enough times, people assume they are true."

"Lies," the man said, lowering his voice and glancing around. "So much of what we are told are lies."

Later Lili talked with a frail looking older woman who spent five years in a tiny unlit cell during the Cultural Revolution as punishment for her "rightist" poetry. "I hate the '*shangshen wenxue*' of our younger authors," she confided.

"'Wound literature'," Chi-Wen translated. "A special category of writing about the Cultural Revolution."

The woman nodded. "These young writers dwell on the flaws of communism and not on its great success".

"But you were a victim of the system," Lili pressed. "Don't you feel bitter?"

"Every revolutionary movement may go a bit beyond its goal," she replied with a gentle smile. "But you don't have to look for bones inside an egg."

Surprising for one who had suffered so much, Lili thought, but these sentiments were echoed by a nearby peasant with a yellow-toothed smile.

"Life is better since Liberation," the man said. "When I was young, village people carried images from the temple to the fields, asking them to kill the insects or bring the rain or keep the river from flooding the crops. From Mao we learned self-reliance. We take pumps and electricity into the fields instead of images. Before, my family starved. Now there is enough for everyone," he remarked as he carelessly tossed the husks of the melon-seeds he was eating into the river.

These two old people measured their present circumstances by what they knew before, Lili suddenly realized—certainly not by an American experience so alien to them

For three days they sailed slowly east, past sampans, dugouts and junks, glimpsing the spectacle of life along the banks of China's largest river. From Wuhan where the 1911 revolution began, ending the last imperial dynasty to Nanjing where Sun Yat-Sen established the first Republican government Lili was struck by China's contrasts: between town and city, imperial past and socialist present, ancient and modern, young and old.

She was also struck by the silences. It happened often, Lili noticed. An almost palpable pall would descend over conversations, bringing them to an abrupt end and people had a strange habit of suddenly looking up or away or lowering their voices. Not like Americans who always plunged ahead, however loudly, however awkward. But of course, in America people weren't imprisoned for writing politically incorrect poetry or sent to the countryside for having the wrong parents.

So far, this country didn't fit any neat romantic or political stereotype. Neither did its people. Not the T-shirted teenagers hawking on the streets, the feminist in the bookstore, the ambitious young honeymooners, the idealistic university students, the cynical hotel bookkeeper, the contented retirees and least of all Chi-Wen Zhou.

Lili understood that his aloofness had not been unfriendliness. It was a wall he needed to erect, to shield himself from the pain of the past. She sensed there were many more secrets hidden away deep within him, in places he let no one see. She wanted to penetrate the mystery of his past, yet she had to respect his reluctance to relive melancholy memories. After all, she had her own.

As they sat on the deck of the steamer drinking warm Tsingtao beer, they talked. Not as she had with Dylan—like comfortable friends—but more tentatively, both still wary of revealing too much. She told him about San Francisco, that she loved American literature and riding motorcycles, that her mother had died of cancer, that she planned to specialize in geriatrics. She didn't discuss her problems with Trenton. She left Dylan out. Chi-Wen was interested, yet sensitive and didn't pry.

He told her about growing up Shanghai, that he loved literature, especially Shakespeare, that he hoped one day to be a great doctor, that his father's sister was his only surviving relative. He didn't reveal the circumstances of her finding an apartment in the city so many years after living in the countryside and he never mentioned Ni-Fu Cheng. When Lili gently sought more details, he just as gently changed the subject.

So that made them both even: each had denied some closeness to the other.

"What's going on?" Lili asked, pointing to several teens huddled in a corner.

"Traditional cricket fighting."

"Can we see?"

Chi-Wen led her to the small crowd that had gathered to watch the gladiator insects spill out of enamel tea mugs into a sand-filled dish. Prodded by owners wielding long blades of grass, the tiny insects locked forelegs in a miniature wrestling match.

The crowd urging their favorites: "*Shan* ! Come on!"

The owners signaled for silence.

Lili was amazed at the tension produced by the miniature battle.

Finally one exhausted cricket scampered out of the arena.

"Next time, give him chili juice," a sage old-timer advised. "It's worked for over a thousand years."

The owner of the defeated warrior nodded, reluctantly handing over a few coins to the champion's manager.

After the crowd dispersed, Lili remained to talk to the boys, surprised they were among a growing group of unemployed youth.

"What about the 'iron rice bowl'?" she queried, referring to guaranteed lifetime work for everyone.

"We are 'waiting' for a job," one of them explained with a smirk, "but I've been waiting for two years now. They only want university graduates, not someone who didn't get through senior middle."

"Unknot and unwind red tape by knowing the right people. That is the secret of life in China today," his friend sneered. "A good education is not nearly as useful as an influential father. Unfortunately, I don't have either."

"The government says get a trading license and sell peanuts or watermelon on the street," another complained. "But we make more money fighting crickets." He lowered his voice to a whisper: "Even though gambling is technically illegal."

Lili wondered if these boys would agree with the old peasant or the woman writer that life was better in China. They represented the younger generation—two-thirds of the nation's population—who, like Chi-Wen, was born after the founding of the People's Republic and who could not compare the new society with the old. But she didn't share her questions with Chi-Wen, sensing that he was uncomfortable discussing politics and unwilling to disturb their still tenuous relationship.

"Would do me a favor?" she asked later that evening as they left the steamer at Nanjing and boarded the train for Suzhou.

"Of course."

"Could you teach me *tai-chi*?"

"It is not something one learns overnight. It is a philosophy, a way of life. I'm a beginner, yet I've practiced for years."

"I'll be in China for a while and

"All right, but I'll ask a favor in return."

"Name it."

"Teach me to ride a motorcycle."

"A fair cultural exchange," Lili laughed, her bright eyes dancing. "Tomorrow, we'll find a rental shop in town."

*   *   *

Beijing, China
Friday, April 21st

In a society where indoor plumbing is a luxury few (even among the highest Party members) enjoy, the public bath is still very much an integral part of Chinese life. For old timers like Deputy Minister Lin and General Pei-Jun Tong, the weekly soaking in three steamy tubs, each hotter than the last, was a ritual to be savored.

It was early evening and most of the usual bath chamber crowd had gone home for supper. Only a few men squatted along the tile pool-side, soaping their armpits or scraping at their feet with hunks of black pumice-stone. In the far corner, three masseurs in galoshes scoured men's chests and buttocks with wooden blocks wrapped in towels. Dark rivulets of dirt ran onto the warm tiles.

Steam swirled around the general as he murmured conspiratorially. "I'm worried. The student movement is getting out of control. Today at noon, at least one hundred thousand marched in Tiananmen Square. Three or four thousand sat on the steps of the Great Hall of the People protesting the beating of students yesterday at Xinhuamen Gate."

The Foreign Minister raised his raspberry-pink torso from the hot water and summoned an attendant to bring a metal tray with a large scissors attached. "You worry too much, my friend," he observed, carefully slicing dead skin from the sole of his feet. "Peng Han has everything under control."

Tong submerged deeper into the tub until only his head remained above water. "Are you aware that students are boycotting classes not only here in Beijing, but in many of the larger cities—Shanghai, Nanjing, Wuhan, Guangchou, Xi'an?"

"I am."

"And you are not concerned?"

Lin carelessly hawked a mouthful of tobacco-colored phlegm into a nearby tin spittoon. "Look, the students' focus is Hu Yaobang. After his funeral tomorrow, everything will calm down."

"What about the girl?"

"She arrives in Suzhou tonight. When Chi-Wen Zhou calls, I'll have him remain until Sunday to avoid the student demonstrations. They'll take the train to Shanghai and Tuesday, they'll fly to Xi'an."

Exhausted by the hot water, Tong joined his friend on the cool tiles. "What about Deng? What does he know about our operation?"

"Nothing," the Foreign Minister replied. "He spends his time inside the walled compound. Any information he gets is directly from the mayor of Beijing who gets his from Peng Han." And then, inadvertently making a pun, Lin added: "So, my old friend, It's strictly our party."

If the general appreciated the humor, he didn't acknowledge. He was lying naked on the tile, legs splayed, snoring loudly, sound asleep.

FIFTEEN

Saturday April 22nd

Suzhou, China

The man in the bicycle shop shook his head. "I don't rent. Only sell. No motorcycles. Only Flying Pigeon, Phoenix, Sea Lion or Forever," he told Chi-Wen, referring to various brands of bicycles.

"What about that one?" Lili pointed to a rusted bright orange Yamaha leaning against the back of the shop.

Chi-Wen asked about the cycle while Lili wandered over to get a better look.

"He says it was left by his wife's younger brother when it stopped working and that was two years ago."

"But it only needs the chain adjusted ," Lili announced. "It's even got a full tank of gas." She had already removed the cotter pin and was trying to loosen the axle nut. "Ask him for a crescent wrench."

"You think you can fix it?"

"Piece of cake."

"Piece of what?"

Lili laughed. "I'm sorry. That's an American expression. It means it will be very easy."

A moment later, Chi-Wen returned with an ordinary wrench.

"That's it?"

"I'm afraid that's all he's got."

Lili thought a minute. "All right, let me try."

On the strength of her assurance, Chi-Wen negotiated with the man, use of the wrench along with a day's rental for three yuan, the equivalent of less than one US dollar. No helmets, but the man threw in two pair of sunglasses, the latest from Hong Kong.

Chi-Wen watched as she bent over the bike: feathery brows arched, full lips pursed; lovely fingers busy with the chain; thin cotton shorts accentuating slender hips and long, shapely legs. The early morning light fell softly on her raven hair, caressing her shoulders. He could see the curve of her breasts tight against her T-shirt, round as steamed buns. How he ached to touch her.

Lin's voice intruded on his musing: *She is Dr. Cheng's granddaughter . She is now the key to his secret....We hope you will make her want to stay in China.... Everything will continue—your aunt's apartment, your job, your future as a doctor- As long as you cooperate."*

Lili looked up at him, smiling. "There! All set. The chain hadn't been oiled."

Chi-Wen closed his eyes, took a deep breath and felt the sun's warmth on his face. Such a beautiful spring day. An omen, he thought. Truly a good day to be alive. Yes! On such a day, anything was possible.

"Chi-Wen?"

He opened his eyes and stared at Lili. She had awakened something in him that had slumbered far too long. Beyond passion, he was beginning to feel hope again. "I'll tell the shop manager about the chain," he replied, pushing Lin's words away. He wanted to enjoy these moments with Lili Quan for now. In a few days they would be in Xi'an. Time enough to face the real world.

"Ready for a dry run?" Lili asked, moving the bike out onto the dirt road just in front of the shop.

"I guess so."

"Don't worry. It's easier than driving a car."

Chi-Wen fixed a bemused look. There were more than a quarter billion bicycles in China, but less than one million cars. "I don't know how to drive a car."

"Then you won't have to forget any bad habits," she said, awkwardly glossing over the faux pas. "Okay. Lesson one, climb into the saddle."

Lili taught Chi-Wen to straddle the bike, balancing his feet while she familiarized his hands with the throttle, spark control, front brake hand lever and clutch control lever.

"Lesson two, start the engine."

Standing beside him, she took him step by step: "Make sure the gearshift is in neutral and open the cutoff." She pointed to the valve between the tank and carburetor. "That's it. Turn the throttle. Not so much. Good."

Chi-Wen followed her directions carefully.

"Now, kick down on the starter pedal and move the choke lever up."

He rotated the left-hand grip, setting the spark control.

"Keep the throttle steady, turn the ignition key and kick down on the starter pedal."

Nothing happened.

"Again."

After several tries the engine idled smoothly.

"Lesson three. Your first ride."

"I'm not ready," Chi-Wen protested.

"Trust me," Lili replied. "Listen carefully." Patiently, she explained the procedure. "Release the clutch and shift into low."

Chi-Wen depressed the gearshift pedal.

"Turn the throttle toward you. Slowly, slowly. You're revving too high!"

Suddenly Chi-Wen squeezed the clutch lever, slammed the gearshift down into low and popped the clutch.

Oh shit!

Too late, he was on the ground while his mechanical mount raced down the street.

"Are you all right?" Lili asked, after retrieving the bike.

Chi-Wen dusted himself off. Except for losing face, he was fine. "In China we say failure is the mother of success."

Lili held out her hand to him. "In America, we say, the only thing to do when you fall off a horse is to get back on again."

"Are you sure?"

"Absolutely."

A few more attempts and Chi-Wen could ride in a straight line. He had never enjoyed himself so much.

"You're a good student," Lili said, smiling.

"And you're a good teacher." He pushed the bike toward Lili. "But I think I'm ready for you to take over."

Lili invited Chi-Wen to sit behind her. "You'll need to hold me around the waist," she prompted.

Tentatively his hands clasped around her.

"I won't break," she laughed. "And I don't want you falling off again."

Chastened, he tightened his grip.

"Great. Here's what you can do after a little more practice." Without warning, Lili gunned the throttle, performed a quick wheelie and accelerated down a shoulderless dirt street paralleling the Shantung River.

The takeoff was so sudden Chi-Wen gasped and clutched her more tightly.

Lili expertly slalomed through the human obstacle course: a woman on a bicycle loaded with live ducks stuffed into a wooden crate, a couple of beat up buses packed with passengers, a man on a donkey.

"We're going to die," Chi-Wen yelled, as they left everyone in their dust.

By way of reply, Lili pointed to a seagull dipping down from the sky, almost close enough to touch. It beat its wings with a slow oaring motion, flying in synchrony and in so doing, seemed to stand still.

Chi-Wen laughed with child-like delight. His panic turned to exhilaration.

For a few more miles, they chased the river traffic, easily outdistancing the slower junks and barges. As the wind whistled past his face, Chi-Wen experienced the thrill of total abandon. A sensation uncomfortable and at the same time, delicious.

At the intersection of Shantang Street and Yan'an Road, Lili brought the bike to a gentle stop. "Fun?"

Still breathless: "That was wonderful!"

Lili smiled at his pleasure. "Now where shall we go?" she asked.

"To heaven on earth," Chi-Wen replied.

*   *   *

Newport Beach, California

Perched ten stories above them, the photographer focused on two men facing each other in profile near the pool of the Four Seasons Hotel. Even with his 300 mm telephoto lens it was difficult to make out their faces. Of course he already knew DeForest. But he'd have to blowup the negatives to identify the second man.

*   *   *

Suzhou, China

According to an ancient Chinese proverb, "In heaven there is paradise; on earth, Suzhou."

Near the edge of a lake, hedged with hills, it was a city less feverish than Guangchou or even Wuhan, its tempo set by the slowly drifting junks, barges and long rafts of uncut logs. Chi-Wen felt it was one of the country's most beautiful cities with narrow cobblestoned streets and arched bridges over a web of canals and waterways. Seeing this "Venice of the East" with Lili, his arms tight around her slim waist, her lovely scent so achingly close, it truly seemed like paradise. A magical day, almost perfect from beginning to end.

"Suzhou was the chief city of the prosperous and peaceful kingdom of Wu five centuries before Christ," Chi-Wen explained as they explored the river scene. "Because of the river and the mild climate, crops could be produced all year round."

"Why the canals?"

"They were carved from the swamp so peasants could sell their surpluses to cities as far away as Beijing."

Seeing the men, women and children in shoulder harnesses leaning forward on their boats, hauling the long ropes, Lili felt like an intruder in history. Her initial reaction was exasperation at the inefficiency of this parade, irked that people still measured their lives step by step along the towpaths of China's seventy thousand miles of inland waterways. Yet as she watched, she found herself swayed by the ancient rhythms. They would come and go, all day, every day, as they had forever, as they surely would forever. Like the moon, like the tide, like eternity itself. "Yes, it *is* beautiful," she mused aloud.

"The gardens are even more impressive." Chi-Wen told her how Suzhou's wealthy merchants employed poets and painters to design beautiful parks and landscaped gardens for their private enjoyment. "Today, however, they are *yiyuan*, open to the public."

"Can we see them?"

"Of course."

After stopping at a local market to buy hard-boiled eggs, meat cooked in soy sauce, candied hawthorn berries on skewers and warm orange sodas, Chi-Wen directed Lili to the center of town. They left the motorcycle on Dongbei Jie Road and walked down a narrow alley to Zhuozheng Yuan , the oldest and most lavish of Suzhou's gardens.

"Most people called this 'Humble Administrator's Garden', but the closest translation is really 'Garden of the Inept Politician'. "

"There's a story there?"

"They say the owner was a corrupt 16th century official who collected bribes from everyone who came to him for favors. The garden was very expensive and took sixteen years to complete, but only a few minutes for the owner's son to gamble it and his favorite concubine away."

Lili laughed.

"This is how officials lived in those days, wasting the people's money and labor for their own pleasures."

"So what else is new?" Lili joked, but Chi-Wen's face flashed a warning.

"In feudal times the rich vied with one another for the best gardens."

"It *is* gorgeous," Lili acknowledged, backing off.

The garden was subdivided into many connected areas, each a balance of plants, trees, grasses, mosses, water, bridges and rocks, defined by walkways and accented by white walls, pergolas or pavilions with patterned window cutouts cleverly designed to frame the views.

"Every garden was conceived as a microcosm of the universe," Chi-Wen explained as they meandered through the grounds. "The rocks represent the earth's skeleton, the water, its veins."

He pointed out the flowers and trees. "Each one is a symbol: the lotus epitomizes purity because it grows out of the mud, but remains undefiled; the pine, an evergreen, is a metaphor for constant friends; the peony is an emblem of love and a sign of spring; the magnolia represents feminine sweetness and beauty." He walked ahead of Lili, so she didn't see the blush spread across his cheek.

"And the pebbles?" Lili asked as they entered the small, intimate Loquat Garden. The geometric patio pavings were all patiently hand-laid, each floor pattern containing different colors and textures in glazed tiles and rounded black and white pebbles.

"Their shapes and textures capture both the timelessness and the *ch'i* or energy of nature. They embody Yang, the masculine side, and when they are placed beside the female Yin of water, such as this," he said, indicating the pool skirting the Fragrant Islet, "together they are most harmonious."

Lili turned to look at Chi-Wen. The wariness and strain of the past few days had been replaced by a softening around his mouth, a glow in his eyes. An amazing transformation—as if talking about this beautiful, fragrant garden filled him with inner peace, relaxing his features. "There is a wonderful sense of solitude here."

He nodded. "Beauty like this is too great for any individual, perhaps even for one country to own, but should be cherished by the appreciative."

They were standing on a little bridge arching over the artificial pond as a pair of Mandarin ducks glided past side by side.

"It's as if they were a couple," Lili commented.

"Oh, but they are." Chi-Wen explained that Mandarin ducks were a unique species who chose only one mate and remained devoted for life."

"Is that true?"

"Yes, of course," he said seriously, then smiled, "but I've heard that if you take them to America, they ask for a divorce within a few months."

This was the first real joke Lili had heard from Chi-Wen and she laughed more to commemorate his breakthrough, than appreciation of humor. "What do you call that?" she asked, pointing to a tree with fan-shaped leaves and yellow fruit boughs.

"A ginkgo tree. They say that one's over four hundred years old."

"A perfect spot for a picnic."

Sitting in the shade of the ancient tree, they shared lunch and conversation, talking about everything from medicine to literature. Aware of Lili's background in American literature and genetics, Chi-Wen marveled at her fund of knowledge. So young to know so much. Suddenly he felt more bitter than ever that the Cultural Revolution had interrupted his education. "What made you study genetics?" he asked.

"I wanted to understand myself."

"How so?"

"The gene is the ultimate unit by which all the characteristics we inherit are passed on to future generations," Lili explained, then cocked her head, struck by a sudden self-revelation. "By understanding the double helix, I guess I thought I could understand why I was different."

Different. There she had said it. After all the years of growing up in San Francisco's Chinatown, after all the efforts to blend in, to escape her roots, her own genetics still made her different. She looked at Chi-Wen. Perhaps not such a terrible fate.

"Is that why you also majored in American literature?"

Lili pondered. Another form of escape? "Probably," she had to admit. "But I think it was my way to correct the injustices in the world, to become the hero who rights wrongs." A self-effacing laugh: "And all without leaving my bedroom."

"Yes," Chi-Wen quietly agreed. "Things are always easier in books."

For a long time they sat, not talking, absorbed in their own thoughts, their silence punctuated by singing cicadas.

Finally, Lili turned to Chi-Wen. "I'm ready for my first lesson."

"What?"

"A deal's a deal. I taught you to ride a motorcycle. Now you must teach me *tai-chi*. You said it is not just exercise, but a way of life."

"That's right. Behind every *tai-chi* movement is the Taoist philosophy of balancing the two opposite forces, Yin and Yang, inside the body."

He pulled a pen and paper from his pocket and drew a circle. "It begins with a circle. There is no start or finish to a circle, only completeness; and total existence is circular. It is the oneness of a cosmos that is always changing."

Across the middle of the circle he drew an 'S'. "Although they are opposites in nature, there is a harmonious relationship between them. Yin and Yang mean completion in the same sense that a coin must have two sides, that there can be no good without bad , no left without right, no heaven without earth." Chi-Wen shaded in one side of the 'S'. "And no black without white."

"Somehow I always thought *tai-chi* was a form of martial arts."

"It is and it isn't," he replied. "In your Western world, exercise concentrates on outer movement and the development of the physical body only. The purpose of movement in *tai-chi* is to transfer the *ch'i* or intrinsic energy to the *shen* or spirit and to use inner rather than outer force. With *tai-chi*, the separation between mind, body and spirit gradually disappears and the student attains 'oneness' with the universe."

Lili's wrinkled brow betrayed skepticism.

"Perhaps showing is better than telling," Chi-Wen said, reaching for her hand and helping her to her feet. "Always remember the circle. Every movement in *tai-chi* is circular and out of each motion comes its opposite. You sink before you stretch, pull back before reaching out, shift left to swing right."

Chi-Wen began to demonstrate. "No matter how complicated your program, always begin standing erect, facing north. Keep your head, neck and torso in one line perpendicular to the earth, but relax."

"Easier said than done," Lili joked.

"Close your eyes and just concentrate on your breathing, as if each breath is silk drawn slowly from a cocoon."

Lili let her breath slow down and gradually deepen.

"Empty your mind. The result will be a look of serenity, representing the state of *wu-chi* or absolute nothingness."

Lili copied Chi-Wen's position.

"Very good. The starting stage of *tai-chi* can be compared to a seed planted in the ground in the spring. Something inside this seed changes to a sprout. In much the same way the concept of practicing *tai-chi* is formed in the very first moment of change. Everything is mobilized in a physical and a mental sense. The transition from outer stillness to readiness for movement is called going from *wu-chi* to *tai-chi*. "

Chi-Wen stood behind her and placed his hands firmly on her hips. "Once the stage of *tai-chi* begins, you are ready to practice *tai-chi chuan*. Your heels should touch lightly as you sink slightly at the knee; then separate your feet, leading with the left foot. Yes. Good."

He spoke slowly and softly. "Above all, the movements come from letting go. From the initial stillness comes motion, slow monotonous, rising and falling with a natural rhythm like the ocean tides."

His voice became hypnotic. "Imagine the air filling your whole body, all the way to your fingertips. With each inhalation, feel the air float your hands and arms out from your body. These small movements are *tai-chi*. They grow from inside out. They are effortless."

Lili enjoyed the firm guidance of his hands.

"Straighten up gradually. Very gradually. Your feet should be shoulder-width apart. Distribute your weight evenly. Do this slowly, testing carefully the weight on each foot. In China we say 'the root of the body is in the feet'. This evokes the image of the earth. In order for the spirit of vitality or *shen* to ascend to the top of the head, it must be held as if suspended by a string from the sky. "

Chi-Wen stopped to observe Lili's stance. "You are doing well. Let your breathing become even deeper ; slower, softer, until your *ch'i* sinks to the *tan t'ien.*" He indicated a point a few fingers just below her navel. "This principle is represented by the image of humanity. The idea is that humanity lives between earth and sky. After you've practiced *tai-chi* for years, you will gradually feel that every movement is the movement of the universe. You and the universe will become one."

Despite her doubts, Lili found herself gradually relaxing.

"We learn from our bodies. Change is motion, *tai-chi* is motion; change in motion. Moving and changing from up to down, from hard to soft, from in to out. "

Lili experienced a sense of lightness, as if she were a feather, floating in complete peace.

"Starting from the center, follow the out-going energy until it folds back on itself. Always return to the center of the circle. "

She didn't realize how long she remained in that position before Chi-Wen's voice gently informed her that it was time to go.

"So soon?"

"It is almost five o'clock."

"You're kidding." Lili checked her watch, shocked that nearly an hour had passed.

Chi-Wen understood. "It is a common experience. *Tai-chi* brings a new awareness of time and space. As you proceed, you will gradually appreciate the continuum of past, present and future. We are all on the same path, but at different points along the way."

"Remarkable," Lili exclaimed. "You may make a believer out of me yet."

"Then you're on your way to becoming a true Chinese." Chi-Wen smiled, then on impulse, blurted: "I'm invited for dinner at my aunt's house. Would you like to come?"

"No. Your aunt won't be expecting another guest. I'd be imposing."

"Please," he said. He didn't want their day together to end. Not so soon. Not yet. Not ever.

Lili felt the same way. "All right," she agreed. "But let me return to the hotel and change."

*   *   *

Xi'an, China

That same afternoon, thousands of students and others gathered at Xincheng Square in front of the Shaanxi provincial government building to mourn Hu Yaobing. Some shouting anti-government slogans clashed with police while attempting to force their way into the government compound. They set fire to a janitor's quarters, a reception room and several cars, buses and trucks near the gate.

The students, alarmed by the violence, withdrew from the Square. The riots continued until evening as the crowd pushed over the western wall of the compound, ransacking provincial court and procurators' offices. Police arrested eighteen looters and suppressed the riot, but not before more than thirty students and one hundred policemen had been injured. A twenty-four hour curfew was imposed.

*   *   *

Suzhou, China

Lili didn't know why she felt nervous, but it was important to her to make a good impression on Chi-Wen's aunt. Rummaging through her suitcase, she found a red washable silk skirt and matching sleeveless blouse that would give her a conservative look, yet make it hard for Chi-Wen not to notice. Red—the Chinese color of happiness. She smiled. Yes. She was happy today.

She dressed carefully, then stepped in front of the mirror for a final audit. With her self critical eye, she acknowledged her beauty, but she was searching beyond the physical in her reflection. Something to explain the imperceptible change. She was becoming less a stranger here, no longer just a visitor.

She touched the jade locket she wore around her neck, running her fingers around the perimeter. A circle. What had Chi-Wen said? It begins with a circle.

Her mother's words: *...wear it always ...so you will never forget...you are Chinese.*

A circle. The continuum of past, present and future.

... you're on your way to becoming a true Chinese.

Impulsively, she slipped off her blouse and put on a red silk bought in Hong Kong. She barely had time to button all the eyelets that came up to the Mandarin collar before there was a knock on the door. When she opened it, Chi-Wen stared at the most beautiful Chinese girl he had ever seen.

*   *   *

Changsha, China
7 PM

After public broadcasts of a memorial service for Hu Yaobang in May First Square, rioters smashed a car and a police box and plundered shops. Several hundred police arrived around midnight, making more than one hundred arrests. They claimed most were hooligans with criminal records and none were students.

*   *   *

Suzhou, China

Two stone lions with chipped faces guarded the doorway of the old style low-story whitewashed plaster and wattle dwelling. Before the Cultural Revolution it probably belonged to a single family. Now more than a dozen households lived there, most with less than one hundred square feet of space per person.

Chi-Wen led Lili through the inner courtyard to a corner room, hidden behind a large broken pot whose one tiny peony had just begun to bud. Contrasted with those flowering so freely in the Humble Administrator's Garden, the lone bud seemed a melancholy representation of spring.

Chi-Wen didn't bother to knock, but opened the door and ushered Lili inside a tiny room illuminated by a single dim light bulb. Lili looked around: a table, a bed that doubled as a sofa, and an old kerosene stove. The only ornaments were a few posters taped on the cement wall and in the far corner, a record player that looked to be vintage 1940. My God, she thought, this drab room serves as bedroom, sitting room and kitchen.

Bending over the stove was a short, round shouldered woman dressed in blue pants and a white blouse.

"Esteemed aunt."

In the faint light, the woman's face appeared worn and tired, her skin as wrinkled as crushed rice paper. Yet the moment she saw Chi-Wen, it was transformed. There was a broad smile on her lips, a sparkle in her black eyes as she ran over to greet them, throwing her arms around Chi-Wen. "Nephew! I'm so happy you have come!"

Chi-Wen spoke a few words in Mandarin before his aunt turned to Lili. "Forgive me, it is just so long since I have seen the boy." She extended her hand. "My name is Fan Zhou. Chi-Wen tells me you come from America."

Chi-Wen had mentioned that his aunt studied in the United States, so Lili was not surprised to hear English. However, unlike her nephew with his slightly British accent, Fan had a Midwest twang. "It is a pleasure to meet you," Lili replied.

"Come," Fan said, urging them to sit on the bed/sofa, then hurrying to retrieve a kettle of hot water on the stove.

While she poured chrysanthemum tea into china cups patterned with flying cranes, Chi-Wen questioned her gently. How was she feeling? What did she lack? Food? Tea? What could he get for her?

To his questions, the old woman waved her hand dismissively. She was fine. Not to worry. "You have done enough for me." But how was Chi-Wen, she wanted to know, studying him carefully. She clucked her tongue. "You look tired." Setting a plate of dry tofu squares in front of him, she added: "and too thin."

She winked at Lili who eyed the scene wistfully, touched by the spontaneity and warmth of the relationship between nephew and aunt. She needn't have worried about the impression she'd make.

To Fan, Lili was the daughter she never had, the talented young woman she herself once was, perhaps a match for her nephew (who knew?) and a welcome interlude into an otherwise lonely existence. "It is so seldom that I have guests."

To Lili, this frail Chinese woman with her round face and kind eyes reminded her of mother and how much she missed her.

Lili answered Fan's questions about family and work, but was more interested in learning about Fan's life. It took little prompting before the old woman retrieved a photograph album from underneath the bed and placed it on Lili's lap. "So many years since I've looked at this," she admitted shyly.

As Lili turned the pages, the history of Fan Zhou slowly unfolded in black and white. There were baby pictures: Chi-Wen's father in 1920; Fan's in 1927. Surprising, Lili thought, Fan looked far older than her 62 years.

Only a few of the two as youngsters with their parents before they stood posing for graduation photos.

"My father became wealthy owning and renting farmland," Fan explained. "But he always placed a high value on education. When we finished high school, he sent us abroad. Chi-Wen's father studied English at Oxford while I became a mathematician at the University of Michigan."

Lili turned to a snapshot of Fan and a handsome bespectacled young man in front of a clock tower. "Ann Arbor," she said. "That's where I met my husband, Joe."

"Joe?" Lili asked.

"First generation Chinese -American. His parents ran a laundry in Lansing, Michigan. I think they named him Joe hoping the neighbors wouldn't notice that he wasn't one of them."

Her laugh was ambiguous, filled with the joy and pain of her memories. "We were both assistant professors in the math department in 1950 when I heard that Mao was inviting Chinese to return home. Many of my friends decided to go. Even my family pressured me."

Her eyes misted. "They said I had become a 'white Chinese' which was the greatest form of insult."

Today they would have called you *banana*, Lili thought, feeling a new connection with this frail old woman.

Fan stared at the faded picture of her husband and sighed. "Joe said I was crazy to go back and live under Communists, but I wouldn't listen. I hadn't learned the word 'patriotism', but I never really meant to stay in the United States. Being an intellectual is a privilege in China. I thought I owed my people something. Besides," she said, looking directly at Lili, "I didn't feel like an American. I always felt very much a Chinese."

"When did you come back?" Lili was suddenly uncomfortable.

"In 1951, when an invitation came from Fudan University to return as a teacher, I accepted." She turned to her nephew. "Your father was already on the faculty and pulled strings to get me the position."

It was the first time Chi-Wen heard the whole story. He knew bits and pieces, but his aunt was never given to nostalgia in his presence. He wanted to learn more. "You lived with mother and father, didn't you?"

"Until you were born," she confirmed, smiling at the chubby little boy in her album.

"And your husband?" Lili asked.

Fan looked away. "We were divorced." The steadiness of her response belied the depth of sadness as she ran her finger over the old photo. "I received a letter about ten years ago stating Joe had died."

She closed her eyes, as if to enhance memories, then opened them again. "It wasn't long before I discovered being patriotic was not easy."

"How so, aunt?"

"America followed me here, nephew. My Michigan education, my husband, my overseas connections made me suspect."

There was a picture of Fan posing with a group of men and women in Mao jackets. "When I arrived in Shanghai, I was wined and dined by officials. But I was watched."

There was Fan standing beside her students in Shanghai.

"After I began teaching, I was questioned by authorities. 'What were my connections in America? Who gave me the money to return?' Over and over again they took down my history, trying to catch me in inconsistencies, to see if I had something to hide."

Fan in Suzhou.

"After a few years, they sent me here to teach. Nothing criminal or counterrevolutionary had been found, but I was never accepted as a loyal Chinese."

She shook her head. "Never. And when the Cultural Revolution began...." her voice faltered for a moment as she stared at a picture of her brother. "You know what happened to your family, nephew. I was put in prison, then sent to the countryside for reeducation."

Fan had not been allowed to return to Suzhou until 6 months ago. Twenty-eight years, Lili thought. An innocent victim who had done no wrong, committed no crime. A survivor of more troughs than crests. Yet she seemed to talk of her experiences in the calm, reflective manner of one who had not only retained her sanity, but discovered a great inner strength. As with the woman writer she'd met on the boat, as with her own mother, Lili was mystified by such equanimity. Accepting joss. Was that what it meant to be Chinese?

As if reading her mind, Fan explained: "At certain points in your life, you can only go one way. That is why I have no regrets. It couldn't have been different for me." She beamed at her nephew. "Now everything has changed. Deng's reforms are working. Life is good. I am back in Suzhou."

Neither Lili nor Fan Chi-Wen's fleeting look of discomfort.

"Come," he said, closing the album, "We've seen enough pictures. It's time for dinner."

*   *   *

For Lili, dinner was itself a picture—a small snapshot of life in China today. She watched Chi-Wen and his aunt bolt down their food, mouths low over their plates, concentrating on feeding themselves as quickly as possible. No talking. Eating as if there would be no tomorrow.

Just like her parents. Lili remembered how ashamed she'd been when she'd first been old enough to understand that Westerners didn't eat like this.

But here she seemed to suddenly understand what her mother had told her. *"Every grain of rice you leave in your bowl will be a tear that you shed before the day is out. "* Her mother could never forget the hungry times. Fear of hunger was always there.

After dinner they listened to 78 RPM records Fan had brought back with her. The classics had been carefully stored for special occasions. It wasn't long, though, before the excitement of their visit and the soothing melodies of the masters put Fan to sleep.

Chi-Wen gently woke his aunt to say goodnight.

"Wan an. "

The old woman hugged her nephew, took Lili's hand in hers and smiled. "I am glad that Chi-Wen has a new friend."

Be wary of new friendships. The fortune teller's warning suddenly seemed long ago and far removed from now.

Yes, Lili thought, returning the smile. I am too.

*   *   *

Strains of "I Wanna Hold Your Hand".

"If I didn't see it with my own eyes," Lili declared as she found the source of the music. "A fully equipped disco in the middle of China!"

In a large room behind their hotel, a live band including the *erhu*—an ancient two-stringed violin—struggled with the Beetles' tune while couples gyrated beneath a pulsating rainbow of colors produced by a rotating stroboscope.

Males outnumbered females at least five to one and no one objected to men moving about the floor together. It was their only opportunity to practice new

steps and their self-absorbed expressions demonstrated their passion for dancing. Lili had not seen so many smiling faces since she'd arrived. She also
noticed there were no Westerners in the room.

"It's for the staff," Chi-Wen explained.

Lili suspected this restriction conveniently kept the Chinese from mixing
intimately with the *waigorens* , but didn't share her thought. Instead, she
moved toward the dance floor. "Shall we?"

"I don't know how to dance," Chi-Wen sheepishly admitted.

"Good. It'll be the blind leading the blind."

They laughed and Chi-Wen's tension fell away. He felt himself drawn
towards her, as she took his hand and led him to the floor.

"I haven't danced since college," Lili shouted over 'She loves you, yeh,
yeh, yeh…' What she didn't mention was that the music was vintage1960.

Chi-Wen wouldn't have cared. For the first time in so long he was enjoying himself, just letting go, and without looking over his shoulder. It felt so
good.

When the music slowed, Lili placed his arm around her waist. He rested
his cheek against her hair, inhaling its scent as if it were perfume. *Don't do
this*, he told himself. *Don't take the risk.*

But it felt so good…

She was reminded of Bernard Shaw, who said dancing is 'the vertical realization of a horizontal desire'… *Be careful.*

Still, as the music ended, they held their embrace, neither wanting to move.

"We'd better go. Tomorrow we leave very early for Shanghai."

"Thank you," Lili said when they'd reached the door of her room.

"For what?"

Her smile was warm. "For today. For the beautiful gardens, for the *tai-chi*
lesson, for introducing me to your aunt, for showing me a side of China that
I could never have experienced without you."

Chi-Wen returned her smile. "Thank you for making me get back on the
horse."

"Tomorrow in Shanghai I'll find my grandfather's grave. Then I'll have
fulfilled my mother's last wish." She turned the doorknob. "Good night. It
really was a terrific day." And then she was gone, closing the door behind her.

Chi-Wen stood alone for a moment, filled with angst.

Tomorrow. What was he going to do?

A terrific day. Yes it had been.

If not for her reminder of tomorrow, it would have been the best day he could ever remember.

SIXTEEN

Sunday April 23rd

Shanghai, China

Boarding a bus in any Chinese city is an experience; in Shanghai it is a trial by fire.

Lili and Chi-Wen started out early, heading for the neighborhood where Lili's grandfather had lived before the Revolution. The parking lot near the bus stop was packed with stalls where young men hawked watermelons and peanuts. A group 'waiting for jobs', Lili suspected.

"Very good melons. Do you want one?"

Lili shook her head. "*Bu yao.*"

"The bus is here."

A sudden surge of bodies advanced toward the open door. Lili was astonished to see Chi-Wen jamming his way into the line, then shoving up to the door where he turned and called to her. "Come on."

"We can wait for the next one." The bus filled to capacity and the rowdy mood of the crowd made Lili hesitate.

"More people will come. Get on," he urged. "Quickly!"

Imitating the pushing, and shoving, Lili squeezed her way to the door handle and placed her foot on the steps.

"Come on!"

She took a deep breath and amid cries and curses, pushed deeper into the bus to stand beside a window where she could cling to the back of a seat. Scowling faces in the crowd reflected disapproval. Their whispers labeled her an outsider. The awkward way she was standing was a giveaway.

Chi-Wen tapped her shoulder. "Turn this way." He showed her how to press her chest against the back of the girl in front of her and her back against Chi-Wen's chest. "Hold the seat with your left hand. Better?"

Lili agreed. As she turned her head, she recognized unspoken approval among the passengers. Facing in the same direction, they formed a straight line, one behind the other, backsides squeezed up against thighs. Packed tight, with barely room to breath, the bus could be filled to maximum capacity. "Very efficient."

"We Shanghainese adapt ourselves to smaller spaces better than anyone."

It was not so much Chi-Wen's pride at this distinctive feat, but its intensity that reminded Lili of her mother. *The cleverest people come from Shanghai,* Su-Wei used to tell her daughter.

The female conductor's voice sputtered over the loudspeaker in Beijing and Shanghai dialects: "Next stop Zhongsham Road East. Anyone getting off, please be ready."

"That's us."

Shanghai is China's largest city and port. Once out on the sidewalk, it seemed to Lili to be the most crowded. Perhaps it was the hot airless morning that drove what appeared to be all twelve million people outside today.

Chi-Wen pointed toward the plane and camphor tree-lined boulevard along the central waterfront area. "They call this the Bund."

Lili shaded her eyes to view the wide, muddy Huangpu River snaking eastward toward the ocean. Five-decked passenger steamers and ocean going liners docked alongside cargo junks, tugs and barges. Among the passengers climbing the gangplank of a liner at the next pier was a man and a young girl. Father and daughter? Lili wondered when they stood at the rail waving to an unseen face in the crowd on shore. Somewhere near here, forty years ago, she thought, Su-Wei had stood on a ship's deck too and waved good-bye to her father, never to see him or China again.

I have returned, mother. For you.

Walking along the Bund with the river on one side and a nineteenth century facade of banks and business houses on the other, Lili realized that after over forty years of Communism, Shanghai was still a monumental symbol of Western influence. The city's architecture reflected the building styles of many nations—bits of London and Paris, a Gothic spire here, a bulbous dome there, Swiss chalets and Colonial mansions built next to new mid-rise apartment complexes. On the hotel restaurant menu Lili had spied evidence of European culinary legacies like borscht, meringues and macaroons. Passing girls with permanent waves and frilly dresses; men in nylon shirts, flared pants and slight heels, she noted that even fashion here was an attempt, albeit a parody at times, to mimic the trendy sophistication of the West. So different from the other Chinese cities she had visited.

Perhaps, though, not so strange. As Chi-Wen pointed out, the modern history of Shanghai went back little more than a century. "Shanghai was founded a thousand years ago, but it remained a sleepy town until 1842 when the Treaty of Nanking was signed."

Lili was aware that when the British won the Opium War, Emperor Tao-kuang signed a treaty giving England Hong Kong and permitting foreigners to establish trading centers in China. The British, French, Americans, Russians, Germans and Japanese came—to set up shops, warehouses, consulates and banks. The great central waterway, the Yangtze River, was little more than ten miles north and not only linked Shanghai with important interior cities like Nanjing and Wuhan, but also connected it to the Yellow Sea. As a result, the city was well positioned to become a conduit through which foreign traders could siphon products from almost half of China. "In less than a century, the little town was a city of four million."

The largest and wealthiest city in China, Shanghai was also the most decadent and squalid—a place where the heights of luxury and the depths of misery co-existed within blocks of each other. Lili recalled Aldous Huxley's writing that Shanghai was 'life itself. Nothing more intensely living can be imagined'. In no other city, East or West, had he ever experienced such a 'dense, rank, richly clotted life.'

But of course, this was a Westerner's view. The richness of Shanghai life was primarily for foreigners; most of those suffering were Chinese. Battalions of deformed beggars, teenage prostitutes and half-starved child-laborers roamed the back alleys. Chinese and dogs were prohibited entrance to the central parks. Without knowing, the Western invaders and their Chinese imitators established perfect social conditions for communism to take root.

"May, 1921 the Chinese Communist Party was founded right here."

"Was Mao involved?"

"He was a member of the original committee," Chi-Wen replied. "But he never felt that Russia's brand of urban proletariat led communism would work for the six hundred million peasants of China. That's why he left Shanghai to convert those in the country-side."

As they walked, Chi-Wen explained how Mao's amateur army of workers and peasants was able to persevere despite disunity, poverty and inexperience. "When the Communist Party was formed, China was in chaos. The government in Beijing had no support and couldn't control the warlords and bandits. The Russians arranged for the Chinese Communist Party to enter into a coalition with the Nationalists and by 1926, the integrated forces overran most of southern China. Chiang Kai-chek moved his Guomindang headquarters to Wuhan. Without warning he dissolved his alliance with the Communists, rounding up and executing as many as he could lay his hands on."

"The Great Betrayal."

"Precisely. Chiang formed a new alliance with the foreigners who supported his take-over of Beijing. He became nominal ruler of China. Shanghai remained as it was. After Pearl Harbor, the Japanese took the city and put the other foreigners in prison."

"And after the War?" Lili asked, knowing most of the story, but curious about Chi-Wen's perspective.

"With the defeat of Japan, China was returned to Chiang. The foreign businessmen were gone, but were replaced by retired warlords, rich refugee landlords, bankers, and businessmen who did nothing to improve the lot of the ordinary citizens. Four years later the People's Liberation Army drove Chiang Kai-chek from China and the Communists returned to Shanghai."

"What happened to Mao's enemies?" Lili asked.

"Mao was surprisingly lenient with them. I suspect he was simply being pragmatic. After all, he had a country to run. His programs required factory production, foreign trade and capital to continue. This meant cooperation from those with knowledge of industry and commerce and with foreign connections—experienced engineers, skilled labor, even capitalists."

"Just as in 1921 they needed Chiang Kai-chek and Guomindang."

Chi-Wen nodded. "According to my father, everyone was surprised at Mao's mildness. As long as they confessed, they were forgiven."

"Until the Cultural Revolution." For a man with Mao's patience, twenty years must not have seemed too long to wait for a day of reckoning with those he blamed for the exploitation of the masses.

"Yes, until then." Chi-Wen sighed, remembering. Until the Cultural Revolution when everything suddenly fell apart for him. He looked around at the city where he was born. Shanghai had once meant so much to him, but now, as if with a twist of a kaleidoscope, he saw it from another vantage point—one that merely evoked the bitterness of his past:

Red Guards shouting slogans: "Earnestly Carry Out Struggle, Criticism, Reform!", "Put Politics in Command, Let Thought Take the Lead!" "Plant the Fields for the Revolution!" "Carry Out the Great Proletarian Cultural Revolution to the End!"

His father's public humiliation and private suicide.

His own banishment from school to the countryside.

That painful journey which had lasted for so many years had begun in Shanghai and for that he could never forgive the city. Its vitality and throbbing energy today expressed the miracle of Deng's reforms, the recovery of sanity, the hope for the future. To Chi-Wen, though, it would always represent the loss of his innocence.

They reached the corner of Nanjing Road East that had once been surrounded by the huge British-dominated International Settlement. It was also the boulevard that still is Shanghai's busiest shopping area. Before 1949, the Big Four: Wing On, The Sun, Sincere, and Sun Sun Department Stores sold everything from ivory back-scratchers and mink coats to green envelopes and pink ice cream. Today, in striking contrast, renamed Number Ten and Number One Department Stores, the Shanghai Clothing Store and the Number One Provisions Store offered only Chinese-produced goods.

Lili felt a growing sense of anticipation, of exhilaration mixed with anxiety as she approached the neighborhood where her grandfather had lived. She tried to imagine the handsome middle-aged man she'd seen in the picture at her mother's home. Past the art deco windows of the Peace Hotel, formerly the Cathay, she wondered if he had mingled with the rich and famous Shanghai visitors like Noel Coward who had stayed there in pre-1949 days.

Or danced with her grandmother at the hotel's roof-top Tower restaurant. Or sat in a sedan chair pulled by coolies dodging and weaving down Fujian Road, then through the maze of narrow, crooked alleys: Jiujiang, Hankou, Fuzhou Road.

"The middle stretch of Fuzhou was called 'culture street'," Chi-Wen said.

"Why?"

"All the great booksellers like Zhonghua, World and Great East had their shops here."

Did grandfather love books as much as Lili? Did he rummage through these book shops searching out a new translation of some European classic? Perhaps he preferred Shanghainese writers like Lu Xun or Chang Ai-ling. God, how she wished she could have known him.

They passed through Renmin or People's Park. In earlier times, it had been part of Shanghai's best known British-run racecourse. Now it was a pleasant thirty acre oasis of trees, pools and decorative rocks, where young Chinese spent most Sundays practicing English. Lili ignored the efforts of one bright looking teenager to engage her in conversation. She was too anxious to get on with her search.

Chi-Wen led her across Xizang Road to Nanjing Road West. Formerly known as Bubbling Well Road, it was a tree-shaded street that housed some of the nicest homes in Shanghai; mansions simulating English country manors stood back overlooking their broad lawns. Most were now government buildings.

"Chengdu Road," Chi-Wen pointed just ahead. "Your grandfather's house shouldn't be far."

Lili's heart rate accelerated as she counted down to Number 7.

She grasped Chi-Wen's hand. "It's gone!" The house where her mother had been born, where her grandmother had died, where her grandfather lived before the Revolution. Lili didn't know what she had expected—a fine mansion, a plain dwelling? She just never considered the possibility that the house might have been torn down. Freshly washed laundry hung out over Number 7 Chengdu Road, a three story worker's tenement.

It can't be. She thought of her mother as she lay dying and of her last wish. I must find him, she thought, I must. She would have asked someone in the building, but she could see no one old enough to have known her grandfather.

Besides, she hadn't brought his picture. How foolish, she scolded herself. "Is the cemetery nearby?"

"Why?"

"I'd like to see his grave."

Panic overwhelmed Chi-Wen. So far, he'd helped her find Dr. Cheng's home before Mao. Somehow that hadn't seemed quite so devious. But the cemetery? How much longer could he maintain the charade?

She grabbed his hand warmly. "Please."

Internal conflict held him transfixed. He felt like a bridge—struggling to span the vast unknown between past and present—old loyalties and newly emerging love. In his mind, he held his aunt's hand in his, unable to let it go, for without him she was alone. But Lili's touch was with him now. And her hand held his. He didn't want to let love go. He wanted to cling to the hours, to stretch them longer, to push the inevitable future further yet. Sighing: "All right."

*   *   *

Newport Beach, California

The room was heavy with the smells of tobacco and sweat.

"Do you want some more, Walt baby?" Asked as a firm, young breast dangled invitingly just above him.

DeForest's response was to ensnare the erect pink nipple in his mouth.

"How's about I give Mr. Piggly Wiggly a little attention, honey?" Yet another voice from under the covers.

DeForest almost bit the nipple as he felt the wet warmth growing around the shaft of his penis. Although he couldn't reach another climax so soon, he reveled in the sensation.

Twenty minutes later, exhausted, the two girls fell into a deep sleep, arms and legs still entangled. DeForest lit a cigar. Inhaling deeply, he studied the sleeping nubile forms. With the accumulation of years, he found himself drawn more and more to the young—boys as well as girls, always looking for new faces, new bodies that never aged. As if he could rejuvenate himself at their source. These women with their smooth faces and firm bodies were mirrors in which he reflected the youth he so coveted. He didn't want to grow old. Shouldn't have to, damn it. Not with all his money.

He blew a smoke ring. Maybe, he thought with delight, he might not.

*   *   *

Shanghai, China

Chi-Wen insisted on lunch first, so it was nearly 2:00 PM before they reached the cemetery.

Glancing around, Lili's face registered shock. Shards of headstones lay strewn over the graves, making identification of the dead virtually impossible. "It looks like there's been an earthquake here!"

"More likely, the Red Guards," Chi-Wen replied.

"But the Cultural Revolution ended almost twenty years ago."

Chi-Wen explained that as an atheist Mao abhorred the idea of hallowed ground. Even after the Cultural Revolution he failed to encourage clean-up of desecrated cemeteries. Because of lack of sufficient living space in most cities, he tried to prohibit traditional burials, promoting cremation instead.

"I never thought of that," Lili declared. "According to the letter my mother received, grandfather died some time in the early 1970's." Maybe he *was* cremated. "Where would I find that kind of information?"

Reluctantly: "The People's Government." Chi-Wen silently cursed his loose tongue. He had spent the last few days agonizing about misleading Lili. Now he was hopelessly drawn deeper into a web of deceit.

"Is it far?"

"Near the Bund."

"Then let's go."

Would she ever forgive him when she learned the truth? Even if the humidity had not weighed so heavily in the air, he would have been sweating. "Lili, I don't think it's such a good idea."

Turning to face Chi-Wen: "Why not?"
"You haven't really dealt with bureaucracy here."
Lili smiled. "That's why I have you."

        *   *   *

Xi'an, China

Foot binding, the rendering of young girls immobile by deliberately maiming them, had been part of the Chinese culture since the eighth century. Some time before the age of seven, young girls had the heel and toes of each foot pulled together and bound tightly with cloth, until the toes were turned under. Bones that resisted were broken by the blow of a wooden mallet. The pain was constant and continued for years until the feet became numb. The result was a teetering, swaying gait regarded as a mark of sexual appeal and endured because a girl's marriage potential and desirability were determined more by the size of her feet than by the beauty of her face. The perverse notion was that this object had been made helpless for her husband. She could not move, stayed where she was put and would serve her master in any way he desired.

Enlightenment came more than seventy years ago when foot binding was finally banned in China. Unusual then to find so many women with "golden lilies" congregated in one place. But then this was the Longevity Facility, a separate wing of the Xi'an Institute where, until Dr. Seng became Medical Director, Ni-Fu Cheng had secretly researched his theories of aging.

At three o'clock each day, Ni-Fu entered the exercise room. Dressed in loose cotton trousers and tunics, their gray and white hair closely cropped, the women in the group looked no different than the men—thirty *tai-chi* players slowly progressing across the white tiled hospital floor. Left foot, right foot, each raised and lowered with the composure of a heron striding through a pond. Watching them, Ni-Fu thought of his earlier conversation with Nien Hu; at 120, the oldest and perhaps wisest of his subjects.

"Hello, doctor."

"How are you, Nien?"

"Old."

Ni-Fu had smiled. "But are you well?"

Sighing: "My parents, my brothers, my husband are long dead. I have buried my children and now my grandchildren are gone. It is not natural."

"What do you mean?"

"I think you know."

Of course.

She touched him with a wrinkled hand. "All who live must die, doctor. To defy this law is to be greedy." Ancient eyes staring into his: "You understand, don't you?"

Yes. Yes. He understood.

And out of that old woman's remark there grew a plan, so quickly it must have lain ready to be discovered.

He waited as arms and legs moved correctly toward the final *tai-chi* pattern. Then, in the completed calm, he saw each of the group let their breath go, just as he had taught them, releasing tension, absorbing the *shen*.

It was time. Slowly, he moved from one to the other, handing each a small vial of colorless liquid that they accepted, then drank in a single swallow. A ritual maintained for almost twenty years. When he reached Nien, his eyes met hers. She nodded as she took the liquid.

Yes. Yes. He understood.

*   *   *

Shanghai, China

The crowd surrounding the Shanghai People's Government building kept Lili and Chi-Wen more than two blocks from the entrance.

"What's going on?"

"I don't know," Chi-Wen replied, wishing he had never agreed to bring Lili here. Strange forces of change filled the air. He had felt the early breezes a few days ago on the campus in Guangchou. And when the wind blew in

China, he knew only too well that the tall trees were the first to be crushed. "Let's get out of here."

"But I must see about my grandfather's ashes."

Lili was already threading her way to the side gate when a guard blocked her path : *"Zou kaio bu xu kao jin!"*

"What's he saying?"

"The offices are closed for today. All workers have been sent home. He says we can return tomorrow."

"But *why* are they closed?"

"It is the government's way of ignoring the demonstration. What it doesn't see, it doesn't deal with."

At least one hundred students marched with homemade *daizibao*.

"What do their posters say?"

"The student movement is for democracy, freedom, human rights, rule of law and modernization."

"How about that one?" Lili asked, pointing to a poster picturing several young men.

"They are sons of high officials like Deng Xiaoping and Zhao Ziyang. The students accuse them of corruption and *guandao*. "

One of the demonstrators lowered his poster and mounted a makeshift platform. Through a hand held megaphone he announced the boycott of classes had been successful in cities across China.

"They're asking the people for support," Chi-Wen explained.

On the faces of the milling crowd Lili saw the kind of excitement and expectation she imagined typified anti-Vietnam demonstrations of the sixties. "The students made good on their promise."

"So it seems." For Chi-Wen, their fervor brought back memories of a China gone mad during the Cultural Revolution. Frightened, he grabbed her arm. "Let's go."

"We might as well stay and listen."

"Lili, this isn't America. It could get dangerous."

"It seems benign. Besides," she countered, " not all demonstrations in the US are peaceful."

Chi-Wen looked at her—this strange young woman rushed into life with a vengeance, embracing it with all its possibilities, but without doubt and fear.

Her direct, single-minded manner unnerved Chi-Wen. How could he make her understand this was China? That life here was different?

"Come with me."

"Where?"

"Please. Just follow me. "

His urgent tone preempted her arguments. He led her inside a nearby gallery, to one of the many scroll paintings on the wall. He paused, watching her puzzled expression. "Tell me what you see."

"Are you serious?"

"Very serious."

Lili examined the painting. It was a Chinese landscape like so many she'd seen and not particularly good, she thought. "Well…"

"Be specific."

"Okay, but I'm not much of an art critic."

"That's not the point of this exercise."

" At the top right-hand corner is a mountain and at the bottom left hand-corner, a bit of land and a moored boat. In between, there's a lake." She hesitated, then added: "Oh, and the sunlight just begins to penetrate the morning mist on the lake. "

"Look again."

Lili spent several more minutes studying the canvas, unable to fathom what she had missed. "What?"

"The lake, the land, the sunlight, the mist and everything else that occupies two-thirds of the canvas is simply not there."

"What are you talking about? I see it all clearly."

"No." Chi-Wen said. "The silk is blank. The artist painted it by ignoring it. Were it not for this emptiness on the silk, the picture would have no meaning. The blank space gives shape to the objects."

Observing the puzzlement in her face: " Look, I'm trying to explain why I can't get involved in the student movement."

"I really don't understand."

"I told you I was a Taoist. That I followed 'the way'."

"So?"

"Taoists believe all striving is futile, even perilous. We achieve content-ment not by chasing it. Our eyes perceive without effort. In fact, we must shut them to keep from doing so. Our ears hear, our lungs breathe, our body grows, all without conscious intervention by our minds."

"Are you saying we make no choices; our lives just happen?" Lili demanded.

He examined her with curiosity before responding. "In the West you think you have freedom to make choices. That is an illusion. Your choices are limited to tiny decisions—will you eat rice or noodles or both; will you sleep late or get up early? The big decisions such as where you are born, how you live, what opportunities you have—these are fated."

"So I can choose to eat when hungry, sleep when sleepy, but I must allow myself to be swept along with the currents of history. Is that it?"

His gaze was long and steady. "Lili, the superior man does not struggle against nature. He knows when *not* to act. His inertia is magisterial, forming a silken backdrop for the futile strivings of others. In other words, the Taoist is the blank part of the canvas. He accepts his lot."

"But that would mean accepting the unacceptable," Lili protested, "to lie down like a dog, to give in without a fight. What about injustice? Don't you need to challenge evil when you find it?"

Chi-Wen shook his head. "You challenge everything."

Frustrated: "And you challenge nothing."

"I told you. Chinese adapt."

"Certainly not *all*," Lili retorted. "What about the students we saw in Guangchou and in Shanghai? They are Chinese and they are challenging the evil they see."

"A newborn calf has no fear of tigers. After it has been chased by a tiger, if not devoured it will become smart. Those who lived through the Cultural Revolution learned our lesson. These young students are naive. They will learn soon enough. The old Maoists will never give up control. They will win. They always do. Then they will purge." He viewed the future with a clarity forged from his own pain.

"I guess I *don't* understand China."

"You think you can come here, spend a few days and suddenly understand one billion strangers."

Stranger? Surprised by the intensity of his response: "No, of course not, but…"

"But, nothing. You are naive, Lili Quan."

How did such a beautiful, brainy woman like you get so naive?

Dylan's words. Funny she hadn't even thought of him before now. Were they both a little right? Dylan and Chi-Wen? Was she just a naive young woman? A brassy American stranger? "Tell me, have you ever read Hemingway?"

"What?"

"Ernest Hemingway. He was a famous American author."

"No."

Lili opened her purse and removed the copy of *The Old Man and the Sea* that she'd bought in Guangchou. "If I'm naive, so was Hemingway. Will you do me a favor?"

"What?"

"Read this." Should she tell him what she had told Dylan? That Hemingway believed that man always loses in the end. That what really counts is how he conducts himself while he's being destroyed. No. She would let Chi-Wen discover the meaning for himself.

Is this some kind of test you make all your prospective suitors pass?

Perhaps. "And keep an open mind."

Chi-Wen accepted the book. He checked his watch. It was almost 5:00 PM. "We have a long bus ride and the hotel won't hold dinner."

All the way back, they didn't speak. The altercation with Chi-Wen had broken the spell of the past few days. When they stood in the hotel lobby, she turned to him: "I'd just as soon skip dinner if you don't mind."

"Aren't you feeling well?"

"I'm fine. I'd just like to go up to my room."

*   *   *

Beijing, China

"Damn it!" He pounded his fist on the desktop.

General Tong entered the Foreign Minister's office. "I see you've read the reports. Should I say I told you so?"

Lin acknowledged the remark by hawking a mouthful of phlegm into the nearby spittoon. "I'd rather you concentrate on helping me plan a counterattack to this student movement."

"Then you're giving up on Peng Han's approach?"

"We still need to give the newspaper campaign time, but I think we should consider additional strategies."

"Such as?"

"Such as taking advantage of Deng's growing paranoia." He lit a cigarette and dragged deeply. "Like Mao, old Deng is becoming more and more terrified of betrayal. We simply manipulate those fears to remove obstacles from our path to power."

The military man smiled. "Yes, it has possibilities. Shall I arrange a meeting with Deng?"

"I'm way ahead of you. It's set for Tuesday."

"And the girl?"

"She's had enough sightseeing. It's time she earned her keep."

*   *   *

Shanghai, China

Too hot to sleep.

Lying across the bed in the sultry night air, hearing the overhead fan whir like a great tireless insect, Lili let her mind slalom through her confusion.

About China—a country so vast it was impossible to characterize in a word or phrase: spectacularly beautiful in places like Suzhou, primitive in much of its countryside, crowded beyond capacity in cities like Shanghai.

About its people: as diverse as the landscape in which they lived: old timers who saw today in relative terms -' better than before Mao', a lost generation who had suffered through the Cultural Revolution and wanted to be left alone, and a third group young enough to be idealistic.

And about Chi-Wen. Part of that lost generation, he had found solace in Taoism. Lili had hoped to know him better, to probe beneath his thin veneer of toughness. In these last few days she had. But was the young man now revealed to her someone she could get close to? Lili sighed, remembering his arms tight around her waist as they cycled through the countryside, his muscular physique as he played *tai-chi*, his earnest face as they talked together in the garden. Someone she could love?

I don't know what to feel, Lili thought. *I don't know what to think or feel.*

She sympathized with all that Chi-Wen had lost , but she rejected his passive approach to life. Ironically, her mother would have approved. How many times had Su-Wei told Lili to 'flow with the Tao' and not make waves? Like a good Chinese daughter.

Oh mother, I never really was a good Chinese daughter!

The heat lay like a heavy quilt over the city. She rose from the bed and opened the window, hoping to catch a breeze. There was an eeriness to the night as she watched the few vans and buses driving with only parking lights or no lights at all (Chi-Wen had said it was to save batteries). Creeping out of a shroud of darkness they seemed like strange, ghostlike creatures. Such a strange land.

What am I doing here ?

Until this afternoon, she thought she'd been right to visit China, that she was learning about her roots, her people.

Ch'uing tou-chi—the past, child, is a window to oneself.

But she'd really found nothing of her past—not her grandfather's house, not his grave, not even the site of his ashes.

Did she really think she could spend a few days and suddenly understand a billion strangers? Chi-Wen had called her a stranger. Maybe he was right. She was an American with a Chinese face in the middle of China. Still, a stranger.

Pent up sadness and frustration surged within her and for the second time in so many weeks, she could no longer hold back tears. She wept as much for herself as for her grandfather—never to have met him, not to have talked to her mother about him so that she might at least have memories. Everyone was gone. No family left to console her melancholy, to celebrate her happiness.

She was a stranger in a strange land and she wept alone.

      *   *   *

The moment Chi-Wen returned to his room, he opened the novel, but couldn't concentrate. His thoughts were of Lili. Why had he scolded her? Called her naive? He shook his head. Because she was. Obstinate too. But he didn't have to be so hard on her. Calling her a stranger was cruel. Especially after they had become so close. He sensed her pulling away. Her silence on the bus had been unbearable.

Frustrated, he threw the book on the bed. Perhaps it was just as well. It was all wrong, all a mistake anyway. He had played a foolish game thinking there could be anything more than a pleasant few days together.

Still, the smell of her perfume filled his nostrils even now—hours after they had been together. He remembered her standing on the little bridge in the garden, staring into the pool. She had not been looking at him, yet he could see the reflection of her lovely face in the still water, a clear mirror under the cloudless sky. He thought of Shakespeare's words, so apt:

Two of the fairest stars in all the heaven,
Having some business, do entreat her eyes
To twinkle in their spheres 'til they return.
What if her eyes were there, they in her head?
The brightness of her cheek would shame those stars
As daylight doth a lamp; her eyes in heaven
Would through the airy region stream so bright
That birds would sing and think it were not night.
See! how she leans her cheek upon her hand;
O! that I were a glove upon that hand,
That I might touch that cheek.

A Chinese Juliet. She was as intelligent as she was beautiful. How he ached for her.

A sharp tap at the door drew his attention. "Yes?"

The desk clerk hurried in. "Comrade Zhou! A telephone call for you. Come!" The clerk led him anxiously down the stairs to the lobby phone. China—still a long way from becoming a "telephone culture."

"*Wei* ? *Wei* ! Hello, are you there?" Chi-Wen yelled into the mouthpiece, knowing the call might be automatically disconnected after twenty seconds of silence.

Nearby, the clerk hovered conspicuously. It wasn't everyday the Foreign Minister called personally. Chi-Wen Zhou must be very important.

Through the shouting and the static, Lin informed Chi-Wen he must bring Lili to Xi'an first thing in the morning. "A military plane will wait for you at Hongqiao Airport. Ten o'clock." No explanations. The Foreign Minister broke the connection leaving no opportunity for reply.

Stunned, Chi-Wen remained holding the phone for several minutes before he finally replaced the receiver.

"Bad news, comrade?"

"Just a change in plans." Chi-Wen forced a smile for the clerk. "Dr. Quan and I will be checking out tomorrow."

"I see. Shall I inform her?" His tone obsequious.

"No, I'll do that. *Wan an.* "

"Good evening."

A moment later, he was knocking at Lili's door.

No answer.

He tried again. "Lili."

Again, no response. He thought he heard someone inside.

Louder: "Lili, are you there?"

Sure of it now. The sound of crying.

Doors in China, contrary to the Western notion of privacy, serve only to keep out light and thus often remain unlocked. Chi-Wen slowly turned the handle and entered. On the bed, Lili lay sobbing. Instinctively, he moved to comfort her.

At the sound of his footsteps, Lili turned a tear streaked face. "You were right."

"About what?"

"About me. I may have Chinese genes, but I'm no less a foreigner than any *waigoren*. " She was thinking that if accepting ones' *joss* was to be Chinese, she never could be. Her mind was too American. "I don't fit here."

Chi-Wen bent over and wiped away a tear. "Of course you do. Didn't I say you were becoming a true Chinese?"

"You also called me a stranger."

"I didn't mean it. Forgive me."

His expression was so earnest. She studied his handsome face. "Tell me, why did you never marry?"

Surprised at the question, he hesitated. "I was engaged once."

"What happened?"

"We met in the countryside where she was born. Although she had no education, she was a good soul. I developed pneumonia one winter from the bitter cold and she nursed me back to health. It had been so long since someone cared about me. I asked her to marry me as soon as I was well."

"She said 'no'?"

"She said 'yes'. It was her parents who wouldn't allow her marry to someone from a rightist family."

Lili didn't know how to respond. She understood the pain of rejection. "I'm sorry."

Chi-Wen shrugged. "It's just as well. We were not right for each other." There was a quiver in his voice that betrayed the swelling of emotions, threading through his iron resolve not to give in. "I know that now." Softly whispered.

Their gaze met cautiously. Although they both sensed what might happen, they shared a long look of puzzlement in that glance, their eyes searching each other's face, trying to answer unresolved questions:

Wasn't this foolish? Chi-Wen wondered. Loving this woman from another land? She questioned everything and feared nothing. Did he really mean it when he said she wasn't a stranger? That she was becoming a true Chinese? He stared into the almond eyes raised up to meet his. How he wanted it to be so. He smiled as he studied her face. Why not? In the soft lamp light she might well be a beautiful Chinese woman from Shanghai. Someone he could hold forever.

What was she doing? Lili asked herself. What about her resolve to be wary? She was not someone who could be intimate in a casual relationship. She knew that. Since Darryl Hamstead, she had been careful to control her emotions. Even with Dylan she had stopped short. Then why take a risk now? Maybe because it was no risk. She was halfway around the world. Nothing could come of it. Should she withdraw before one of them got hurt again? Her head said 'yes', but her heart cried 'no!' as Chi-Wen reached out to her, pulling her to him.

"Lili."

His touch was electric. "Yes."

So it was decided. He knew from her sigh, from the release of tension in the body he now held close. They remained embraced for a time, savoring the realization that it was decided, that they no longer needed to question or analyze. No turning back. It was happening, inevitably happening. Nothing else mattered. They were alone. A man and a woman. No past, perhaps no future. American. Chinese. These things were unimportant. Against his body, hers was familiar, without nationality.

Slowly they undressed each other. Naked, Chi-Wen lowered Lili to the bed, gently exploring her soft curves. She was surprised by his tenderness as he wrapped his arms around her, declaring his feelings with little kisses, moving his slim hips against hers. Her own body moved in rhythmic response. It had been a long time since she experienced this urgency and she gave in to her growing passion, savoring the smoothness of his hairless chest, the power of his hard muscles.

Chi-Wen was a considerate lover, tempering his own desire until she sought and found him and pulled him into her. Together they rode the wave of their pleasure. When they reached the crest, they collapsed into each others' arms, exhausted, sighing contentedly in the darkness.

He: "*Ah shi.*"

She: "Oh yes!"

*   *   *

Washington, DC

"Honey, you almost done?"

"Another minute." He placed the light-tight cover on the developing bath, lifted it out of the temperature control bath and tapped the bottom of the tank lightly against the table. This was to dislodge air bubbles that might otherwise transfer to the film.

"Can't I come in? I'm lonely out here all by myself."

He switched on the darkroom light and opened the door a crack. "Sure, but put out that cigarette first, uh..." he couldn't remember her name—Judy or Sherry or Cathy or...

"Sandi—with an 'i'." She did a poor imitation of Bette Boop.

"Sure, sweetie." He'd picked her up on the plane back from California a few hours ago. Another young girl coming to Washington with a good body and no skills, full of dreams about getting close to the center of power. When Halliday told her he worked for a Senator on the Hill, she practically leaped into his bed. One of the perquisites of a divorced male in a town where eligible women outnumbered men five to one.

"Whacha doing?" she asked as he agitated the fixer-filled tank for the third time.

The timer signaled the end of the cycle. "Developing pictures I took in Newport yesterday." He adjusted the faucet, letting the water run slowly to protect the film emulsion.

"For the Senator?"

Remembering his lie: "Yeah. He wants them on his desk first thing tomorrow."

Dropping the name of the powerful man was apparently an aphrodisiac to Sandi with an 'i'. "Too bad you have to work so hard." She rubbed her erect nipples against Halliday's back until he was aroused.

"Yeah." He set the timer for thirty minutes, then pulled her into his arms. "But I don't think he'd mind if I took a short break."

SEVENTEEN

Monday, April 24th
Shanghai, China

Dawn crept over the horizon.

At the window, Chi-Wen watched Lili sleep, half-hidden by the cotton bedcovers. Unable to sleep himself, he had eased out of bed hours ago and began reading *The Old Man and the Sea*. Hemingway's simple, direct style was easy to follow.

"He was an old man who fished alone in a skiff in the Gulf Stream and he had gone eighty-four days now without taking a fish."

Almost three months without a catch. The men of Santiago's village said the old man was definitely *salao*, which, as Hemingway explained was "the worst form of unlucky." Bad *joss*, Chi-Wen thought. Something he could understand.

"Everything about him was old except his eyes and they were the same color as the sea and were cheerful and undefeated…"

Chi-Wen sighed. Cheerful and undefeated. With so much against him, how was that possible? Like Lili, this old man seemed to think you could transcend what everyone believed to be impossible.

Lili. The first rays of daylight fell across the bed, illuminating the gentle rise and fall of her breathing. No matter how many times he replayed last night, nothing could change his feelings. Making love to Lili had been extraordinary. He hadn't planned or even expected it. But when she responded, moved eagerly into his embrace, he was overwhelmed. Abandoning all fears, he succumbed to the sheer magic of the moment. Now, with daylight nigh, he had to confront reality.

Reality. He almost laughed at the irony. For so long he'd closed himself off to love in order to endure. Then he'd met Lili and tried to convince himself love would help him to endure. Now in the cold light of day he knew love would be his destruction. And hers. This is how Shakespeare's Juliet must have felt. Love and pain were indeed inseparable.

Impulsively, he slipped on his pants and tiptoed past the bed and out the door. At the lobby he found the clerk with his head on his arms, snoring. It took several shakes to wake him.

"Comrade Zhou."

"Dr. Quan and I will be leaving in thirty minutes. Would you arrange a taxi?"

The clerk rubbed the sleep from his eyes. "Of course, Comrade. My pleasure."

On his way back to the room, Chi-Wen checked his watch. 6:30 AM. If he hurried, there would be time. Time enough to buy a ticket and catch the 8:00 AM train back to Guangchou.

*   *   *

In the lobby, the desk clerk followed Chi-Wen with his eyes until he disappeared up the stairs. Then he turned his attention to the figure lurking deep in the shadows—the young cadre who had been following Lili since Changsha.

*   *   *

Chi-Wen tiptoed back into the room and as he did, his shadow fell across Lili's face.

She stirred, opening her eyes. "Good morning." Stretching lazily. "You should have woken me."

"You were sleeping so peacefully."

"How long have you been up?"

"A while."

She studied him. "What have you been doing for 'a while'?"

"Just thinking."

Sensing his agitation, Lili wondered if its source could be remorse. She hadn't had time to analyze her own feelings. "Chi-Wen?"

"Yes?"

"Is something wrong?"

Averting his gaze: "No, it's just that I confused our schedule. We have to leave in thirty minutes." No point in telling her the danger she might be in. It would only complicate things. Just get her out of China—fast.

A loud knock at the door precluded further questions. Lili grabbed her robe. "Shouldn't you get that?"

"You answer it." No time to explain that in China it wasn't wise to be caught visiting an unmarried woman in her hotel room. Chi-Wen stood out of sight.

Two men waited in the half-light of the hallway. The younger one bowed and asked in broken English. "Where Comrade Zhou?"

"Why he's right here," Lili replied without hesitation.

Reluctantly, Chi-Wen stepped from his hiding place. "What do you want?" he demanded in Shanghainese.

"Comrade Zhou?"

"Yes?"

"Foreign Minister Lin has asked me to accompany you and Dr. Quan to Xi'an."

"I see." The fact that the desk clerk stood behind the young cadre was not lost on Chi-Wen. No one could be trusted in this new China of *hou-tai* and *guandao*. His heart tightened with pain. But he had known the truth before the door opened. He had known it from the instant he conceived his hasty plan.

To escape with Lili was hopeless—as hopeless as his love for her. They were doomed from the start.

He thought of the garden they'd visited yesterday and its beautiful, enclosed spaces. Enclosure. That's what he hadn't been able to explain to Lili. Whether of the world behind the garden walls, the courtyard of the household, the person in the family, enclosure was a fundamental organizational principle in Chinese society. So different from Western concepts of individuality, a Chinese would always be surrounded and defined by an enclosed world.

You can't stop fate ! he wanted to scream at Lili. It was foolish to think so. Not here. Not in China.

Defeated, he sighed. "We'll need time to pack."

"Of course. We don't have to be at the airport until ten. I'll wait outside." Before leaving the young cadre looked pointedly from Chi-Wen to Lili, to the unmade bed. "By the way, the Foreign Minister asked me to tell you your indiscretion with our overseas Chinese guest won't become public. He said you would understand."

Yes, Chi-Wen thought with bitterness. It was a warning he understood only too well. As the old Chinese saying went, "You listen to the man who feeds you." The Foreign Minister was reminding Chi-Wen that he owned his soul. If he didn't cooperate, his aunt would probably lose her apartment, her only hold on life. Chi-Wen would jeopardize his chance for medical school and there would likely be punishment for him at a labor camp for "rehabilitation."

"What was that all about?" Lili asked when they were alone again.

" Dr. Seng has sent a plane to take us to Xi'an."

" Dr. Seng?" She had the feeling that man was tracking her every move. "Doesn't he think we can find our own way there?"

Chi-Wen stared blankly out the window. Maybe it was just as well that things were turning out this way. After all, Lili would have to remain in China. That was what Dr. Seng and Foreign Minister Lin wanted. But wasn't it what Chi-Wen wanted too? "There's someone in Xi'an anxious to meet you," he said softly.

"What are you talking about?"

He turned to face her. "Lili?"

"Yes?"

Her eyes were large, dark pools. He stared into them, lost in their depth. At the moment he saw only trust there. He tried to imagine what feelings those eyes would project when she heard what he had to say—what he must say. He couldn't hide the truth any longer. "Your grandfather is alive." *Please don't hate me!*

"What?" Lili didn't know exactly what she was expecting, but it certainly wasn't this. "That's ridiculous. My mother got a letter from the government. I saw it." She said it mechanically, unwilling to believe what she'd heard.

Chi-Wen shook his head. "Dr. Ni-Fu Cheng is very much alive. He's working in Xi'an. At the Institute."

Shock registered on Lili's face. "You mean, all this time my mother thought he was dead and..." She hurled an accusing look at him. "And you knew!"

"I didn't know Dr. Cheng had *any* family until last week. I'm just a messenger, Lili. I was sent to bring you to Xi'an."

So much to absorb. She thought about Dr. Seng's visit to Los Angeles and the way he lured her to China. "I don't understand. Why all the subterfuge? It doesn't make any sense. All Dr. Seng had to do was tell me my grandfather was alive and I would have come willingly. Why go through all this convoluted, complicated rigmarole?"

"Because we are Chinese."

"Damn it, what does that mean?"

"Since the dawn of time Chinese motives have always been a mystery." Mounting bewilderment, dismay, frustration, anger. Lili wanted to scream. "Chinese motives. If that's some Taoist drivel, it's not good enough, Chi-Wen. Not after this week! Not after last night!" Her eyes were on fire. "You say you didn't know about me until last week. I'll have to accept that. But tell me why did you let me continue to think he was dead —why did you take me to the cemetery, let me search for his ashes? And why are you telling me now? I want to know!"

"You want an easy answer," he said, fighting the turbulent emotions that threatened to engulf him. He had struggled most of the week trying to figure out a way to tell her about Ni-Fu Cheng. But every time he'd played out the scene in his head, it came out wrong. Each time Lili ended up hating him for what seemed to be a betrayal. He stared glumly out the window.

"I just want the truth."

"The truth?" he asked, feeling his heart tearing. "The truth is I never expected what happened this week."

"Exactly what *did* happen?" she demanded, her tone full of confusion and pain.

I never expected to fall in love! How could he tell her now?

"Chi-Wen?"

For a long time, he remained with his back to her, gazing out at the city just waking up. "What happened?" He turned to face her. "From the moment I met you, I was overcome. I knew if I told you earlier, I'd never have had a chance to spend time alone with you." Struggling with feelings he'd kept in check for so long: "I...I didn't want this week to end, Lili. Not ever." His voice trembled. "I love you." He'd said it. "That's the truth."

He moved to the door and waited until his hand was on the knob before adding: "I'm sorry." Then he was gone.

*   *

Washington, D.C.

Under a white light, Halliday examined the processed contact sheet with a magnifying loupe to determine which negatives to enlarge.

Damn. It wasn't the clarity of the pictures that was going to be the problem. It was the fact that the man who'd met with DeForest in Newport was not a local player. Too many years on the desk in D.C., Halliday had lost touch with the international set.

Well, he thought, as he dialed area code 703. He'd just have to get the information he needed some other way.

EIGHTEEN

Shanghai to Xi'an

Less than two hours in the air and Lili knew why so many American tourists in China preferred the train to flying. She only hoped the Russian turbo-prop Ilyushian engine worked better than the toilet or air conditioning. A stewardess had passed out hard candy and fans just after take-off, then disappeared before explaining emergency procedures. Probably a futile exercise, Lili reasoned, observing that seat belts, flotation devices and oxygen masks were nonexistent.

Fortunately the weather was picture perfect. Had the Civil Air Administration of China (CAAC) possessed radar equipment, it would have been needless. The plane flew low enough so Lili could appreciate the lushness of the landscape south of the Yangtze River—the "land of rice and fish" where every inch of rich, black soil was neatly cultivated to the very edge of the narrow footpaths. The square sails of a junk moving over the tops of mulberry trees seemed to be sailing on land.

She glanced over at the young cadre curled up in his seat beside her, dozing. Chi-Wen sitting by the window, gazed silently out, his face pale and strained. Since their confrontation in the hotel room, they had barely spoken.

She wondered what Chi-Wen was thinking as conflicting ideas and emotions jostled together in her own head.

Your grandfather is alive.

How her heart leapt at the words. She closed her eyes, trying to imagine the man pictured with her mother. Alive! She realized that she hadn't asked Chi-Wen a single question about him.

He's been working in Xi'an. At the Institute.

And you knew.

I'm just a messenger.

...you knew.

Your most cunning enemy will first seek to be your ally.

I didn't want this week to end.

She hadn't either.

I love you.

The plane's bumpy landing jolted Lili back to reality. She looked over at Chi-Wen, still staring vacantly out the window.

The voice of the stewardess crackled over the loud speaker: "Ladies and gentlemen..."

Remembering how she felt in his arms last night—so excited, and warm and...

"...we have reached Xi'an."

...and right.

I love you.

She knew Chi-Wen well enough now to appreciate that his declaration had not come easily.

"Please   watch   your   step   as   you   exit   from   the   plane." It seemed so long ago.

Chi-Wen's words in the garden at Suzhou: *We are all on the path, but at different points along the way.*

Sighing. For a moment, their paths had crossed. How long, she wondered, would they remain at the same point along the way?

The plane came to a stop at the terminal gate.

What they had started had been interrupted, Lili thought as she grabbed for her knapsack. Only time would tell if it would remain unfinished.

*   *   *

Xi'an, China

Ni-Fu carefully rolled the tip of his calligraphy brush in the pool of black ink, then with a dancer's grace, moved it rhythmically across his *shuan* paper, keeping his body almost still. The characters flowing in one stroke emerged on the page in perfect, aesthetic balance. *Ai* , love: a heart under a roof , symbolizing the joining together as one. For Ni-Fu it meant Lili, his only family. How he yearned to see her.

He held up the paper for only a moment before crumpling it.

"Why do you always destroy your work, Dr. Cheng?"

"Ah, Dr. Seng, I didn't hear you come in." Ni-Fu returned the brush to the inlaid box on his desk. "The joy of calligraphy is in the creating, not the saving."

"So I've heard you say. But so few remain who are as skilled in this ancient art. It seems a pity not to keep your work."

Ni-Fu turned to look at the Medical Director still standing in the doorway of his room. "I must be dreaming. An avowed Communist speaking reverently of the past."

Dr. Seng laughed good-naturedly. "You are not dreaming, Comrade. Even Communists have learned that destroying the past is not necessarily the way to move ahead."

Ni-Fu nodded, thinking how much art and literature, destroyed during the Cultural Revolution, could never be replaced. "It is a good lesson to learn. However late."

Feeling the sting of criticism, Dr. Seng abruptly changed the subject. "Well, I have good news. Your granddaughter will be arriving late this afternoon. I've arranged for you to meet her tomorrow."

Ni-Fu couldn't hide his happiness.

"I know you will help us make her stay here enjoyable."

"What is it you want from me?"

"Nothing more than I've wanted all along, doctor. Your secret."

"And I've already told you, my work isn't complete. I can't give you the formula for longevity until it is perfected."

"Can't or won't?"

Ni-Fu volunteered nothing.

"Come now. Thirty people on ward #1 all living well over 110 years? Even a non-researcher understands the odds of that being anything but a measure of your genius is astronomical."

Silence from Ni-Fu.

"Dr. Cheng, you and I are both men of science." Seng's voice assumed a tone of reason. "I think I understand your point of view and I commend your regard for ethics. What troubles me is your reluctance to trust in the good sense of our leaders; to appreciate that they will see that your discovery is used in whatever way best serves China."

Will they? Or will they simply use it to keep power for themselves? Let politicians decide how it should be used? It must never get into their hands. Never! It was his discovery. It should be his choice. A man with a soul and a conscience.

Ni-Fu would have welcomed the opportunity to challenge this opportunistic toady. But any philosophical debate would have to wait for another time, another place. Now he had to control his emotions for the sake of his plan. For Lili's sake. He remained quiet.

Seng's patient veneer vanished. "Very well," he said abruptly. "Let me put it to you a different way. My instructions are to offer you the alternatives. Give us your secret and you and your granddaughter can have a nice visit together and then she'll go home. You can continue the life you've been leading, working in your laboratory, seeing patients. Not a bad life."

"And if I don't?"

Seng's smile was menacing. "Do I really have to spell it out?"

"No." Ni-Fu knew Seng to be an ambitious bureaucrat, capable of anything that might advance his position in the Party. Nothing—including killing was beyond him. "Let me think about it."

"Just don't take too long. My superiors won't wait more than another ten days. In the meantime, the less your granddaughter knows, the better off she'll be."

"You mean I'm to hide the fact that I'm a prisoner here?"

"Prisoner seems such a harsh word. Haven't you been comfortable?"

If he hadn't been so anxious to see Lili, Ni-Fu might have asked what comfort was without freedom. Instead, he replied, "She won't learn anything."

"Good, then I'll let you rest for tomorrow." At the exit he turned and added: "Please remember, Dr. Cheng, there is no place, even among the scientific elite, for counter-revolutionary tendencies." The door slammed shut.

As soon as Dr. Seng left, Ni-Fu found a fresh sheet of paper, raised the sheep's hair brush and dipped it into the ink several times until he felt it was properly loaded. A familiar ache in his left jaw almost took his breath away before it disappeared as quickly as it had come—without traveling down his arm. Even if it had, Ni-Fu would have ignored it. There was no time for self-indulgence. Not now. Not if his plan was going to work.

He held the brush just above the page for a moment before beginning the smooth calligraphy. For almost five minutes he worked, filling the paper with the characters of a poem he'd composed. When he finished, sweat glistened on his forehead.

This, he thought, would be one creation he would never destroy.

*   *   *

Dubbed the land of kings and emperors by Du Fu, China's most famous poet, Xi'an was at various times the capital of eleven dynasties. Once called *Chang An*, Everlasting Peace, the city lying on the broad, sluggish Wei River in Shaanxi Province commanded the approaches to Central China from the rugged mountains of the northwest. It was the serendipitous discovery in 1974 of first emperor Qin Shi Huangdi's burial site, however, that catapulted Xi'an to world renown. With the unearthing of eight thousand life-sized terracotta soldiers buried over two thousand years ago, the city quickly became one of the most popular tourist destinations in China.

Xi'an also served as the origin of the Silk Road along which Chinese merchandise was transported as far west as the Mediterranean during the seventh and eighth centuries. Then, Lili imagined, leisurely paced nomads on foot vied peacefully with equally unhurried camels and donkey carts for the right of way. Now, as the Santana, a Shanghai manufactured Volkswagen sedan, rattled down the dusty airport road at sixty miles an hour, oncoming cyclists swerved from its path screaming abuse. Drivers in rickety-looking trucks and vans removed their straw hats and waved them furiously to disperse the thick dust clouds produced by the speeding car.

The Santana didn't slow until they reached the outskirts of the city. By then the sun was just beginning to set and Chi-Wen leaned forward and tapped the driver on the shoulder. The driver decelerated immediately and maneuvered the sedan more carefully around the cyclists pedaling unlit bikes, several abreast on both sides of the tree-lined road.

Although modern Xi'an seemed plain and businesslike, Lili sensed the more pretentious flavor of ancient times as they passed the moat and sections of the fourteenth century old city wall with its crenellations, sentry posts and crossbow-width towers. She could almost imagine the men and women living here six hundred years ago, strolling along the wide avenues, perhaps stopping to admire the fur pelts or hammered brass pots and pans that were probably offered in the market stalls. Today the vendors sold cheap clay replicas of the terra-cotta soldiers.

Because of the clammy heat, occupants of the apartment buildings that stretched like red brick cliffs along both sides of the street squatted in the dust on the unpaved sidewalks. Most of the men had stripped to the waist, while the women and girls rolled their baggy blue trousers up above their knees in an effort to keep cool. Lili wiped the sweat from her brow and closed her eyes, overwhelmed by fatigue.

Only a moment later she was jerked awake as the driver braked sharply in front of a massive stone facade. "Where are we?"

"Xi'an Institute," the cadre informed her.

The outside wall was at least eight feet high and made of untreated concrete blocks—dreary enough in itself, but rendered particularly forbidding, almost sinister, by the fact that it was topped with barbed wire. More like a prison than a hospital, Lili thought.

After checking with the uniformed guard at the gatehouse, the driver passed through its heavy curved portals to an inner courtyard. A short drive took them near the entrance of the Institute, a nondescript five-story brick building connected directly to the Shaanxi People's Hospital. Although a research facility, it housed many workers for both the Institute and the hospital.

As soon as the car stopped, Chi-Wen silently unloaded their bags while the cadre led Lili to the registration desk.

"You are Dr. Quan?" the young woman behind the window asked in halt-ing English.

"Yes."

"I will need your passport."

"For how long?"

"It is required for all foreign visitors."

"When will I get it back?"

The question came as a surprise. "Ask Dr. Seng. He is the medical director."

"Ah yes, I know Dr. Seng."

The churlish tone was lost on the young woman who shrugged and handed Lili a key. "You are in room number 504." She pointed to the far stairs.

Lili perused the lobby. Built in 1952 by Soviet technicians, the building reeked of incipient decay typical of Russian construction. "What about the elevator?"

"Out of order." The receptionist laughed a Chinese laugh of embarrass-ment. "Also the hot water."

Chi-Wen started to carry her bags to the stairs when the young cadre spoke to him in Chinese. His response was a curt nod. Although she understood none of their conversation, Lili sensed from the flush on Chi-Wen's face and the rapid pulsation of the artery in his neck that whatever transpired had clearly upset him.

"Anything wrong?"

For a brief instant they locked glances. In that moment Lili noted that Chi-Wen's eyes which had softened during their week together showed their old wariness.

He looked away. "I'm afraid I can't come up with you. Regulations. It is not allowed."

"Why not?"

"Men and women are separated. Unless... " He lowered his voice. "...they are married."

Lili took her bags from him. "I see." Always superiors, always regulations. She had to remember this was Chi-Wen's world. "When can I meet my grand-father?"

"First thing tomorrow."

"Why not tonight?"

"Dr. Seng thought you should rest tonight."

"Always looking out for my best interests," she replied sarcastically.

"Lili, you look exhausted. Relax tonight. Tomorrow will be here before you know it."

"All right," she grudgingly agreed. She *was* exhausted. The revelations of the last twenty-four hours had left her emotions taut and frayed.

He started to retreat.

"Chi-Wen?"

"Yes?"

"Will you be there tomorrow?"

"I don't know." As if an afterthought, he turned back and handed her a Fax. "This came to the Institute. It's for you."

She didn't read it until she thought he had gone." Glad *you arrived safely. Miss you. Love, Dylan.*"

Watching from behind the doorway, Chi-Wen saw her smile and his heart almost broke.

Miss you.

Had he been a fool to fall in love with someone from such a different world? This woman who expected so much, he couldn't help but disappoint her?

Love, Dylan…

One last look before he headed for the entrance to the Institute's Administrative Offices. Perhaps it was just as well that he hadn't told Lili the whole truth. Dr. Seng expected him right away and from the cadre's tone, the summons seemed ominous. Chi-Wen feared he might not see her again.

Never to see Lili again. The thought produced a sudden and overwhelming sense of despair.

*   *   *

Beijing, China

David Kim was fuming when he finally located Lee Tong on the Beijing University campus. He didn't like unexpected meetings. He was especially annoyed by the distance to the northwestern suburbs. Even in a private taxi, it had taken over half an hour.

"Why all the mystery?" There must have been five thousand students crowded in the quadrangle. Kim had to shout above the commotion.

"I need your help."

Kim felt a twinge of alarm. Everything depended on Tong's promise to deliver the secret of longevity. Nothing could go wrong. Not now. "You're not able to keep your end of the bargain?"

"It's not that. Dr. Quan arrived in Xi'an today. Everything's going exactly as planned."

A sigh of relief. "So what's the problem?"

"Look at that," he said, pointing beyond the crowd to the bevy of foreign reporters and photographers. "The demonstrators are gaining support."

"Aren't you over-reacting? From what I hear the student leaders can't even agree among themselves. Do you believe they're going to change the structure of the entire Chinese government?"

A pig-tailed girl holding a white cardboard donation box stopped to solicit a few yuan. "It's okay if you don't give much money," she said after Tong had dropped in only a fen. "The point is to let the masses know what's going on." "I'm telling you," Tong said when she was out of earshot, "something's happening. Last week a Chinese businessman who had been taking bribes and embezzling from the government was found guilty in court."

By now Kim knew that Tong always kept a cigarette lit. His voice was shaky as he spoke, letting the smoke puff around his face, never looking at Kim. "Yesterday that man received his sentence. He was executed Chinese style: a bullet in the back of the neck."

"Surely your *hou toi* will protect you."

Tong shrugged. "Who can tell? If the moderates in the government want to show their good faith, anyone may become a target."

Kim was familiar enough with Chinese politics to appreciate the truth in Tong's words. "You said you need my help."

Tong lit another cigarette. "You must get me out of China." He cast a nervous glance at the crowd. "I've got to get out!"

Kim feigned a cough, mostly to avoid showing his reaction. This was an unexpected and unwanted development. "It won't be easy." He tried to order his thoughts. "I certainly can't do anything until you get hold of the longevity formula."

Tong nodded. "Of course not..." His smile was ingenuous. "Naturally, we'll still be equal partners," he added casually.

Greedy bastard. Kim controlled his anger by fingering the collar of his hand loomed shirt. A sharp contrast to Tong's sweat stained pullover. "Naturally."

It really didn't matter what he promised this poorly dressed fool. Their partnership had been doomed from the beginning.

*   *   *

Xi'an, China

The conversation meandered like the Yangtze for nearly fifteen minutes. But then, Chi-Wen thought, the Chinese had perfected the art of seeming to waste time and exchanging irrelevancies while discussing business, only striking at the last moment. The strike finally came.

"So you told her about her grandfather." His tone was soothing, his face a mask of politeness.

Chi-Wen was speechless. He stared into his mug of hot green tea, the leaves uncurling like green flowers at the bottom. *Seng knew! Of course. They knew everything. This was China.*

Dr. Seng's calm eyes watched his reaction. "Ordinarily, there would be serious consequences for defying orders, but as it turns out, your—how did the Foreign Minister put it? Yes, indiscretion—is quite compatible with our plans for Dr. Quan."

Chi-Wen gave no sign of acknowledgment, concentrating on the dregs of his tea, grown cold.

"As expected, Dr. Cheng returned to his work after hearing his grand-daughter was on her way to China". He smiled. "We Chinese have always had a strong sense of family. More hot water?"

Chi-Wen declined.

"This afternoon I had a little talk with Dr. Cheng and I think he will reveal his secret soon. " The medical director poured himself a fresh cup. "Hopefully, he will do it willingly. That's why we've taken such pains to keep everyone happy—so far. Of course," Seng said, sipping the steaming brew, "with his granddaughter in China, there are always more unpleasant ways to get results."

Chi-Wen drew a sharp breath, trying to disguise alarm. "You promised no harm would come to Dr. Cheng or Lili." He wiped sweaty palms on his pants.

Laughing. "So it's Lili, is it?" Dr. Seng shook his head. This lost generation had no sense of political passion. They only cared about getting from one day to the next. Occasionally, it was possible to manipulate emotions. Love always seemed to transcend politics. "It's true, I made such a promise. But that promise only stands as long as we get what we need."

Just as Lin, Han and Tong, Dr. Seng had no qualms about using people to his advantage. He never doubted it was for a greater good. If the moderates wrested power from the old timers, chaos would overrun the country. "You continue your relationship with Dr. Quan and work with Dr. Cheng as before."

No response from Chi-Wen.

"The Foreign Minister has been too patient with you. Time is running out. He wants the formula by May 4th."

The irony was not lost on Chi-Wen. That date marked the seventieth anniversary of the May 4 Movement of 1919, the prelude to the founding of the Chinese Communist Party two years later. Since 1939, Mao had designated May 4 as China's Youth Day. Routinely celebrated by the students of China, Chi-Wen sensed that with the increasing unrest he'd already witnessed on several campuses, this year that date would mark trouble.

"You have ten days to convince Dr. Cheng to reveal his secret," the medical director was saying. "Use your powers of persuasion." His tone became mocking. "From the scuttlebutt, I understand they are formidable."

Chi-Wen's crimson cheeks betrayed his loss of face.

"You cooperate with us and I mean cooperate this time," Dr. Seng underscored the point. "That way we can avoid any unpleasantness for you, for your aunt, for Dr. Cheng and for your Lili Quan." He emptied his mug. "I think we understand each other. You may go now."

Dr. Seng never asked for Chi-Wen's formal consent, nor was he given it. He believed Chi-Wen had no choice.

*   *   *

As Lili looked around in the twilight, the stark details of her tiny room assaulted her—reminding her of shelters she'd visited in San Francisco when she'd worked with the homeless—the two army cots covered with thin khaki blankets and too-often washed sheets, the unrelieved grayness of the concrete walls, the metal dresser, the bare brown linoleum floor, the incessant buzzing of the unballasted fluorescent tube in the ceiling. She wasn't sure what she had expected. Certainly not the Peninsula Hotel. But this was a far cry from the sparse dormitory-like facilities she'd known as a resident. She supposed the fact that she wasn't sharing the room was a concession to being a foreign guest.

Perspiration dripped from her forehead. Set amid the yellow burning drought of the loess, Xi'an suffered unbearable heat and humidity—even in April, even at 8:00 PM. She tried to open the heavy-steel framed window to let in air, but the crank stuck. Exasperated with the futility of her effort, she sat on the bed and then, in spite of her exhaustion, was suddenly embarrassed by her easy American expectation of comfort, her American presumptions. This was China- for all its advances, still a developing third world nation. She'd learned that much traveling through the countryside this past week.

What else had she learned about this strange land? She sighed. That nothing and no one was as they seemed. She thought how Dr. Seng had manipulated her into coming here:

Perhaps you would be interested in spending a few months at the Xi'an Institute as a visiting fellow. You could learn much from our approach to aging. And then: *it happens that a young resident from Harvard was scheduled to come in April and canceled at the last minute.*

So convenient. So neat. But why? At least she knew her grandfather was alive. Why not just tell her in LA? Her mind churned with questions.

We would welcome your coming home.

What did Seng mean? What was going on?

She lay down and closed her eyes, fighting contending emotions of indignation and anticipation. Tomorrow she would get answers. Tomorrow she would see her grandfather.

Somewhere within this facility, she thought, Ni-Fu Cheng waited for her. What would he would be like? She tried to imagine forty years added to the picture in her mother's lacquered box. There was so much she wanted to ask, so many memories she wanted to share—about her mother, about his life in China, about his work. *Ch'uing tou-chi*—the past, her mother had said, is a window to oneself. Yes, ultimately about herself.

As she began to drift off, she wondered what time it was in Los Angeles. So nice of Dylan to send her that Fax. He *was* nice, she thought, yawning. Someone who was exactly as he seemed. She smiled in her sleep. A good friend...

NINETEEN

Tuesday, April 25th
Xi'an, China

The snap of a twig woke her.

Startled, she realized she'd fallen asleep dressed in her jeans and T-shirt. Another sound from outside made her leap from bed and hurry to the half-open window. The brick wall around the Institute was high enough to block out the distant view and reduce her horizon to the confines of the tiny court-yard below.

In the pre-dawn light she could barely make out the figure until he turned and she saw his face: Chi-Wen—immersed in the movements of *tai-chi*, jab-bing and parrying as if he faced an opponent, unaware that she was watching. She envied his serene contemplation and for a split second, wanted to join him, to do *tai-chi* together, to extend their intimacy beyond the bedroom. But it was a fantasy. He hadn't been very friendly since yesterday; she sensed he wouldn't welcome her now.

She decided to exercise alone. In the middle of her room, she stood silently, eyes closed, concentrating only on her breathing and the progression of the *tai-chi* forms.

Empty your mind of thought. The result will be a look of serenity, repre-senting the state of wu-chi or absolute nothingness.

She raised her hands, palms outward in front of her chest.

The transition from outer stillness to readiness for movement : wu-chi to tai-chi.

She lunged slowly to one side, bent her knees, insinuated her hands through the air as Chi-Wen had taught her.

From the beginning stillness comes motion, always slow monotonous, ris-ing and falling with a natural rhythm like the ocean.

Gradually straightening, her movements graceful, the tempo, slow.

...the spirit of vitality or shen ...must be held as if suspended by a string from the sky.

Her body began to feel limitless, the rounded motion of arm and leg draw-ing the world outside herself, that world merging into the spaces encompassed by her motion.

Starting from the center, following the out-going energy until it folds back on itself. Always returning to the center of the circle. Until your ch'i sinks to the tan t'ien.

A soft knock.

Her mind collapsed back into her body.

"Dr. Quan?"

She opened her eyes. In the completed calm, she was alert only to the shapes and colors and sounds immediately around her: the angularity of her room, the golden rays of the sunlight playing off the ceiling, the buzz of the cicadas just outside her window. She looked out to find morning come and Chi-Wen gone.

The knocking intruded on her senses.

Opening the door, she faced the receptionist. "Yes?"

"Dr. Seng would like to see you now."

"Good," she replied. "I'm ready." Now she would get her answers.

*   *   *

When Chi-Wen entered with the breakfast tray, Ni-Fu was asleep in the chair beside his bed. Watching his shoulders rise and fall, the words in the *Old Man and the Sea* came to mind: "*They were strange shoulders, still powerful although very old and the neck was still strong too and the creases did not show so much when the old man was asleep and his head fallen forward....*"

Like Manolin of Hemingway's story, Chi-Wen loved this old man, this Santiago who had taught him so much and who had loved him unconditionally. Would he betray him now? Could he? He had wrestled all night with the question.

Ni-Fu's eyes opened, meeting Chi-Wen's intense stare and like a guilty child, the young man looked away.

"I missed you, son."

"And I you, Dr. Cheng."

For the briefest moment a flicker of pain shadowed Ni-Fu's face.

"Dr. Cheng, what is it?"

The professor shook his head. "Nothing. Just a toothache. "Come, " he said, reaching out a hand. "Sit on the bed and have tea with me."

While Chi-Wen complied, Ni-Fu studied his lab assistant's face. "How is my granddaughter? They haven't harmed her, have they?"

"She's fine. She's safe."

"Tell me about her."

"She's terrific," he blurted, almost pouring the hot water onto the floor. "So intelligent—she studied literature and genetics in college. A wonderful doctor." His eyes glowed as he explained how Lili had saved the young boy's life on the train. "In many ways she reminds me of you, Dr. Cheng."

"Is she pretty?"

"Very," Chi-Wen admitted, blushing naturally.

"It sounds as though she's found herself an admirer," Ni-Fu observed. Though unspoken, he sensed Chi-Wen's love for his granddaughter. "You know why they brought her here?"

Sighing: "I know."

Ni-Fu put aside his teacup. "When I began my work almost forty years ago, I never considered the possibility that a discovery to prolong life could be used for anything other than good." His laugh was bitter. "Call it naiveté of youth. Or arrogance. Either way, I didn't see this future. A few old men hoping to use it to cling to power."

"Will you give them what they want?"

"What would you do?"

"Perhaps it would be best to let them have the secret now," Chi-Wen spoke carefully. "They promised not to harm Lili if you did."

"And you would believe them?"

Softly: "I want to believe them."

Ni-Fu put his hand on Chi-Wen's shoulder. "Don't be misled. These are ruthless men. They'll stop at nothing to get what they what. And they'll sacrifice everyone who stands in their way to do it—me, you, even my granddaughter."

The implications hit him hard. More than anything, he wanted Lili to be safe. He looked into the older man's eyes. "It just seems so hopeless." Chi-Wen quickly reviewed his aborted plan to get Lili back on the train to Guangchou and somehow out of China. "They are always watching. The moment we make a false move, they know."

"Tell me, what is the essential Chinese character?"

Chi-Wen shrugged. "I don't know."

"Of course you do," the professor pressed. "What is the essence of being Chinese?"

Sadly: "Sometimes I feel, deep inside, that to be Chinese is to be weak."

"Why?"

"Because for so long we have accepted so much pain and sorrow, injustice and suffering without rising up, without complaining. To be Chinese is to accept your *joss*, your fate without question."

Ni-Fu sighed. "No, my son. To be Chinese is to be strong. Otherwise we would not have lasted over five thousand years. Forbearance and endurance are strengths; willingness to make sacrifices is strength. Even to have the imagination to try the craziest social experiments is strength. But," he added, "it is also Chinese to hope."

"Hope?" The word was bitter on his tongue. "I stopped hoping when I saw my father beaten and humiliated because he was a teacher; when I saw my aunt return to China from America to help her country and finding distrust and ridicule; when I was forced to give up my education and spend ten years of my life working in the countryside for a society that professes equality, but rewards only those who have connections." He shook his head. "No, professor, for me, hope is dead."

"Listen, son. You and your generation have been weaned from the concept of hope. I understand that. But it is not dead!" Ni-Fu declared. "It is still within you. Like the resiliency of a thin branch bent to the ground by the winter's snow. When the snow melts, it springs back. *That* is your *joss*."

"You really believe that?"

"I do. Absolutely." Ni-Fu surveyed the room. "I think I know a way to rekindle hope."

"You have a plan?"

"I have a plan." He motioned Chi-Wen to lower his voice. "You never know who may be listening," he whispered.

*   *   *

Xi'an, China

"Ah, Dr. Quan," Dr. Seng declared as he rose from behind his desk. "Come in, come in. I took the liberty of pouring your tea. It's always better if it has a chance to steep a bit."

Refusing to be mollified by Dr. Seng's congeniality, Lili ignored his outstretched hand.

Dr. Seng said nothing, but Lili thought she saw a grin slip across his lips before he sat down. He motioned for her to take the chair opposite his desk. "How do you feel this morning, Dr. Quan?"

"Furious!" Lili snapped, staring directly into Dr. Seng's dark eyes. Dressed in khaki bermuda shorts and sandals, the round-faced man looked more like a scout leader than a medical director. A sharp contrast to Tex Trenton's immaculate appearance. "I feel deceived and manipulated."

"I regret the need to deceive you in any way, my dear." Dr. Seng's voice exuded sincerity.

"If you regret it, why do it?" Lili angrily gripped the Victorian antimacassar protecting her armchair. "You knew my grandfather was alive when you visited LA Medical, yet you never told me."

"Yes, and I'm sorry," he said, his face softening. "I couldn't risk anyone else knowing."

"I don't understand."

"It was shortly before I made the trip to Los Angeles that I learned Dr. Cheng had any family."

"Even if I believed you, it doesn't explain why you didn't tell me the truth when you met me," Lili retorted.

Dr. Seng held up his hand. "Please, I'm getting to that. There *was* a compelling reason for my silence. You see, Dr. Quan, your grandfather has been doing some very important research. In England he became an expert in pharmacology. When he returned to China he studied the use of Chinese herbs as medication." He stopped to sip his tea, aware Lili was following every word. Better then to tell half the truth. It made the lie easier to conceal.

"Through his work with Chinese herbs, your grandfather has been able to isolate several new drugs including innovative treatments for hypertension and diabetes. As you might imagine, the market potential for such discoveries is enormous."

"And you're afraid of espionage?"

"Precisely. Until we are up to the manufacturing stage, there must be no leaks outside China."

"I see." Lili felt at a loss. Dr. Seng made it sound so reasonable. If her grandfather was involved in drug research, she could understand the need for secrecy. From her conversations with Dylan she appreciated the intense competitiveness of the research world. Still, she wanted to know more. "Why try to lure me to China with a story about a fellowship? Why not tell me my grandfather was alive?"

"The answer to the first question is easy. We value family above all. Even with our communist practicality, we haven't overcome the centuries-old tradition of ancestor worship. Your grandfather had recently become depressed; he felt he was aging with no family around him. When we learned there was a relative living in the United States, we hoped bringing you to him would cure his melancholy. The fact that you are a doctor was a wonderful coincidence. Hence, the offer of the fellowship. Which," he added, "is quite legiti-mate. There is much you can learn here about Chinese medicine."

"And the answer to my second question?"

"Not telling you your grandfather was alive was a decision I made after meeting you, my dear."

"I beg your pardon?"

His smile was indulgent. "If you'll forgive my saying so, Dr. Quan, you are an impulsive young woman."

Lili looked away, refusing to acknowledge the truth of his words.

"I was afraid you might inadvertently share that information with others. The Americans believe Ni-Fu Cheng is dead. If they knew he was alive and involved in the work he's doing, they might be inclined to lure him out of China. It's already happened with a few of our best scientists. Our country needs to keep good people here."

"Provided they want to be here."

"I assure you, Dr. Cheng wants to be here."

"I'll need to prove that to myself."

"Of course."

She did not know what to say. She'd come to this meeting filled with suspicion, expecting to hear about some international plot, not even sure she hadn't been kidnapped. Now it seemed the Chinese were simply paranoid about losing the edge on their drug research. Getting her there had certainly been convoluted. Why? *Perhaps because we are Chinese*, Chi-Wen had said, Inscrutable Chinese? Was it as simple as that? Maybe. "What about my passport?"

Dr. Seng opened his top desk drawer and showed her a packet including her passport and travel papers. "Here they are. Stamped and approved. You can have them any time." He spoke in the velvety voice of a seducer. "This drawer is never locked." Buying her confidence was worth the small price of losing control of the documents. Besides, it didn't matter. Now that she was in Xi'an, it would be impossible for her to escape.

Lili looked at him, chagrined. Her mind had worked overtime, invented conspiracies and international plots. Suddenly she saw that all her presump-tions had been wrong. She felt like a fool. "You keep them. I'm sorry for being difficult, Dr. Seng," she said quietly.

"No need to apologize, my dear. I'm glad you're here. Come," he said, standing up, "Let me take you on a little tour of the hospital and then we'll join your grandfather on rounds."

*   *   *

Langley, Virginia

Welcome to Busybody. Please Logon.

He sat at the keyboard console facing the fourteen inch computer screen and punched in a six digit security identification number.

Thank you. Enter Password .

It was a new program—still highly classified. But he'd managed to "borrow" the secret code from a colleague from Data Control who owed him a favor.

Thank you.

He was in! Once the negative was fed through the scanner and the image digitized, Halliday quickly accessed the extensive database stored in the CIA's mainframe computer. Photos of anyone ever fingerprinted anywhere in the world had been cross-referenced with identity information.

No file found.

Shit! Then he remembered. His colleague had told him the computer system did not use the new "fuzzy logic" technology. It required that the photo be taken at precisely the right angle to make the ID. He found another snapshot and fed it through the scanner.

No file found.

He checked his watch. Five minutes. Jesus H. Christ! If he stayed on the system much longer he'd be caught. Starting to sweat, he scanned the last photo.

Thank you.

Thank *you.* Third time's always a charm.

Seconds later, the answer flashed on his terminal. He stared at the screen. So that was it! Well, he supposed he shouldn't be shocked. After all, Halliday had been willing to double-cross the CIA. Why shouldn't DeForest do the same to him?

*   *   *

Xi'an, China

The line coiled around the outpatient clinic like a snake, its tail lengthening every few minutes. Some of the sick sat on wooden benches outside the examination room, waiting for the doctors to open the doors. The small area could barely accommodate the number of patients who, Lili noticed, seemed to be accompanied by at least one family member.

"That's because in China, no one would dream of going to the doctor alone," Dr. Seng explained. He checked his watch. "Ten o'clock."

As if on cue, the dispensary doors opened and the crowd surged forward destroying the uniform contour of the snake. Unperturbed, a doctor dressed in a white coat over Bermuda shorts began to question one old man who'd come with his wife and eldest son.

"*Zhong yi huo zhe xi yi ?*"

"He's asking whether he prefers Chinese or Western medicine," Dr. Seng translated. "Whatever the answer, the consultation will be very similar."

Seng introduced Lili to Dr. Yang, a slender bespectacled man in his fifties, who invited her to join him at his examination desk as he interviewed the old man. "I spent one year at the University Medical School in San Diego," he declared in excellent English, "so I like to mix Chinese with Western medicine."

The patient's chief complaint was cough and fever. Lili listened to Dr. Yang ask him about smoking history, pain, night sweats, weight loss, character of his cough, all the while making notes on a small chart.

"The client, not the clinic keeps the record," Dr. Seng told her.

After each question, there was a long consultation between the man's wife and son whose comments were apparently contradictory. However, Dr. Yang displayed none of the displeasure or impatience typical of American physicians in similar situations. He merely smiled, nodded and kept writing. After a great deal of questioning and a short examination, he diagnosed mild bronchitis and asked the patient what therapy he would like. "For colds you can have nose drops, ear drops, throat lozenges, vitamins for overall strength. For bronchitis, I recommend an herbal mix and an injection of antibiotics, with some nose drops and vitamins."

The old man agreed to the combination therapy and Lili followed him and his family to the pharmacist who filled the tonic prescription, mixing a variety of herbs, bones, meals and dried flowers on a tall pile of newspapers, deftly twisting a sheet into a series of cones, one cone per infusion. "Two injections a day of this antibiotic," he said, handing the patient a cardboard box filled with ten glass vials of saline and ten capsules of powder.

"The sick person takes care of the medicine himself," Seng explained to Lili as the group proceeded to a small room off the pharmacy where the injection nurse waited.

Without pretense of privacy, the man was instructed to climb up the three steps onto the highchair and pull down his pants to expose his thigh. The nurse selected an enormous syringe from a huge sterilized pile lying on the white tray, fitted it with a reusable needle, mixed one capsule of antibiotics into a vial of saline and injected the medicine very, very slowly.

When Lili wondered aloud at the possibility of an allergic reaction, Seng told her Chinese antibiotics were weaker than Western drugs because doctors in China were afraid of over-medicating. "People here rely so much on natural remedies, they tend to be more sensitive to Western medications."

As he led her down the hall, he expounded on the philosophy behind Eastern medicine. "We Chinese know that general health is primarily a matter of interior harmony in which all parts of the body work smoothly together, guided by a tranquil mind. We know too, that a disorder in one part of the body can bring pain to another."

They entered a room where several patients lay supine on benches, each as placid as a walrus despite the long, thin needles stuck into various parts of their flesh.

"We believe there are hundreds of points along the nervous system which can be stimulated to trigger responses in other parts of the body, helping to bring all the elements back into balance and restore natural order. This is essentially the belief underlying acupuncture, a practice over two thousand years old."

"It's funny, I guess," Lili confessed. "But I've never actually seen acupuncture performed."

"You'll have ample opportunity to learn the technique here if you desire." Seng pointed to one of the benches where a young man lay with one pant leg rolled up above his knee, three threadlike silver pins implanted in his tibia.

Lili watched the doctor, bent low, palpate his ankle until she found a spot and pressed it with what looked like a ball-point pen, leaving a pin in place, shot in by a spring. She twisted it very gently until it entered about an inch before exploring the hollow of his heel, seeking a location for yet another pin.

Lili noted that the man showed no sign of discomfort, but lay completely quiet and still, as if under sedation.

"What's wrong with him?" she asked.

"Headache," Seng reported after consulting his doctor. "I can assure you he's already been evaluated for various causes of headache," he added, responding to Lili's look of skepticism. "We've ruled out eye problems, high blood pressure and infection. He's scheduled for a CAT scan in a few days. Meanwhile the acupuncture treatment will relieve tension."

"A CAT scan? I guess I just assumed you didn't have any modern technology."

Seng shook his head. "CAT scanners, respirators and computers. These days we are always willing to learn from the West all which is clearly useful and worthwhile." He looked at her. "But you in the West do not seem prepared to learn anything from us, which is a pity, since in some ways we might be wiser than you are."

Lili felt the same discomfort under his piercing gaze that she'd experienced in Los Angeles. "I didn't mean..."

Seng held up his hand. "I understand what you meant. When you look at things in China, you are still seeing them with the eyes of a visitor. It will take time to adjust your mental and emotional focus to understand our way of thinking. This case, for example," he said, referring to the acupuncture patient. "It is not the Eastern way to search insistently for a single 'why' or to try to prove conclusively what 'is'. In medicine, as in our way of life, we leave room for a variety of feelings and beliefs which together make a completeness."

Completeness. Yin and yang. Like *tai-chi* ? Like Lili and Chi-Wen? A momentary muse. They had reached the end of a long corridor. Without thinking, Lili reached for the handle of one of two doors placed at a ninety degree angle to one another and discovered it was locked.

"This one," Seng said, leading her quickly through the door connecting the inpatient and outpatient clinics. "It's time to meet Dr. Cheng."

Had Lili been more attentive, less anxious to meet her grandfather or more understanding of the Chinese way of thinking, she might have wondered about the locked door. As it happened, it wasn't until some time later that she even remembered and thought it odd.

*   *   *

Beijing, China

A long crooked stack of hot ash toppled from the end of Deng's Panda-brand cigarette and splashed across the lapels of his crumpled jacket. He removed the glowing stub from his mouth, holding it between tobacco stained fingers that trembled with age. At the same time, he covered his mouth with his other fist to smother the sudden rasp of his chronic smoker's cough.

Waving away his anxious-looking nurse, the diminutive leader straightened in his seat to stare belligerently at the three men who had insisted on meeting in the early morning hours. "Are you questioning my reforms? There are those who say we should not open our windows, because open windows let in flies and other insects."

Although his shoulders sagged and his jowls quivered, Deng's eyes burned with a fierce brightness that belied his eighty-four years. "They want the windows to stay closed, so we will all expire from lack of air. But we say 'Open windows, breath fresh air and at the same time, fight the flies and insects."

It was a part of a speech he had given many times, but now the effort of talking provoked another coughing spasm. Foreign Minister Lin waited for it to pass before responding. "Just so, Comrade Chairman. Open the windows by all means." He leaned forward in his seat opposite the Party chief. "But there is someone 'sleeping by your bedside' who would see you fail."

"Who?" the old man demanded, understanding Lin meant someone very close to him.

"Zhao Ziyang."

"Nonsense, he is among my most trusted supporters."

"I'm afraid it has come to my attention through my Intelligence sources," Peng Han said, "that the General Secretary of the Party blames the problems of inflation and the failure of economic reforms on you. He hopes to distance himself, so he may take over."

Deng's face flushed with fury. He half-rose. "How dare he?"

"I also have information that he is openly siding with student demands for a more liberal society, encouraging protests across China, trying to create national turmoil." The Intelligence officer briefly recounted how classes on campuses from Guangchou to Changsha to Shanghai to Xi'an had been boycotted, carefully highlighting any violence resulting from the demonstrations.

"If this chaos is allowed to continue, it will develop into a counterrevolutionary rebellion. The leaders wish to overthrow the Communist Party and the socialist system," Lin added. "They want to topple you and transform the People's Republic of China into a bourgeois republic."

There was a silence then, long and tense. If what his old friends were saying was true, Deng thought, this represented the biggest challenge to the authority of the party since the Cultural Revolution. A final shameful discrediting of the legitimacy of his rule. And the biggest loss of face. Everything he had worked for—the supremacy of the Communist Party, the unity of China, maybe the future of socialism—threatened by a bunch of kids demanding democracy. At last: "General, what do you advise?"

"Harsh measures are called for," Tong declared. "You must repress the student movement no matter what the bloodshed."

Suddenly exhausted, Deng sank down in his seat . "All right. Do what you have to do."

*   *   *

Xi'an, China

Dr. Seng cut the hospital tour short for Lili's sake. Still, in less than an hour he had showed her pediatrics, obstetrics-gynecology, intensive care and surgery. It was an odd experience—seeing the old and makeshift juxtaposed with the new and modern: jaundiced neonates in rusted bassinets under bilirubin lights; IV aminophylline delivered to asthmatics through dirty, cracked, brown rubber tubing; pneumonia patients on respirators set beside phlegm-filled spittoons. Seng had said they were learning; acknowledged they still had a long way to go.

The hospital's statistics were certainly impressive: 1500 outpatient visits per day; 300 inpatient beds, always occupied; 1200 births per year; 297 medical personnel, of whom 100 were doctors, an equal number of nurses and 45 technicians. Lili was particularly interested to learn that more than half the doctors were women and all of the doctors in OB-GYN were women.

"Western physicians look on themselves as an elite class. They feel they are above the masses and beyond criticism," Dr. Seng related. "With us it is quite different. The idea that a doctor should regard himself in any degree superior to other people is ludicrous. In China the doctor is an integrated member of the community. He has particular functions which are no more important than those of a school teacher, a cadre or a factory worker."

As they walked through the hallways, Dr. Seng told her this attitude could be demonstrated in the relationships between members of the hospital staff. "We are all here to serve the patient and we do so according to our skills—even if it sometimes means a doctor emptying a bedpan or a nurse writing orders. The efficiency of any one person will depend on how much he is willing to identify with the masses. This is the message of our great leader, Mao."

"And no one complains?" Lili mused out loud, wondering how such an egalitarian theory worked in reality.

"All Chinese are not one hundred percent virtuous or idealistic, it is true, but because of Mao we have a national sense of direction."

Proselytizing about Mao? Even in the short time she had been in China, Lili knew few held the Great Helmsman in high esteem. Some said he'd made 'mistakes', others simply didn't mention him at all. Almost no one gave him unqualified praise anymore. She turned to Seng and saw the same expression that had made her uncomfortable in Los Angeles and again this morning—a fanaticism burning in his eyes that seemed ominous.

Seng studied her shrewdly. "Ordinarily our staff has political meetings in the afternoon, but since your visit is special, we will excuse Dr. Cheng today. Here is the medical ward," he motioned towards a group in white coats. "Rounds are just ending."

The scene was so familiar that Lili was immobilized. Doctors gathered around a patient's bed, discussing the relevant points of the case. But this was China after all. Seven thousand miles from her home. And the man in the center of the group, gesturing, explaining, all faces focused on his—the slender, elegant figure was…her grandfather. Her gasp was audible clear across the room. He turned and met her gaze.

"Granddaughter."

She came towards him and as if in slow motion, the decades rolled back, returning Ni-Fu Cheng to the day, forty years before, when he'd sent his daughter Su-Wei on her journey to America. The light caught the jade locket around Lili's neck and he was on the Shanghai dock again:

Do you know what this means?

Shou? It means long life?

Wear this always and never forget that you are Chinese. Someday you will return to your country and we will be together again.

Ni-Fu held his arms out to Lili as he had forty years before to Su-Wei and held her close, too overwhelmed to control the tears that rolled down his cheeks.

*   *   *

In his room, Chi-Wen tried to read the *Old Man and the Sea.*

"Now they have beaten me, he thought. I am too old to club sharks to death. But I will try it as long as I have the oars and the short club and the tiller." Santiago never lost his courage, fighting until the bitter end, even though he recognized the hopelessness of bringing in his fish. A nice story, but what did any of it have to do with him, with his life?

Chi-Wen slammed the book shut. Ever since his talk with Dr. Cheng, his mind kept wandering back to another meeting almost twenty-five years ago. As if it were yesterday, he could still remember:

The doleful quality in his father's voice imploring Chi-Wen to help him, to speak for him, to save him. *"Please."* So hard for a Chinese father to beg a son.

"I can not. " Not if he wanted to save himself.

The anguished look as his father recognized betrayal in Chi-Wen's eyes. *Father.*

He'd criticized him publicly, the despair and loss of face eventually had driven his father to suicide.

How could I have done that to you?

Lili had excused him, saying he was young—only 8 years old. But Chi-Wen could never adequately describe to her the pain he suffered still at the memory of his betrayal. Pain that beat like a hammer on the anvil of his soul. Always there.

Now Dr. Cheng was asking for his help. And like so many years ago, Chi-Wen was expected to betray someone he loved to save himself. A man who'd become almost a father to him.

He was preoccupied with Dr. Seng's ultimatum. Nine more days. That was his deadline. Time was running out.

Ren, joss. Doubt about the supreme validity of the Taoist Way had never troubled him before.

Hope? Love? He'd assumed that the liberation of the heart from the disruptive influence of unbridled passion, the spirit purified of desire, was the ideal to strive for; that the way of acceptance was superior to the way of action.

A black wave of despair, such as he had never known, washed over Chi-Wen. Alone, unable to think, he fled his room, seeking the anonymity of the street.

*   *   *

All afternoon Lili and Ni-Fu talked, trying to catch up on the many years lost between them. Dr. Seng had offered the meeting room just off his office: "Tonight we have a banquet planned. Right now you two should be alone."

Lili thought the gesture especially thoughtful, reinforcing her earlier reversal of opinion about the medical director.

Ni-Fu, of course, knew better and while he welcomed private time with Lili, was certain the room was bugged. No matter. For Lili's protection, he would not reveal the true nature of his work—at least not yet. He only spoke in generalities, preferring to gaze at his granddaughter—so much of Su-Wei and Qing Nan in her features—and learn about her life. In three hours he'd discovered a great deal about this beautiful independent-minded young woman who refused to learn Chinese, raced motorcycles in high school, spurned sororities in college, and fought for programs for the homeless in medical school. "So you didn't think your Dr. Trenton would give you the geriatrics fellowship over Ed Baxter. That's not the reason you decided to leave your residency and come to China, is it?"

"Why do you say that?"

"You don't strike me as someone who'd run away from anything."

It took her a moment to recover from surprise. He was so perceptive. "You're right. It wasn't that. It was everything at the same time—Dr. Trenton, Ed Baxter, Mrs. Manley, Mr. Sanderson, the fellowship, Dylan, Dr. Seng, mother's death. I needed to get away, to find myself." The moment the words tumbled out she realized how wholly American was the concept of finding oneself, how self-indulgent it must sound to someone living in China and she wanted to explain, but Ni-Fu said simply, "I understand."

So natural. As if he understood everything about her. Lili looked at her grandfather. Tall, thin, sharp cheekbones and smooth skin peculiarly ageless for a seventy-five year old man; dark, clear eyes that looked at the world with calm appraisal; this handsome, gray-haired man who spoke perfect English with the same British accent Chi-Wen had. He was a wonderful listener with the bedside manner of Marcus Welby.

She'd been flustered and nervous, talking too much, but then it wasn't every day you met a grandfather you grew up thinking was dead. Ni-Fu put her at ease, sometimes smiling, sometimes laughing as she shared the vignettes of her life. He listened and sympathized. A kind man, she thought, peering into his eyes; marveling at the comfortable intimacy that had sprung up so quickly between them. Only a short time and she felt she had always known him. "Mother loved you so much."

Ni-Fu's eyes filled. A whole lifetime lost. Was it worth the sacrifice? "Tell me, granddaughter, was your mother happy?"

Happy? How to answer? Lili remembered the picture of her parents standing together, not touching, not reacting for the camera. Not happy, not sad, just accepting. Contrasted with the one of Su-Wei as a child with her father. Ni-Fu would have remembered that little girl, confident, carefree as she held his hand. Probably the last time Su-Wei was really happy. Before her own mother died, before war broke out, before her life changed forever.

She touched the locket around her neck. *Someday I hope you will return to China for me. I will live in you now.*

Happy? Somewhere Su-Wei knew she had come home. "Yes, grandfather, I think she was happy".

Ni-Fu seemed comforted by her words. "I hope so."

Lili wanted to ask how he could have sent her off alone to America, but sensed this wasn't yet the time. Later she would press him about that and more. She sighed.

"What is it, child?"

"I'm overwhelmed. I mean finding you...alive... It's all such a shock..."

Ni-Fu took Lili's hand in his. "For both of us."

She smiled at him. "I am glad I came to China."

Ni-Fu would have liked to say he was glad too, but though he returned her smile, it was counterfeit, concealing his fear for this granddaughter he already loved.

*   *   *

After walking aimlessly for several hours, Chi-Wen found himself near Xin Cheng Square. As he rounded the corner, he saw a crowd of several hundred students and teachers from Jiaotong University demonstrating in front of the provincial government complex. More than a thousand citizens on both sides of the street joined in clapping hands and shouting slogans. "Down with guandao!", "Long live democracy!, "Down with rule by individuals, long live rule of law!", "Freedom of the press!"

So the winds of change were now blowing in Xi'an, Chi-Wen thought. For a second he was about to turn away and then, drawn by some irresistible force, he moved closer to several intense looking young men sharing a podium and a loudspeaker.

"Comrades, my name is Zheng Tu, " one of them announced in a clear high-pitched voice. "Two days ago more than thirty students were hurt by police who tried to stop us. A twenty-four hour curfew was imposed."

Grumbling from the crowd.

The dozen or so armed policemen who lined the periphery remained passive, but Chi-Wen wondered for how long.

"Do not despair, friends. We will not be defeated! Our pro-democracy movement is just beginning." Zheng jumped down from the podium to shake the hands of a few of the guards and suddenly cheers went up for the soldiers.

"People's police have the love of the people! "

"We love the police!"

"My good friend here, Chen Mingyuan, a philosopher from the Chinese Academy of Science, has come today to tell you that our Constitution guarantees freedom of speech, press and association and the right to demonstrate."

A burst of applause from the audience.

"Our leaders have trampled on the Constitution," Chen declared. "We defend it! Our rally is to get those in power to pay attention; to make them take a firm stand. We must straighten the bent backs of the old tree trunks!"

"Those old trunks love their power too much," someone in the crowd asserted. "They will never listen!"

"You cannot change the soup without changing the ingredients!" another agreed. "Forty years they have ruled. It is time to step down!"

"They will never give up their power and they have already shown they will use force against Chinese citizens who make peaceful statements in favor of democracy."

"Didn't Mao himself say that revolution is no picnic," another chided.

Zheng held up his hand for quiet. "We will accomplish our goal without violence as an example for our leaders. It will not be a battle of tanks and bullets. We will make a peaceful petition asking for negotiation." He held up a two-inch thick Xeroxed *Manual for Nonviolent Action*. "This is our weapon. We will fast and sit-in and parade and give out flowers until the People's Congress meets on June 20th."

Chi-Wen listened as Zheng spoke passionately of the problems. Like the words of student leaders in Guangchou and Shanghai, Chi-Wen knew them to be true. Demands for higher education, satisfactory jobs, decent housing, protection against arbitrary exercise of authority and a modicum of self-expression were justified. Unhappy memories of the Cultural Revolution and the struggle of recent economic reforms amid rampant government corruption fueled the protesters appetite for change. But could reasoning, parading, fasting, and flowers accomplish the peaceful end Zheng promised? Could it transform China into a country where one could live freely?

As if reading his mind, Zheng said: "Let me tell you a story of the swimmer who was picked out of her cradle by Olympic scouts, taken from her family and trained to be a star. She was lucky enough to get into an accident that ruined her swimming career. Now she's free to do something else with her life."

A rousing cheer.

"It is time we were free to do what we wish with our lives!"

A woman next to Chi-Wen gave a victory sign and at once the entire group raised their hands.

"Come on! Come on!" the woman elbowed Chi-Wen. "Aren't you going to join us?"

No longer deniable, he thought. It is changed. His life. Ever since he met Ni-Fu. And Lili. Feelings growing inside him for months suddenly overpowered him. His longing to right the wrong against his father, to cry out where he had been silent, to stand up against evil men like Seng and Lin, to fight for love was so intense he trembled with the pent up emotions of a lifetime. What was a future as a doctor if the price demanded was his soul? To betray his friend, to lose his love, to forsake his country?

Ren. For so many years he had endured. Could he continue?

Joss, he thought. Or was it?

Hope. Dr. Cheng said it was not dead. It merely needed to be rekindled.

"It is not dangerous to dream," Zheng declared.

"Well?"

Chi-Wen stared at the woman, waiting for his response.

"Will you join us?"

Of course, he knew the answer; had always known it somehow. I must not let this happen. Not to Ni-Fu. Not to Lili. Not to China.

Smiling, he raised both his hands in the sign of the V. "Yes, comrade. I will."

*   *   *

6:00 PM

Said to be the most intimate social contact available to Chinese not related to one another, the banquet offers a lot more than good food. It is a way of honoring special guests in a carefully controlled atmosphere of exaggerated conviviality.

Such was the case with the banquet prepared in Lili's honor. There was plenty of good natured teasing, lots of jokes, endless talk about food, but nothing that could be construed as serious fare. Lili didn't mind. It was the first time she had relaxed since arriving in Xi'an. Her cheeks flushed with too much *maotai*, the fiery 106 proof Chinese liquor, she found the ritual a delight.

Her only disappointment was that Chi-Wen had been seated at the far opposite side of the room. She had dressed especially carefully, her tight silk sheath accentuating her curves. The one time she caught him looking at her, his gaze quickly slid away. Well, damn it, if he wasn't interested in her, she'd ignore him as well.

At least a few dozen members of the Shaanxi Province Hospital and Xi'an Institute staff were seated at several round tables where all glasses were kept full and plates were piled high. Dishes were served according to the prescribed palate-stimulating sequence, starting with cold appetizers and continuing to over ten courses that balanced the five basic tastes of Chinese cuisine: sour, hot, bitter, sweet and salty. As guest of honor, Lili received the choicest part of the fish as well as the entire chicken drumstick. Out of politeness she continued to eat beyond bursting.

Dr. Seng who sat between Lili and her grandfather, stood and raised his glass for the third time. "We have welcomed our honored guest, Dr. Quan and we rejoice in this family coming together again," he said, pointing to Lili and Ni-Fu. "Now I would like all of you here to join me in a toast to their continued good fortune. "*Ganbei*." In the time-honored tradition. he emptied his glass with a single chug.

"*Ganbei*!" the crowd responded.

"To long life and happiness!"

Although Ni-Fu raised his glass, he was not fooled by the purpose of the evening. A staged presentation for his benefit alone, a

not-so- subtle reminder of who played which parts: Ni-Fu the puppet; Seng the puppeteer, pulling the puppet's strings even in the midst of this crowd. Seng understood only too well that China was a nation inured by thousands of years of feudalism. To expect a public outcry if one or two people quietly disappeared was to misunderstand the Chinese soul. Ni-Fu drained the bitter drink. "Ganbei!" Lili's view was blocked so she missed the look that passed between Seng and Ni-Fu. And even if she had seen it, she would never have appreciated its significance or the irony of that toast.

*   *   *

While Seng toasted, Chi-Wen left the room, indicating a need to relieve himself. Instead of heading for the toilet, he slipped into the administrative offices and turned on the fax. Carefully, his heart beating wildly, he dialed the memorized overseas number, then placed the message from his pocket into the machine. With the telephone lines controlled, this was the best way the students could inform the outside world of their activities.

The 'transmit' signal flashed briefly, then lost the connection.

Shit.

Chi-Wen stood back and expelled a long breath. How many minutes had passed? Three? Five? More? If he was away too long, he'd be missed. One more try.

Sweat formed on his brow. With shaking hands, he redialed the US number.

Shan !

It was only minutes, but seemed like an eternity. Nothing happened. *Come on!*

It had to work! With a muted beep, the fax came alive, slowly devouring the page, then, seconds later, like a ruminating cow, disgorging it again.

Quickly, Chi-Wen turned off the machine and slipped the page back into his pocket. As his racing heart gradually returned to normal, he experienced the exhilaration of success. He had taken a risk, challenged fate. And it had been so easy.

Smiling to himself, he remembered. Lili would say it had been 'a piece of cake!'

*   *   *

Seoul, Korea

When David arrived at his father's home in Kwahun, a fashionable suburb of Seoul, he was surprised to find the senior Kim at the dining table, surrounded by the managers and division heads of Kim Company including his cousin and rival.

"Please sit." His father nodded toward the vacant chair beside him.

A white-gloved young woman served him *sinsallo*, a casserole of vegetables and eggs mixed with pine and ginkgo nuts, *kimchi* and bean curd cakes while another filled his glass with *sujonggwa*, a drink made with persimmons and ginger.

"What is the occasion?" David asked.

"Hangwap."

"But your birthday isn't until next month."

The senior Kim nodded. "If I had time, we would wait. As it is, time is a commodity I am short on." A sudden pain produced a grimace. "I am dying."

David's reaction was genuine grief. He loved his father as much as he feared him. "I didn't know."

"None of you did," he replied, addressing the table. "But now it is clear that I will not last another fortnight." Shin-yung Kim waved away the whispered murmurs of concern. "I am satisfied by the latest financial reports from our China operations that David is a suitable heir to Kim Company." He reached out in a rare physical gesture to grip his son's arm. "It is time for you to take over."

"I don't know what to say."

"Nothing to say. Just make me proud." The senior Kim smiled through his pain. "Now, I hope all of you will join with me in a toast to my son's success as our new chairman."

"To our new chairman!"

"*Gunbai* !"

David was so overwhelmed he barely heard the congratulations or tasted his *sujonggwa*; his only thought, Kim Company was finally his. In a few weeks he'd have the secret and the future of his *choebel* would be secure forever.

*   *   *

Xi'an, China

In her room after dinner, Lili found the covers on her bed turned down and her pajamas laid on the pillow. Who was responsible for that little gesture? A parody of gentility in a country without hot water or indoor plumbing. Had the man or woman who unpacked her pajamas also been through her things? There wasn't anything of value, but she checked her suitcase anyway. Dylan's fax was still on the bottom of the case where she'd hidden it under her blouses. Nothing seemed to have been disturbed, though of course she couldn't tell for sure.

Well, no matter. Too groggy from *maotai* to speculate further, she turned off the overhead light and got into bed. The cicadas had begun their evening lullaby. Closing her eyes she had a glimmer of a thought, like a curtain fluttering in her mind—something about a locked room. But as quickly as it came, it disappeared and she drifted into an alcohol-induced sleep.

*   *   *

Seoul, Korea

Later that evening Shin-yung Kim fell into a deep coma from which he never awakened. With the confirmation of death, his body was covered with a quilt and arranged to face south. Although he'd requested no formal wailing or *kok* , David, the eldest male member of the family, followed the ancient tradition of *ch'ohon* by carrying his father's coat to the roof of the house, crying loudly for his soul to return to the body.

TWENTY

Wednesday, April 26th
Xi'an, China

Ni-Fu put his fingers to his lips, then turned up the speed of the centrifuge. "The walls have ears." He moved closer.

Chi-Wen nodded. "I've thought about your plan. The American embassy may be reluctant to provide sanctuary if they feel it could jeopardize relations with China."

"You have a better idea?"

"I might." Without explaining Ni-Fu's role in his epiphany, Chi-Wen told the professor he was now committed to the student movement. "I have decided to question."

Ni-Fu placed his hand on Chi-Wen's shoulder. "That is good, son. Be careful."

"Don't worry," Chi-Wen assured him. "The students are setting up an underground network to help political dissidents escape to Hong Kong. "I've agreed to help them transmit messages to the West. Perhaps in exchange I can convince them to help you."

Ni-Fu considered the idea. "It's a good contingency plan."

"By May 4th everything should be in place. Will you be ready?"

"Report to Dr. Seng that I'm perfecting the formula. Tell him I need to complete one last experiment."

"Okay."

"Tell him he'll have what he wants on his desk by the deadline." Ni-Fu didn't mention he'd already altered the potion he'd been giving to the thirty old souls imprisoned in the Institute's Longevity wing. It would take nine days for the reversal to take effect; for the aging process to accelerate. By May 4th, they would die.

He touched his jaw; the recurrent ache was increased by anxiety. Everyone dead. Including himself. No regrets. No second thoughts. This was the only way to get his secret safely out of China. Lili would have to make her escape alone. With Chi-Wen, she'd be in good hands. "I'm proud of you, son."

"You said hope was not dead."

"So I did."

"Why all the whispering? Am I interrupting?" It was Lili, dressed in navy slacks and a plain cotton blouse.

Even without make-up, Chi-Wen thought she looked beautiful. His eyes feasted on her hair and eyes and lips. Desire was like a fever. It took all his self-control to contain his feelings.

Brushing past him without even a 'good morning', Lili placed a kiss on Ni-Fu's cheek. "I hoped to catch you on rounds, but I overslept. That *maotai* is unbelievable."

"*Jiu bu zui ren ren zi zui ; she bu me ren ren zi me ,*" Chi-Wen remarked softly.

"Do you mind translating?"

"Just an old Chinese saying," Chi-Wen said.

"What does it mean?"

"'It is not wine that intoxicates people, they intoxicate themselves...' You had more than a few glasses."

"I didn't realize you were counting." Despite her tone, Lili flushed with pleasure knowing he'd noticed.

For a brief moment, his dark eyes bore into hers. Then, he quickly averted his gaze.

Insufferable! Lili thought.

Ni-Fu interrupted the uncomfortable silence. "Perfect timing." He stopped the centrifuge, its purpose as background noise fulfilled, and emptied the water-filled glass cartridges. "Chi-Wen and I are finished. I postponed rounds."

"Great." She looked around the lab. " Dr. Seng told me about your research…"

The glass dropped from Ni-Fu's hand. "…using Chinese herbs as medication."

Shattering into a dozen tiny shards on the floor.

"You've cut yourself," Lili cried, hurrying to help him.

"No, I'm fine. It's just a nick." Ni-Fu wrapped a handkerchief around his fifth finger. "Did Dr. Seng tell you anything else?"

"Anything else?"

"About my work."

She noticed his upset, misdiagnosed the cause. "Don't be angry with Dr. Seng, grandfather. He said you've discovered some innovative drugs for hypertension and diabetes. Nothing more specific."

"I see."

"He told me that after I insisted he explain the roundabout way he lured me to China. I understand your research must be kept secret. It's no different in the US."

Chi-Wen chose that moment to head for the door.

"Aren't you coming?" Lili queried, weakening in her resolve to ignore him.

He stopped and turned around slowly. "I must meet with Dr. Seng."

"What about my *tai-chi* lessons? Have you given up on me?"

His face seemed troubled. "You'd have to make it very early."

"Say when."

"First thing tomorrow morning. In the courtyard. Five o'clock."

"Fine."

He nodded, then abruptly disappeared.

"You know Chi-Wen didn't complete the translation of that old saying."

Lili turned back to her grandfather. "Oh?"

"'*Jiu bu zui ren ren zi zui*—It is not wine that intoxicates people, they intoxicate themselves; *she bu me ren ren zi me*—neither do women beguile men, men beguile themselves.'"

"What are you telling me?"

"Chi-Wen loves you."

"He has an odd way of showing it."

Ni-Fu shook his head. "Though I haven't left China for forty years, I suspect one thing that has remained the same the world over is the tumultuous nature of the human heart." Thinking of his years with Qing-Nan, he sighed. "No matter what else you find on this earth, Lili, remember one thing. Without love, life is not worth living." He put an arm around her. "You love him too, don't you?"

She did not answer at first, searching for the proper response. "I'm not sure, grandfather, I think I do."

"Then take the advice of an old man. If you do, stick with him."

*   *   *

Washington, DC
13 hours earlier

"Do you have the elixir?"

Halliday recognized Carpenter's voice. "Damn it, Marty, I told you not to call me. I'll call you."

"But I'm in trouble here. Aligen just posted first quarter losses that could mean a pink slip for me."

"Don't you think you're being a bit paranoid, old friend? You've been with the company over twenty years."

"Seniority in the private sector doesn't mean diddly-squat. You were smart to opt for a secure government job."

Halliday winced at the unintended jab.

"Two VP's from marketing were canned last week. Both were with Aligen almost as long. With the economy going to hell, everybody's downsizing. I'm telling you, I'm next. I feel it." He spoken rapidly, without a pause.

"Calm down. What do you want me to do?"

"The project I funded at LA Medical is going nowhere. If I could announce a potential winner on the horizon, I'd have a shot. Do you happen to know if this concoction is an herb?"

"Why, would that present a problem?"

"Not at all. Americans spend over eight billion dollars a year on prescription drugs derived from plants. The World Health Organization estimates eighty percent of the world relies on traditional botanical medicines for primary health care."

"So if it turns out to be a natural substance, the potential market would be huge."

"Right. Now what do you say, Charlie, can I leak it to my boss?"

"Still too early. But listen, we're talking a month at the most. Can't you hold out? You'd look like a fool if this is all a hoax."

"I guess you're right."

"Thatta boy. How about dinner tomorrow? We'll discuss it over steaks and beer."

"Like old times. Sounds good."

"Meet you at Roxbury Park near the bridge. Eight sharp. And do me a favor."

"Sure."

"Don't mention our meeting to anyone. Until this operation's over, it's all got to be on the QT."

"I understand."

Hanging up, Halliday took a deep breath. Damn it, that was close. He never counted on Carpenter being a problem. On the other hand, what was one more problem when you were talking about a potential billion dollar payoff?

*   *   *

Xi'an, China

Chi-Wen endured the prolonged scrutiny by staring a foot above the medical director's head, toward the bottom edge of a framed portrait of Deng.

"So, the good doctor has finally agreed to give us his formula," Seng said at last.

"Yes. Once he completes one final experiment."

"He understands there can be no extension?"

"He understands." Chi-Wen stammered, avoiding direct eye contact.

"Good." The medical director stood, signaling the conclusion of the meeting. "A week from now I expect to be shaking your hand for a job well done."

Chi-Wen made a quick exit.

Too easy, too pat, Seng thought, staring after him.

A moment later he called for the young cadre waiting just outside. "Follow him!"

*   *   *

Ni-Fu nodded towards the patient. "Mr. Jing was admitted complaining of fatigue as well as total body edema." He pointed to the swelling of the man's limbs and abdomen. "A physician practicing traditional Eastern medicine would say Mr. Jing has the pattern of 'deficient kidney fire, unable to rule water'. He would prescribe warming herbs, including aconite and the use of moxibustion, burning substances such as mugwort to stimulate specific acupuncture points."

"Would that treatment work?"

"It helps. Aconite is a potent cardiotonic. Chinese medicine describes it as a warmer of the kidneys which are said to rule the grasping of *ch'i*. "

"Fascinating," Lili exclaimed. "So some ancient medicine was somewhat scientific."

"Of over three thousand extracts I have tested in the last forty years, more than two hundred have shown biological activity. From the *ma huang* twig, a time honored Chinese cure for asthma, I extracted ephedrine. Chinese rhubarb, *ta huang*, contains the same active ingredient as cascara root and senna leaves, widely used as a laxative. I also found an analgesic, a muscle relaxant that could aid delivery and an anti-depressant."

Lili was impressed. She could understand Dr. Seng's concern about secrecy.

"Unfortunately," her grandfather lamented, "the work is painfully slow. Most prescriptions contain five to ten ingredients traditionally brewed in water or soaked in wine; the resulting liquid drunk like tea. What happens when the herbs react with each other during preparation, not to mention the chemical reactions in the stomach, is still a big mystery." He smiled at her. "It's like trying to determine the nature of an egg by analyzing an omelet."

She laughed as they moved to the next patient.

By late afternoon, Lili and her grandfather had examined and discussed most of the patients on the geriatrics ward. More than grandfather and grand-daughter, they were colleagues, sharing their medical knowledge and experiences. It was another bond between them—based not on genealogy, but on mutual professional respect.

Lili updated Ni-Fu on the latest treatment for scleroderma—plasmaphoresis—making her grandfather aware of how isolated from advances in Western medicine he'd been here in Xi'an; Ni-Fu demonstrated a case of ginseng overdose that she'd misdiagnosed as Cushing's syndrome, a disease caused by the body's excess cortisol production.

"You're not way off base. The steroid in the ginseng root causes the same result," he said, pointing to the man's moon face and buffalo hump. It's a common home therapy for impotence. Legend has it that the more the root looks like a human figure, the better it works."

Lili laughed. "When you hear hoof beats, think horses, not zebras."

"Pardon me?"

"Oh, a lesson we were taught in med school. Don't diagnose exotic diseases when there's a more obvious explanation for your patient's symptoms. In China, think ginseng, whereas in the US, adrenal tumor might be more likely."

Ni-Fu nodded.

"I must tell you, grandfather, I'm surprised most of your cases are similar to mine."

"Because of the improved overall delivery of health care," Ni-Fu explained, "Chinese are living into the seventh decade. With longer life comes newer diseases. Less than twenty years ago, when life expectancy was fifty, this hospital handled very few cases of heart disease, stroke, cancer or Alzheimer's."

It was the same in the States. "Chronic diseases," Lili agreed. "That's what geriatrics is about. Until someone comes up with a way to slow down or stop the aging process altogether." She thought of Dylan, wondering how his research was coming. "That would be something, wouldn't it?"

Ni-Fu looked off into some private distance, letting the question hang. "Come," he said, putting his arm around her. "We have a few more patients to see and I have a political meeting before dinner."

*   *   *

Los Angeles
LA Medical Center
16 hours earlier

Dylan studied the latest batch of electron micrographs and shook his head.

Damn. Still no good. He pulled his lab book from his desk and noted that as of April 25 at 9:15 PM, sample # 12 was still inert.

No change! Another promising lead fizzled. His project remained stalled at the same point it had been almost six months ago. No breakthroughs after so much work. Grand expectations turning into false hopes. He was growing desperate. None of his experiments so far could explain how the main histocompatibility complex regulated DNA repair.

Dylan washed down a bite of tuna sandwich with a cup of coffee from his thermos. Leaning back, he gazed out the window. A Santa Ana condition had blown the smog out to sea so that the Santa Monica mountains in the distance stood sharply against the night sky as if etched by a jeweler's hand. His genetically inbred mice roamed noisily around their cages, but he was used to them, easily tuning out their squeaky chatter, so no sounds intruded on his thoughts.

He had always preferred the solitude of the laboratory to the tumult of the hospital and patients. That's what he tried to explain to Lili. Research, though, was no bed of roses. It came with its own pressures—impossible grant deadlines, Institutional Review Boards requiring reams of paperwork for a single modification to an experiment already authorized, people like Aligen's Martin Carpenter who assumed funding your work meant owning you too.

He spent several more minutes admiring the view before making another entry in his lab book: sample #13. Yawning. He'd probably be here all night. Well, no matter. He wasn't giving up. None of these pressures could compete with his own blind ambition—driving him to succeed at all costs.

*   *   *

Beijing, China

A smile crossed General Tong's face as he perused the editorial in the People's Daily. Excellent, he thought, reading the quotes lifted from Deng's speech at the secret Politburo meeting yesterday. Even better that Zhao Ziyang, on a state visit to Korea, had been absent from that session.

"A handful of people with ulterior motives... have resorted to big-and small-character posters to smear, scold and attack our Party and government leaders. They have wantonly violated the Constitution to advocate opposition to the Communist Party's leadership and the socialist system. They have established illegal organizations in some universities to seize power from the official students' unions.

Some have instigated class boycotts in schools, using force to prevent students from attending class. They have pirated names of workers' organizations to spread counter-revolutionary leaflets. A well-organized conspiracy to sow chaos... to poison people's minds, sabotage political stability and create national turmoil."

Tong was pleased. By branding the student movement a "turmoil" or *dongluan*, Deng had finally sent a clear message that student protests would no longer be tolerated. He knew the word had powerful resonance because it evoked memories of the nightmarish Cultural Revolution, often referred to as "ten years of turmoil". Deng obviously intended to identify dissent with a chaotic period in Chinese history and thereby galvanize popular support for government repression.

Deng's message was clear. Any citizen reading the editorial would understand that participation in this movement meant defiance of Deng himself—and that would be tantamount to treason.

*　　　　*　　　　*

Macao

"So you heard?"

"Of course," Ng told the caller, drawing hard on his cigarillo. "Information on my side of the Pacific is as up to the minute as yours."

"No doubt," the caller chuckled. "It's why you and I make such good partners."

Ng plucked the tojang from his desk. "With David Kim officially head of Kim Company we can safely accelerate the second phase of our plan. Do you agree?"

"Absolutely. Have you thought about what to do with him once we've accomplished our goal?"

This time it was Ng's turn to laugh, but not a chuckle—it was the insane, maniacal laugh of a dangerous man. "Absolutely. We will kill him."

*　　　　*　　　　*

Beijing, China

If the editorial in the People's Daily was meant to frighten the students, it had the opposite effect. "An outrage," a Beijing University student declared, "its verbiage sounds like a Cultural Revolution tirade." After a lengthy debate, the students decided to call Deng's bluff by organizing a gigantic march the next day. That evening many prepared for what they thought would be their final conflict by writing "last wills" exchanging farewell toasts and sharing a last supper.

*   *   *

Xi'an, China

The hot night air trapped her in its moist embrace.

Faster, faster, she urged her weary feet. Lili wiped perspiration from her brow as she ran. She had to find him before they caught her.

Grandfather!

Heart pounding, she ran down one winding corridor after another; a rat in maze, unsure which way to go.

It is a very difficult and dangerous journey.

Screaming: *Where are you?*

Lili, is that you?

Somewhere in the distance, a shadowy figure waved to her.

Grandfather?

She ran toward the shadow. A man in a white suit vanished in a cloud of cigar smoke and another appeared.

You have come home, my dear.

She couldn't see his face, but the words. Oh my God. It was Dr. Seng!

I'm looking for my grandfather. Where is he?

Laughing, his hand outstretched. *Come home...*

Yes !

Suddenly there were others, all smiling and holding out their hands to her: the people she'd met on the steamer, the girl in the book shop, Fan Zhou, Chi-Wen's aunt.

Come home.

Where is my grandfather?

The figures reached out and almost touched her, but she turned and ran.

Faster, faster. Her breath was ragged as she hurried down the seemingly endless corridor.

A door. She turned the knob. It wouldn't budge.

Help me ! she screamed, pounding on the door. *Chi-Wen? I need you.*

You are becoming a true Chinese.

Chi-Wen, is that you? Help me!

I can not.

Louder and louder, she heard the pounding.

"Lili?"

A tap on her shoulder.

She was afraid to turn around.

"Lili?" Shaking her. "Wake up!"

Bathed in sweat, Lili opened her eyes. Chi-Wen sat on the edge of her bed, a concerned expression on his face. "What are you doing here?"

"I waited in the courtyard to begin your *tai-chi* lesson. When I heard your screams, I ran up."

"The door was locked."

"Doors are never locked in China."

Her head felt fuzzy, her heart only now beginning to slow down. "I was dreaming. A nightmare." It was still dark in the room. "What time is it?"

"A little after five." He paused. The desire to touch her was almost overwhelming, but he forced himself to suppress his emotions. For her sake, he told himself. "Are you all right?"

She nodded. "Yes, it's fading now. Just images, nothing concrete. I dreamed my grandfather was..." she searched through her mind, "lost. Somewhere in the Institute. A locked room. I called to you, but," she looked thoughtfully at him, "you said you couldn't help me."

A stab of fear pricked Chi-Wen's heart. "Just a dream," he said, but he held her gaze for a long time before he rose from the bed.

"Where are you going?"

"I shouldn't be here. I'll wait for you outside."

"Chi-Wen?"

"Yes?"

"Please," she whispered, reaching for his hand. "Don't leave. Not yet." Without thinking, Lili pulled him close to her. She shook her head: "For God's sake. I'm in love with you. Can't you see that?" It had come to her in that instant, clear and definite. The answer to her grandfather's question. "I love you," she repeated.

The sweet scent of her skin filled him and unable to fight his own emotions, he found himself returning her embrace. "And I you," he murmured as his lips met hers.

TWENTY-ONE

Thursday, April 27th
Xi'an, China

Two hours later their bodies were still entwined.

Lili stirred, opening her eyes. "Good morning."

"Did you sleep well?"

She nestled her head into his shoulder. "No dreams this time. And you?"

"I dreamt of the clouds and rain."

Lili smiled, recalling Dorothy's speculation that Asian men were all tigers in bed. "We Chinese do have such a poetic way of describing lovemaking, don't we?"

"You have definitely become a true Chinese." Chi-Wen gathered her hair, loosely twisting it in his hands and softly kissing the nape of her neck. "So beautiful Your body. Your name…"

"What about it?"

"Li Li." He pronounced it the Chinese way. "Flower." A soft sigh passed his lips. "I can't believe you'll be leaving China." He never meant for the words to slip out.

"I'm not leaving for a while yet. "

"I know." He tried to recover. "It just seems so soon."

Her fingertip traced its way down the line of his jaw. "Are you planning to miss me?"

He looked at her for a long time. "Is there someone missing you in America?"

"You are one weird Chinaman, Chi-Wen Zhou," she teased.

"When we first met, you hardly noticed me. In Changsha, we became close enough for you to share your past. We made love in Shanghai. Two days ago, you were cold again and now…"

"Now?"

"Now I believe you're showing signs of jealousy."

"You didn't answer my question."

"It's a silly question."

"Lili…" His words coming with difficulty. "I am serious. I know about Dylan."

"You read my fax!" she snapped.

"Yes."

Her cheeks flushed angrily. "I know there's no word for privacy in China, but that doesn't mean you can read my mail."

"I'm sorry." He took her hand and held it tightly. She couldn't pull away. "Growing up, I never saw people hold hands; never saw married people touch one another. Not even my own parents. It wasn't the custom in China to show affection publicly. It's changing, but only among the younger generation". He shook his head. "Do you remember telling me in the garden at Suzhou how you struggled all your life against being different?"

Lili nodded.

"I didn't tell you then how much I envied you. In your country you can be different. Here it is almost impossible." He looked at her. "I've been so lonely, Lili. For so long. Then I met you in Guangchou. You thought I despised you…" He sighed. "It was hardly that. I was afraid."

"Afraid?"

"Yes." He couldn't tell her everything, but everything he told her was true. "I never thought I could ever love someone. Not like this."

Shaken, seeing his vulnerability, Lili's anger turned to tenderness. She took his other hand and drew him toward her. "It's all right. " She closed her arms around him. "Dylan and I are just friends. It's you I love."

"I'm glad." Together like this, they were in a tiny world, cocooned against the outside. Nothing else mattered. "Lili, I love you so much," he whispered. " So... hopelessly," he added.

His lips met hers, muffling the words. I'll never stop loving you, not ever, he thought. Even if in the end we cannot be together.

*   *   *

Beijing, China

Only 8:00 AM and Lee Tong, sitting in his director's office at the Beijing No. 1 MSG Factory, was already staring at his first crisis of the day. A big one: his factory was short of raw materials. Low government prices were discouraging farmers from growing soybeans and supplies had shrunk, throwing factories like his into a turmoil. Already several MSG companies had been forced to close.

During the daily meeting with his top aides, Tong presented an emergency plan. One vice-director was to go to their usual supplier and purchase as much as available—even if he had to pay a premium. Another would try scavenging from their competition. Tong would lean on his contact through the government supplier, a longtime personal friend of his father, the general. He'd ask for an increase in his monthly quota at the state subsidized price—fifty-five percent below market.

"It helps to have connections," one assistant said.

"With a little luck," another chimed in, " the enterprise can locate enough material to keep operating for at least few months".

Yes, Tong thought, as he wrestled a cigarette from a limp pack of Kents. And with a little luck, well before then Dr. Cheng would reveal the secret of his longevity elixir and he could chuck the MSG business altogether.

*   *   *

Washington, DC

Halliday opened the door to the parked black Lincoln Town Car and slipped into the passenger seat. "This sure beats my beat-up '82 Pontiac."

Carpenter shrugged. "One of the perquisites of working for a big firm. Aligen leases a fleet of these."

"Nice," Halliday said, caressing the leather seat. He opened the brown bag he carried with him and removed a bottle of Cutty Sark and one glass.

"What's that for?"

Halliday poured a glass and handed it to Carpenter . "Here, have a drink."

"Now? Can't it wait until we get to the restaurant?"

As Carpenter started to hand the glass back, Halliday drew a 357 Magnum from the bag and leveled it straight at his friend. "Not really."

"Come on, Charlie, is this some kind of joke?"

"No joke. It's really pretty straight-forward. I'm going to kill you."

Carpenter's voice filled with panic. "But why? What did I do?"

"It's more a question of what you didn't do," Halliday replied evenly. "I needed you to provide a cover while Lili Quan was in LA. Once she left for China, your job was done. Had you kept quiet, this might not have been necessary." He waved the gun in Carpenter's direction. "In about a month, I'd have called to tell you the intelligence information we received from China was false and that no longevity drug existed."

He pointed to Carpenter's glass. "Drink that. You've got a whole bottle to finish and my story won't take that long."

Reluctantly, Carpenter downed the scotch.

"Good." Halliday refilled his glass. "See, I never planned to give Aligen the secret. For one thing, I'd have a lot to explain to my boss at the Company."

"You said this was a CIA operation."

"I'm in the CIA, aren't I?" Halliday's laugh was sinister. He shook his head. "This was strictly my operation. A one man show. A few months back, I happened to intercept a routine intelligence report on Chinese traveling to the US. When I saw Dr. Seng's name, I remembered he'd been on an old list of operatives out of Russia in the '60's. Then a buddy in the China section of MI-5 sent me the internal memo from the Chinese Foreign Ministry. Based on

Browning's testimony after the war, the Brits were convinced Cheng couldn't possibly have solved the secret of longevity. Didn't think it was worth digging into their budget to finance a look-see."

Halliday took a slug from the bottle. "That's the trouble with bureaucracies. Penny wise and pound foolish. Their loss, right? The way I figure, the money from Cheng's discovery will set me up for the rest of my days." He laughed again. "I probably won't even mind the alimony checks anymore."

"Okay, so don't give Aligen the drug. But why kill me? I won't say a word."

Halliday's voice filled with genuine sorrow. "I'm afraid you've played your part."

"For God's sake, Charlie, I've got a wife and kids."

"They'd be better off without you. You said it yourself, you're due for a pink slip." He gestured to the glass and Carpenter gulped his second whiskey. "If you have a little accident because you drank too much and drove off this bridge, your family collects the insurance. College tuition, the house payments, everything taken care of. Actually," he said, handing the bottle to Carpenter. "When you think of it, I'm a godsend."

"Please..." Carpenter began to sob. "Don't do this."

Halliday leaned back against the car seat and sighed. "I don't relish an embarrassing scene. Do me a favor, Marty."

"I'll do anything, anything..."

Halliday looked at him for a long time, then said: "Finish the bottle and die like a man."

TWENTY-TWO

Friday, April 28th through Monday, May 1st

Over the next few days, Lili quickly fell into a routine: *tai-chi* with Chi-Wen at dawn, rounds with her grandfather in the morning, acupuncture clinic in the afternoon when Ni-Fu attended political meetings or begged off to do his research. She eagerly immersed herself in Chinese medicine. Fascinating how so many physicians integrated Eastern and Western methods of treatment; their results were impressive. She anticipated sharing her insights with colleagues back home.

Home.

Suddenly Los Angeles seemed a universe away.

I can't believe you'll be leaving soon.

Lili shook her head. She wouldn't deal with that now. She was happy here. In only a few weeks, China had changed her.

You will lose part of yourself before you find yourself. The fortune teller's words. In that sense, she supposed, he'd been right. She'd found her Chinese self here—in Shanghai's streets and Changsha's monuments; in students' defiant shouts and oldsters' nervous whispers; in the sweet smell of peonies and the sharp taste of Hunan peppers; in her grandfather's quiet, distracted gestures; in unexpected moments of intimacy with Chi-Wen. In losing part of herself, she had found her roots. She *had* come home. Full circle. *Always return to the center of the circle.*

She wasn't ready to think about leaving. Not yet. Today she wanted everything to remain as it was. Like Scarlet O'Hara, she'd think about it all tomorrow.

                    *   *   *

Chi-Wen's involvement in the student movement rapidly intensified. He continued to fax reports to the outside world late at night. During the days, while scheduled to work in Dr. Cheng's lab, he slipped away to help the students prepare for their demonstrations.

On April 27th, more than a hundred thousand students descended on Tiananmen Square, joined by one million Beijing residents. Xi'an also staged its biggest anti-government demonstration in the forty year history of the PRC. Singing the national anthem 'March of the Volunteers' and the Internationale, students broke through police barricades and charged down the streets calling for democratic reform, freedom of the press, *toumingdu* or openness in official matters and an end to abuses by officials.

"Don't hit them!" people in the crowd shouted at the line of policemen. "Like watching an iron bar bend", one bystander remarked joyfully.

Because Zheng Tu had urged him to remain under cover, Chi-Wen observed from a safe distance. Exposure would mean more than mere censure, Tu had warned. "By telling the world what's happening, you are helping us in the best way you can." He had proven himself to be one of them.

Still, the sight of the marchers stirred feelings he hadn't experienced for so long. As if he had awakened from a long dream, from a sojourn in a passionless world. Suddenly, a strong sense of purpose and meaning directed his life. Perhaps, everyone *did* have an ultimate destiny. It was all going to happen anyway. But maybe Lili was right too. Maybe that shouldn't prevent you from reaching that destiny in the manner you chose.

"They've agreed to a dialogue!" a student leader announced to the crowd after talking by phone to his counterpart in Beijing.

Surprised by massive public support for the widespread student demonstrations, government leaders had obviously miscalculated the mood of the people. The crowd was jubilant.

"What will you do if Party officials reject your demands?" Chi-Wen asked his new friend.

"There is always May 4th," Tu replied. "An auspicious date, don't you agree?"

Chi-Wen felt a tremor of apprehension; a chilling breeze in that tropical heat. May 4th. An auspicious date indeed. The fate of everything and everyone he loved might well be decided that day.

*   *   *

In the shadows farther down the street, a cadre stood, silently watching, carefully noting every move so as not to forget a single detail when he reported back to Dr. Seng.

*   *   *

Washington, D.C.

News of Martin Carpenter's death was carried in the Wall Street Journal, both the US and Far East editions: "Car Over Bridge; VP of Aligen Drowns in Potomac". According to the account, the victim had been drinking heavily and crashed through a guard rail, plunging into the river. While there had been early speculation that Carpenter, distraught over Aligen's losses that quarter might have tried suicide, insurance investigators were now satisfied his death was indeed an accident.

Although most who read the article concurred, one individual with serious doubts was determined to conduct his own investigation.

TWENTY-THREE

Tuesday, May 2
Seoul, Korea

The *ch'ulssang* or carrying of the bier to the grave site was accomplished with much fanfare.

The coffin itself was built of six planks of wood, each eight centimeters thick—the heaven plank, the earth plank, and the east, west, south and north planks. Inscribed inside the top was the Chinese character for heaven; the character for sea, at each of the four corners. Once the top was nailed down, the name Shin-yung Kim was written on it. Decorated with banners and paper flowers, his bier was borne on the shoulders of relatives and members of the funeral *kye* , preceded by friends holding funeral flags and burning incense. David, as the eldest son, was followed by the rest of the mourners, all dressed in black with armbands of coarse ramie fabric.

After arriving at the grave site, which had been prepared to exact specifications divined by the geomancer, incense burned and the grave was cleansed of evil spirits. Amid formal bows and appropriate wailing, David watched the coffin slowly lowered into the pit.

I have fulfilled my filial duties according to the basic teachings of Confucius. Though I have not always honored you in life, in death I have shown the proper respect for my ancestors. Good-bye, father.

Sighing, he turned toward his waiting limousine. Going through the ritual burial had liberated him. It was time to begin living his own life, free from his father's disapproval. From now on, he would do things *his* way.

As he slid into the back seat , a manicured hand reached out to him. "*Shillye-hamnida*. I'm sorry, cheri."

"Camille, what are you doing here?"

"I came to be with you, darling," she purred, "to take your mind off your sorrow." She tapped the closed glass partition, directing the driver to Tuksom Track. "I have a tip on a filly running in the fourth race. If we hurry, we'll make it before the gate closes."

David was aroused by Camille's closeness. Her perfume hinted of lilacs and jasmine. "I should go to the office."

Her eyes half-mocking. "I thought you were in charge now." Moving still closer, her hands began to loosen his belt. "Surely the boss can take one day off." Her voice a husky whisper.

The boss. It sounded good. David's heart pounded as Camille unzipped his trousers. "I guess you're right."

Her hand encompassed his throbbing shaft. "Of course I'm right."

By the time the limo passed the Kim Building, resolve to visit the office had slipped away. If David had entered, he would have noticed unusual activity on the South Korean Composite. Someone was buying up huge blocks of Kim Company stock in David Kim's name.

*   *   *

Xi'an, China
midnight

It felt so right. Lying in Chi-Wen's arms. Everything new and exciting, yet old and familiar. They had made love twice, quickly, and then an hour later, a third time, more slowly. It was as if they were trying to store memories—just in case—each afraid to discuss the possibility of future separation.

When they were both exhausted, Lili lay, content, in his arms, her head resting on his chest. "Are you being careful enough?"

"No one was watching when I slipped into your room. I'm sure. And I'll leave well before morning."

"I meant your work with the students. Grandfather told me what you're doing."

"He shouldn't have."

"It *is* dangerous, isn't it?"

He kissed the tip of her nose. "I'll be fine."

"Why are you doing it?"

Chi-Wen sighed. "For a lot of reasons—family, country, you."

"Me?"

"You've been my inspiration. Your Mr. Hemingway made me see there may be something beyond blindly following one's 'duty'."

Lili smiled. "I must have been seven or eight years old when I questioned my Chinese tutor. He taught me the five bonds Confucius claimed as the true basis for an orderly life."

"You remember them?"

"Wives must be subject to husbands, children to parents, brothers and sisters to the eldest brother, friendships subordinated to family relationships and everyone subject to the ruler."

"No doubt that didn't sit too well with the independent Lili Quan."

"No doubt," Lili laughed. "Poor mother. She never understood my need to be my own person."

"She wouldn't. She was born here. It must have been hard for her—10 years old, steeped in Chinese customs and culture—to flee to a foreign country."

Lili understood that more easily now that she had seen China. "It was," she agreed. "Mother had no one to help her adjust to her new life."

"I thought she was sent to your grandfather's sister."

"Yes, but Auntie Tan was old and as wedded to the ancient ways as mother." Lili looked into Chi-Wen's eyes. "You, on the other hand, would have me."

For a moment, Chi-Wen did not respond. There it was. Even though unspoken, they knew what she meant. "That would be wonderful," he said finally, shutting his eyes to hide his doubts and fears. "Wonderful," he whispered, holding her close, matching his breathing to hers, until both of them finally drifted off to sleep.

*   *   *

"And they are together now?" Dr. Seng questioned the cadre whose telephone call had just disturbed his own sleep.

"Yes, sir. Shall I arrest him?" Even with the relative easing of restrictions between the sexes, Chi-Wen's punishment for cohabitation would, at the very least, be expulsion from the Institute.

"No. Let them be. For now. Continue to keep watch. Report to me in the morning."

"Yes, sir." The cadre clicked off.

Seng returned to bed, lost in thought. Something was up. He was sure of it. Some kind of double cross. He didn't believe for a moment that Ni-Fu would reveal his secret so easily—even with his granddaughter's life in jeopardy. As long as he kept his eye on Lili and Chi-Wen, he was certain he'd discover it. Seng wanted them to feel as free as possible.

Patience.

Very soon, like unsuspecting insects tiptoeing onto the web, they'd be ensnared in the spider's trap.

*   *   *

Five AM.

A sudden urgency in her bladder aroused Lili from a deep sleep. She sat up, forcing her way back to consciousness. In the half-light of pre-dawn, she could see the gentle rise and fall of Chi-Wen's breathing. She'd expected him to be gone by now. Well, she'd wake him the moment she returned.

She pulled on her jeans and a T-shirt, cursing the location of the community bathroom at the far end of the hallway. If not for the overwhelming mephitis of human waste, she might have missed it in the darkness. Squatting over the open hole in the floor, Lili wondered how people survived without simple flush toilets. But then, she speculated, what they hadn't experienced, they couldn't miss.

She rose, splashed a few drops of water coaxed from the rusty faucet, wiped her hands on her jeans (in lieu of hand towels) and backed into the hallway, walking in the direction she thought her room to be. Progress through the corridor was frustratingly slow in the pitch blackness. She had to grope her way along the wall.

Damn, was this the right way? Should she have turned left? Within moments she had become disoriented, finding herself turning into another corridor and farther down, yet another. Though she continued blindly, she was sure she was lost. A rat in a maze! Lili leaned against the wall, eyes shut, heart hammering. Just like her nightmare, she thought, experiencing the sense of confinement. The walls seemed to press in on her with a suffocating closeness. Sweat beading on her forehead, in her armpits, and between her breasts came more from fear than the relentless Xi'an humidity.

A noise ahead.

She froze in her tracks, afraid to be discovered by some cadre who'd insist on escorting her back to her room. If Chi-Wen was found there, they'd both be reported to Dr. Seng. At the far end of the corridor she heard someone unlock a door. Also like her dream. And from the recesses of her mind, Chi-Wen's words: *Doors are never locked in China.*

A narrow streak of white light swept the hallway. For an instant, it shrouded a figure coming through the door. Her grandfather! At least from a distance it appeared to be. For some unknown reason Lili remained silent, watching. Immediately, the door shut, wrapping her in total darkness again. What was going on? Where was grandfather going? Why did she feel so terrified?

She willed herself to calm down.

Think !

There had to be a rational explanation. She must have wandered into the corridor connecting the staff quarters with the Institute. That door must be the one she'd found locked during her tour with last week. But *why* was it locked? What was behind it? Lili slowly edged her way along until her hand found the knob. She tried to turn it several times, but it wouldn't budge.

Damn !

About to retreat, she dug into the pockets of her jeans. Her hand grasped a few bobby pins she used to keep her hair up. It was worth a try. She bent one back and inserted it into the keyhole, moving it up and down until she heard the soft click of the tumbler.

She paused at the door before twisting the knob. Unsure what she might find, she held her breath, carefully cracking it open. Its unoiled hinges groaned faintly in protest. Lili froze, praying the noise would not betray her entry. No one appeared, so she eased the door a little further, until she could pass through. She breathed normally again.

A soft fluorescent light illuminated another long empty hallway. Her ears strained, but she heard nothing except the quiet rasping of her own breath and the hammering of her own heart. Yet she knew that, beneath the eerie silence, there was something else. Trepidation mixed with curiosity as she quietly inched her way along the corridor until it opened into a large room. Its stark white windowless walls and tiled floor embraced and magnified the quietude.

Lili stood rooted to the spot. The scene had a surreal quality: thirty men and women dressed in loose cotton trousers and tunics gliding in a slow motion ballet across the floor. She felt hypnotized watching them. She recognized a few of the *tai chi* forms Chi-Wen had taught her, though some were new. The grace and control of the players impressed her, but of course they'd had many years to practice.

As she watched, she was struck by their youthful appearance—every face unlined. She looked more closely. Something *was* odd. For a few moments it nagged and tugged at the edges of her consciousness until finally it struck her—the feet.

That's it!

All the women had tiny feet. She'd read about the ancient practice of foot binding, but had never actually seen any of its victims. Each foot couldn't have been more than three inches long. My God, she thought, how could anyone call such grotesque extremities golden lilies? Thank goodness, this barbaric practice had been officially banned. When was it? Over seventy years ago. That would place these women well into their eighties.

From a smaller room just off this large one, Ni-Fu emerged carrying a tray of vials filled with clear liquid. Unaware of Lili's presence, he handed each person one vial, waiting until they had drunk it before moving on to the next. No one spoke; they drank—a single swallow, then reassumed *zhan zhuang*, the rest position. Lili was spellbound, her mind suddenly filled with scattered thoughts and images:

Dr. Seng told me about your exciting research.

The glass dropping from her grandfather's hand, shattering into a dozen tiny shards on the floor.

Using Chinese herbs...

Ni-Fu had seemed so upset. At the time Lili had simply explained it away as justified concern about confidentiality. Now she wondered if she might have misdiagnosed the cause.

Did Dr. Seng tell you anything else?

Anything else?

About my work.

Her grandfather was standing over a tiny white-haired woman. Although he whispered, Lili was just close enough to overhear his words. "Nien," he said softly, in English. "This is the last treatment. It will all be over soon".

The woman drank, then touched Ni-Fu with a wrinkled hand. "It is better this way."

Anything else?

About my work.

Maybe it was fatigue mixed with curiosity, fear and more than a touch of paranoia, but Lili's mind made a fantastic leap. My God, this was her grandfather's secret laboratory and these people were his subjects. But for what purpose?

Her involuntary gasp made Ni-Fu turn. "Lili."

"Grandfather, what's going on?"

He put his fingers to his lips and motioned her into the small room where they could not be heard. Closing the door, he faced her.

For the first time since she'd arrived, Lili noticed deep lines of worry and fatigue etched around his eyes.

"I didn't want to get you involved, child, but I suppose it is too late."
"Involved? In what?"

"Those people in there. How old do you think they are?"

"How old? I don't know. About 80," she guessed, based on the foot binding. "Perhaps a little more. Although they look younger."

Ni-Fu shook his head. "The youngest is 110. Nien Hu, the oldest, is 120."

Lili was incredulous. Surely he must be joking. "What are you saying?"

"That I've discovered the secret of longevity."

Skeptically: "I don't understand."

"I'll explain." Ni-Fu nodded towards a chair. "But first sit." He filled two porcelain cups with hot water. "And have some tea. I have a very long story to tell you."

*   *   *

Twenty minutes later, Chi-Wen stirred restlessly in his sleep, than abruptly awakened. It wasn't his usual protracted waking, the relaxed emergence from a cocoon of sleep that he always enjoyed. Instead it was a sudden sharpening of all his senses, a tensing of his body, as if some unseen danger lurked nearby.

Eyes still shut, he listened for the sound of Lili's even breathing. Nothing. He reached beside him. Empty. Lili was gone! Relax. Probably just a trip to the bathroom.

He shook his head. Less than three weeks seemed more like a lifetime. Funny how in such a short time this strange, wonderful young woman had managed to insinuate herself into his heart. He realized that he loved Lili Quan beyond salvation.

He sat up. Amber rays of sunlight struggled in through the dirty window. He'd slept too long. Soon the Institute would come alive and he'd never get away unseen.

Hurriedly, he dressed and tiptoed barefoot out into the hallway.

*   *   *

What Ni-Fu Cheng remembered from the moment he was old enough to understand was the instability of the times into which he was born.

China's imperial government, mortally weakened by corruption and its inability to compete militarily with the West and Japan, had survived the 19th century only by dint of its own inertia. Three years after the Empress Dowager's death, the revolution overthrowing Manchu rule began. City after city repudiated the Manchus and in February, 1912, the child emperor, Pu Yi, abdicated.

"I was only eight years old. The new Chinese Republic, under its founder Sun Yatsen, had problems from the beginning as various factions vied for control. Followers of General Yuan Shikai consolidated their power in Bejing, while Sun Yatsen set up the Guomindang in Guangzhou. We lived in Shanghai where my father and his brother ran a prosperous export business, trading with the West. If not for World War I, we could have ignored these internal struggles. I was thirteen when my father left to fight on the side of the Allies. I was fifteen when the message came that he'd been killed.

My mother and my two brothers came to live in my uncle's home. Business after the war was better than ever. We ate well, even drove in chauffeured limousines, while around us the city spawned urban slums, rumbling bellies and growing discontent. Under Shanghai's glittering surface festered opium dens, brothels, crime syndicates and rampant corruption; its gutters were littered with the corpses of the poor who had died from exposure and starvation.

While my brothers and I played in the streets, workers began organizing strikes to fight foreign rule and influence. Our experiences touched each of us differently. Daqin embraced my uncle's way of life and eventually took over the business. Hao was drawn into the tempestuous struggle around him. He wanted to change the world with guns; he joined the Communist Party after the first National Congress. Four years later he helped organize the demonstrations and strikes known as the May 30th Movements."

Ni-Fu wiped a tear from his eyelid. "Hao was twenty-one when Chiang Kai-chek's troops shot him during one of these uprisings."

"I'm sorry." It seemed an insipid remark and yet, Lili was deeply touched by her grandfather's account of his life. She wanted him to know she felt his pain too.

He touched her hand.

"What about you?"

"I smelt the stench of greed and killing and wanted to run away. When my mother died a few months later of typhoid, I begged my uncle to send me to England to study medicine. I hoped to help China too, but not with bullets and not with yuan. I felt that only with modern science could our people ever truly compete with the outside world."

"Is that where you learned English?"

"I knew a little from my uncle who did business with *waigorens*. But it wasn't until I got to Oxford that I became fluent." He looked at Lili. "It was a magical time for me. My whole world had opened up as I discovered the tradition of the greatest men of science—Hippocrates, Aristotle, Galen. In order to read from their original writings, I studied Arabic, Greek and Latin and spent all my spare time in the historical archives. I found that even though the earliest Egyptian medical papyri were replete with ritual prayers and spells against demons, a more rational, empirical practice had also developed. This involved the use of drugs derived from plants—castor oil, senna, colchicine, even opium. It occurred to me that while surgeons had their role to play, the future of medicine lay in the discovery of new drugs.

One day I met a Chinese scholar who claimed that the Chinese pharmacopoeia was the most extensive of the older civilizations. I began to comb the stacks for anything from the ancient dynasties. That's how I stumbled on the quest for *shou*.

"Longevity," Lili said, fingering her necklace.

"Yes, I came across a two thousand year old account of a physician who had ministered to Emperor Qin. He kept a diary, recounting events of the day. Since it was written lyrically, most scholars passed it off as bad literature, not science."

Lili smiled, easing her tension and acknowledging the humor.

"Emperor Qin was a man obsessed with immortality. He sent explorers throughout the world in search of potions. They were to find an island called Penglai. Legend placed it beyond the Eastern Ocean, beyond the impassable wind and mist where phoenixes, unicorns, black apes and white stags supposedly lived amid magic orchards, strange trees and plants of jasper. If they returned empty-handed, Qin cut off their heads.

It sounded like a fairy tale.

"Most never returned. In fact, they say the Japanese are descendants of one such group of explorers. A few did come back, boasting they'd found the secret."

"I take it they all lost their heads."

"All but one," Ni-Fu said. "It seems one young man returned with a species of butterfly—probably from South America. It had iridescent wings and an unusually long life span. The emperor bred these butterflies in captivity, hoping to learn the secret of their longevity. But the creatures died once they were caged. Qin ordered the young man back to the countryside with the remaining butterflies, instructing him to return once he had discovered the secret."

Lili was on the edge of her seat. "What happened?"

"In the caves north of Xi'an the butterflies survived, but did not live extraordinarily long. Then one day the young man noticed that after a few had eaten the leaf of a particular herb, they remained in the caterpillar stage for much longer than those that ate from other trees. Convinced this herb held the secret, he returned to the emperor with an extract. Unfortunately, it only gave the emperor diarrhea. The writings state that the young man disappeared into the hills and was never heard from again."

Disappointed. "So there was no secret?"

Ni-Fu continued without responding to her question. It was a long story. He would reach the end soon enough. "The account only described the herb, but did not give its name or reveal its content. Before discarding it as pure folly, I wanted to do some research. My professors had other ideas. They insisted I spend more time with my patients; less time in the library or the laboratory. I dropped the project, completed my medical studies and remained another two years as a fellow in the department of pharmacology. It was 1937 and Hitler was rising to power. Everyone sensed that war in Europe was inevitable, so I returned to China."

Ni-Fu's silence forced Lili to prompt him. "What happened?"

"It was to change my life forever."

*   *   *

The cadre was hidden deeply in the shadows just outside Lili's room. Chi-Wen walked right by him without realizing he was there. And he didn't notice the young man following discreetly ten steps behind.

*   *   *

Fascinated, Lili listened.

"Nowadays Yan'an is just an out of the way market town. But in 1937, it served as the headquarters of the Communist Party. Of the ninety thousand who began the Long March, fewer than half reached Yan'an. Then as now, the summers were miserably hot and many sought sanctuary in the innumerable cave dwellings up in the dry loess hills. Ravaged by the two and a half year trek through central and western China, Mao Zedong and his followers set up camp, planning to rest and reassess his political and military strategy.

It happened that I had also set up camp in one of those caves. I avoided the Communists. My only interest was to find the secret.

"For months after returning to China I searched the area described in the ancient text until I finally came to Yan'an. The hills were covered with the herbs I had read about. I studied them and used them to treat the peasants who came to me when they were ill. I made *qingmuxiang* from the root of *Aristolochia* debilis as an antihelminthic, *haifenteng* from *Piper futokadsurae* for asthma and arthritis, *cha-tiao-qi* from the leaves of *Acer ginnala* for acute dysentery, and the root barks of *Pseudolarix kaempferi* for fungal infections. But I still had not found the one herb I was looking for.

One day I was digging in the hills when a soldier from Mao's army abducted me at gun point. I expected to be killed on the spot; instead he led me into a cave where I came face to face with Mao himself. Despite the hot summer day, Mao lay on his cot, covered with blankets, shaking from fever. It was clear why I had been brought there. The soldier knew I was a doctor. One of the peasants had told him I could cure Mao. I promised to try and I remember even now the soldier's diabolical smile as he warned that I better do more than try. If I failed to save Mao, not only would I die, but so would the peasant's daughter. "

Ni-Fu stopped to sip his tea.

"Malaria?" Lili ventured.

Ni-Fu nodded. "Yes, that was my diagnosis. The problem was finding cinchona bark from which to make the quinine."

"I don't understand."

"The tree is not indigenous to China, but rather the mountainous regions of South America. I tried to explain, but the soldier gave me three days to return or the girl would be shot."

Lili shuddered. "How awful."

"Mao always believed that power grew from the barrel of a gun." Ni-Fu spoke with uncharacteristic bitterness. "For two days and nights I hiked up and down the mountainside. My effort seemed futile. Perhaps it was *joss* or just plain good luck. I finally discovered a trail to the highest part of the hills. There under the moonlight, I found the tree. I peeled the bark and dried it quickly to prevent the loss of alkaloids. When I returned to the cave, I made a final extract for Mao. In a week his fever finally broke and in another two he regained his full strength.

While Mao convalesced, I was kept close by. I finally met the young peasant girl held hostage." Ni-Fu still remembered the first time he saw Qing Nan. Long black hair flowing like a silken coat over her shoulders, her gentle smile and her sparkling black eyes betraying an independent spirit. So much like the young woman seated beside him now.

"Your grandmother was the most beautiful woman I'd ever seen. " The memory swept over Ni-Fu like a giant wave. His eyes were suddenly wet with tears. He missed Qing Nan so much.

Her arms around him, Lili hugged him gently. "Tell me about her." "She was nineteen and not yet married—a tragedy for a poor family that valued a woman less than a cow or ox. They couldn't afford a dowry and she was too old to sell as a concubine. If Mao's men had killed her, there would have been no mourning. As a captive, she listened to the Communists speak of equality for men and women. She decided if she survived, she would leave her family and live alone."

"You mean she wanted to join the revolution?" Lili asked.

"No, she was too spiritual to be a revolutionary. And like me, she wasn't interested in politics. The opportunity to experience another side of life and broaden her view of the world excited her. She was eager to learn and I was a willing teacher. I also longed to share my secret. I remember her face when I told her of the butterfly. She smiled, took my hand and led me to a cave I'd never seen before.

Growing up, she had spent many hours alone in those caves and knew their twists and turns by memory. She said to possess the secret, you must become the secret. On a ledge deep inside, she showed me what I could never find on my own: a Sedum sepaea plant, exactly as described in the monograph. Camouflaged beneath a leaf was a butterfly pupa, smooth and elegant, hanging by a silken pad. I could see its well-developed wings through its translucent cuticle. Oddly, it was already summer and the pupa still had not completed its metamorphosis. That's when I first thought I was really on to something. Strange, something in the plant seemed to slow its progression to adulthood.

Naturally, I had to study the life cycle of the butterfly to test my hypothesis. I needed a real laboratory. By then, Qing Nan and I both knew we had to be together. We were married in those hills; Mao was a witness and, with his blessing, I was allowed to return to Shanghai.

It was late 1937. The Japanese were at the gate. Shanghai's days of glorious excess were being blown away, leaving the stench of defeat in the hot summer air. I found death and disease everywhere. Corpses lined the boulevards and hutongs while rats and dogs feasted. I joined the overworked doctors at the Shanghai University Hospital, treating the wounded as best we could in makeshift surgical suites in overcrowded corridors. Although I could only grab a few hours here and there for my research, I had followed the butterflies through several cycles. I knew my theory was correct. Meanwhile, Qing Nan worked tirelessly as a volunteer, stopping only to give birth to your mother in 1939."

Lili remembered the picture of her mother and grandfather—how happy they'd looked together. "And your brother?"

"His business flourished until 1941 when most of the city's foreigners were interned by the Japanese so he could no longer trade with them. He became involved with the Guomindang. By 1945, when Japan was defeated, he was a lieutenant in Chiang Kai-chek's army.

When the Japanese occupied China, our people lived on wheat chaff or warehouse droppings. Some were constipated, others had diarrhea, When they were near death, the Japanese often buried them alive. Once the Nationalist troops arrived, people expected life would be better. Instead they suffered inflation and rationing. A family of four had to survive on a grain allotment for one. Inflation was so high that a lifetime's savings might buy just a single kilo of rice.

In April, 1949, one US dollar could be exchanged for 3.75 million Chinese yuan. Chinese money was worth less than the cost of printing it. Financial chaos merely fueled the corruption and greed of politicians and entrepreneurs. When the first columns of the People's Liberation Army entered the city late in May, the prevailing attitude was overwhelming relief."

"How did you feel?"

"Certainly the old China needed change. For most, the Communists brought new hope. I was more skeptical. To me, Communism was neither better or worse than other systems. It was devised and implemented by men and therefore corruptible."

"And grandmother?"

Ni-Fu sighed. "That same month, Qing Nan died giving birth to our son. I was numb with grief and then word came that my brother had been killed. Suddenly your mother was all I had left. I didn't want to lose her too."

"So you sent her to America," Lili said, beginning to appreciate Su-Wei's feelings for her father and China.

"I had to."

"Why didn't you go too?"

Ni-Fu's laugh was sardonic. How could he explain his feelings at the time? "I loved China. I wanted to help build a new country. Looking back I suppose we were naive to believe that the Communist Revolution would help China's progress. Yet this belief led many of us to remain here in those years."

"I understand," Lili said, thinking of Fan Zhou's deep love for China and her desire to serve her country.

"I was not a Communist," Ni-Fu continued, "but those in the Party were impressed when I volunteered to go wherever a doctor was needed. No matter that I expressed no interest in joining. A doctor could be morally neutral. Poor people need medicine under any regime."

"And your research?"

"I put it on hold. There was too much else to do. Our new nation required great personal sacrifice. Not what I want, but what does China need? The government told its citizens they had to sacrifice to survive. People had nothing—no basic necessities. For several years I practiced the most primitive medicine in every tiny village and town between Shanghai and Xi'an. Then in 1952, another knock on the door. A soldier from the People's Army placed me under arrest."

"For what?"

"For being the brother of a Nationalist." Ni-Fu's smile was bittersweet. "In China, my child, no matter how far you go, you cannot outrun the shadow of your family. I was sent to prison without a trial. I would have died there, but for another piece of luck."

"What happened?"

"One day, after almost three years, Chairman Mao arrived to inspect the prisoners. Somehow he recognized me. I was little more than skin and bones; my hair had turned completely gray. He demanded to know why I was being held. I had saved his life once, he said, and therefore would always be his friend. Naturally, the prison commander, eager to ingratiate himself with the Great Helmsman, assured him he would correct the "mistake". I was released within the hour."

Ni-Fu poured himself another cup of tea. "More?"

Lili shook her head.

"Mao had me treated for malnutrition. When I recovered, he came to see me. By that time I decided the only way I could ever complete my work would be to trust him with my secret. I told him as much about my theories as I dared. Mao immediately understood the implications. He was already 62 and there was still so much to accomplish. If he could only live another fifty or sixty years!

He arranged for me to work at the Xi'an Institute. The Medical Director knew little medicine, but was a loyal Communist. If Mao wanted me to conduct my research in secret, he would comply with his wishes. I was given everything I needed—my own laboratory, my own subjects. No one disturbed me. During the day I saw patients in the Shanaaxi Provincial People's Hospital and taught science and medicine at Jiaotong University. At night I searched for *shou*. "

"And you succeeded."

Ni-Fu nodded. "After many fits and starts. For years I assumed I needed to find the right dose of the herb from which the butterfly pupa fed, but as my subjects continued to age and die normally, I soon realized something was missing in the formula. If it hadn't been for Nien Hu, I might never have stumbled on the answer." He winced as he rubbed his jaw.

"Are you in pain, grandfather?"

Though the uncomfortable sensation had begun radiating down his left arm, Ni-Fu refused to give in to it. Not yet. "It's nothing, " he insisted. He had nearly completed his story. He wanted to finish. "Twenty years ago. Nien was the only one of the first group still alive. Though one hundred, she appeared as youthful and vital as if she were only sixty."

"Perhaps she just inherited good genes."

"I had deliberately picked subjects whose families had all died relatively young. No, it was something altogether different. Nien was a devotee of a certain school of *tai-chi*. One day she repeated a story told by an ancient Taoist philosopher. Tsan-Tsu dreamt he was a butterfly, happily flitting from tree to tree. When he awoke, he could not tell whether he had dreamt he had become a butterfly or whether the butterfly had become him." Ni-Fu's ebony eyes locked with his granddaughter's. "That story provided the solution."

The frown creasing Lili's face reflected her confusion.

"The answer was in the power of *wu-chi*. "

"How?"

"Absolute nothingness achieved through certain tai-chi movements reproduces the butterfly pupa's metabolic state. That combined with a specific formulation of the herb eaten by the pupa turns off the body's aging mechanism." He pointed to the other room where thirty ancient souls stood perfectly still, as if in a state of hibernation. "Those people there—my butterflies—are living proof of shou."

Lili wished Dylan were here. He'd been looking at the problem from a typically Western point of view.

Somehow the MHC regulates DNA repair. By finding what turns these genes on and off, we might be able to control the rate of aging, prolong human life span to 120, 150, who knows how long.

Her grandfather had found the control mechanism using an Eastern approach. No doubt the complete explanation required a merging of these two views. But like many great discoveries, the ultimate solution to unlocking the secret of longevity seemed so elegant in its simplicity.

Unable to contain her excitement, she hugged Ni-Fu. "What you've accomplished is a miracle!"

Ni-Fu shook his head. "I'm not sure I believe that anymore. For many years I convinced myself that all the sacrifice, the years in prison, even the loss of Su-Wei—would mean something because I was helping my country. " He sighed. "Forty years later I admit my motives were not totally altruistic. Ego was part of it. To be the first, to do what no man had ever done before. I was obsessed with the passion and fervor of discovery."

Like Dylan. "But there's nothing wrong with that."

"Perhaps not, but questions of ethics and responsibility were far from my mind. The only issue was how. I can't describe the excitement I felt. I thought I was on the verge of something that would save China. My secret would add years to our greatest minds. I never considered the potential problems."

"Such as?"

"Such as the effects of such a discovery on an already overpopulated planet. In 1909, when I was five years old, there were two billion people on earth. Sixty years later, in 1969, there were three and a half billion—a seventy-five percent increase. Only ten years later, in 1979, the population had grown to 4.2 billion. In one decade, the number of human beings on earth had increased by seven hundred million, nearly the population of India. The total numbers are increasing faster now. Lili, we'll end this decade with a world population edging over five billion, twenty percent of which is in China."

"So what are you saying?"

"That with an average life span of say seventy, we have natural growth already overburdening our food, energy and shelter resources. What if people didn't die at seventy, but lived twice as long, to say one hundred and forty? If we can't feed five billion today, how are we going to feed eight or sixteen billion more? The result would be total economic and social chaos. Most of the world's people are clustered in underdeveloped nations—places like China where increasing population begets increasing poverty, less available land for agriculture, less firewood for fuel."

Ni-Fu paused only long enough to catch his breath. "Almost fifteen million acres of forest are cleared each year and by the year 2000, half the present forests on earth may be gone. Forests conserve soil and prevent violent runoff of excess water. Trees release water into the air instead, cooling and moistening it. Forests also produce oxygen at a rate higher than any form of vegetation replacing them. Soil in rain forests will soon be leached of nutrients by crops planted in them, while rain runoff will gully and destroy the soil altogether. Vanishing rain forests will become deserts."

"You can't play God, grandfather," Lili interrupted. "If you're able to keep people alive longer, you should."

"At what cost? Even without the issue of overpopulation, there is the question of the quality of those extra years. I have not found the key to immortality. Cells will still age. They'll just do so more slowly. And for some individuals—say with Alzheimer's disease or severe arthritis or terminal cancer—that means more years of suffering. Or, suppose like those thirty souls in there," he pointed to the people waiting in the other room, "their friends and families have all died. They are alone—prisoners in an empty world, their lives devoid of love and meaning." He thought of Nien's words: "For them, it may be easier to die than to go on living."

Lili's thoughts were in turmoil. And her emotions. She appreciated some of her grandfather's arguments, but ultimately rejected the notion that death could be better than life. "Surely if science can solve the secret to longevity, it can also solve the problems created by its discovery."

"I think that's true—given time and proper consideration of the best and worst case scenarios. I'm suggesting that at this particular moment in man's history, perhaps the greatest single threat to the human race is not the bomb, but the possibility of prolonging life without insuring that such a discovery won't be misused."

"You can't be suggesting that we bury probably the greatest discovery in history?"

"Not necessarily bury it. Just remove it to a safe place." Ni-Fu hesitated for a few seconds, before plunging ahead. "Finding *shou* could probably have only succeeded here in China where so much is done in secret. Unfortunately, such secrecy is intrinsic to Communism's dark side: the pervasive venality and duplicity of the ruling cliques, the corrosive spirit of blind obedience fostered by the Party and the wide-spread perversion of the ideals of the Revolution.

Eighty percent of China's people live in the countryside. They understand the power of nature—the wind, the rain, the sun. They endure and accept their government as they endure and accept the calamities visited on them by the great forces of nature. Many are still illiterate, most still retain their ancestral beliefs in ghosts and superstition—even if they hide it well. Their rulers are as remote from their daily lives as the forces that cause floods and earthquakes. Yet their strength can be harnessed for remarkable works."

He smiled. "The muscle of one billion people is awesome." Sighing. "Unfortunately, the passivity of the Chinese also makes us the most compliant on earth. Even today only the ambitious few fight for power, their petty intrigues no different from those of the imperial past. Despite the great ideals of Marxism, little has changed in three thousand years. And the changes are as transient as my calligraphy." A note of bitter despair tinged his voice. "I realize now that in China today there is no hope *shou* will ever be used for anything but evil."

He explained how Dr. Seng had taken over as Medical Director six months earlier. Unlike his predecessor, he made it a point to monitor all research. Once the implications of Ni-Fu's work became clear, Seng didn't hesitate to exploit his contacts in the Party. "A promise for a promise. Seng's career advancement in exchange for the secret."

Hadn't she sensed the danger in the man? Despite the heat, Lili experienced a sudden chill. "You said you didn't want me involved. What did you mean?"

"I suppose there's really no way for me to keep this from you." Ni-Fu squeezed Lili's hand in his. "About four months ago, the Foreign Ministry chief demanded that I reveal my discovery. I replied that it was meant for all the people, not a small group of old Party leaders clinging to power. Seng responded that by saving these old men, I *would* be helping the people. When I refused, he had me tortured."

Lili gasped.

Ni-Fu dismissed her shock. "Lin realized that I was worthless to them dead, so he devised a more diabolical way to persuade me to talk. You."

Silence as she slowly absorbed the thrust of the conversation. Finally, it was all laid out before her—the most fantastic story she'd ever heard. Her grandfather had made the most earth shattering discovery since the atom bomb and was being imprisoned by Dr. Seng. She had been lured here to force him to reveal it to three old Party leaders who meant to keep it for themselves. Lili's heart raced as she realized the full extent of her peril. My God. She was no less a prisoner here than Ni-Fu.

As if divining her thoughts. "I have an escape plan."

"An escape? How? When?"

"To America. But, the less you know, the better. Chi-Wen has promised to help. This much I will share with you," he said, beginning to slowly tap along the edge of his desk in the same manner that physicians percuss a human chest, its resonance or dullness indicating the relative tissue densities. "Listen carefully."

The sound Ni-Fu produced were the low tones of solid wood...

Lili's brow furrowed in concentration.

...except for one small spot, easily missed in the intricately carved wood.

"Hollow," Lili diagnosed, suddenly understanding. She pushed down on the place where the pitch had been higher, revealing a tiny, hidden compartment.

Ni-Fu removed several folded sheets of paper. "My notes."

"Very clever!"

"Seng turned this place upside down, but never found a thing. Too bad he's not as good a clinician as you."

Lili smiled at the irony.

"The state is determined to save us from ourselves. But we can't let that happen, Lili. People of science need to control their discoveries. Not the government. In America you have that freedom."

"Yes, but even there it's eroding. Because we don't appreciate it. Little by little, America's changing. So slowly it's imperceptible." She thought of Dr. Trenton and Mrs. Manley. "Bureaucrats making rules—controlling doctors' practice, their priorities."

"At least you can still fight the system. You can demand to be heard."

"Of course, you're right, grandfather. In America, you and I will demand to be heard."

You and I...

He wondered how to answer. The intensity of the pain in his jaw and left arm suddenly crescendoed, this time accompanied by a new sensation—a crushing, searing pressure in the center of his chest. Ni-Fu placed a fist over his sternum and slid to the floor. His other hand gripped his notes. Panic and desperation filled his consciousness. Not now. Not when he was so close! "I...."

Lili's eyes widened. "Help!" As she stooped over her grandfather, she knew he was having a heart attack.

*   *   *

Newport, California

Halliday helped himself to a Hoyode Monterrey from the old man's alligator case. "Not your best side, I'll admit, but then it was difficult to find a flattering angle from ten stories up."

DeForest fingered the black and white prints spread on the table, his expression impassive. "I was hoping you wouldn't know about this."

"I like solving puzzles." Halliday slowly unwrapped the cigar, lit it and took a long, reflective drag. "Especially ones that have blown up in my face."

DeForest's eyes did not flicker. "I see." He rose and sauntered to the wet bar that filled almost an entire wall of his richly paneled den. It wasn't so much a desire for a drink as his need to buy a little time. Only after selecting a glass, dropping in some ice, then pouring in the Dewar's, did he turn to face his adversary. "Would you believe me if I said it's not what it seems?" he asked, taking a sip of scotch.

The CIA man's lips curled into a thin smile as he savored the moment. Few ever got the best of Walter DeForest, self-made billionaire, giant among men. The thought gave him a great deal of pleasure. "Not a chance."

*   *   *

Xi'an, China

Chi-Wen was turning toward the hospital side of the Institute when he heard the cry for help. Though faint, he knew it came from the Longevity unit. This door should be locked, he thought, as he reached out and tried the handle. It turned without resistance. Quickly, he pushed the door open and ran down the corridor to the main room.

"Help!"

"Lili?"

"In here!"

At the doorway to the tiny inner office, Chi-Wen stopped, unsure what to do. Lili was hunched over Ni-Fu.

"Please, I need you," she called, looking up for a split second. "And you," she added, acknowledging the young cadre who appeared just behind Chi-Wen.

*   *   *

Newport, California

"So you only needed Ng to guarantee delivery of the formula."

"Right, Charlie," DeForest asserted, his tone still disingenuous. He gulped his second drink. "Our deal was never compromised."

"You expect me to believe that shit?" Halliday tsked. "You disappoint me, Walt. Frankly I'd expect a little slicker lie from someone of your reputation."

"Look, I can see you're upset. There's no reason we can't modify our deal. What say we double the ante?"

Halliday snorted derisively.

"Not enough? No problem. Name your price."

Halliday shook his head. "You still don't get it, do you? I *know* about your joint venture with Zee Enterprises and I *know* about the recent activity on the South Korean Composite."

The clinking of ice cubes against his glass betrayed DeForest's sudden anxiety. "I see."

"You never really intended to cut me in. You and Ng planned to screw David Kim." Halliday moved to where the old man stood." And you, my friend, planned to screw me."

"But…"

"But nothing. The ruse is up." Halliday's eyes turned stone cold. "And like you, I've made contingency plans." He now stood nose to nose with DeForest. "It's what I call my 'one screw rule'. You screw me,…"

The CIA man removed what looked like a fountain pen from the breast pocket of his suit jacket. In less than a second, he'd discarded the pen top and depressed the tiny atomizer, releasing a small but fatal dose of hydrogen cyanide vapor.

The liquor had slowed DeForest's reactions, though even under normal circumstances he could not have prevented the outcome. Just time to register surprise and disbelief.

Stepping back far enough to avoid inhaling the gas himself, Halliday watched DeForest begin his agonal throes with detached fascination. In a few seconds, the rapid respirations progressed as the old man tried to inhale great gulps of air, became dizzy and tumbled to the floor. His tormented convulsions turned his lips blue and streaked his cheeks with blood. Halliday heard the hiss of his last expended breaths and smiled at the utterly still, limp body with its empty eyes staring upward. Like spraying a roach with RAID.

"…you're screwed."

*   *   *

Xi'an, China

No time to think that it was her grandfather lying there, barely conscious. Lili quickly assessed his medical condition. ABC: Airway clear; Breathing, shallow; Cardiac: pulse thready and rapid. She closed her eyes, mentally counting the beats. One hundred eighty. Much too fast. Was the source of the tachycardia, supraventricular or ventricular? A definitive diagnosis required an electrocardiogram.

Damn.

She surveyed the room wishing she had the familiar equipment at LA Medical—EKG monitors, portable defibrillators, Swan-Ganz catheters and the kind of highly trained team where everyone knew their job so well, few words were necessary. She had no choice—she had only Ni-Fu's old stethoscope lying on the desk to determine his arrhythmia and Chi-Wen and the young cadre to help her.

Pressing the bell of the stethoscope to her grandfather's chest, she listened carefully while watching his neck veins filled. Detecting no cannon waves, she felt somewhat relieved. Their absence made the more malignant, ventricular type of heart irregularity unlikely. If she was right, Ni-Fu had a much better chance for survival. If she was wrong...

She looked at Chi-Wen. "Grandfather's heart rate is too fast. I need to find out why—quickly. Gently hold his head while I press his carotid artery. This should slow his heart," she explained. "Meanwhile, ask our shadow to run for an IV, some morphine sulfate and a gurney to move him to the hospital."

A rapid fire exchange in Chinese persuaded the cadre to reluctantly depart.

"He'll bring Dr. Seng," Chi-Wen said, suddenly realizing that the cadre had been following him. For how long?

Lili merely shrugged. All that mattered now was saving her grandfather's life.

"Okay. Ready?" Lili breathed deeply and prayed.

Please, God. Let this work.

Too little pressure and the rapid rhythm would continue, further compromising oxygen supply to his heart; too much and she could precipitate a stroke. Carefully, she massaged the artery on the right side of Ni-Fu's neck.

"Can you take a pulse?"

Chi-Wen nodded, placing his fingers over the professor's radial artery.

"All right. When I tell you, start counting... Now." She continued her carotid massage.

"150, 140, 120..."

"Good, it's slowing down." A little more pressure.

"110, 100."

Lili stopped for several seconds as Ni-Fu gradually stirred. "Grandfather, can you hear me?"

Ni-Fu nodded weakly.

"How do you feel?"

"Much better." He tried raising his head, but Chi-Wen retained his gentle hold. "Where do you think you're going, professor?" he admonished.

"Lili?"

"Yes, grandfather." She leaned over him.

"Is it...?" His voice was barely a whisper, but Lili heard and knew what he was trying to say. Before Chi-Wen and the cadre had arrived, she'd stuffed Ni-Fu's notes in her pocket.

Sotto voce: "Don't worry, grandfather, it is safe."

"Good." Though he smiled, his face was drawn and pale. Suddenly he seemed old, frail, desperately tired. "Some water, please."

"Of course," Lili said. "Chi-Wen, could you get a pillow for his head?"

The moment she and Chi-Wen stepped away, Ni-Fu removed the last vial of clear liquid from his pocket and drank it down.

"You know how lucky you were?" Lili asked, when she returned with the water. That jaw pain was angina. But I don't have to tell *you* that. You just ignored the symptoms."

"I'm sorry to upset you, granddaughter."

Fear and fatigue had produced the reprimand, not anger. "Nothing to be sorry for. It's..." her voice trembled with pent up emotions, "...I don't want to lose you." She took Ni-Fu's hand. "I just found you after all these years."

Ni-Fu squeezed her hand in response. "You can't lose me. I'll always be with you. Remember that."

Something in his words produced a sensation of foreboding. "Of course. As soon as you're well enough, we'll find a way to get out of here."

He shook his head. "No. I'm not going with you to America."

"What are you talking about?"

Ni-Fu peered into her shadowed face. "When we're healthy and the world seems good to us, the thought of death is remote. We feel immortal. Death is for others, not for us. We reject and fear what we cannot comprehend." He stopped for a moment to catch his breath. "But we should not be afraid. There is a time to live and a time to die. I have chosen to make my time now." Ni-Fu's eyelids fluttered.

Lili checked his pulse. It had gone from brisk and regular to barely palpable. "Grandfather!" she screamed. "What have you done?"

"I've completed the circle," he whispered. "For Nien, all the others in Ward #1 and me." He pointed to the clear vial lying on the floor beside him. "There is nothing now between me and death."

"No!" She had just found her grandfather and now he was leaving her. "What will I do without you?"

"The wind will still ride the mountain; the Yangtze will still ebb and flow."

"But I need you. You're my only family. Please, don't die," she pleaded.

"No tears, granddaughter. There isn't time. I want you to understand. I have left you a heavy burden to carry." His voice little more than a whisper as he struggled to speak. "You alone now hold the secret. You will decide whether or not to reveal it to the world."

"How will I know what to do?"

"You will know. " His strength quickly waning. "Just remember—it has the power to save or destroy."

Lili bent close to kiss him.

"Be careful. Chi…" Then he shuddered.

"Grandfather?" Lili felt for a pulse that was no longer there.

The past was gone forever…

BOOK THREE

THE FUTURE

The future is purchased by the present

Samuel Johnson

We do not know much of the future
Except that from generation to generation
the same things happen again and again.
Men learn little from others' experience,
but in the life of one man, never
the same time returns

T.S. Eliot

TWENTY-FOUR

Wednesday, May 3
Xi'an, China

Dr. Seng couldn't fall back to sleep.

His thoughts were filled with Ni-Fu Cheng. After many months, he knew the professor well. A man from a different era. Typical intellectual, son of bourgeois liberals, never really had to suffer. Not like his own family. Seng's parents were peasants. Only after the Revolution could their youngest son get an education and become a doctor. Seng's life would have taken a very different path without the Party. People like Cheng could never really understand that. The power of the Party; the beauty of the Party; the People's Party.

Before Seng became Medical Director of the Institute, Ni-Fu never attended the required weekly political meetings. He felt above all; better than others. That's what tipped Seng off. Ni-Fu had been protected for years by the former administrator. But why?

It took no time to discover that while Cheng was indeed developing drugs from Chinese herbs, his real research lay elsewhere. Then, one night, Seng followed him and discovered Ward #1. What a revelation: *shou*—the ability to prolong life. Utterly fantastic. And what an opportunity for Seng. He sought out the Foreign Ministry chief and obtained Lin's promise of a more prominent position in the Party for the gift of longevity.

Of course, Seng hadn't expected Cheng's intransigence. Who knew the old man could endure such terrible torture? Or that he would keep his secret from Chi-Wen? But Lili Quan. There was a stroke of luck—Peng Han's discovery that a granddaughter existed. If Chi-Wen could not extract the secret, Seng had no doubt Lili could. Love and trust of family still counted above all else in China.

Seng also understood Cheng's passion for his work. He may have refused to reveal it to Lin, but he certainly wouldn't go to his death without assuring that his secret lived on.

Seng smiled. Every contingency was covered; the culmination of a long and careful plan finally within his reach. No more delays. Tomorrow he'd interrogate Lili to determine what she already knew, advise her that unless Cheng cooperated, she, Cheng and Chi-Wen would suffer the consequences. Even if torture proved necessary, the girl could never endure the torment her grandfather had. Soft American, he thought contemptuously.

For Lili Quan, there would be no escape.

It wouldn't be long now. Soon he'd leave this stinking city behind. No more second cadre. So close, he could almost feel the wonderful tumult of Beijing. A real city. Close to the heart of the power.

His reverie was interrupted by a banging on his door. " Dr. Seng! Come quickly! Dr. Cheng has collapsed."

*   *   *

"Lili, we've got to get out of here!"

She was weeping uncontrollably. "Grandfather."

Gently, Chi-Wen pulled her up from the floor. "There's nothing more we can do for him. He's at peace now." Chi-Wen held her against his chest until her sobs subsided. "Come on. We've only got a few minutes before Seng shows up." He grabbed her hand and led her, like a child, from the ward.

"Oh my God," Lili gasped. "Chi-Wen, look." She pointed to the thirty men and women who'd been part of Ni-Fu's experiment. Where an hour before they had been performing graceful, surreal *tai-chi*, they now lay on the floor, eyes closed, in peaceful repose. "They're dead."

"He said he was completing the circle."

Lili shook her head. "A time to live and a time to die." But grandfather, she thought, sadly, for us there was so little time.

*   *   *

Newport Beach, California

It wasn't until morning that DeForest's body was discovered by his house-keeper. In keeping with her boss's obsession with privacy, she called in Dr. March rather than the police. As far as the family doctor was concerned, his longtime patient was a man who'd lived too hard for many years. He'd tried often to get him to slow down. So, despite the fact that March hadn't been with the old man in his final moments, he had no qualm signing the death cer-tificate, certifying the cause as "natural".

*   *   *

Xi'an, China

They'd reached the corridor between the hospital and the Institute when they heard the sound of footsteps clicking against tile. And though the voices were low, they recognized them. Seng and the cadre coming towards them, still out of sight.

They froze.

Chi-Wen pointed to the door leading to the hospital, but Lili shook her head. Taking that route risked being seen by medical staff who would likely report back to Seng. Instead, she indicted the elevator. It was not only closer, but coincidentally settled on their floor. She'd seen workmen there yesterday. Hopefully it had been fixed.

"Okay," Chi-Wen mouthed. He led the dash to the elevator, pulled open the heavy door and slid the rickety metal gate just enough to allow them passage. Its loud creaking sound echoed off the corridor walls.

Please God, Lili prayed as she frantically pressed the button for ground. Let it work!

From outside, the footsteps grew fainter. Seng and the cadre had turned off the main corridor.

Seconds passed as if hours. Finally they heard the machinery start up inside the shaft.

Numb with fear, Lili pressed against the back of the car, her eyes shut tightly, her hand clutching Chi-Wen's. With agonizing slowness the Russian built elevator descended: five, four, three, two, ground floor.

*   *   *

"What the…"

Seng surveyed the thirty corpses, then hurried into the small office where the cadre pointed to Ni-Fu's body. Seng stooped to take a pulse, but he knew Cheng was dead too. Why? He saw the tray of empty vials and his face reddened with rage. Damn it. Cheng *had* gone to his death with the secret. Unless…

He stood up. "Where's Dr. Quan?" he demanded.

"Gone," the cadre reported. "So is Chi-Wen Zhou."

Ni-Fu must have told her the secret.

Then he saw it—the tiny compartment in Cheng's desk. Open and empty. In the confusion, Lili had neglected to shut it again.

That's where he had stashed his notes! Clever bastard. Seng had spent weeks searching the Institute. He'd almost believed the old man's story that it was all in his head. Nothing on paper. For security reasons.

He studied Ni-Fu's inert body. Well, my friend, I guess at the end you were no less a liar than the best of us.

He turned to the cadre. "Find Dr. Quan," he snapped. "She's got to be somewhere in the Institute."

Somewhere, he thought, almost smiling, with the secret in her pocket.

*   *   *

Xi'an, China

In a small classroom at Jiaotong University, the mood was somber. Despite several all night meetings with Yuan Mu, the State Council spokesman in Beijing, there had been no resolution of the students' primary issue: a call for dialogue. The stalemate included who the government would talk to: the leaders of the moderate government-recognized student union or the more aggressive, independent group. Wuer Kaixi, newly elected president of the independent student union walked out midway through the session, declaring that no dialogue was possible until the government recognized the legitimacy of his organization.

Now, after speaking with their counterparts in Beijing by phone, the students in Xi'an argued strategy.

"The battle lines between the students and government are drawn. Us against them," Zheng Tu declared. "We must step up our demonstrations, Beginning tomorrow, May 4th, we will march -all across the country, from Guangchou to Beijing."

"Be careful," someone warned. "Tomorrow is not only the historical seventieth anniversary celebration, it's the same day the Asian Development Bank will hold its annual meeting. If we march, Party conservatives will claim students and reformers sabotaged the opportunity to show the world China is ready to take its place as a leader in business relations. The consequences will be as in 1987, when reformers were blamed for social unrest and Hu Yaobang was made the scapegoat and ousted."

"We know how important this meeting is for international business," another agreed. "It results from the open-door policy of the past ten years. It proves reform has been successful. We must do nothing to disrupt the progress of reform."

"Look," a math graduate student who'd lived through the Cultural Revolution said, "we know the Asian Development Bank meeting is important for China. But this is our opportunity to demand the government talk with us."

A young woman in the back stood up. "Many of you believe there is a distinction between reformers and conservatives. You are wrong and if you believe this, you are hurting the reformers. Everyone knows full well what the situation is: there is an internal Party struggle between Li Peng and Zhao Ziyang. I hope we all proceed cautiously or our movement will hurt reformers like Zhao Ziyang. The hard-liners want to use our actions to blame him and those like him in the Party for promoting social unrest."

"You undergraduates are too young to understand," the math student asserted. "The government lied and ignored us again and again. We only want them to talk to us and admit we are not traitors."

"And what if they don't?" the girl challenged.

"If they don't," Zheng Tu responded, "we are ready to die, to use our lives to pursue the truth. We will sacrifice ourselves."

"*Qiuhousuuanzhang,*" someone intoned, bringing an almost instant, palpable chill to everyone in the room. It meant 'one settles scores after autumn'. If they didn't succeed in convincing the government, they would all surely be punished after it was over.

For the girl in the back of the room, such a possibility was unacceptable.

*   *   *

The elevator stopped; the doors opened. Lili remained inside, her fingers poised over the "door-close" button while Chi-Wen scanned the lobby.

Empty. At five minutes to six, the day clerk hadn't yet come on duty. The night clerk was probably still at breakfast. He motioned to Lili to exit the car.

"We'll never get out of here," she whispered. Even if they made it outside, they couldn't climb over the wall. Not with barb wire. Less likely they could slip by the guard at the gatehouse. It was only a matter of minutes before Seng alerted him they were missing.

"Look!" Chi-Wen pointed to a canvas-covered lorry parked outside the Institute entrance. "That farmer just made a vegetable delivery." Puffs of smoke rose near the front of the vehicle where the driver stood, his back to them, enjoying a cigarette before taking off. "Come on!"

"Are you crazy?" she hissed. "I can't drive that out of here. The guard will stop me."

"We're going to be passengers," Chi-Wen explained. "We'll hide under the canvas. The farmer will drive us outside the Institute walls. No one will see us."

Lili held back, uncertain.

"He's bound to head back to the countryside. As long as we get far enough from the city, I can hitch a ride to the university. My friends will help us."

Lili could offer no alternative. If they remained, they'd surely be caught. "Okay."

The driver hawked a bolus of phlegm into the street, then resumed his smoking.

"Now!"

Although they affected nonchalance, their steps through the lobby to the front door were hurried. Following Chi-Wen's lead, Lili climbed into the back of the lorry. As quietly as possible, Chi-Wen pushed aside enough empty vegetable crates to create a nest into which they could settle. They faced each other, using a couple of old burlap bags smelling of ripe turnips as a makeshift blanket. Chest to chest, it was difficult to tell whose heart hammered more loudly.

The slam of the truck door was followed by the rattle of the motor turning over. Overhead, their vault of olive-drab canvas fluttered.

Lili squeezed her eyes shut.

"Don't worry," Chi-Wen whispered.

The lorry inched toward the gatehouse.

"*Zao an.* Good morning, comrade."

Lili imagined the zebra-striped gate being lifted.

"And to you," the farmer returned the greeting.

The truck surged forward causing several crates to fall with a loud bang.

"Shall I help you tie your cargo down?"

Chi-Wen translated.

Dear God, we're done for, Lili thought.

"No, the crates are empty. I'm used to the rattling."

"Okay, see you next week."

"*Zai jian.*"

A sudden bump as they pulled outside the Institute walls onto the main road. Still, Lili waited several miles before breathing normally. "In Hong Kong we stay at the Peninsula Hotel," she murmured into Chi-Wen's ear. "The beds are softer."

Within five minutes, lulled by the rocking motion of the loosely-sprung lorry, she surrendered to her emotional exhaustion, falling into a deep, dark sleep.

*   *   *

Washington, DC

Waiting for the final call to board the jumbo jet for Hong Kong, Halliday savored the last of DeForest's cigars and pondered the permutations of death: two down, he thought with a secret smile; one to go.

*   *   *

Xi'an, China

When Lili drifted up from the blackness, it was much hotter under the canopy. Sprawled supine in the bed of the truck, she opened her eyes. Chi-Wen hunkered at the tailgate, his tired face in need of a shave, his left hand holding one of the rear flaps open. Through it Lili spotted a sliver of bright, azure sky. "How long did I sleep?"

"Shh, he might hear us."

Lili doubted anything could be heard over the noisy rumbling of the lorry's engine, but she lowered her voice. "Sorry."

"Less than an hour."

Her head ached. Standing up, Lili carefully crawled through the vegetable crates to Chi-Wen. He was peering over the tailgate, an odd, pensive look in his eyes—as though he sensed that a decisive moment in his life had arrived. She wondered whether he foresaw their liberation or their doom. Fearing his answer, she asked: "Where are we?"

"About a mile from the railway station, I think," he whispered. "We'll get off here and walk the rest of the way. I'll use the public phone to call my friends at the University."

An involuntary spasm rumbled through her stomach.

"We can grab some breakfast too."

"I'm not hungry."

He looked directly at her. "You'll need your strength for the ordeal ahead."

No time to interpret his expression. The truck suddenly slowed as the driver maneuvered around a sharp corner. Chi-Wen grabbed her hand. "Now. Jump!"

Seconds later, they both cleared the tailgate and stood, breathless, in the middle of the dusty road, watching the lorry gradually fade into the distance.

*   *   *

Washington, DC

As soon as all passengers boarded the 747 for Hong Kong, the man watching from the far side of the terminal returned to a bank of telephones and dialed the long number he'd memorized. The connection was immediate.

"Halliday's on his way," he reported.

No response. Just the click of the receiver as it was dropped back into its cradle.

*   *   *

Xi'an, China

More than an hour passed before Seng would admit Lili and Chi-Wen had literally evaporated. He had the cadre check with his contact at Jiotong University—a pretty undergraduate convinced that informing on her fellow students was the only way to survive the inevitable upcoming purge.

*   *   *

Just inside the Long-Hai Railroad station, Chi-Wen bought Lili a breakfast of steamed buns and tea.

"Aren't you eating?"

"I have to make my call first." He pointed towards the platform across the room. "I'll meet you there."

"Don't be long."

At 7:30, the station was already a beehive of activity. Lili edged through the noisy crowd with deliberate slowness, hoping it would swallow her up and offer concealment. She must remain calm, remove fear from her eyes. At least here she looked enough like everyone else to avoid attracting attention. The irony of the thought almost made her smile.

"Lili Quan?"

Startled, Lili turned. The face beneath the flat-brimmed parody of a Hakka woman's hat belonged to Dorothy Diehl. "Hello, Dottie."

"What a small world. I thought I recognized you. I'm glad we bumped into each other. With only a day in Xi'an, I never had time to look you up."

"No problem," Lili replied, distracted. She hoped no one overheard Dottie call her name. If Seng had alerted officials, the train station would be a natural place to search. "I've been busy…at the hospital…"

"What are you doing here?"

"Uh… I'm meeting a friend," she replied, glancing in the direction of the telephones. Pointless to say more. There was no way anyone could help her. Except, of course, Chi-Wen. Surely he wouldn't be much longer.

"Well I hope it's a handsome *he* ." Dottie produced her Dr. Ruth giggle. "Me, I've had no such luck. But, then there's still Guilin. That's next." She pointed to the group huddled in the far corner of the hall.

Miss Pu, the pert, cheerful tour guide, was handing out tickets for the next leg of their journey.

"What a bunch." Oblivious to Lili's peril, Dottie brought her up to date:

Ed, the anemic accountant and Abigail, the spinster librarian, had become lovers. "Can you believe that one?"

Charlotte was barely speaking to her. "I told her to keep her opinions about men to herself and that was that."

The Witticks made themselves unpopular by refusing to pay for an orange soda one hot day because "we've paid for this trip already and this ought to be included."

"Only two yuan. Can you imagine?" Dottie quipped.

An Australian from another tour group had called them "ugly Americans" and the Witticks were threatening legal action. Virgil was close mouthed, but his wife Alice had become the life of the party- apparently downing several Tsingtao beers at every meal.

They'd bought bargain souvenirs, lacquer ware, rugs, chopsticks, brassware and fans. "Everyone was nice, but they never *heard* of fortune cookies!"

Lili resisted the urge to tell her fortune cookies were the brainchild of San Francisco entrepreneurs, not a Chinese invention. She realized Dottie and her group had toured many of the same cities she'd been in, but wondered how much they'd seen through windows of their air-conditioned minivans and soft sleeper-cars. Perhaps it wasn't fair to be critical. 'China Off the Beaten Track' notwithstanding, this group of Americans had come to get a brief glimpse of a foreign country.

Everyone was tired and irritable, Dottie confided. Like a school outing that had gone on too long. "This morning I wrote in my journal: 'Day number 18, we've gone over two thousand miles and believe me, it hasn't been a picnic'. Thank goodness we leave for Guilin today and then to Hong Kong."

"What did you say?" Only half-listening until that moment. "You've been keeping your journal?"

...in China today there is no hope that shou will ever be used for anything but evil.

"Yes, indeed." The ex-geography teacher opened her over-sized purse and removed her lined copybook. "For that novel I told you about. With some of the shenanigans going on, I expect to give Jackie Collins a run for her money."

"And you're returning to Hong Kong?"

You can't be suggesting that we bury probably the greatest discovery in history?

"We'll arrive on Saturday at one."

Not necessarily bury it. Just remove it to a safe place.

"Dottie?"

"Yes, my dear."

A long ringing bell announced the next train.

"That's me!"

"Could I ask you for a small favor?"

By the time Chi-Wen returned ten minutes later, Dottie's train for Guilin had departed, along with the secret of *shou* slipped inside her lined copybook.

*   *   *

Seng nodded as he considered the cadre's report. This was the break he'd been hoping for. "All right. Get down to the station right away. Make certain you're on their train," he snapped. "No slip-ups this time."

"Yes, sir."

As the cadre left his office, Seng chuckled. By tomorrow morning Chi-Wen Zhou and Lili Quan would be hand delivered to Lin. After that, the Foreign Minister wouldn't dare delay his promotion any longer.

*   *   *

"Beijing?"

"Chi-Wen's idea really," Zheng Tu told Lili. "But I discussed it with the other students and they agreed." He handed Lili and Chi-Wen train tickets. "They will expect you to go south. This way you'll be safe."

"You're a good friend."

Zheng Tu smiled at Chi-Wen. "Your faxes helped get our message to the world. The foreign press is pouring into China. Tomorrow's rallies should get even more attention." To Lili: "I'm sorry about your grandfather."

"Thank you."

He checked his watch. "I must go. When you reach Beijing, someone will take you to a safe house until the plane leaves for Guangchou. From there you'll follow the underground railroad to Macao."

"Dr. Seng has my passport," Lili said. "How will I get past customs?"

"Don't worry," Zheng Tu assured her. He wrote the name and address of another contact in Macao. "He'll provide a counterfeit passport and visa to Hong Kong."

"How can we thank you?" Chi-Wen asked.

"Just be careful," he said seriously. "There are many spies and plainclothes police."

TWENTY-FIVE

Thursday, May 4th
Beijing, China

The driver steered the limousine along the special lanes used on Beijing streets by privileged travelers. A thick, seemingly solid pedaling column of bicyclists gave wide berth to the long black car.

"There's a crowd up ahead, sir. Probably part of the May 4th celebrations."

David Kim rolled down his window. They were less than a block from the New China News Agency building. Several dozen policemen had lined up at the entrance, arms linked to prevent journalists from getting outside where hundreds of students were marching with banners and shouting slogans: "Never forget the spirit of May Fourth', 'Down with graft, fight official corruption'. All at once, several journalists broke through the police barricade and fell in line behind the marchers, defiantly shouting demands for freedom of the press.

"This looks like more than the usual holiday crowd," Kim said, as the driver turned onto Changan Avenue toward Tiananmen Square.

From a few blocks away, it was clear the demonstrators converging on the square numbered in the tens of thousands.

"Shall I try to go through?"

"No," Kim responded. "Just return to the hotel."

He leaned back and shut his eyes. It didn't matter. The Asian Development Bank meeting was merely a convenient cover. He'd return to his room and wait for word from Lee Tong. And with Camille along, he anticipated that wait to be very pleasant.

*   *   *

Ten minutes outside of Beijing Chi-Wen woke. "Did you sleep?" he asked.

Lili shook her head. "Not a wink." For twenty-one hours she'd remained in the uncomfortable hard seat section, afraid to move, terrified to call attention to herself. Could she trust the woman with the baby or the old farmer or the young couple if they suspected she was on the run?

Thankfully, her fellow passengers had expressed no curiosity—dozing through most of the trip, waking only to spit or smoke or slurp tea or eat whatever snacks they'd brought with them. With the loudspeaker announcing their impending arrival, the compartment emptied. Like a Chinese fire drill, Lili thought, imagining the passengers jammed up against one another at the exit, panting and pushing, waiting to make a mad dash the moment the train reached the station.

Every muscle ached as she stood to stretch. The fact she hadn't had even the Chinese version of a shower in over twenty-four hours compounded her discomfort. "I think I know what they mean by Chinese torture," she complained.

Chi-Wen threw her a curious look that she would later interpret as sinister. Now she merely ascribed it to his own fatigue.

The train lurched to a halt at Beijing Central Station. Lili followed Chi-Wen to the compartment door.

"You stay here," he said. "The train won't depart for another fifteen minutes."

"But... "

"You'll be safer here. As soon as I find Tu's contact, I'll be back to get you."

Chi-Wen disappeared before Lili could protest. Alone in the compartment, she felt uneasy. She knew it was accumulated exhaustion and emotional stress, but she couldn't control her anxiety. Through the window she scanned the station platform, wondering how Chi-Wen could find anyone in the crowd. Hurry, she silently urged.

A soft tap at the door made her jump. "*Shir* ? Yes?"

"More tea?"

"No, thank you," Lili responded before she realized the question had been in English.

Too late. The door opened. "Dr. Quan, so nice to see you again." It was the cadre from Xi'an.

"What do you want?"

"You're to come with me."

"Where?"

" Dr. Seng thought you should meet our Foreign Minister."

If Lili *had* contemplated escape, the two soldiers standing just behind him quickly dispelled the notion.

*   *   *

Had David Kim attended the morning session of the Asian Development Bank group, he would have heard Zhao Ziyang's speech. By suggesting that the students' concerns might be valid and proposing to meet their demands for reform, the General Secretary of the Party openly challenged the conservative old-timers and Deng himself. It may have improved Zhao's image with the students, but that speech sealed his and ultimately their fate. Weeks later, when he'd been deposed, it would be officially branded as "a turning point for the escalation of the turmoil."

*   *   *

Outside his office window the din was deafening.

Lin would have shut it if not for the stifling heat. His fan provided little relief. He stood, fists clenched, watching thousands of citizens of Beijing lining the streets to Tiananmen Square to cheer the students, bringing them food and drinks, joining their ranks to demonstrate. He shook his head. "I thought we had a news blackout."

"In the official press," Peng Han acknowledged, joining the Foreign Minister at the window. Sweat soaked his porcine face. "But the students seem to have a better network than we anticipated."

Someone was singing a newly composed hymn, Beijing University's Pledge: "Fear not, fear not, to shed blood for the people, fear not…To demonstrate in our quest for people's rights, to oppose corruption and *guandao*, advance, fear not!"

"People's rights!" Lin sneered. "They have no idea what they want. Anarchy, chaos. That's what all this will bring."

"It's May 4th," Han said. "There's nothing we can do today. But starting tomorrow, if the class boycotts don't end, Deng is committed to cracking down. He says he will sacrifice two hundred thousand lives in the square to buy twenty years of stability."

"It may come to that, old friend."

General Tong barged in without knocking. "The girl is on her way here."

Lin nodded. "And Chi-Wen Zhou?"

"He eludes us for the moment," Tong reluctantly admitted. "But we'll find him."

Lin quickly weighed his future against the present political value of people. "When you do, kill him," he said dispassionately. "The fewer witnesses the better."

Silence reflected the others' consensus.

*   *   *

He was stunned.

Far enough away and camouflaged by the teeming station crowd, he could see without being seen. He didn't believe it possible. How did they find her? He trembled with frustration and rage.

"Come on. Let's get out of here."

Only Bin Go's strong grip on Chi-Wen's shoulder held him as he help-lessly watched three men, including the cadre from Xi'an, push Lili into a gray Shanghai and whisk her away. He looked at Go, ashen faced, drained. The cadre had followed them on the train. It was his fault. "I can't just leave," he said, his voice filled with anguish.

"What can you do?"

"I don't know," he admitted, "but I *must* help her."

"First, let's get you to a safe house." The student smiled, hoping to convey more confidence than he felt. "I'll try to find where they've taken her."

* * *

Two hours later, the phone in David Kim's hotel room rang.

"Yes?"

Kim recognized Lee Tong's voice. "Good news. The package has been delivered."

* * *

She was in an office. Totally disoriented.

They had brought her there blindfolded. The blindfold had been tied over her eyes the moment they forced her into the limo, so she had no way of knowing exactly where she was—only that she was probably still in Beijing.

"Good afternoon, Dr. Quan. I am Deputy Foreign Minister Lin. This is Peng Han and General Tong." Lin's voice was polite as proffered a packet of cigarettes. "Smoke?"

So it was afternoon. But how many hours had passed? Three? Four? For Lili, physically and emotionally exhausted, time had lost its structure, its pre-dictability. Sitting opposite Lin's desk, she watched in fascination as he lit a cigarette with the butt of an old one and inhaled, leisurely drawing the nicotine deep within his lungs, as if it were a substitute for oxygen.

Summoning all the bravado she could, she shook her head. "Didn't anyone ever tell you that smoking was bad for your health?"

"American propaganda, I assure you," he replied, making noisy use of the spittoon beside his desk. "I am eighty-three years old. I went on the Long March with Mao." Smiling : "Do I look unhealthy to you, Dr. Quan?

Impatient: "Why have I been brought here—like a prisoner? What do you want from me?"

"It should hardly be necessary for us to spell out the position we have reached. Your grandfather discovered the secret of longevity. There are those in the government who want it. We think he passed it to you just before he died. Therefore we must compel you to disclose what you know." As he spoke, the smile never left his face. Nor did it warm. He looked at Lili inquiringly, to see if further explanation was needed.

"Grandfather was overcome with pain when he died. He was ranting, but he didn't mention a secret. I can't help you."

"We know you have his research notes," Tong said.

"Is that what Dr. Seng told you? Your people searched me—quite thoroughly I might add—and found nothing." Despite the fact that she was sweating, Lili forced her voice to remain steady. "Can't you see? Seng's so ambitious for power, he'd make up any story. If my grandfather had the secret of longevity, he took it with him to his death. He told me nothing. And since he is dead, it is best for me to return to America as soon as possible."

"I'm afraid that isn't possible." Lin did not sound regretful.

"Are you telling me I'm not free to go home?"

"Your old life is gone. Forget about America. China is your home now. You can choose to be part of this great country and live and work here or sit in prison, labeled a counter-revolutionary, enemy of the State."

"What if I want neither?"

"You don't have a choice." He grinned broadly despite the fact that Lili's level gaze was unusually self-possessed for a Chinese woman, betraying no hint of fear.

"Listen," Peng Han interrupted. "My Intelligence branch has devised many ways of extracting information. Some are scientific, some are...shall we say, more crude. The scientific methods—drugs- are powerful, but dangerous. There are two reasons for this."

He used his chubby index finger to emphasize each point. "First," he said, jabbing the digit in the air, "once the chemical effect is set in motion, it cannot be halted. The optimum dose for each individual varies and if too much accumulates in the bloodstream, anything can happen. On more than one occasion these drugs have destroyed the mind of our subjects before they could communicate what they knew."

Lili's eyebrows shot up, revealing alarm for the first time. She couldn't believe Han's words. These men were mad.

"Second, it is possible for a person of average strength and intelligence to resist drugs for a long time, either giving us false information or talking nonsense. You, my dear can never be accused of being average. From what I hear, you have a strong will and clever mind. In your case, we may be forced to resort to the cruder methods I mentioned."

His eyes wandered from her face, briefly focusing on the guard behind her. "In the past, I have been forced to employ physical methods, but I must say, it has never been something I've enjoyed."

Outraged, Lili jumped up. "You're not serious. I'm an American citizen. You can't keep me here." Her voice sounded strong and confident, masking inner terror.

The Foreign Ministry chief nodded slowly. "We can and we will."

Lili turned pale. Her calm exterior began to wither. She was more frightened than she had ever been in her life.

Lin came around from behind his desk and stood beside her. The unsought, imposed intimacy had an unnerving effect. "Perhaps a little time alone will help you decide." He motioned curtly to the guard. "Take her to the detention cell."

The guard took Lili's arm and roughly guided her to the door.

"Until the morning…"

What did that mean? Fifteen, eighteen hours maybe. A small reprieve, though the tenor of all three men left no doubt in Lili's mind that no further delay would be tolerated.

*   *   *

Los Angeles, California

"What the...?" Dylan stared transfixed at the strange message just transmitted over his home fax. He had no idea who had sent it, but the words were clear: Lili was in trouble and needed help. Now.

Without hesitation, he made several calls, left a few messages and began packing his bags. Less than an hour later he had locked his apartment. Downstairs, the cab was already waiting for him. "LAX, Pan Am Airlines and step on it," he told the driver. "My plane leaves in forty minutes."

*   *   *

Beijing, China

The room where Lili was taken was no larger than a cell, furnished with a bed and chair. There were no windows, so she sat in the chair in total darkness, her head in her hands. Lin had taken her watch, but at least several hours had passed since the surly guard brought her a dinner tray of rice cakes and tea. Too distraught to eat, the meal delivery merely provided a sense of time. She figured it must be somewhere around eight or nine o'clock in the evening.

My God, she thought, what have I gotten myself into? And Chi-Wen? Where was he? Lin hadn't mentioned him and she'd been too afraid to ask. She assumed he'd been captured too. Had they tortured him? Or worse, was he dead? No, no, she couldn't even conceive of it. And yet, hadn't her grandfather told her what monsters Lin and his cronies were?

She thought about tomorrow. What would happen to her? Suppose Lin made good on his threats. Could she stand up to his torture? She didn't know. Her grandfather had died to protect his secret from these men. How could she simply hand it over to them? She refused to accept fate. She would turn it into an instrument of her own will. But how? She couldn't think anymore. Tears of rage, frustration and despair coursed down her cheeks until exhausted, she lay across the bed and drifted into any uneasy sleep.

Hours later, she was startled awake by a small sound. A light flickered in the room. Someone stood near her bed, silently watching her. For a second she thought it might be Chi-Wen, but the figure was shorter.

"Who's there?" she cried out.

A hand clasped over her mouth. The intruder put his lips to her ear. "Don't make a sound," he commanded in a strident whisper. "I came to take you out of here. Quickly, follow me." He removed his hand.

"I'm not going anywhere until you tell me who you are."

"Shh," he hissed. "If we're discovered we'll both be killed." A second match was lit and the man held it just below his face, offering her a quick look. "My name is Lee Tong."

"Why do you want to help?"

He frowned. "My father is General Tong."

One of Lin's fellow conspirators.

"He may be my father, but he represents the worst of our country. Until people like him are eliminated, China will never change. By helping you, I keep him from his dream to remain in power," Tong lied easily. "Now no more questions. There isn't time."

"Do you know what's happened to Chi-Wen Zhou? Is he a prisoner too?"

"Chi-Wen Zhou works for my father."

"What are you talking about?"

"He's been spying on you since you arrived in China."

Lili struggled to get oriented. Her panic soared. "It's not possible. Chi-Wen was helping me escape."

"That's what he wanted you to think. But tell me, how did the cadre know where to find you?"

Was it mere coincidence that the moment Chi-Wen left her on the train, the cadre appeared? Lili reeled inwardly.

Beijing?

It was Chi-Wen's idea really.

How did the cadre know where to find you?

You stay here... As soon as I find Tu's contact, I'll be back to get you.

"He deceived me? Was it all a trick?"

"I'm afraid so."

She felt faint. If Tong's words were true, Chi-Wen had lied to her from the beginning. She had trusted him. She had loved him! Was it all just part of a clever plan? Now she remembered that sinister look on the train. Oh God. How could she have been such a fool? Ironic-he'd called her naive. The only honest thing he'd said. Shocked and disillusioned, she wanted to scream.

I'm just a messenger.

It was simply a job to him, deluding a naive American to get control of her grandfather's secret.

Be wary of new friendships. The most cunning adversary first seeks to be your closest ally.

Why hadn't she heeded the fortune teller's warning?

She was shaken, scared and filled with rage. Chi-Wen hadn't just tricked her. He'd deceived her into falling in love with him. How he must have laughed at her. She despised him.

"We've got to get out of here," Tong urged. "I've put some milkwort root in the guard's tea. He'll sleep for at least another half hour." He handed her a gauze mask. "Wear this over your mouth and nostrils. It will help disguise your face."

Lili knew men and women wore these on the street when they had colds and were obeying rules to avoid spreading infection. She took the mask, then closed her eyes for a moment, trying to master the surge of emotions within her. This was not the time for feelings. She had to suppress them to remain alive. *Keep control!* Emotions were luxuries for later.

Opening her eyes, she turned to Tong. "I'm ready," she said, wondering if there ever would be a "later".

*   *   *

Hong Kong

Traveling west to east halfway around the world often left even the most experienced traveler disoriented and Halliday was no exception. He needed a few hours sleep to let his body catch up with the time zones, but didn't have a second to waste. The moment his plane landed in Hong Kong, he headed for the telephone kiosks to check his messages and grabbed a cup of black coffee. Then he found a taxi to take him to Yaumati dock where he caught the eleven o'clock jet foil for Macao.

*   *   *

Beijing, China

They emerged from the walls of the Foreign Ministry building to a hot, moonless night.

"Stay close!" Tong whispered.

As the blackness swallowed them, Lili's heart pounded against her ribcage, her lungs burned and her legs ached. All her senses were focused on one thing: escape. She ran, adrenaline propelling her onward. Crouching, hiding in the shadows of doorways whenever cars came near, looking over her shoulder to see if anyone followed them. Even though the small, back streets were virtually empty, she expected armed cadres to appear at any moment. She hoped Lee Tong had a real escape plan. Her chest heaved as she took in gulps of air.

"You okay?"

"I'll be fine," she wheezed. "As soon as we're out of China." Hot beads of sweat had formed on her forehead and cheeks. "Where are we going?"

"Not far. Near Tiananmen Square. Just two more blocks. "

*   *   *

...Slammed into wakefulness from what had been a pleasant dream, General Tong was annoyed. After hearing the cadre's report, he was furious. Incompetent fools! First they let Chi-Wen Zhou escape at the train station.

Now they'd lost the girl. In frustration, he pounded his fist on the night stand. How could they lose someone in the middle of the Foreign Ministry Building?

"There is something else," the cadre stammered.

"What?"

"Your son helped her escape."

His own son? The color in Tong's cheeks rose to a bright fuchsia as he considered the betrayal. But he shouldn't be surprised. That was the problem with the country today. Young people had no loyalty to tradition, no respect for their elders, no filial piety.

"I want them found," he snarled. "Tonight. " He knew his son would have to be silenced. He had no choice. "When you do, bring them directly to me. Do you understand?"

"Yes, sir."

"They can not be allowed to leave the country."

If only Lin had listened to him and kidnapped the girl when she'd first arrived in China. They'd have the secret by now and be done with her. Dammit. Everything had become so complicated.

The cadre was halfway to the door when Tong decided. The matter was too delicate to delegate. "On second thought, comrade, wait for me outside. I'm coming with you."

*   *   *

Half past ten, Bin Go returned to the safe house, an empty apartment on the eleventh floor of an abandoned fourteen story building. "She's escaped."

"Are you sure?"

The young student nodded. "I don't know how, but evidently someone helped get her away. It happened less than an hour ago. I had one of the students watching the Foreign Ministry Building. He didn't see her leave, but he overheard a couple of cadres who'd run outside just after she'd disappeared."

Chi-Wen started for the door. "I must find her."

Go shook his head. "Forget it. In Beijing she could be anywhere. There are still hundreds of thousands of students and citizens marching in the streets. Our May 4th rally was a bigger success than anyone anticipated." Smiling: "If anything, she has a perfect cover to escape."

Chi-Wen considered this information. Perhaps Go was right. He'd never find Lili here. And if she had escaped, she would likely try to make her way to Macao. She'd need a passport to enter Hong Kong. He hoped she remembered the address Tu had given them. "I've got to get to Macao as soon as possible."

Go produced a plane ticket for Guangchou. "It's all arranged. Including the fax you asked me to send."

Chi-Wen hadn't eaten or slept since Lili was taken that morning. His stomach grumbled in protest and he yawned deeply.

"I'm afraid that will have to wait 'til you reach your destination. We've got to leave for the airport now if you're going to catch your plane. It takes off in one hour."

*   *   *

Near Changan Avenue, they slowed their pace, their footsteps echoing on the pavement.

Just before midnight, the area around Tiananmen Square bustled with activity, the atmosphere more of a holiday parade, than a political demonstration. The fact that it was still May 4th, a traditionally festive day, coupled with the oppressive humidity, explained the reluctance of most to leave. Near the Gate of Heavenly Peace, mothers and fathers bounced babies on their shoulders, teenagers giggled with friends, old men argued with one another while they cracked melon seeds between their teeth. Many carried posters calling for freedom and human rights like those Lili had seen during the past three weeks. What made this rally different from the marches in Changsha and Shanghai, was the swell of ordinary citizens who openly participated. It was as though they suddenly embraced the possibility of real change.

Lili and Tong joined the protective coloration of the throng until they reached the corner of Dongdan Street. "There," the general's son hurried over to a willow tree where he'd locked his bicycle. "We can ride from here."

"How far do we have to go?" Lili asked, eyeing the ancient one-speed black Flying Pigeon with concern.

"The airport. About forty kilometers. My friend has a private plane ready to take you out of China."

Twenty-five miles, Lili thought, doing a quick conversion. "We'll never make it on this bike. Not if Lin or your father send men after us."

"Then I don't know how..."

"A motorcycle," she said. "Like that one." Lili pointed to a young boy astride a Honda 175CL. It had a flat seat for two. "Ask him if it's for sale."

Tong shook his head. "Flying Tiger Brigade. He'll never part with it."

"What kind of brigade?"

"*Feihudui, liumong* ! " Tong replied. "A bunch of hooligans. A few months ago they roamed the streets in groups of forty or more scaring people. Now they've taken on the cause for democracy. They ride around Beijing giving students information about the police." Tong's contempt was transparent.

"And you don't approve?"

"Of course, I support the student movement," Tong insisted with conviction. "It's just the kids," he improvised. "I don't trust them."

"We could use his cycle."

Reluctantly, Tong stopped the boy and began to haggle. At the same time, Lili scanned the crowd.

"Lee Tong!"

Lee, without a face mask, had been recognized.

Lili's stomach gave a sickening lurch. A block away, she spotted the same black Shanghai in which she'd been kidnapped yesterday. Beside it stood General Tong, staring at them.

"It's my father!"

"Give the boy whatever he wants," Lili urged, her heart pounding again. "We've got to get out of here!"

"Sixteen hundred yuan. That's almost five hundred US dollars."

Lili jumped on the bike. "When we get to Hong Kong, I'll pay you back."

The general got back in the car. The crowd prevented his driver from moving more than a few feet at a time.

"Okay," Tong relented, reaching into his trouser pocket and handing the boy a wad of *renminbi*.

"Hurry!"

Tong took his place behind Lili.

She turned the ignition key and kicked down on the starter pedal, praying silently the engine would start. It coughed to life. *Thank God.*

"Hold on," she shouted, remembering not so long ago, she'd asked Chi-Wen to do the same. Gunning the throttle, she accelerated, plunging into the thick and restlessly moving stream of marchers and bike riders.

*   *   *

Chi-Wen held his breath as the immigration officer dressed in white jacket and red-starred cap checked his papers before boarding the CAAC flight to Guangchou. He was traveling on a Philippine passport stolen four hours earlier in a crowded restaurant. Fernando Sison had been inebriated at the time and would likely not miss it until morning. The papers said he was *huaqiao*, Overseas Chinese, first generation born in Manila. Chi-Wen could expect special status—provided the credentials passed scrutiny. Fortunately, the passport already had an authentic visa stamp from the Chinese consulate in Beijing. Even the hastily pasted photo of Chi-Wen seemed impressive enough to convince the casual eye. He prayed he wouldn't be asked to speak Tagalog.

The official smiled at Chi-Wen. "Have you had a pleasant trip, Mr. Sison?"

"Very," Chi-Wen replied in Chinese, painfully aware that the business suit Go "borrowed" from his father was one size too big. The official never noticed. "*Zai jian*," he said courteously, as he placed the final exit stamp on the passport and waved Chi-Wen through the gate. "Have a good flight."

*   *   *

Lili maneuvered sharply around the pedestrian traffic as Tong directed her through the side avenues of Beijing. Dongdan Street to Dongsi Street to Dongzhimennei Road and onto Dongzhimen Wai Street.

"I think you lost him," Tong shouted above the motor.

When they turned onto Jing Shun Road, the four lane, willow-lined boulevard leading to Beijing International Airport, Lili rocketed the motorcycle forward until it reached its maximum speed of sixty miles per hour.

Safe!

"Oh no!"

Lili looked back to where Tong was pointing. Bright headlights glowed in the distance. Unusual since drivers in China always used parking lights at night. It was moving up fast. A black Shanghai. Lili gasped. The general obviously figured they were heading for the airport and took a shortcut to the highway. It moved closer. She thought quickly. "Is there another route?"

"The old road. But it's badly paved."

A quick backward glance. She could not judge how far they were, but they were closing quickly. "I've got to try."

Tong indicated a spot just ahead. "That way."

Gravel flew like machine gun fire from under cycle's spinning treads as it took the hairpin turn.

Tong tightened his grip around Lili's waist.

The Shanghai swerved onto the narrow, dirt road.

Oh, my God. I can't be caught.

Grimly, Lili clutched the hand levers, fighting to keep the wheels under control. She knew they were going too fast for safety, but she had no choice. The Shanghai would soon be right behind them.

She passed several modest farm houses and rice paddies before she saw it. Two hundred yards ahead, obscured at first by darkness, was a pedestrian bridge with a cat walk not more than three feet wide. It was worth a try. In the moonless night, the driver of the Shanghai would not realize the danger until it was too late.

Lili slowed the cycle until the general was just two car lengths behind.

"What are you doing? They'll catch up with us!"

"Don't worry," Lili tried to reassure Tong, at the same time gunning the throttle. It didn't respond. Her heart beat wildly. The Shanghai was only one car length behind.

Come on, dammit!

Again she raced the motor. This time the cycle lurched forward, whipping easily over the narrow bridge.

As Lili predicted, the Shanghai followed her tail. But just as the driver reached the bridge, he saw he'd never make it. A sudden swerve to correct his mistake brought the front end of the car over the edge. Too quickly for the evasive action to be effective, it lunged into the irrigation ditch. Headlights disappeared beneath the muddy water.

"It's stuck!" Tong breathed.

Lili nodded, but didn't look back. If they were lucky, they had a few miles lead, if they were really lucky, the car would remain stuck for hours. Either scenario, she was determined to outride them. "Which way?" Her heart pounded as she continued toward the airport, unsure what lay ahead.

The next fifteen miles were no less nightmarish with only the cycle's dim headlight to guide them through the twists and turns of the one lane alternate road. At one point, Lili fishtailed dangerously to avoid a large branch lying across her path. Just as she did in Westwood months ago, she produced a controlled slide-out that stopped her dead, narrowly avoiding a collision.

Thirty minutes later they reached the airport. Tong directed her to a private airstrip a quarter mile away. "There it is!" he pointed to the Kim Company Learjet parked across the field.

From the cockpit David Kim saw them and ordered the pilot to start up the engines.

A noise behind alerted Lili. "What the...?"

The Shanghai had reappeared! They must have gotten the car out of the ditch and returned to the main highway, she thought, screeching to a halt. "Get off," she told Tong. "We'll have to make a run for it."

Together they bolted across the field.

The heavy whine of the jets was deafening.

The cabin opened and a Korean called to her in English. "Dr. Quan. Hurry!"

A burst of rifle fire jangled every nerve in Lili's body.

"Run!"

Tong, sprinting, tried to close the gap between them.

A bullet ricocheted off the cockpit door. A second one exploded just above Lili's head.

"Don't shoot the girl!" General Tong ordered in Chinese.

"Hurry up!" Kim screamed.

Lili summoned whatever reserve she possessed and bolted up the stairs. Lee Tong followed a few feet behind. When she reached the top, Kim pulled her inside the plane, pushed the steps away and slammed the cabin door shut.

"Help me!" Tong pounded on the fuselage.

"Open the door," Lili demanded.

David Kim ordered the pilot to begin the takeoff.

"But he'll…"

The sound of guns firing over and over again.

The jet began to taxi.

Lili looked outside the window. Lee Tong lay crumpled on the tarmac, dead.

The plane barreled down the runway.

"You let them shoot him!" she screamed. "Why?"

"He was expendable," Kim said simply.

Bewildered: "I don't understand. Who are you?" she asked, fighting back panic. This man was no friend. She began backing away, aware that once again she'd been betrayed. "Get away from me!" Her voice was weak.

"I suggest you sit down and enjoy the flight, Dr. Quan. You're not going anywhere."

Blindly, Lili tried to rush past Kim, but he caught and spun her around like a rag doll. Then someone was behind her, smelling of jasmine and holding something in her hand. A needle. A syringe.

"No!"

Camille plunged the needle into Lili's left biceps. "Sleep tight, cheri."

Too late. Lili felt the hot squirt of the liquid enter her muscle. Almost instantly everything went black.

*　　　　　*　　　　　*

On the field General Tong was shaking.

Anger and sorrow rose simultaneously. He shook his head as he watched the jet disappear into the dark night. Lili Quan had escaped. She had beaten him. He could forget *shou*. Wanting to live forever, he reasoned, was just fear of dying. As a soldier, Tong never feared death. For him, immortality lay in defeating China's enemies. Now that Deng had sanctioned force against the students, General Tong could control the ultimate outcome. Like his son, some students would die so that China could remain the dragon it had always been.

TWENTY-SIX

Friday, May 5th
Macao

A pair of tree sparrows courted one another in the early morning light, their melodies echoing across the tiny Portuguese province. Parked as if to sight-see, Halliday aimed his telephoto lens not at Macao spread below, but at Ng's gated estate perched on a flattened mound of Guia Hill. Even with the windows open, the air in his rented Mercedes 300E was stifling. He swiped lazily at a long legged insect hovering near his face.

It had been a long time since he'd been a field agent stalking criminals around the world and despite the physical discomforts, he reveled in the sense of being his own man. In the field, the Company wasn't bogged down by the bullshit of legalities and bureaucracy. This would be his last stakeout. He had one task to finish before heading back to Hong Kong.

A photo of the man DeForest had met in California lay on the seat beside him. Halliday put down his Nikon 8008 and studied the face seamed down one side by a strange Z-shaped scar. Paulo Ng. An ugly son-of-a-bitch. But a damn smart one. At least according to his dossier. Dealing with him might not be as easy as DeForest. But then again, he had the element of surprise on his side.

As he sipped cold coffee from a Styrofoam cup, Halliday wondered just how long he'd have to wait for Ng's return. Last night the houseboy said his boss had taken his yacht for a sail. He was expected home some time today. That was fine. He'd be back.

Unconsciously, he patted the .45 automatic he wore in a shoulder harness under his jacket. After all, he thought, he'd waited this long. He could wait a few more hours.

*   *   *

Just before seven AM, he heard the sound of engines.

Ng trained his binoculars on the horizon, sweeping them to find the plane. Suddenly it appeared, a growing dot racing toward him. He jumped from his limousine and switched on the warning lights at the end of the makeshift runway. The Lear jet whistled overhead once, banking sharply to the east, circling out over Castle Peak Bay and sweeping back a second time over the pair of desolate islands known as The Brothers for a landing on the larger of the two 'sibs'. Barely ten miles long and just two miles wide, the thin strip of hard land floated in the South China Sea like a won ton in a teacup. But it was precisely its total isolation that suited Ng's needs.

A few minutes later, the plane touched down in a cloud of sand. The cabin door opened immediately and Kim disembarked.

"You have the girl?"

Kim nodded. "Camille had to keep her sedated."

"No problem. We'll transfer her to my yacht. By the time we reach Macao she should be able to talk."

"What about my plane?" Kim asked.

"Send it home." Ng put his arm around Kim's shoulder. "You'll be my guest for a few days. Don't worry. I'll see that you get back to Seoul."

*   *   *

Hong Kong

The first red glow of dawn streaked the horizon as the 747 swept in low over the bay and banked into Kai Tak airport. Dylan felt a surge of excitement. Part of it was being in Hong Kong again. Only once, years ago, but the island held fond memories of exotic sights and sounds and smells—a place of endless intrigues and infinite possibilities. Most of it, though, was the anticipation of seeing Lili again. What had happened to her in China, he wondered. He hoped to see her soon to get answers.

As he passed customs, he heard the page. "Attention, arriving passenger O'Hara. Please contact Pan American information…"

"I'm Dr. O'Hara," he told the petite Asian woman at the Pan Am counter.

"A message for you," she said pleasantly, handing him a sealed envelope.

His face must have registered surprise as he read the note inside. "Anything was wrong?"

"No, not at all, " he replied without looking up.

"May I be of further assistance?" she queried. "A taxi perhaps?"

Her voice interrupted his musing. He'd been thinking about the message. "I would appreciate that."

"Where to, sir?"

"The Peninsula Hotel."

*   *   *

Guangchou, China

Chi-Wen's eyes swept over the faces of waiting relatives and friends.

He had no idea what the student sent to meet his plane would look like— only that he (or she) would wave a People's Daily, smile and deliver a pre-arranged greeting. No one in the crowd seemed to be waiting for him and he couldn't leave the airport until his contact showed. He followed the disembarking passengers down the station concourse to a breakfast stall where he purchased a small bowl of salted fish and rice, the strain of the past twenty-four hours manifested in a rapacious appetite. Two yuan bought him a second bowl which he ate slowly, savoring the smoky flavor.

"Papers, please." An airport security guard accompanied by an army officer initiated an inspection at the far end of the breakfast line.

Waves of nausea overwhelmed Chi-Wen as his stomach twisted in panic.

Next to him, a young man in a suit as baggy as his own, banged down his rice bowl and began a frantic search through his jacket pockets. "Damn nuisance!" he grumbled in Mandarin. "Do they think we're all spies?"

Spies? The word brought frightening images of irrefutable accusations, inevitable arrest and the sound of cell doors clanging shut with irrevocable finality.

"Here they come."

The two uniformed men stood in front of Chi-Wen's neighbor who handed over his yellow ID card and travel permit. The army officer's eyes narrowed and his lips pursed. "Step out of line," he ordered.

"Anything wrong?" the young man asked in a surprised tone.

"You are going on to Shatin?"

"Yes, I have business there this afternoon." Spoken with an air of self-importance. China's new breed of entrepreneurs.

"You'll need a correct date stamp, then. This one is for yesterday."

The young man squirmed. "I couldn't get an earlier flight from Beijing."
"It's against regulations. You must have the proper stamp."

"But that could take hours. I'll miss my meeting." He leaned slightly toward the security guard, hoping he might be more sympathetic than the bureaucratically indoctrinated army man. "Comrade, it's just one day off. Can't it be overlooked?"

The guard merely shrugged as if to say the matter was out of his hands, then moved on while the officer escorted him away. "Your papers."

Chi-Wen fought to control his anxiety as the man's dark eyes studied him. *Stay calm.*

"Passport."

"Of course." Chi-Wen yawned to affect indifference, though his body prickled with tension. Behind the guard, he glimpsed the airport exit, a freedom he would never reach. In a moment he'd he discovered and carted off to jail.

"Thank you."

"Fernando!" A skinny girl in shapeless gray pants and white blouse was hurrying toward him, pushing through the crowd, waving a People's Daily over her head. "Cousin! What kept you? Everyone is waiting outside!"

The security officer turned to look.

Chi-Wen felt his knees weaken as he realized this was the Zhongshan University student he was to meet. He was certain he was done for.

Distracted by the noisy entrance, the guard handed back his papers with an avuncular scolding. "You shouldn't keep family waiting."

The girl embraced him. "The name is Mei Ling," she whispered in his ear. "Hurry! We must get you out of here!"

Chi-Wen returned the embrace, then gratefully followed her to the airport exit. As he pushed open the door, his hand shook. *That* was close, he thought. Too close.

$$*\qquad\qquad *\qquad\qquad *$$

Near New Territories

Ng's seventy-five foot custom English cutter sliced silently through the South China Sea toward Macao. Sleek and low in the water, the craft's exterior resembled a racer more than a yacht. In fact, it had been fashioned after the old cutters used in the early nineteenth century to pursue smugglers; its sliding bowsprit and topmast provided speed and easy handling. The interior, however, was designed for different sport—complete with a large main salon fully appointed with rosewood pool table and marble wetbar, a master suite with king-size bed and Jacuzzi, ample quarters for two other guests and a galley befitting any gourmet chef.

While Camille guarded Lili in a guest bedroom, David Kim sat in the main salon reading the papers Ng had put before him with growing confusion. And fear. It wasn't possible. Despite the air conditioning, he reached inside his suit and peeled his sweat soaked handmade shirt from his clammy skin. "I don't understand. This looks like Zee Enterprises has somehow bought a controlling interest in Kim Company. I never okayed any stock purchases."

Ng laughed at the look on his face. "It was quite easy." His eyes gleamed. "I simply used your *tojang* to make the transactions. A legal signature, I assure you."

"But why? You said Zee Enterprises was to be a subsidiary of Kim Company. Nothing more. You promised...."

"Promised?" Ng found the notion hilarious. "I'm a businessman, pure and simple. I'm motivated by profit, not ideology or politics. Certainly not morality." He spread out a wad of chits. "Your debts. I'm afraid you've run up quite a hefty tab these past few weeks."

"I'll pay it back."

"Where do you propose to get the money?"

"I'm head of one of the most successful companies in Korea," he said with genuine indignation. "I'm good for it."

Ng's smile disappeared. "You're good for nothing, my friend." He shook his head. "If only your father had paid more attention. Though I suppose it's understandable. Having his own flesh and blood, his only son, inherit the business. He was blinded to the facts. He believed the improved earnings and increased market share in the China plants were a sign you'd given up your decadent ways, had settled down. But of course, we both know you hadn't changed at all."

Ng leaned forward. His scarred face was close enough to make Kim pull away. "I had to make a business decision, David. Kim Company was on the brink of disaster before your father died. With you at the helm, it would have fallen off the edge. I bought these shares," he said pointing to the stock portfolio. "To protect my investment."

Kim tried to recover. "We're still partners," he stammered.

"No, we're not. I dissolved our partnership."

Bewildered: "How?"

" Also with your *tojang*. " Ng didn't bother to mention his short-lived relationship with DeForest. The man's untimely death was fortuitous. "*I'm* the sole owner of Kim Company now."

For several minutes David sat stunned as the news settled like lead in his stomach. He could not believe he had lost his company, though he held the proof. Zee Enterprises owned Kim Company and Paulo Ng was Zee

Enterprises. He knew it was his own fault. He had betrayed his father's trust. Still, it seemed unjust. To lose everything. He appealed first to an imaginary court. Couldn't he make amends? It wasn't too late, was it? Then to the pirate: "What can I do?" he whimpered. "I'll do anything."

Ng looked at Kim's shaking hands, disgusted by the manicured nails, the soft fingers. "You've brought dishonor to the Kim name. If you were your father, you would consider suicide."

"You're crazy!" But the perspiration along his hairline attested to his panic. Instinct told him he was in mortal danger.

Ng ignored the outburst. He clapped his hands and two men, one the ex-Sumi wrestler from the casino, entered. Each took one of Kim's arms and dragged him toward the door.

"What are you doing?" Kim screamed.

"I understand your generation rejects the old ways," Ng said evenly. "That's why I've decided to help you."

*   *   *

Beijing, China

Deputy Minister Lin was less sanguine than General Tong about Lili's escape. "She's got the secret, Peng Han. I want her found."

"The same informant who told us where to find her in Beijing claims Chi-Wen Zhou is headed for Hong Kong. Evidently, he plans to meet her at the Peninsula Hotel."

Lin smiled for the first time since Lili's escape. "Then that's where *I'll* meet her."

*   *   *

Near Macao

She was a lost soul in a raging sea, screaming wind, tossing deliriously on the backs of giant black waves. Then the waves opened up, folding her into walls of water, sucking her beneath the surface, into the darkness. Somehow the blackness passed and she was rising once more toward the light, toward the torrent.

Help me! Don't let me die!

As if her prayers had been answered, the wind died down and the waves became soft rolling hills, rocking her in a gentle cradle.

No!

A pair of hands shaking her from side to side. She was not floating outside on calm waters, but lying on a hard bunk in a cabin.

"Can you hear me, Dr. Quan?"

The face was not Asian, yet not European. Speaking to her in English, with a heavy accent. In the fog she couldn't place it. Not Chinese. She tried squinting to see properly, but it slipped in and out of focus. She thought there was mustache and a scar. Like a Z. How funny!

"Can you hear me?"

The voice was coming closer again.

"Dr. Quan? Can you sit up?" the voice queried.

Lili felt hands shoved under her, pushing her to a sitting position. Reluctantly she moved until she was upright. Her head began to spin and for a moment she feared blackness would return.

"Do you want to be sick?"

She closed her eyes until the dizziness passed. "Where am I?"

"You're on my yacht headed for Macao." He put a cigarillo in his mouth.

Yacht? How did I...? Slowly it all came back, nightmarish images—her wild escape from Beijing, Lee Tong's shooting, the strange Korean, someone injecting her and blacking out. Lili opened her eyes fully. A man in a white suit was smiling. Why did he seem so familiar? "Who are you?"

Flicking his gold lighter so the dragon etched on the side seemed to belch fire. "The name's Paulo Ng." He lit his cigarillo and took a long drag.

Blue smoke, white suit, something about his voice...

'win-win. It's essential that everyone's special needs be satisfied'

Like a curtain rising, Lili pulled the scene from her memory. "You're the man at the Peninsula Hotel."

"And the dim sum restaurant."

'I'd leave room for the saan tat if I were you...'

My God, she thought, three weeks ago in Hong Kong he'd been following her. "What do you want, Mr. Ng?" she demanded.

The pirate's admiring look was genuine. "A direct woman. I like that. I suppose that explains how you've managed to outwit three of the most important men in the Chinese government."

Sensing danger, Lili was deliberately evasive: "I don't know what you're talking about."

"Of course you do, my dear." Skipping details, Ng explained he was a businessman who had made a deal through David Kim with Lee Tong. He knew Ni-Fu Cheng had discovered the secret of longevity and before he died, passed it on to Lili. "You give me the formula and you'll be free to go," he said reasonably.

Lili tried to swallow her fear. This man was lying. He'd never let her go. He couldn't afford to have a witness survive. "You're even stupider than you look," she said contemptuously.Ng roared with laughter.

"Excuse me." Camille entered. "We'll be docking in a few minutes."

Ng nodded. "Dr. Quan, we can finish our little chat at my villa." To Camille: "Tie her up. We wouldn't want our guest to disappear again."

* * *

Guangchou, China

The girl was silent during their bus ride from the Baiyun Airport.

Through the downtown commercial area of Guangchou toward Zhongshan University. Everywhere he looked, Chi-Wen felt a disturbing sense of deja vu—the Beijing Road bookstore, the fast food noodle house, the White Swan Hotel—familiarity a bittersweet reminder of the time he'd spent with Lili. Less than three weeks ago he was walking down these same crowded streets with her, frustrated by her ingenuousness, fascinated by her independence—

falling in love. Now he was returning alone, not sure if he would ever see her again. The thought made him shudder.

Mei Ling tapped him on the arm to indicate they'd reached their destination. "I'm taking you to an apartment near the university," she explained. "You can rest there."

"How soon can I leave for Macao?"

The girl shrugged. "Since the student coalition announced more class boycotts, the government threatened a crackdown. They've already detained a few student leaders, so we're planning a hunger strike."

Chi-Wen was stunned. He had no idea so much had happened in the last twenty-four hours.

"We'll have to wait 'til dark. If police security at the airport and train stations picks up, we have to find another route to get you out."

"What would that be?"

The girl looked at Chi-Wen for a long moment before she responded. "Do you swim?"

*   *   *

Macao

Headlights swung onto the driveway and stopped.

"Open the gate, dammit!"

"Sorry, sir. The remote's not responding."

"Get out and move it manually!" Ng ordered the bodyguard who doubled as chauffeur.

The silence of the black night was broken by the driver's footsteps echoing off the gravel of the long twisting driveway. Beside the massive wrought iron gate, he casually hunched down to inspect the motorized mechanism, assuming the circuit breaker had been tripped. As he leaned closer to reset the toggle switch, he was surprised to find it already in the correct position. Puzzled, he noticed a six inch iron bar carefully wedged between the chain and the sprocket wheel jamming the entire assembly. Buddha! This could only be the work of a saboteur. He'd better warn the boss.

It was his last thought. In one swift movement, a piano wire was wrapped around his neck from behind and pulled tight, dragging him breathless and dying into the bushes.

Silently, Halliday removed the coil and rewrapped it around his left wrist.

From within the Rolls, Ng grew impatient. "Find out what's keeping that idiot!" he snapped at his bodyguard.

The guard was almost fifty feet up the driveway when the poison dart struck his jugular. Brushing frantically at his neck, he thought a bee had stung him. Until his limbs grew numb and his breathing seemed to stop.

The occupants of the Rolls Royce did not hear the heavy thud of his body hitting the ground.

"All right," Ng told Camille a few minutes later. "I'd better handle this myself. Lock the doors and watch the girl." He stepped out of the limo and squinted into the darkness. The night air was still and muggy. "Pei-Jun?" So quiet he could hear the blare of a ship's horn far off across the water. "Yu?" Where were those pox infested sea slugs? He took his gold lighter from his pocket , flicking it this way and that, but the shadows gave up nothing.

"Put it out, please."

Ng froze, trying to locate the voice.

"I *said* shut it off."

Ng flicked off the lighter and was cloaked in darkness.

"That's better."

He felt a presence approaching just behind him.

"Good evening, Mr. Ng."

Furious someone had infiltrated his compound, unwilling to lose face. "Do I know you?" he asked in a conversational tone.

"Let's just say I was also a partner of the former Walter DeForest."

"He never mentioned you," Ng said.

"I'm not surprised. Loyalty wasn't one of Walt's strong suits."

"Loyalty and business don't always mix."

"So I've learned."

Ng began to turn his head, but was dissuaded by the barrel of Halliday's .45 against his neck.

"Don't do that," the voice in his ear ordered. "And don't try anything. I know all about your deal with old Walt. And David Kim and Zee Company."

"I see."

"I'm not sure you do," Halliday said. "Lili Quan would never have gone to China if I hadn't orchestrated her trip. The secret of *shou* is rightfully mine. Now, hand over the lighter."

Ng did as he was told. Whoever he was, this man was obviously no fool. Ng would need to keep his cool if he was going to reverse his position.

"Throw down your weapons."

Slowly, Ng reached in his pocket and withdrew his cigarillo case. "I have no weapons. Just this." He opened the case, holding it up for Halliday. "See."

The ex-CIA man patted him down carefully. "Okay, turn around," he said.

"Would you like one?" Ng offered.

"No thanks."

The Macanese shrugged and took one before returning the case to his pocket. "I could never get our mutual friend to try them either," he said putting the cigarillo to his lips. "I suppose DeForest preferred the more macho image of a cigar smoker."

Halliday flicked the flame as if to offer a light, but used it to watch the pirate's expression. "That was not an intelligent move, Mr. Ng."

The scarred face contorted, a mass of twisted fury as he vainly blew on the end of the cigarillo . "What the…?"

"I'm afraid your Dobermans won't be able to hear that," Halliday clucked, grabbing the high-pitched whistle. "They've been dead for hours."

The dark orbs grew narrower as Ng realized Halliday had gotten the best of him. "My compliments, Mr.…."

"The name's Halliday."

"Mr. Halliday. You are quite a resourceful fellow. Look," he said trying again to regain his composure. "I own Kim Company."

"So?"

"So you still need a way to market the formula."

"I'm listening."

Ng smiled to cover his disgust for the greedy foreigner. He'd sweet talk him now. Later he'd screw this fornicating *waigoren*. "You and I can be partners."

"Walt once told me, 'never work for a company you can't own'."

"Good advice."

"Yes," Halliday agreed. "But I'd add one thing."

"What's that?"

Halliday cocked his .45. "Never take partners." And squeezed the trigger. "It's too risky." Blowing Ng's brains out.

At the sound of gunshots, Lili, huddled in the back seat, bound and gagged, produced a low, throaty cry of terror.

A harsh slap from Camille. "Shut up!" she hissed, then climbed into the driver's seat. "We've got to get out of here." Shifting to reverse, she floored the accelerator and raced blindly down the driveway.

Halliday was ready.

Whack!

The first bullet blew the left rear tire. The Rolls swerved, but Camille kept going.

Whack!

The second hit the right rear tire and the limo skidded to a bumpy stop.

Halliday moved to the front of the car and stood in the glare of the head-lights. "Out!" he yelled.

Panicked, Camille shifted to drive and tried to gun the engine. Too late. Halliday fired. The sputter of erupting radiator fluid ensured that the Rolls wasn't going anywhere. Then, aiming directly at the driver, Halliday fired again. The sound of shattered glass and another *Whack!* The Eurasian woman went limp, a dark red hole in her forehead.

Halliday opened the passenger door and yanked Lili out. On the edge of hysteria, she tried to pull away, twisting her body from one side to the other. "Dr. Quan, listen to me. I'm Charlie Halliday, CIA. I'm here to rescue you."

Tears streamed down her face as he untied her hands and removed the gag. "Are you all right?"

Lili tried hard to regain her composure. She nodded. "I'll be fine." Between ebbing sobs she massaged the pain in her wrists. Then she saw Camille draped over the steering wheel and Ng lying on the driveway a few feet from the car. "Did you have to kill them?" she cried. It seemed so sense-less. Like Tong's killing. Kim had said Tong was expendable. On the way to the villa, Ng had boasted about terminating David Kim. Expendable, terminate—words meant to justify. What? The chance to prolong life? The irony was almost laughable.

"I had no choice. They would have killed you."

She supposed he *had* saved her life. But why? Questions began piling up like waves on a beach. Why was he here? What did he want? How did he know where to find her? How long had anyone known about her plight in China? Answers no easier to catch than the surf. "What's going on, Mr. Halliday?"

He took her arm and led her toward his Mercedes parked at the edge of the hillside. "I suggest you get in the car. If the houseboy heard the shots, he'll call the police. They'll be here any minute."

"So?"

Exasperated. " I don't have time to deal with them now. Besides, this is hardly a local police matter. What I do need is to get you to a safe place for debriefing." He unlocked the passenger door and opened it for her.

Debriefing? She stared at him, bewilderment and fear converging in her look. "How do I know I can trust you?" She had already made the mistake of trusting three men who'd betrayed her.

"Typical American. Doesn't trust anyone," Halliday laughed easily. "Listen, I'm an American too. And I'm on your side."

"You say you're with the CIA. What does the CIA want with me?"

"I don't have time to answer your questions now." His voice took on a hardened edge. "Let's get going."

She bent to get in, stopped and straightened. A swirling mist of doubt. Something didn't feel right.

"Get in the car," he said harshly.

She backed away. Her mind leapt back and forth, mental circuits of paranoia arcing through exhaustion and terror. "I'd rather wait for the police."

He'd been standing with his hands outstretched as he attempted to convince her. Now his right hand slipped into his jacket pocket.

"No!" she screamed, moving further toward the edge of the road until her foot slipped on a loose stone. As she lost her balance, she fell backwards, hitting the ground, then rolled and twisted until she finally banged up against a tree midway down the hill. Instinctively she pressed herself flat, hugging the earth. She stayed for a moment, struggling to catch her breath, listening for the sounds of gunfire or an indication that Halliday was following her. But all she could hear was the rush of breath in her own throat and a hot breeze whispering through the trees. At seven, the sun had already set. The moon, dimly lit though the clouds, outlined everything in eerie shadows.

"Dr. Quan, come back." The crunch of footsteps, then the glare of a flashlight. For a second her heart stopped as she waited inevitable discovery. But the beam wasn't pointed toward her. It probed the upper edges of the hill, silhouetting trees and bushes like an old time sepia photograph.

Muffled curses filled the air as the arc swept closer. "Damn bitch!"

Lili lay pressed down. *Dear God, please don't let him see me.*

"I know you're there. No point in hiding. It's only a matter of time until I find you."

The light so close she was just outside its circular beam.

A siren wailed through the darkness and at once the light died.

Lili held her breath.

The sounds of running, a car door slamming, the engine starting and stones scattering, as the Mercedes pulled away.

The siren wailed above her. The police, Lili speculated. Alerted by Ng's houseboy. Would they help? Without a passport and papers, she'd be as likely a murder suspect as anyone. At the very least, she'd be delayed. There wasn't time. Dottie would be in Hong Kong the day after tomorrow. No, she thought. From now on, she'd trust no one but herself.

She waited five minutes in the darkness before sensing she was safe; five minutes more before she pushed herself up to a crouch and began to run.

Run for her life.

*   *   *

To Halliday, Lili's escape was a major setback, but not an irrevocable obstacle to obtaining the secret. As long as he knew her ultimate destination, he'd catch up with her. Driving back to the Outer Harbor on the

Avenida da Amizade, he returned the rental car, then hopped the hydrofoil back to Hong Kong.

*   *   *

Numb and confused, she ran, her breathing ragged.

She could see nothing clearly, but sensed what was there. The events of the last thirty-six hours swirled round and round in her head, transforming every-thing into something sinister and menacing. In the shadowy light, she con-jured up ghosts—her overworked imagination convinced her that anything was possible. Drenched with perspiration, exhausted by the exertion of run-ning and scrambling several miles through scrub and backyards, down the twisting roads from Ng's house near Guia Hill.

She would have liked to find a spot, hidden beneath a tree or bush, where she could curl up for a few hours and rest, but she dared not close her eyes. Halliday couldn't have given up so easily. He must have some trick up his sleeve. She had to maintain her vigilance.

At Avenido do Conselheiro she finally stopped to catch her breath, won-dering what to do next, where to go. Then she remembered the name and address Zheng Tu had given her. If she could find it, perhaps she'd be safe.

*   *   *

Seventy miles south of Guangchou

Mei Ling peered at Macao's brightly lit shoreline three miles away. "I'm afraid this is as far as we can take you," she whispered. "You must find your way on your own now. Good luck."

Chi-Wen swung his legs over the side of the sampan and lowered himself into the water. He was barefoot, his shoes hung around his belt. "Thank you for all your help." The trip from Guangchou had challenged the university student who'd commandeered a series of cars and trucks to transport him seventy miles down the coast to Nantou on the east side of the Pearl River delta. She'd found a fisherman to take him as close to Macao as he dared.

"Chi-Wen Zhou?"

"Yes?" Treading water, legs scissoring to stay afloat.

"When you've found your friend, will you think about returning to China? The democracy movement needs you."

In the few seconds Chi-Wen took to consider an answer, the fisherman had already brought the little sampan about, heading it back toward the mainland.

Something brushed by his foot. A shark? He must be very still. Mei Ling had said they were extremely sensitive to motion. Heart in his throat, he waited, imagining the predaceous fish swimming below him, readying to open its crescent-shaped mouth and devour him. But whatever he felt passed by and was gone. The distant sound of waves slapping against the retreating hull underscored his aloneness.

You must find your way on your own now.

His fate was in his own hands, he thought, suddenly reminded of Lili and Santiago of *The Old Man and the Sea*. Denying the ineluctability of fate, winning against all odds, taking risks. Soldiers, bullfighters, fishermen, Chinese students. Staring up at the winking stars, he resolved to be one of those who meet the pain and difficulty of their existence with stoic courage.

Good luck.

He'd need that too, he thought, shivering in the frigid water. He began a slow side stroke, swimming across the current, toward the shore.

*   *   *

Macao

She found the address with surprising ease.

It was a small tailor shop on cobblestoned Rua do Campo, its sign and window grimy with years of dust. She knocked and waited a long time until at last a shape emerged from behind the net curtain that covered the door. The lock turned and the door swung open slowly. The owner was a pockmarked Chinese Lili guessed to be close to seventy. Although round-shouldered and pale from years of sitting in the half-light at his sewing machine, the eyes that scrutinized her were sharp and the hands he held to his chest did not shake.

"*Shir* ?"

"I'm an American. I've lost my passport and I need a new one."

"Then go to the American embassy. They will help." His English was remarkably good. An expatriate from the mainland, Shen Minghad once dreamed of traveling to America. Forty years later, he'd made his peace with his lot in life, though from time to time he helped others get there. As he started to close the door, Lili placed her hand on it, a look of urgency on her face.

"I don't have time. Please," she said. "You must help me. I'm a friend of Zheng Tu, one of the student leaders. He gave me your name and address. He said you could get me papers and a passport."

The man's eyebrows lifted as he looked more closely at Lili.

"Zheng sent you? Why didn't you say so? He is my sister's grandson. If he thinks it is important, it must be so." Now he noticed her shabby appearance. "Is your life in danger?"

Lili sighed. "Yes."

"In that case, come in."

Lili stepped into the shop. Shen ushered her through a door at the back, into a small room that served as his kitchen, dining room, living room and bedroom. She thought of Fan and for a moment, Chi-Wen.

The tailor misinterpreted the anguished look on her face. "I'm afraid it isn't much. But it serves. My wife died four years ago. We had no children. I don't need much." He motioned Lili toward a chair and sat opposite her. "When do you need these papers?"

"As soon as possible."

Shen pointed to a short wave radio on the table. "Tell me, I hear on Voice of America that the student uprising is sweeping China. Is it true?"

Lili nodded. "Three weeks ago, it was just the students. Now ordinary people are starting to listen. On May 4th, I saw thousands near Tiananmen Square. And Zheng said there would be marches from Guangchou to Xi'an to Shanghai as well."

The old man was silent for a moment, filled with memories of his own efforts as a boy to change China. "Maybe this time they will succeed," he said finally. He looked and Lili and smiled. "It is late. Let us begin."

*   *   *

HongKong

As Lili sat with Shen in Macao, a news item was being typeset for the Hong Kong Daily's early morning edition:

Disfigured Body Found in Car Park.

Police are trying to establish the identity of a man in his 30's whose face-less body was discovered in a container car-park in KW Change last night.

KW Chung Assistant District Commander (Crime), Chief Inspector Jim Thomas, said, "We are unable to establish how the man was killed until a post-mortem examination is carried out."

Part of the man's face is missing, probably cut away with a sharp instrument, but there were no signs of any other wounds on his body.

No identifying documents or money were found on the body, except for a chip from a gambling casino.

"We are trying to establish whether the man was a patron or an employee of one of the casinos in Macao," said Chief Inspector Thomas.

*   *   *

Macao
5 AM

Three hours after first jumping into the icy, oily-tasting water of the Pearl River, Chi-Wen could feel the und ertow pull his barefeet into the sand. Arms wrenching in their sockets, he struggled against the strong current for the few remaining yards until he finally reached the beach. Exhaling his relief. He had made it!

Exhausted, he lay pressed flat against the crushed seashells. Just ahead, the lights of Macao shimmered, a welcoming crown of iridescent jewels. Those of Nantou in the distance were dimmer, more diffused. Would he return to China? he wondered. First he had to find Lili. Perhaps then he'd know.

He remained where he was for almost half an hour, shivering, but afraid to move lest someone see him. The stretch of coast where he had landed seemed deserted, but Mei Ling had warned of patrols looking out for potential illegals from the mainland. When he'd become accustomed to the sounds and shadows, he stood and began walking up the beach.

TWENTY-SEVEN

Saturday, May 6th
near Hong Kong

Lili could barely breathe.

She was in the trunk of a car. After preparing her passport and papers, Shen had persuaded a friend to take her by ferry to Hong Kong. He explained that too many people watched the hydrofoil and jet foil docks. She would hide in the trunk for the two and a half hour trip. Once they landed, she could walk off the ferry to freedom.

Alone in her sweltering cocoon, she fought images causing her to break out in a cold sweat.

Running, hiding, gunshots, death....

Her head ached as she thought of those who'd wanted to kill her for her grandfather's discovery. Mad generals and government officials like Pei-Jun Tong, Lin, Peng Han and Dr. Seng, driven by memories of a China that could no longer exist in the twentieth century, rejecting a world they found weak and ineffectual. Such men would make a pact with the devil as long as they retained their hold on the country; old men stealing life from the young for power. And then there were the corrupt businessmen like the general's son,

David Kim, Paulo Ng and Walter DeForest and the disenchanted bureaucrats like Halliday—each willing to exchange their souls for money.

What about Chi-Wen? A sickening hollowness spread through her as she conjured up his face in her dark tomb. His betrayal hurt her most, the one she could least reconcile. So certain his feelings for her had been real. How had she been so blind?

Or was it simpler than that? Perhaps he was a man who would always believe in the immutability of fate. LIke Hamlet, who claimed 'there's a divinity that shapes our ends, rough-hew them how we will...', Chi-Wen must have felt his survival required Lili's betrayal. She shuddered despite the heat. It wasn't the answer she desired. And it didn't soften her pain—knowing she'd probably expected too much from him—a man born into another world, one she could never truly understand or be a part of.

A knock on the trunk and a whispered message: "We dock in five minutes." Shen's friend helped her out of the trunk.

"Thank you."

As she drifted into the crowd readying at the ferry's bow for disembarkation, she counted herself fortunate. Chi-Wen may have stolen her heart, but he hadn't gotten the secret. No one had. Tonight she would retrieve her grandfather's notes from Dottie Diehl's copybook.

That is, if Shen's papers passed muster at customs.

*   *   *

Beijing, China

Several hundred students demonstrated on the campus of Beijing University, calling on others to continue class boycotts until the government met their demands for a substantive dialogue. They were prepared to launch a country-wide hunger strike during the Gorbachev visit on May 15th. Tragically, these students underestimated the determination and convictions of old revolutionaries who would use any means they thought necessary, including a bloody military crackdown to safeguard their position.

*   *   *

Hong Kong

Lili need not have worried. Shen's papers were accepted by the border guards without demur. The tailor had correctly guessed they would never question an American passport—especially one carried by a beautiful girl in tight jeans and T-shirt. The few mainlanders who tried coming through Macao generally forged Hong Kong passports, but lacked Lili's independent manner or command of English to pass the scam off successfully.

Still it wasn't until the cab let her off in front of the Peninsula Hotel that she really felt safe.

*   *   *

Macao

It was almost ten by the time Chi-Wen found the tailor's shop.

"You say you and this girl are good friends?" Shen eyed the wiry young man dressed in oversized trousers and filthy white shirt still damp from his swim with suspicion. How could he be sure he wasn't a spy?

"Please, you must tell me if she'd been here." Chi-Wen explained he and Lili had been separated in Beijing, that she had managed to escape before he could find her and that his only hope was she might have come to Shen's shop for a passport." He looked away. "*Yi yan ji chu si ma nan zhui.* A promise cannot be taken back once it is made."

"And what promise was that?"

"I promised her grandfather I would make sure she reached Hong Kong safely."

"Is that the only reason you want to help her?"

Chi-Wen shook his head. Softly: "No, I love her."

"The moment of finding is always a surprise, like meeting an old friend never before known."

Chi-Wen recognized the old Taoist saying.

"It is how I felt when I met my dear wife." Shen pointed to her framed picture on his table. "Dead more than four years and I still miss her terribly." He smiled at Chi-Wen. "Your Dr. Quan left for Hong Kong a few hours ago."

At least she was safe.

"Did she mention me?"

"I'm afraid not. I take it you want papers too."

"Just a visa." He'd have to risk using the Philippine passport for now. If he decided to leave China for good, he'd return for appropriate documents later.

The tailor nodded. "I'll throw in some clean clothes too."

*   *   *

Hong Kong

It was only when she saw him standing in the lobby that she realized just how frightened she still was. "Dylan, my God, I can't believe you're here!" She was shaking, breathing in swallows and gasps as she started to tell him everything that had happened. "They tried to kill me!"

"Whoa!" he said, his blue eyes full of concern. "I want to hear all about it, but the doctor's ordering a stiff drink first."

"Actually a STAT bath would be more like it," she laughed, self-consciously brushing away a stray wisp from her brow. "I must look awful."

"You look wonderful." He started towards the elevator.

"Where are we going?"

"I thought you wanted a bath. My room's on the third floor."

Hesitating.

"Lili, I heard the concierge say the hotel was filled. I've got a suite…"
She raised her eyebrows.

"…it was all they had. Bedroom and living room. So I can stay on the couch. Of course, If you're still not comfortable, I'll find a room somewhere else and you can stay here."

She shook her head. "I wouldn't hear of it. Forgive me, it's just that so much has happened…"

"I understand."

She looked up at him, suddenly perplexed. "How did you know….?" Her call from Macao to Los Angeles had only reached Dylan's answer phone. Even if he'd gotten her message, there wasn't time to hop a plane for Hong Kong.

As if reading her mind. "How did I know you needed me?"
She nodded.

A shrug. "Call it lucky intuition." No mention of the fax he'd received. "It *was* luck, wasn't it?"

His wonderful smile made it easy to shrug off her uneasiness. She pressed her forehead against his chest and closed her eyes, clarity of thought eroded by emotional exhaustion. "Yes, it was," she sighed. He was here now. That's all that counted.

*   *   *

Dressed in his dark double-breasted suit and conservative navy tie, Foreign Ministry Chief Lin affected the air of a successful Hong Kong businessmen taking morning coffee in the Peninsula's lobby. He had no doubt that with a closer look, Lili would recognize him. That was why he looked away until she and Dylan passed his table and entered the empty elevator. Once the doors closed, he paid his check and sauntered over to the hotel manager's desk.

"May I help you, sir?" The assistant manger's studied modish look and accented English suggested a young man not long from Shanghai. "I just wondered where to get the People's Daily?" Lin said, then added in

Mandarin: "So many years gone. It is a way to keep up with the news from home."

"*Shir*," the young man agreed. "Our gift shop carries all the out of town papers."

"Thank you." He smiled at the assistant manager. "You also have family in China?" An innocent question.

"Yes, my parents and younger brother."

"And they are well?"

A shrug. "They live a quiet life."

Lin clamped a hand over his. "Would you like them to stay that way?"

The young man's cordial smile was replaced by a look of alarm. "I beg your pardon?"

Lin showed him his official ID. "I am the Foreign Ministry chief. I want information."

"What kind of information?" The assistant manager had no doubt if the credentials were genuine, Lin was in a position to change his parents life any way he wished. It was that fear that kept many PRC immigrants from involving themselves in anti-government politics abroad.

"I want to know what room Dr. Lili Quan is in and who she's with."

"I cannot tell! The Peninsula has a policy to protect guests' privacy." Although he spoke Mandarin, *privacy* was in English since no such word exists in Chinese.

Lin leveled a pointed look. "You can make an exception this time."

The manager walked by and the young man resumed English, trying to control the trembling in his voice. "Have a seat, sir and I'll see what I can do."

*   *   *

Fifteen minutes later, Lili emerged from the bathroom wrapped in a Peninsula terry cloth robe, a towel around her just-washed hair. "That *was* just what the doctor ordered," she said, sitting on the bed.

"Take your medicine." Dylan handed her a steaming mug. "Hot brandy, water, sugar and spices. Better than any of your prescriptions. Guaranteed to calm the nerves."

Lili sipped the hot toddy. "Thanks."

Dylan sat down beside her. "Think you're up to telling me what happened?"

"It's a long story."

"I'm not going anywhere."

Lili gazed into his deep blue eyes. Whether the bantering was motivated by friendship or something more, she didn't care. The brandy was already producing a comforting warmth that Dylan's closeness only augmented. She was glad he was here; glad she had someone she could finally trust. "I never expected any of what I found in China," she said and began to recount the events of the last few weeks.

"Jesus," he exclaimed, when she had finished. "What a story! And you're certain your grandfather has really found the secret of longevity?"

"I saw the results with my own eyes. Thirty subjects all living well into their twelfth decade. If he hadn't stopped the experiment, I'm not sure how much longer they might have lived."

"Unbelievable. The greatest discovery of all time." Dylan was clearly caught up in the excitement. "Amazing how your grandfather managed to keep it a secret all these years."

"Even more amazing how I spirited it out of China."

"You've got it with you?"

"Not exactly." She picked up the bedside phone and dialed the desk manager.

"What are you doing?"

"I almost forgot." She put her fingers to her lips to indicate that the call had been picked up. "My name is Dr. Lili Quan. I'm staying in room #322. Could you refer any messages for me to this number."

"What was that about?" Dylan asked, as she hung up.

"Just before I got on the train in Beijing, I slipped my grandfather's notes to a tourist I'd met on the plane over."

"Was that wise?"

"As it turned out, if I hadn't, I would have been killed the moment Lin and his cronies found it. This way, I bought time and managed to escape." She yawned, the hot toddy's effect.

"Where's this tourist now?"

Eyes half-closing. "On her way to Hong Kong. The tour gets in this after-noon. She's to call me as soon as she arrives."

It was only eleven.

Dylan gently pushed her down on the bed.

"Taking advantage of a lady's vulnerability?" Lili slurred.

"I wouldn't think of it." He lay a blanket over her. "I like my women wide awake and excuse-free."

"How about a rain check?" she mumbled.

Dylan placed a platonic kiss on her forehead. "You got it."

Exhausted, Lili sank into a dreamless sleep.

*   *   *

Downstairs, in the hotel lobby, the assistant manager tapped Lin on the shoulder. "I have that information for you."

*   *   *

Hong Kong assaulted Chi-Wen. Its sights, its smells, its sounds were at once chaotic and exciting.

Even in Guangchou he had not seen so many cars or heard so much noise or smelled so many intermingling odors. Most people he passed on the streets were Chinese, yet something in their self-confident gait and open stares was in sharp contrast to the Mainlanders. He stopped to scan the horizon. Just north, across the harbor, the dark hills of China almost drifted in the murky, humid air. So close, yet worlds away. There people walked with closed faces and little bounce, aware every move was observed, afraid to draw attention to themselves.

Both places were chaotic, but China's chaos was government created, while Hong Kong's was of the peoples' making. Knowing that didn't change the fact that he felt different here.

Different. Another reminder of Lili.

He asked a passerby the time and learned it was close to five. Rush hour traffic just beginning to fill the narrow streets. "How far is the Peninsula Hotel?"

"Two blocks. Salisbury Road. You can't miss it, sir." Evidently the clean tailored suit provided a facade of confidence Chi-Wen lacked.

"Thank you," he replied and hurried up the street. Only a matter of minutes until he finally saw Lili again.

*   *   *

Two rings before the telephone woke her.

"Lili, is that you?"

"Dottie ?" Lili checked the bedside clock: five after five. She'd slept all afternoon. "Where are you?"

"You'll never guess," the ex-geography teacher gushed, oblivious to Lili's urgency. "After almost a month in China, I finally ran into the man of my dreams!"

"That's wonderful, Dottie." Lili sat up and rubbed the sleep from her eyes.

"A widower from London. I met him on the Li River cruise. Although I wouldn't actually call it a cruise." That Dr. Ruth giggle. "Just a floating barge, but the view of the Guilin hills is magnificent..."

Interrupting. Lili was fully awake now: "Dottie, you still have what I gave you?"

"Your grandfather's private letters?"

That was the cover story Lili had used. "Yes."

"Sure." Another giggle. "I feel like a regular Mata Hari. It'll make a good chapter for my book."

"Did anyone try to stop you?"

Almost disappointed. "No one. The advantage of a tour, I guess." Lili's racing heart slowed. "Where are you now?" she repeated.

"I dropped my group. It's the last day and Fred promised to show me the same sights. He travels regularly to the Far East. We're heading for the Tiger Balm Garden now. I thought you could meet us there. At quarter to six."

"I'm on my way."

"I'll be the one with the Hakka hat and the handsome guy in tow," Dottie laughed and hung up.

Lili pulled her robe around her and ran into the living room.

Dylan stood near the phone. "I'm sorry the call woke you."

"It was my friend. She's brought grandfather's papers. I'm meeting her at six at the Tiger Balm Garden."

"I'm coming with you."

Lili smiled at Dylan. "A bodyguard would be nice." She started back into the bedroom. "Give me a minute to get dressed."

*   *   *

"A woman just called."

"And...?"

Beads of sweat appeared on the young man's brow. He wiped them away with a silk handkerchief. "...and Dr. Quan asked if she had her grandfather's private letters."

"And...?" Lin had no patience for this gutless idiot.

"The woman said yes."

Earlier the assistant manager had informed Lin that Lili was expecting an important call. Now it seemed Seng had been right after all. Lin could barely contain his excitement. All these years Dr. Cheng had hidden his research notes at the Institute. Dying, he gave them to his granddaughter and she'd managed to pass them along before being caught in Beijing. Clever girl.

"Dr. Quan plans to meet her at the Tiger Balm Garden at quarter to six."

Lin nodded. "You've done well, my friend. Good fortune will shine upon your family."

It was the absence of bad luck most Chinese hoped for.

"Please call me a cab."

*   *   *

"Tiger Balm Garden." Dylan hung up as Lili entered the suite's living room.

"Who were you talking to?"

"I asked the concierge to reserve a cab. I didn't want you to be late for your meeting."

"Did I tell you how glad I am you're here?" Lili moved close to him.

"You did, but I'm a glutton for compliments." Dylan put an arm around her. "If we don't get out of here in a hurry, I'm going to expect that rain check right now."

*   *   *

Chi-Wen arrived at the Peninsula just as Lili and Dylan stepped into a taxi.

Lili. Pent-up emotions assaulted him, the memory of the feel of her body and the sound of her voice overwhelmed him. Though he longed to touch her, to hear her speak again, he refrained from calling out to her. Instead, he observed the way she was smiling up at the handsome young man, how the two held their faces close together. A terrible ache in his chest.

Be glad she's fine, he told himself. After all, it was he who had contacted Dylan by fax. Still, the twinge of jealousy was beyond his control.

"Tiger Balm Garden."

He watched as the taxi pulled away from the curb, wondering what to do. Perhaps he should leave. No sense interfering. He'd promised Dr. Cheng to make sure Lili arrived safely in Hong Kong. He'd fulfilled that obligation.

His musing was interrupted when someone jumped into the next cab in the queue.

"Follow them!" a man in a dark suit ordered.

Chi-Wen did a double take. He glimpsed the man in profile and was certain it was Lin! What was the Foreign Ministry chief doing in Hong Kong? How had he found Lili? He hailed his own taxi.

"Where to, sir?"

"Tiger Balm Garden," he told the driver.

Chi-Wen had no choice. Lili was in trouble.

The cab headed toward the Cross Harbor Tunnel that led from Kowloon to Hong Kong Island.

"And hurry."

                *   *   *

Dusk.

In the shadowy blue light, the plaster figures surrounding the Haw Par Mansion appeared particularly grotesque. Dylan and Lili began climbing the steep hillside looking for Dottie. Apt, Lili thought, that the sixteen million Hong Kong dollars it took to build this eight acre monstrosity had come from Tiger Balm patent medicine. Indeed, if Kim or Ng or Halliday had been able to exploit grandfather's secret, they could have easily bested old man Aw Boon Haw's fortune by billions.

"You're sure she'll show ?" Dylan checked his watch. "It's quarter to six."

"You're more impatient than I am," Lili replied. "She'll get here. Let's check out these horrible statues?"

"The figures depict Chinese folktales or Buddhist stories," a tour guide sing-songed to her group.

"What's this one?" someone asked, pointing to a particularly lurid set of figures.

"It represents the Ten Courts of Hell."

"Not a pretty sight," Dylan quipped.

"Lili! Over here!" Dottie from just below them near the Tiger Pagoda. Dressed in her Hakka outfit, her arm possessively hugged a thin, bald-headed man at least six inches shorter than she.

"Sorry we're late," Dottie apologized when they'd reached her. "Fred wanted to show me the Aw family's jade collection. It's in the mansion. If you have time, you must see it." She squeezed the little bald man's arm. "This is my new friend, Fred Delbert."

"Pleased to meet you." Fred had a decided British accent.

"And this is my old friend, Dylan O'Hara."

"Ah." Dottie winked. "The fellow you were meeting in Beijing."

"Well, actually…"

But Dottie expected no reply. "Fred was just in China on business," she reported.

"Oh?" Lili felt obligated to make polite conversation.

"I'm trying to sell the Chinese on nappies," Fred explained. "You know those split pants all the babies wear. If even half the population switches over, my company stands to make a bundle."

Dottie beamed at him, clearly smitten. "Isn't he something?"

"The Gardens close in ten minutes," a uniformed guard announced.

Most of the crowd had dispersed.

"We'd better get going, love," Fred told Dottie. "We don't want to miss our dinner reservation."

"Fred's taking me to Lung Wah's. He says the steamed pigeon and snake soup are superb." Dottie opened her purse and handed Lili an envelope. "Your grandfather's letters are inside."

"Thank you. I really appreciate your help."

"Nonsense, my dear. I'm only sorry it was so easy. I'll have to embellish the story if I ever write that book."

Lili smiled. "Well, be sure to send a copy when it's finished."

"Actually, I'm giving up the idea of writing for the moment. Fred has talked me into returning to London with him." Dottie gave her a hug. "Wish me luck," she whispered.

"Have fun," Lili whispered back.

As soon as Fred and Dottie disappeared down the hillside path, Dylan took the envelope from Lili. "Imagine the single greatest discovery mankind will ever know."

Even in the dim light, Lili recognized the same fire in his eyes she'd first seen the night he'd described his own work on longevity. For a moment she studied him, wondering if the chill she was feeling came from the breeze over Causeway Bay or something else.

*   *   *

Lin's cab stopped a block from the Tiger Balm Garden.

Chi-Wen waited until the Foreign Ministry chief had paid his fare, then followed him up the steep hillside. Afraid to call attention to himself, Chi-Wen kept his pace steady, though considerably slower; tennis shoes muffled urgent steps. At the garden's entrance he lost sight of Lin as several tour groups burst en mass through the gates toward their buses.

Damn.

Straining in the fading daylight, Chi-Wen studied the maze of paths and levels beyond the mansion, reminded of a great labyrinth. Bizarre multicolored plaster statues, effigies from Chinese mythology, life-size plastic figures of Chinese emperors and huge extravagant animal sculptures were all scattered amid stairs, grottoes and small, but meticulously tended terraces: a perfect blend of artifice and chaos.

Which way had he gone ?

Murky shadows made his search difficult, though few people remained on the eight acres so near to closing time. Finally, he saw the dark suited figure: Lin hurrying several levels above where Chi-Wen stood. He followed, reaching the top breathless, heart pounding just as the Foreign Ministry chief ducked inside the white pagoda, a sacred multi-story temple and symbol of the Tiger Balm Garden.

From the opposite side, Chi-Wen tiptoed into the open building, deserted except for Lin and himself. Footsteps echoed off tiled stairs. Chi-Wen silently made his way up to the third story where he slipped behind a pillar, giving him a shadowed view of Lin.

What was going on ?Where was Lili ?

Five minutes passed. Chi-Wen knew that the garden would close in less than ten minutes. Something had to happen soon. Hiding among the shadows, he edged closer until he was near enough to follow Lin's unwavering gaze to the grounds below. In the semi-darkness, he recognized Lili and Dylan talking with a bald headed man and a woman in a Hakka hat. Too far away to hear their conversation.

What was the Foreign Ministry chief up to ?

Chi-Wen's mouth suddenly went dry with apprehension as he sensed Lin's plan. He's stalking her! Waiting for an opportunity to kidnap her again!

The woman in the Hakka hat handed something to Lili, then gave her a hug and turned to leave. Lin jerked up an arm. Even at a distance, Chi-Wen recognized the shape of a pistol in his hand. With a silencer on the end.

He's going to kill her! Gasping.

Lin heard the sharp intake of breath and turned. "Who's there?"

In that same instant, Chi-Wen quickly circled. "Too much time behind a desk has made you careless, comrade," he whispered, jabbing his pointed finger into the Foreign Minister's back.

"Chi-Wen Zhou!"

"Don't turn around or I'll shoot. Hand over the gun."

Lin did as he was told.

Holding the pistol against Lin's skull, Chi-Wen wondered if he could be capable of pulling the trigger.

As if reading his mind: "You know the penalty for murder."

Chi-Wen couldn't help chuckling. "I suspect I'll be considered a hero when Deng finds out you tried to steal the secret of longevity for yourself. It is you who will face the firing squad."

"Don't be a fool," Lin hissed. "Too many people owe me favors. Your word against mine? No one will believe you."

"I guess I'll have to take that chance."

"Why take a chance?" Lin tried to strike a rational tone. "Help me get the secret from Lili Quan and I promise you a life of privilege."

"No!" Chi-Wen's voice was filled with disgust. He despised this man whose lust for power had almost destroyed his spirit. "The students are right. Men like you must step down. You have corrupted all that is great in China."

"I can save China."

"You're no savior. You and your cronies want to keep us slaves to the past."

"Freedom," Lin spoke with scorn. "Your Dr. Quan can rhapsodize about it, our students can yell slogans about it, but what do *you* know of it? People who have never known freedom, who have lived one way for over forty years with everything taken care of for them—jobs, marriage, homes—suddenly present them with freedom and you'll get anarchy and chaos, not utopia."

"China belongs to the people," Chi-Wen replied, pushing Lin toward an alcove where he'd be hidden. "Unbuckle your belt and hand over your tie."

"What are you doing?" Lin's voice suddenly cracking.

"Don't worry, I'm not going to kill you."

Quickly, Chi-Wen secured Lin's hands behind his back with the belt. "Lie down on your stomach," he ordered. He bound Lin's ankles together with his shoelaces, then used the tie as a gag.

"Don't leave," he whispered. "I'll be back."

                    *   *   *

"Let's get out of here. This place gives me the creeps."

Nearly six, they seemed to be the only two people left on the grounds.

"In a minute." Dylan removed the notes from the envelope. "Jesus, they're in Chinese."

"Of course, what did you expect?"

"I don't know. I guess I just assumed…I mean, you said your grandfather spoke English…" Dylan pulled a cigarillo from his breast pocket. "Have you read them yet?" he asked.

"No, he died just after he gave them to me and from that moment until I slipped them to Dottie, I was on the run."

Dylan shrugged. "Well, there's plenty of time now." He put the cigarillo in his mouth.

"Dylan?"

"Yeah?"

"When did you start smoking?"

"It's a nervous habit I've kicked off and on over the years." He took a lighter from his pocket, fumbling with it until it ignited.

Gold lighter... . "Where'd you get that?"

"What?"

"That lighter."

"I don't know," he replied, returning it to his pocket. "What's the difference?"

Cigarillos, gold lighter—coincidence? She was trembling. "Can I see it?"

"We ought to get going."

"No, I want to see that lighter."

"Why all the questions? I'm not asking about the man you met in Beijing. What interest could you have in a silly lighter."

"The man is history." She didn't want to talk about Chi-Wen now. "He doesn't need to be explained. But that lighter—I think it belonged to Paulo Ng—the man who kidnapped me. When Halliday killed him, he stole it. Which means..."

Trying to think things out as she spoke, the fire in her mind grew, spreading, until she was suddenly consumed by an extraordinary possibility. "Don't tell me you're mixed up with Halliday?"

He stubbed out the cigarillo. "Lili, you've been through a lot. You're still running on overtime. You're bound to feel some residual paranoia, but..."

"Don't patronize me, Dylan. Let me see it. "

Reluctantly, he handed her the lighter.

Confirming her worse fears, a dragon was etched on the side. "It's true. You are involved with Halliday."

A look of irritation. "What if I am? "

"How? Why?" She struggled to control herself. "The man's a murderer."

"Halliday recruited me in med school. Trenton was my mentor, remember. He worked for the CIA off and on until his wife died. Halliday was his contact."

"I'm not surprised to hear that Tex Trenton might be a spy, but *you* ?"

"Spy's a little too dramatic, Lili. The correct parlance is civilian intelligence operative."

"And what exactly does such an individual do?"

"Odd jobs. At first it was nothing more than information gathering—reporting on the latest developments in immunogenetics and related fields. The CIA didn't want any other country scooping us the way Russia had with space stations or Japan with computers. The work helped pay the bills and I got to see a little of the world." He smiled. "My very first trip was to an international conference in Hong Kong."

"And later?"

"Later, I moved on to low profile operations."

"Meaning?"

"After Iran-Contra, the CIA couldn't afford to be implicated in any so-called 'dirty tricks'. Independent civilians like me provide appropriate fronts."

"Was this a low profile operation?"

"Exactly," he responded, ignoring her sarcasm. "Halliday arranged for the Aligen Company to finance my project at LA Medical. That way I could keep an eye on Aligen and you."

"Me?"

"He learned your grandfather had perfected a longevity drug and that certain people in the Chinese government planned to lure you to the mainland to get him to reveal it."

"Lin, Han and Tong," she said. Monsters. But any more than Dylan? "And what was your job?" she asked, still fighting control.

"First, to see that you went to China. Hopefully, your grandfather would give you his formula. After that, I was to get it from you."

Lili shook her head. "But you had your own work."

"It wasn't going well. I was years from making a breakthrough. You said it yourself—your grandfather's work showed success in humans. Even if I had located the gene that turned off the MHC, in the US it would have taken years to get the FDA and Human Subjects Committees to approve human testing. Especially given the current public paranoia about genetic engineering. If I helped Halliday get your grandfather's formula, he promised to share it with me."

"And you'd pawn it off as your own discovery? That's fraud."

Sighing: "You think research is honest, Lili? That's a delusion. All your dreams, all your tilts at the windmills of justice—you should be reading *The Man from La Mancha* , not *The Old Man and the Sea*. I find the secret to pro-long life and I become the most famous man on earth. You're talking Nobel Prize and more."

Lili was silent for a few moments, then asked: "Is that really what you're in it for? For the prizes and the money?"

"Do you want me to lie to you? Tell you it's for a higher, moral purpose? Of course I'm in it for the prize. People who get hung up moralizing get nowhere fast. All that matters is the result. In the big picture, the end justifies the means. And screw the rest. I suppose you can't understand that."

The real horror was that Lili did understand. Back in LA, Dylan had told her how important winning was. She had simply chosen to ignore his words; seduced by the assault of his calculated charm. What did that say about her? She saw the sparkle in his eyes that she'd taken for love and now discerned as something foreign. Her stomach tightened. "You used me!"

"You and Trenton never saw eye to eye. Ed Baxter wanted the fellowship. Your mother was dying. Dr. Seng offered you an opportunity to get away from your troubles. Halliday and I merely set you on a stage."

"You sent me to China knowing I would be in danger? How did you think I'd get out of there alive? Or didn't you care?"

"Halliday always expected to have to get you out himself, but as it turned out that wasn't necessary."

"I don't understand."

"Soon after you left LA, he got wind of a double cross and stumbled onto Ng. The pirate planned to smuggle you out of China."

"What you did was despicable". Her mind was at once numb and on fire. She could not believe the depth of Dylan's depravity. The thought that he had once seemed so attractive sickened her.

"Lili, I said it before, you're naive." Dylan shook his head. "It's too bad; we could have worked together.

"And what now?" she asked.

No response.

"Are you going to kill me?"

His grim expression terrified her. "Are you really capable of murder too?"

"He may not be, but I've got no qualms." Halliday emerged from the shadows pointing a gun. "Dr. Quan, we meet again."

"You bastard!"

"Such lovely talk from a lady," Halliday quipped. He nodded toward the papers still in Dylan's hands. "Is that it?"

"Her grandfather's research notes. They're all here."

"Good work, my friend." To Lili: "Let's get going." He used the gun to urge her ahead of Dylan.

"Where are you taking me?" Stay calm.

"It's such a warm evening. I thought you might like to take a little ride."

He really did mean to kill her. "And if I scream?"

"Check around you. Everyone's gone. Eight acres. Lots of bushes. I could plug you now and no one would find you for a week."

"Someone would hear gunshots."

"In Hong Kong? I doubt it would cause anyone to look up from their Mah-Jongg game. But just in case," he said, pulling a silencer from his pocket, "I brought this along."

Lili turned to stare at Dylan, but he averted his gaze.

"You two have a falling out? Once they've been to America..." the CIA man tsked. "When we're done here, Dylan, I'll buy you a nice compliant Chinese gal on Wachai Street." They had almost reached the top of a steep path.

Desperate, Lili had to save herself. But how? Think! As she started to walk down the path, she recalled an afternoon in Suzhou:

Somehow I always thought tai-chi was a form of martial arts.

It is and it isn't. In your Western world, exercise concentrates on outer movement and the development of the physical body only. Movement in tai-chi is to transfer the ch'i or intrinsic energy to the shen or spirit and to use inner rather than outer force. With tai-chi, the separation between mind, body and spirit gradually disappears and the student attains 'oneness' with the universe.

Standing with her head erect, Lili closed her eyes and concentrated on breathing. *As if each breath is drawn slowly from a cocoon.*

"Come on, get going."

Gradually deepening, emptying her mind of thought. *Wu-chi.*

Her heels touched lightly as she crouched slightly; she separated her feet, leading with the left foot. *Tai-chi.*

With each inhalation, she felt the air float her hands and arms out from her body. Effortlessly, her movements grew from inside out.

From the initial stillness comes motion.... With a smooth, unhurried motion, she pivoted with her right foot.

Gracefully, almost effortlessly, Lili sped into her attack before Dylan could react. She jumped high, her left knee jerking up, then twisting in the air while her right foot snapped toward Dylan's head in a roundhouse kick. He fell crumpled in a heap on the floor, dazed.

In that same instant, Halliday cocked his gun and aimed at Lili.

"No!"

The CIA man pivoted to face Chi-Wen.

"No!" he screamed again. Without thought, without the slightest hesitation, Chi-Wen lunged to place himself between Lili and her attacker.

Halliday fired.

Instinctively, Lili dove to the ground, ducking a hail of bullets.

Chi-Wen fired Lin's gun. Though the bullet only grazed Halliday's wrist, he reflexively released his weapon. Chi-Wen grabbed it as it fell to the floor. He turned to Lili. "You did well," he said, indicating Dylan, still semi-conscious on the ground.

"I had a good teacher." Trying to sound calm, her voice had an edge of pain, despair and bitterness.

"Are you all right?"

If she hadn't known better she might have believed he was genuinely concerned. Damn him! "I'm doing just fine!" she hissed. "I thought coming to China was my choice and now I find it was a well- orchestrated plot to use me to steal my grandfather's work. Of course, you would just call it my fate," she hurled the words like spears.

"Lili…"

Interrupting: "And better yet, everyone I trusted..." her voice broke, "everyone I loved has either betrayed me or died." A tear hovered at her lower lid before starting its slow descent down her cheek.

Chi-Wen moved toward her.

"Don't touch me!" She wiped the tear with the back of her hand. "What are you doing here? " She looked at the gun he had leveled at Halliday. "Are *you* also planning to kill me for the secret?"

"Lili, I've been searching for you since you were kidnapped in Beijing."

"You betrayed me in Beijing!"

"No, it had to be one of the students. Remember Tu said there were many spies and informers." He studied her face, hoping to convince her. "Please, believe me, I would never betray you."

That stopped her cold. She scrutinized Chi-Wen's face. There had to be yet another trick. But looking into his eyes, she saw pain as great as hers. "You didn't tell Lin where I was?"

"Of course not. After you were taken, I tried to find you. Tu told me you'd escaped."

"Actually General Tong's son kidnapped me."

"I don't understand."

"He'd made a deal with the devil."

Chi-Wen's furrowed brow conveyed confusion.

"It's an American expression," Lili explained. "Apparently, he'd overheard his father's plan to lure me to China and realized the enormous economic potential in a drug that could prolong life. He made a deal with his Korean business partner. Unfortunately for him, David Kim never planned to honor their contract."

"What happened to Tong?"

"His father shot him." Lili shuddered at the memory of the scene on the tarmac.

Ironic, Chi-Wen thought. Cadre children like Lee Tong plunging headlong into capitalist schemes, assuming they were above the law. But everything was a circle, wasn't it? In ancient China, the punishment for not showing filial piety was death.

"Kim had made his own deal with a Macanese pirate." Lili continued. "I ended up bound and gagged on his ship."

"How did you escape?"

Lili gestured towards an impassive Halliday. "This man saved me only to betray me. Once I managed to escape from him, I ran right into Dylan's arms."

Chi-Wen looked at Dylan. "That was my fault."

"Your fault?"

"I couldn't be sure I would find you so before I left Beijing I asked a student I trusted to fax him a message that you were in trouble and to meet you at the Peninsula Hotel."

"How did you know where to find Dylan?"

"Remember he sent you a note when you first arrived in Xi'an. I went to your room the next night and copied his fax number."

Lili recalled wondering who had rummaged through her things. "And the Peninsula Hotel?"

He reminded her of what's she said on the truck: "In Hong Kong we stay at the Peninsula Hotel"

"Ah yes."

"I was a fool, Lili. I thought Dylan was your good friend."

No more than I, she thought, remembering the fortune teller's warning. *Your greatest enemy will try to be your closest ally.* Dylan was the friend she should have distrusted. All that time it had been Dylan. "Oh Chi-Wen, I'm so sorry I doubted you."

"No need to apologize."

"How did you escape Beijing?"

"I figured you might head for Macao. Because the government is looking for student leaders, it's harder to get out of China. I had to swim to Macao. When I got there, you'd already left."

She was deeply touched by his strength of spirit, his tenacity.

"When I arrived at the Peninsula, I saw you getting into a taxi. Just behind you was Foreign Deputy Lin."

"My God, he followed me too?"

"Whoever betrayed us, must have told him you were heading for the Peninsula. At first I thought he planned to kidnap you again, but Lin meant to kill you."

The fact that Chi-Wen had said "us" didn't escape Lili. He had no way of knowing she'd slipped the notes to Dottie in the Xi'an train station. "Dr. Seng must have found the secret drawer in my grandfather's desk and guessed where he'd been hiding his research notes all these years. When Lin 's men searched me in Beijing and didn't find them, he assumed I'd hidden them somewhere." Lili told Chi-Wen how she'd passed the notes to Dottie."I'm sorry I didn't tell you."

Chi-Wen shrugged. "I didn't need to know."

Lili nodded. "When Lin heard I was heading for Hong Kong, he put two and two together and followed me. Once he saw the exchange, he decided I was expendable." She looked around. "Where is he now?"

As they talked, Halliday slowly unwrapped the piano wire around his wrist.

"Tied up in the white pagoda."

With lightening speed, Halliday grabbed Lili from behind and held the wire tautly against the soft skin of her jaw.

"Let me go," she shouted, but Halliday's hold was too strong.

He looked at Chi-Wen. "If you want her to live, drop that gun. "

"Don't listen to him," Lili screamed.

"Do it or I'll kill her right now."

Chi-Wen had no choice. He followed Halliday's instructions.

"Kick it away."

Chi-Wen put the toe of his shoe against the stock and pushed it down the path.

"Smart boy. Slowly raise your hands. Clasp them together over your head. " He pushed Lili towards Chi-Wen. "You too."

"Stop there," another voice ordered. "CIA. You're under arrest." Two men in dark suits appeared, each brandishing revolvers, covered Halliday and Dylan. Throw your gun on the ground, Halliday."

"Come on, guys, I'm one of you."

"Your gun."

"What's the charge?" Halliday asked after discarding his weapon.

"For starters, the murder of Martin Carpenter."

"The coroner ruled his death as accidental."

"Until Dr. Trenton yelled foul. Lucky for us, too. We had no idea you were running your own renegade mission. California, Washington, Macao, Hong Kong; Carpenter, DeForest, Ng. You've been a busy bee, my friend." The taller of the two turned to Lili. "Dr. Quan? I'm Bill Nesbit, this is Tony Lucca." Nesbit flashed his ID. You okay?"

"I think so." Not sure how to react. Why should she suddenly trust these men any more than Halliday or Dylan? She edged over to where Dylan lay and picked up the research notes scattered beside him.

"Sorry we took so long. After we tapped Halliday's last phone call from Dr. O'Hara, we rushed to get here. Unfortunately, we didn't know where in the garden you'd be meeting Miss Diehl."

That was all she needed to hear. Friend or foe—what did it matter? Everything that had happened since she'd left for China had been because of these.

She thought of her grandfather's dying words:

You alone are now the keeper of the secret. You will decide whether or not to reveal it to the world.

How will I know what to do?

You will know.

"We'll take those now," Lucca said matter-of-factly.

You will know...

She flicked Ng's lighter, igniting the papers. Lucca tried to grab them, but Lili extended her hand and in seconds, held a burning torch.

"Stupid bitch!" Halliday screamed. "You just destroyed the greatest discovery the world has ever known."

"Your opinion, Mr. Halliday. It might also have been the world's greatest nightmare." She watched the ashes begin to float across the grounds.

Just remember—the secret has the power to save or destroy.

"Either way," she said sadly, "it seems mankind just isn't ready for *shou* yet."

"Lili!"

Chi-Wen held his left arm close to his chest. "I have to tell you..."

"My God!" The front of his shirt was stained with blood. "You've been shot!"

"It's nothing…" but the edges of his field of vision were starting to blur and he no longer heard her voice clearly.

"Chi-Wen!"

Suddenly he was at the end of a darkening tunnel, fighting an almost irresistible drowsiness. "I love you," he whispered before he was enveloped in blackness.

TWENTY-EIGHT

Sunday, May 7th
Hong Kong
7:00 PM

Spectacular.

A tepid offshore breeze had cleared the air, magnifying the brightness of the stars twinkling against Hong Kong's night sky. Staring out at the horizon, Lili recalled another such night, a little over three weeks before.

When you look outward you see the past.

How true the fortune teller's words seemed now as she gazed at the hills of China in the distance. She had found her past there, losing part of herself in the process. But as the one-eyed man also predicted, she'd discovered so much more.

The past is a window to oneself. Her mother's words.

In examining her past, she'd come to understand her Chineseness, to appreciate being "different". Her roots were deep and rich.

Dear mother, dear grandfather. Quietly weeping. *How I miss you.*

She touched the jade locket she wore around her neck.

Wear it always...so you will never forget...you are Chinese.

No, mother, I never will forget.

Her finger outlined the perimeter. A circle. Just as Chi-Wen had said. It begins with a circle. The continuum of past, present and future.

Thinking not of the past, but the future, she turned from the window."Lili?"

Smiling at Chi-Wen. "You're awake."

"You've been crying."

She dried her cheeks with the back of her hand. "It's nothing."

"How long did I sleep?"

She sat beside his hospital bed. "Since last night."

"And you've been here all this time?"

Nodding. "Of course."

"What happened?"

"You don't remember?"

"I remember everything getting dark and then…"

"You fainted. One of Halliday's bullets hit your left arm and tore through an artery. You bled enough to lose consciousness."

Chi-Wen raised the full arm cast. "Why this?"

"The bullet also shattered bone. Your arm is broken."

"Broken bones can be mended."

Softly: "What about broken hearts?"

The silence that engulfed them was a complex one.

She gazed into his liquid eyes. Weeks ago, she hadn't been able to define what she'd seen in them—a certain vulnerability, yes, but something more. Much more. "You're going back, aren't you?" As much an expression of her fear for him as an accusation.

"China is my country. That's where I belong."

"It's too dangerous right now. Those CIA men have let Lin go. Apparently the US government doesn't want to upset relations with Deng Xiaoping. If you return, you'll be arrested or worse…" Her voice trembled.

"I plan to be very careful. Besides, the democracy movement is a success. You saw that. By the end of the summer we'll oust the old-timers. Then it will be Lin and his cronies in jail, not me."

She took Chi-Wen's hand in hers. "Listen, I talked with my chief, Dr. Trenton. I have misjudged him. Although he once worked for the CIA, he broke ties with them after they tried to involve him in their "dirty tricks". He never had anything to do with Halliday's scheme. It was Dylan." Gripping his hand tightly. "He's offered me the geriatrics fellowship in July."

"Congratulations."

"As long as I leave Hong Kong right away and complete my residency."

"I see."

"Chi-Wen?"

"Yes?"

"He offered you a job in his lab. You can study at night, finish college in the United States and go on to medical school."

Sighing. "A month ago, I would have jumped at such a chance."

"And now?" Knowing his answer, yet afraid to hear it spoken.

"Now I must do what I believe is right." He brought her hand to his lips and gently kissed her fingertips. "Would you respect me if I did not?"

"Respect?" She wanted to shake him. "I'm talking about love, damn it! You and me. Yin and yang. Together. Always."

"I feel the same way, my dearest Lili. But it is because of my love for you that I must stay in China and help the students."

"Then I'll stay with you."

"No. You belong in the United States."

"I thought you said I had become a true Chinese."

"You always were. You just never knew it." Chi-Wen was quiet for several seconds. "You are also an American."

We are all on the path, but at different points along the way.

For a brief time their paths had crossed and now it seemed he was saying they could no longer remain at the same point. "So that's our *joss* ? To fall in love, then never see each other again?" Her eyes misted, the thought too much to bear.

"To accept such a fate would be to accept the unacceptable."

Smiling through tears, she acknowledged his paraphrase of her own words.

"No," he said, "we will meet again. And I promise, when it is truly safe, when the chaos is banished, you and I will march hand in hand through a changed China."

"Promise?" she asked, searching his eyes for the truth.

"Promise."

"Well, it better happen soon, " she pouted, embracing him. "Otherwise, I'm coming to get you."

*   *   *

Two days later, Chi-Wen recovered enough to leave the hospital and drive with Lili to the airport. They sat together in a quiet corner of the International Terminal, holding hands, each wrapped in their own private thoughts. So much to say, so little time.

Dr. Trenton wired money for her ticket home and a change of clothes so she was dressed in a red silk skirt and matching blouse with Mandarin collar similar to the outfit she'd worn at Fan's home. A magical evening she would always remember. Oh God, she was going to miss Chi-Wen.

"Final call for Flight 431 to Los Angeles."

"That's you." Chi-Wen stood.

Hope momentarily flared in her eyes. "You can still change your mind about coming with me."

He shook his head. "You know I can't."

"I know." Lili came to him and embraced him one last time. "Good-bye, my love."

"*Zai jian* !" He squeezed her tightly. "I love you."

She didn't want to let go, but the plane was waiting. "How will I know you are safe?"

"I'll get word to you. Don't worry, we will be together again. Your grandfather once told me the strength of the Chinese is our ability to hope. Otherwise we would not have endured over five thousand years."

"I'll remember that," she replied, smiling through tears.

EPILOGUE

For democracy, for freedom,
We should not hesitate,
We should not be silent.
For the people, for China,
We should work together as one.

Do you understand?
Do you realize?
I may fall and never rise again.

lyrics to song written for the democracy movement, 1989

**Beijing, China
Sunday, June 4th
2 AM**

It was a moonless night and Tiananmen Square seemed darker than usual. Flags and banners fluttered lazily in a gentle breeze. Student loudspeakers affixed to the Monument to the Revolutionary Martyrs blared the national anthem and the Internationale, while inside makeshift tents and canvas shelters classmates huddled together and sang, accompanied by the soft sound of guitar music.

Just outside a large green tent audaciously christened the "Democratic University", Chi-Wen helped students prepare for resistance. They dipped face cloths and shreds of banners in buckets of water, then tied them over their mouths with surgical masks.

"This time, they'll use more than tear gas," someone ventured. "They're going to kill us."

"Impossible." A young boy defiantly gave the "victory" sign.

"It's possible," countered another.

Chi-Wen had to agree. Foreign Minister Lin and his cronies had finally managed to wrest power from the moderates. In just over a month, the dream of a new China was coming apart. As he listened to the students solemnly pledging their willingness to die for the cause of freedom, he closed his eyes and thought of the last five weeks.

Using forged papers, he had sneaked back into China, plunging headlong into the democracy movement. And though he'd seen the ousting of Zhao Ziyang and the implementation of martial law, he'd also experienced the sense of *tongxin*—the same heart—with hundreds of thousands of students and ordinary citizens who participated in sit-ins, rallies and hunger strikes. On May 30th, when the Goddess of Democracy was unveiled, he traveled with fellow dissidents to Beijing to see this symbol of defiance and hope, joining over one million people protesting in the streets.

Five days later, on a warm, balmy night, he stood alongside many of those same people, waiting for the army that few doubted would be coming—despite crude barricades thrown across many of the city's intersections. Forty years earlier, Beijingers had gathered to cheer the arrival of the People's

Liberation Army—the patriotic force that liberated the country from the Japanese and the despised Nationalists. On this Sunday in 1989, the citizens were doing everything they could to keep the same army out.

"I swear, for the democratic movement and the prosperity of the country, for our motherland not to be overturned by a few conspirators, for our one billion people not to be killed in the white terror, that I am willing to defend Tiananmen, defend the republic, with my young life. Our heads can be broken, our blood can be shed, but we will not lose the People's square. We will fight to the end with the last person."

Two AM.

A volley of tracer bullets heralded the arrival of the PLA convoy at the square.

"Do you know what you're doing?" an agitated woman shrieked. "You should be protecting the people, not hurting them!"

The soldiers stared back, some cradling AK-47 machine guns, others holding spiked whips , truncheons, tear gas and cattle prods.

"You cannot do this! You have a conscience!"

The menacing column of tanks and armed soldiers were lined from the northeastern corner of the Great Hall of the People as far back as the eye could see.

"Look!"

Chi-Wen turned to see billows of smoke and flames pouring forth from the direction of Changan Boulevard- the street of Eternal Peace. Someone lobbed a Molotov cocktail at Mao's portrait, eerily lighting his impassive gaze.

"Good, good!"

"Down with Li Peng!"

"Long live the people!"

What sounded like firecrackers popping mobilized the throng in the Square to rush toward the tanks. Chi-Wen found himself moving with the human wave, a prisoner of the crowd.

This time the sound was obviously gunfire.

"*Bu yao pa* ! Don't be scared! They're only blanks!"

A sustained burst of bullets and a ricochet zinged off the ground near Chi-Wen.

"Fascists!"

A blood-curdling scream.

"They really are shooting people! This is no joke."

Bicycle bells, ambulance sirens, helicopter rotors, frenzied cries of disbelief and terror.

The troops were surrounding the Square. In the distance, flames silhouet-
ted a tank as it rolled over an elderly woman standing in its way, crushing her
as if she were a bug.

"No! No! The People's Army loves the people!"

Chi-Wen continued to move forward, his mind filled with the thought of
Santiago's determination to fight against the sharks until the end: *They have
beaten me... I am too old to club sharks to death. But I will try as long as I
have the oars and the short club and the tiller.*

"Real bullets!" someone screamed. "*Real* bullets!"

The barrage of machine fire now continuous.

Beside Chi-Wen, a young boy dropped, his face covered in blood.

The lights on the Square went out and Tiananmen was filled with the sound
of absolute chaos.

"Lili!"

*   *   *

Los Angeles, California
one month later

Only the soft ping of wind chimes disturbed the perfect silence. She stood facing him for a moment, then raised her arms. He followed the movement until
their fingers touched, each bringing their arms back to their bodies in a slow,
gentle circle.

Always remember the circle.

Her left hand gracefully sliced the air as did his right, nearly brushing their
fingertips. His body shifted, unfurling a sweeping arc with his right hand as
he turned to face that direction, his left hand "grabbing air" to anchor the

movement. Simultaneously, she executed the reverse image of each gesture. Yin and yang.

Two partners performing the stylized reflection of the other, beginning together, sweeping apart, then coming together throughout the entire sequence of tai chi. The reflected dimension of perfectly mirrored timing and distance between two moving bodies.

Balancing despair and hope.

As they turned and advanced, whirled and retreated, struck and parried, joining every neuron, bone and muscle into a finely integrated whole, time and distance between them disappeared.

Lili and Chi-Wen.

For a moment together again.

Movement and stillness.

A perfect balance.

Lili reached out, expecting the brush of fingertips, feeling nothing.

Chi-Wen !

The image vanished.

Don't leave me !

Only the deafening sound of the chimes remained.

Sitting bolt upright in bed, Lili tried to hold back her sobs. Bathed in sweat, she trembled. For nearly a month it was always the same. Since the massacre at Tiananmen Square. Night after night she'd watched the news reports of the violence in China, never knowing whether Chi-Wen had survived. So far, no word. And as the days dragged on, she was losing hope.

The sound again. But not wind chimes. It was the insistent buzzing of the doorbell.

She climbed out of bed, grabbed her bathrobe and walked into the living room. "Who's there?"

"UPS."

She opened the door.

"Lili Quan?"

"Yes."

The delivery man handed her a small package. It was stained, dog-eared and carried a Hong Kong stamp.

Oh God!

"Could you sign here?"

Lili hurriedly scribbled her name on his clip board.

"Have a nice day."

She slammed the door shut. Hands shaking, she tore off the wrapping. Oh my God! It was a well-worn copy of *The Old Man and the Sea*—the one she'd given to Chi-Wen in Shanghai. Her heart pounded as she flipped through the pages, searching for a message. She found it: two thin, folded sheets of paper wedged inside. One was a letter from Chi-Wen.

"Dearest Lili,

If my friends in Hong Kong manage to get this to you, you will understand I have survived Tiananmen Square. I cannot tell you where I am, only that I am safe. The democracy movement is not dead. It has only gone underground.

I sent you a poem from your grandfather. I had to hide it when we escaped from Xi'an in case we were caught. He asked me to not to give it to you until you were safely in America. Read it carefully. And remember what I told you in Hong Kong. Your grandfather was right.

All my love,

Chi-Wen".

He was alive! She wanted to cry with relief. Dear God, he was alive!

She unfolded the second paper he had sent her, recognizing her grandfather's beautiful calligraphy. Unfortunately she could read Chinese only slightly better than she could speak. Yet Chi-Wen's letter insisted the poem bore an important message.

Read it carefully. And remember…

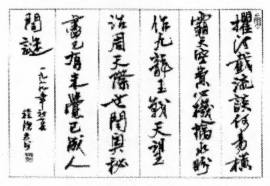

She pulled her Chinese-English dictionary from the shelf.

"To a Chinese," her grandfather had told her, "each ideogram is like a musical scale, or a pattern of given notes on which a composer may make variations within the chosen key. It is possible to put every expression into the characters of these ideograms."

Like a puzzle, Lili thought, studying the forms. A message from beyond the grave.

Slowly, painstakingly, the words emerged and she began to translate:

"Stop the water and seize the river.

Take hold of the air and possess the sky.

Such foolish struggle.

To seize the river...become the river.

To possess the sky...become the sky.

To possess the secret...become the secret."

Become the secret, become the secret, Lili repeated to herself. Nudging her memory. What did it mean? For several minutes she stared at the beautifully styled letters, trying to recall her grandfather's exact words:

For months I searched the area described in the ancient text until I finally came to Yan'an.

Mao and his followers set up camp.

Your grandmother smiled and led me to a cave I'd never seen before. ...She said that to possess the secret, you must become the secret. On a deep ledge inside the cave she showed me what I would never have found on my own.

Lili removed her locket from around her neck and studied the picture of Qing Nan. Only when she looked very closely did she see what she'd missed before. The pieces had just come together and the irony almost made her laugh. The terrible responsibility she thought had been lifted, was now thrust upon her again

To possess the secret, become the secret.

In the picture, Qing Nan stood in front of a cave. Of course. Another copy of grandfather's formula was still buried in China! That had to be it. Somehow it made perfect sense. Her grandfather recognized that man might not be ready for *shou* now. But perhaps someday.

Your grandfather once told me that the strength of the Chinese is our ability to hope. Otherwise we would not have endured over five thousand years.

Chi-Wen must have figured out the significance of the calligraphy. That's what he meant in his letter. A second copy would represent that hope. Now she knew where it was buried.

She removed Ng's lighter from her pocket, flicked it and held the poem to the flame. As all traces of the ideograms disappeared, she made a promise: Someday, grandfather, Chi-Wen and I will return to China and find *shou*.

Hope. I will remember.

She stared at her reflection in the hallway mirror. This time she didn't turn away. Smiling, she thought, I *am* Chinese.

It is Chinese to hope.

THE END

Glossary

Amah—a Chinese nurse or nanny

Cadre—White-collar employees of all kinds—both functionaries (members of the large administrative apparatus) and party members. They exist at all levels. When the Communists took over, people in these positions no longer wanted to be called *guan* or "officials" since it was too reminiscent of the old society. Instead a new word was coined—*ganbu* —doer or cadre.

Ch'i—intrinsic energy

Daizibao—character posters

Dim Sum—literally "touch heart". These are lunchtime tidbits of different items from pork buns to shrimp rolls that are chosen from trolleys.

Foot binding—the rendering of young girls immobile by deliberately maiming them had been part of the Chinese culture since the eighth century. It was begun very young by pulling the heel and toes together, wrapping them tightly with cotton binding until the toes were turned under. Bones that resisted were broken by the blow of a wooden mallet. The pain was constant and continued for years until the feet became numb. The result was a teetering, swaying walk that was a status symbol for being well-born since a woman who tottered on her feet couldn't work for a living. It was regarded as a mark of sexual appeal and was endured because a girl's marriage potential and desirability was determined more by the size of her feet than by the beauty of her face. The perverse idea was that this object had been made helpless for her husband. She could not move, stayed where he put her and would serve him in any way he wished. Even when the binding was discontinued, victims were left with deformed, undersized feet.

Fung shui—it means 'wind and water' and refers to the Chinese art of locating anything, from an ancestral grave to the premises for a new factory, so that its placement will ensure the most auspicious topographical relationship with the mountains, wind, waters and spirits of dragons. Water means prosperity, for example, and still water facing the premises means easy money. Mountains are said to be the underpasses of dragons and a good fung shui expert will be able to determine which range of hills the local dragon spirit is moving through and how far he has reached. Since there is nothing luckier than to be on top of a dragon and his lair, this would be a good location on which to build. In pre-war Shanghai even the position of the boss's desk would be decided by such an expert. Although Mao eliminated such superstition, Chinese living outside of mainland China—especially in Hong Kong— still spend many dollars consulting a fung shui expert before building an expensive high-rise or selecting the proper burial site.

Guandao—The so-called "official" racketeering engaged in by sons and daughters of Chinese party members

Hakkas—the farming people of the new territories

Hutongs—narrow alleyways

Huaqiao—overseas Chinese

Hou-tai—meaning literally "behind the stage", a term indicating the support and protection from persecution a person might enjoy from people who hold power. However, one's hou-tai only reaches to a certain level.

Joss—fate, luck, the will of the gods.

PRC—People's Republic of China

Ren—to endure

Shen—spirit of vitality

Shuo ku—tales of the evil social conditions of pre-1949

Tai-chi—a disciplined form of shadowboxing that combines the mental and the physical

Waigoren—foreigner

Wu-chi—absolute nothingness

Yin and yang—the interaction of two opposites. Yin is earth, feminine, negative, passive, weak, dark, even, moon. Yang is heaven, male, active, light, strong, odd, sun. Yin contracts and yang expands and so the universe breathes. Not warring forces, they do not conflict, but intertwine. There is a small part of yin in yang's sector and of yang in yin's. Yin and yang mean completion in the sense that a coin must have two sides, there can be no good without bad, no left without right, no heaven without earth.

Yi shen—doctor

Yiyuan—public gardens

Ziyou shichang—free market. One of Deng's reforms, this allows anyone to do business and keep the profits. Street traders can earn up to five times a factory workers' salary.

Zhongshan suit—Sun Zhongshan was the other name for Sun Yatsen. In summertime, the jacket is removed and a short-sleeved open-neck shirt or blouse is worn. In winter suit is worn over numerous layers of warm underclothing.

About The Authors

Deborah and Joel Shlian are both physicians who practiced Family Medicine for over ten years before returning to UCLA for MBAs. They have since balanced medical management consulting with writing. They often write together, producing several medical mysteries as well as non-fiction books and numerous magazine and journal articles on healthcare and medical management issues. They recently moved from Los Angeles to Boca Raton, Florida.